THE FALLEN

Volume One of the Book of Souls Saga

To Becky.

Thought you might like a nice
version to keep.

Thanks again for all your help.

M

Mark Ashbury

To Lisa.

Without your support, this book would never have happened.

Love you heaps.

CONTENTS

ACKNOWLEDGEMENTS

Thanks to Lisa and Becky Reynolds for their valuable input into the story lines and my dodgy use of the English language.

Thanks to my publishing team at Kindle Book Publishing for help in getting my book published.

Inspiration for Tom's robotic arm were taken from the Open Bionics Hero Arm (www.openbionics.com). Liberties were taken with the features of the arm, but this site proved to be a great starting point.

Most of my research for the team's weaponry was gleaned from Wikipedia, Military-today.com and eliteukforces.info.

The makeup of the team and their previous lives in the armed forces were researched using Wikipedia, the British Army website at apply.army.mod.uk and the article *Afghanistan: Life with the Bomb Hunters* published by Channel 4.

Useful information on the mechanics of how to remove an arrow from a wound was found on youtube.com. Tod's Workshop posted a video called *How to Remove Medieval Arrows* which was very useful indeed
 (https://www.youtube.com/watch?v=YxHcSSyOTd0).

The field bandage used to bind Sam's arrow wound was based loosely on the Olaes® Modular Bandage
(https://www.prometheusmedical.co.uk/equipment/haemorrhage-control/olaes-modular-bandage).

Lastly, thanks to Johnson Controls and Boris Johnson for putting me on furlough for five months due to the Covid-19 pandemic. Without this time at home, this book would not have surfaced for a number of years. The Covid-19 pandemic has been a tragic event for a great many families, but hopefully many people like me will have used the unexpected time it gave us to do something positive and re-evaluate what we really want to do with our lives.

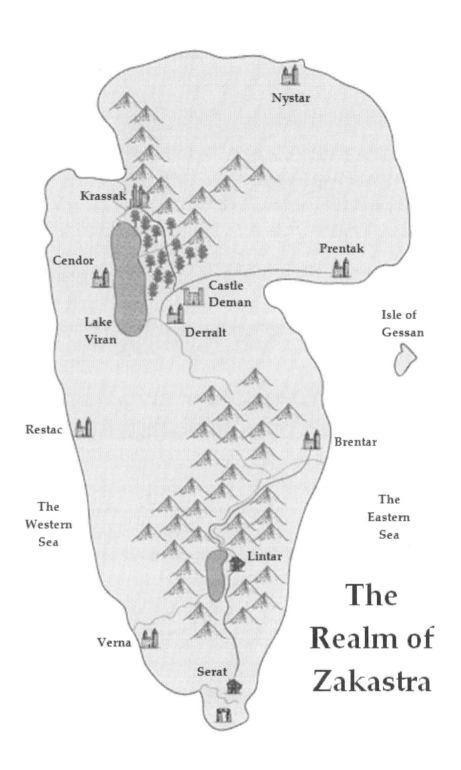

Nystar

Krassak

Cendor

Prentak

Castle
Deman

Lake
Viran

Derralt

Isle of
Gessan

Restac

Brentar

The
Western
Sea

The
Eastern
Sea

Lintar

Verna

The
Realm of
Zakastra

Serat

CHAPTER 1

Near the Western coast of Zakastra

Lalitha could hear the horses crashing through the trees behind her. She gritted her teeth and ran. The pine needles and sticks dug into her bare feet, but she tried to ignore the pain and keep going. They couldn't catch her. If they did, it was all over.

She had been running for what seemed like hours, ever since the atrocity that had befallen her family in the Tower at Krassak. How had it come to this? She still couldn't believe how her world had fallen apart so quickly. There was hope though; she still had the Book.

She heard voices coming from behind her, and she dug to find a deeply hidden reserve of energy as she raced on through the undergrowth. Brambles and branches clutched at her and scratched her skin as she scrambled through them.

Lalitha noticed that the trees were starting to thin out. The sea must be close. She knew that if she broke cover too soon, the riders would be on her, but what choice did she have? She needed to get to the cove where she knew there would be boats pulled up on the sand. She clutched the Book to her chest even more tightly and raced on, her heart pounding as if it would burst at any moment.

This was it. The trees parted, and as Lalitha ran through the bracken towards the open grassland, she heard a sudden shout behind her.

"I see her my Lord Gask. She makes for the sea."

"No!" she screamed to herself. "Gask is with them. I cannot let him catch me. I cannot."

Lalitha plunged onwards, up the slope through the long grass. Was that the sea she could hear? She was close. Behind her she could hear the riders breaking cover from the woodland.

"We almost have her!" shouted the lead rider. "My Lord, she is here."

Lalitha could hardly breathe with the exertions of the chase and the fear that was rising within her. As she neared the top of the hill, she looked back over her shoulder and saw at least eight riders bearing down on her. She looked forwards again and suddenly the world seemed to fall away in front of her.

With a scream Lalitha managed to stop herself mere centimetres from the edge of the cliffs that fell away hundreds of metres to the crashing waves of the Western Sea below her.

"I should not be here," she cried. "I am lost."

Behind her, the horses slowed and came to a stop. Lalitha turned slowly to face them and she felt unbridled rage begin to boil in her chest. A large grey charger with a tall rider, clad in leather armour and chain mail, came to the front of the pack, the others parting to let him through. The rider raised the visor on his helmet to reveal his face. His handsome, angular features were framed by long dark hair, but the expression on his face was full of anger and bitterness.

"Findo Gask," spat Lalitha, "I curse you for what you have done, you murdering bastard."

"Princess Lalitha," he replied, "give me the Book and surrender yourself. It is over. There has been enough tragedy this day."

Lalitha clutched the Book tightly and felt its heat against her. The Book knew that danger was close. Slowly, slowly the whispering began, quietly at first but gradually getting louder and more insistent. She edged away from the riders, her heels getting closer and closer to the cliff edge.

Gask dismounted and took a step towards her, his hand outstretched.

"Lalitha," exclaimed Gask, "you need to stop and you need to give me the Book. There is nowhere to run. Give it to me."

"No," she screamed in reply, "you cannot take it from me. The Book will not let you. You will pay for what you have done, Gask!"

The voice was no longer a whisper in her head, it was loud. It was repeating the same words over and over again.

"He must not take us. He is not Chosen."

Gask came closer, he could almost touch her now.

"You are correct, Lalitha, I cannot take the Book from you, but I have one with me who can."

From within the group of horses, a figure clad in a long black robe stepped forwards, his face hidden within the depths of his hood. He moved slowly towards Lalitha, his hand outstretched.

"Give the Book to him," Gask hissed. "If you do not give it up, he will take it by force. The King is dead and your family's rule is ended."

The hooded stranger moved closer and closer. Lalitha waited for the Book to tell her what to do, but the otherworldly voice did not speak, she was on her own.

With her heart hammering in her chest, Lalitha watched the hooded figure's hand as it reached out towards her. The fingers brushed the front of Lalitha's dress. Why was the Book doing nothing?

Suddenly, she knew what she must do. She closed her eyes, took a step backwards into the void and fell.

The stranger lunged to catch her, but his fist closed on nothing but air.

Lalitha fell. The air rushed past her and took her breath away. She saw the sea smashing against the rocks below as they rushed towards her, but the voices were so loud in her head that she could no longer hear it. Suddenly, as she plummeted towards the ground, she heard herself shout a single word.

"DESSAT!"

As soon as the word left her lips it felt like the world was somehow folding in on itself. Lalitha screamed in pain and before she hit the rocks, everything went black.

From his vantage point at the top of the precipice, Gask and the hooded stranger watched the small body fall and then, with a noise like the crack of lightning, there was a blinding flash and Lalitha vanished before she hit the waves.

Gask stared down angrily at the waves below.

"She has escaped us," he whispered viciously.

He strode back to his horse, climbed up onto its back and rode quickly back towards the woods.

CHAPTER 2

West London, England

It was the usual kind of night in *The Drum*. Tom McAllister took a long pull from his pint and turned back to the animated conversation that were going on around the table. Alex was debating the latest developments in whatever bullshit TV reality show she was addicted to at the moment, whilst Sam and Jimmy were more concerned about the rumours of some strange flu-like disease that was making itself known in China. Danny was, as usual, telling anyone that would listen about the latest adventures in his life as a West End nightclub doorman.

Tom struggled with these drinking sessions with his old team. It was great to see them all, but being with them was a painful reminder that things were very different now. It wasn't so long ago that they had been a tight-knit unit trying to make a difference in the anarchy of Helmand province, but an IED and the loss of an arm unceremoniously slammed the door shut on that life.

Tom looked down at his left arm and moved the fingers on his robotic replacement. He had mixed feelings about his robo-arm. It allowed him to live with some degree of normality, but at the same time it reminded him of the life he had been robbed of.

He flexed his skin-toned polymer fingers and gripped his glass. Sensors buried in the sleeve beneath the plastic detected muscle movement in what was left of his lower arm, and translated these signals into the electronic control commands for the hi-tech hand. As his fingers closed on the glass, haptic feedback in the arm vibrated gently to let him know the grip was successful. He lifted the pint pot and took another swig of lager. There was always the risk that he would drop beer everywhere and make a total prat of himself, but the more Tom had used the arm, the more confidence he had gained in its technology – which was just as well since the thing had cost him a small fortune.

"Boss! Jesus, are you even listening to me?" asked Sam.

"Sorry, Sam, what were you on about?"

In Helmand, Sam 'Slaphead' Franklin had been part of the security detail for the ordnance search and disposal unit, but now he earned a living servicing four-wheel drive SUV's for a civvy mate who owned a local garage. He was a stocky figure who had put on some weight since their army days. That was one of the dangers of working in a garage across the road from a Greggs bakery, too many pies and sausage rolls. Sam knew that he was lucky to have found a trade after coming out of the forces. The others had not all been as fortunate. Jimmy had ended up working nights stacking shelves in Tesco.

"I said, come on tightwad. It's your round!" repeated Sam in his broad Mancunian accent.

"Give it rest, Slapper," sighed Alex. "You know the boss is skint. I'll get them in."

Alex got up from her chair and playfully slapped Sam on top of his bald head as she passed him on her way to the bar.

In her past life, Corporal Alex 'Moonshine' Aluko had been the unit's Electronic Counter Measure Operator. It was her job to make sure that the bad guys couldn't remotely detonate a device while the team was trying to diffuse it. Without Alex blocking the radio frequencies used to trigger the explosive detonators, the unit would have met a grizzly end on more occasions than Tom liked to think about. Alex was unflappable and Tom could rely on her to back him up no matter what the situation.

These days Alex worked with a different kind of electronics. She sold burglar alarm systems to householders that watched too much Crimewatch, and lay in bed at night worrying about the state of the country. As well as being on her feet a lot of the day door-knocking for sales, she had kept in shape since leaving the team, going to the gym three times a week. The regular exercise kept some measure of routine in her life and the circuit training gave her a trim, athletic figure, which definitely came in useful when selling alarm systems to her male customers.

"Skint my arse!" grumbled Danny with a grin. "The Boss is the one that got the big wedge from the government when the shit hit the fan."

"Here we go again," thought Tom. "This record never gets old."

"Anytime you want to saw your arm off and swap it for a few quid, go right ahead," he threw back at Danny.

Raised on a Southwark estate, Danny 'Fester' Adams had not had the easiest of upbringings. His father didn't hang around after his birth and had headed back to Jamaica at the first chance he got. Danny was tall and had a muscular build and it had not been long before his 'in-your-face' attitude to life had attracted the attention of the local gangs. It had only been the intervention of an uncle in the Royal Engineers that had prevented Danny from going the way of so many of his peers. Violence, drugs, crime and ultimately incarceration at Her Majesty's pleasure. Thanks to the armed forces, the routine and discipline of army life had helped him to get through his twenties without ending up behind bars.

Since leaving the forces, Danny had worked in a multitude of low paid roles, but had ended up odd jobbing in the private security sector. As well as the legitimate work he did at gigs and nightclubs, Danny still had some very dodgy contacts from the old days that threw titbits his way now and again. Tom didn't really want to know what this work entailed, mainly because he was sure most of it was the wrong side of legal and there was a fair chance that Danny would end up neck-deep in trouble again.

"Yeah yeah," Danny muttered. "You got it easy man. Nice easy monthly cheque and nothing to do but sit in your armchair and set your robocop arm to jerk-off mode."

"Fester, you're a dickhead sometimes," Sam grinned.

Danny laughed in reply, "You love me that way though don't ya?"

Sam swallowed down the last of his pint and stuck a middle finger up in Danny's direction. Danny loved to wind people up and enjoyed nothing more than a good argument, but under it all he was a solid mate and, when it mattered, when you were in a tight spot, you knew you could depend on him to do something. It may not always be the right thing, but life was never boring when Danny was around.

Alex arrived back with a tray of drinks.

"What did I miss?" she asked.

"Just Fester being an irritating sod," said Tom.

"Nothing new there then, Boss," she laughed.

Boss. The moniker still stuck after all this time. Captain Tom McAllister had been a decorated Ammunition Technical Officer for the Royal Logistics Corps detachment based at Camp Bastion and had led Danny, Jimmy, Sam and Alex on over fifty IED search and destroy missions. They had been an effective and prolifically busy team, once disarming nine devices in a single day. After so many successful missions, their final shout together had not even been their most difficult. Perhaps that was the problem. A small device hidden under a parked car should have been a straightforward job, which is why Tom took it on even though the light was starting to fade. The wires had been more difficult to identify in the falling dusk, and an incorrect cut had caused the explosion that took his arm and left him lying unconscious in a hospital for three weeks. Thankfully, the others had only received minor injuries and nobody had lost their life. It could have been so much worse.

After spending months in a military hospital in Surrey, Tom had found himself living back in West London, his time occupied with counselling, physiotherapy sessions, prosthetic fittings and a serious bout of depression. He was no use to the army any longer and the abrupt loss of the routine and security of life within the armed forces was a major culture shock. Tom found himself spending hours and hours locked away in his flat eating cheap microwave meals and watching the mindless crap that they put on the TV through the day. Slowly and painfully, he had come through those dark days without succumbing to any of his more self-destructive urges and had eventually started to come to terms with his place in this new world.

The team had continued in the field under another officer, but after two tours in Afghanistan, they each decided that enough was enough, and as their terms came up, none of them felt the desire to re-enlist. For better or worse, civilian life seemed a safer bet.

The conversation around the table in *The Drum* meandered around for another half hour. Sam and Danny spent most of their time partaking in one of their favourite pastimes. Jimmy Baiting. Jimmy 'Cod' Lang was the youngest member of the team at only twenty-five. He was a quiet character most of the time and, in a masochistic kind of way, enjoyed the piss-taking from the lads. It made him feel part of a family, something he had never experienced growing up in the child care system that claimed him after a car crash killed his parents. Jimmy had joined the army straight out of school and had been involved in many combat situations in his time in both Afghan and other war zones around the world. After the other team members had left the forces, Jimmy had become disillusioned with the way of life and decided to not re-enlist once his contract was up. He had regretted that decision ever since. He struggled to adapt to civilian life and had found employment in civvy street hard to come by. Life out there was radically different from what he had been used to.

After the adrenaline rush of firing bursts of 5.56mm rounds at insurgents to defend the boss while he defused an explosive device, unpacking crates of baked beans in an empty supermarket at two o'clock in the morning left him feeling dead inside. Away from work, Jimmy tended to hide away in his bedroom and spend hours at a time gaming online. His long-standing addiction to the Call of Duty series of video games had earned him his nickname 'Cod'. Jimmy enjoyed these unit get-togethers because it got him out of the house. The stories and camaraderie reminded him of times when the action had been real and not just on a forty-inch TV screen in a dark, dingy bedroom. They were times he had felt needed. Felt important. Felt part of something that mattered.

Tom looked at his watch. Nearly eleven o'clock.

Danny downed the last of his drink in one big gulp and stood up.

"I gotta go. Got a delivery to do for Alexey tonight."

No-one said anything. Alexey Petrov was bad news and Danny's late-night delivery job was bound to involve something distinctly iffy.

"Just don't mule drugs for Christ sakes," said Tom eventually.

"No, Mum," he quipped. "Definitely no drugs involved."

"Bet there is, you dickhead," Sam chirped, pulling a face in Danny's direction.

Danny grinned, stood up and grabbed his jacket from the back of his chair. It signalled that the evening was done. Everyone took this as their cue to wrap things up.

"OK, so 'til next time," said Danny as he made a mock salute and headed for the door. "See y'all next time."

Everyone else drained their glasses. There was the exchange of customary hugs, and the team left the warmth of the pub and made their way outside into the cold February night. It started to rain.

"You ok getting home?" Tom asked Alex as Jimmy and Sam tried to flag a black cab down.

"Yep. No problem I'm only just around the corner."

"Well, keep in touch and I'll see you soon, ok?"

"Will do."

Alex stretched up and gave Tom a peck on the cheek before turning and walking off down the dark high street. She turned in the light of a shop window to give him a last smile before disappearing around the corner.

"You want to share a cab?" Sam asked.

"No thanks, Slaphead, the walk home will do me good."

"Suit yourself. Jimmy… there's one with its light on. Flag him down."

Jimmy waved frantically at a cab whose yellow roof light was switched on and it swerved towards them, pulling up at the curbside nearby. The lads threw cheery V-signs at Tom as they climbed into the back and slammed the door closed behind them.

"See ya, Boss," they shouted through the window as the car pulled away into the Friday night traffic.

Tom smiled to himself and started to walk towards home. It was quite a distance, but he didn't mind the cold or the rain, and the walk would help him sleep.

CHAPTER 3

West London, England

It was still raining as Tom got to the end of his street. It had taken him nearly forty minutes to walk all the way home. The weather was getting worse and his teeth started to ache as happened sometimes when high-pressure weather systems closed in, but he felt better. Being out in the fresh air always helped to clear his head.

After his stay in hospital, Tom had been housebound for a long time, not wanting to see anybody or to let the world see his disfigurement. Once he had used some of his compensation to buy his prosthetic arm, some of his old confidence had returned, (partially at least) because he did not look obviously disabled any longer. Since then, he had taken up running which had improved his state of mind considerably, and his fitness levels had returned. The extra few pounds that he had been carrying since the accident soon dropped away, and Tom's frame returned to its toned condition.

Tom looked up the street before crossing over to his little flat. A red double decker turned into the end of the road, the streetlights reflecting off its wet windows. There was plenty of time to get across and Tom stepped off the kerb and made towards his front door on the other side of the street. As he did so, the rain abruptly turned to hailstones the size of garden peas that began to hammer down around him. As Tom fumbled in his pocket for his keys, there was a bright flash and a deafening clap of thunder behind him.

"Jesus," Tom exclaimed out loud, holding his left arm above his face to protect his eyes from the hail onslaught, "was that a lightning strike?"

He turned back sharply to see the driver of the approaching bus hit the brakes hard. The big vehicle started to skid, the road surface now slick with a layer of icy hailstones. In the midst of the bouncing balls of ice, where Tom was sure the road had been empty just a moment ago, a girl now lay on the tarmac. Where did she appear from? Had she been struck by the lightning? The bus was slowing as it skidded, but not quickly enough. It was going to hit her.

Acting without thinking, Tom lunged for her, grabbed her with his good arm and just managed to pull her out of the way of the on-coming bus. He set the girl down on the pavement and crouched down beside her. She was breathing and Tom found a pulse in her neck. A strong, regular one. Thank God.

The bus had come to a standstill beside them and the driver sat shaking his head, a shocked look on his face. After a few seconds he threw open his window and leaned out.

"What's she doin' lyin' in the middle of the bloody road?" he demanded. "Stupid bitch! One second the road's empty, the next there's lightnin' and she's just lyin' there. Where'd she come from?"

"I don't know," Tom answered. "She's got a pulse and she's breathing ok, but I think the lightning might have hit her. She was right there when it struck".

"I don't know 'bout that," the driver exclaimed. "All I do know is that it was nothin' to do with me. And look at her! She's hardly wearin' anythin'. In this weather! She's not even got shoes on 'er feet. Bloody junkie prob'ly. I'd leave well alone if I were you!"

"I'll sort it. I live just here," answered Tom, gesturing at the building next to them. "I'll get an ambulance out to look at her."

"Get the cops too. She looks a right state to me. A night in a cell might make 'er think about the poison she's stuffin' into herself. Good job I wasn't in service. If a passenger'd been hurt, there would 'ave been hell to pay!" cursed the driver.

With a last shake of his head and a with disgusted scowl fixed firmly on his face, the driver slammed his window shut, released his airbrakes with a loud hiss and drove away into the night.

Tom's heart rate was banging after the shock of the near miss and he breathed heavily as he looked back down at the girl. She was wearing an outlandishly flimsy dress. Her legs were scratched and bleeding and the driver was right, she had no shoes on and her feet were a mess. He touched her skin and she was cold. Really cold.

Tom realised that she was also clutching some kind of ancient looking book tightly to her chest.

"Shit," muttered Tom to himself, "I need to get that ambulance."

He pulled his cellphone out of his pocket and tried to unlock it using his thumb. Dead battery.

"Typical!"

The rain and hail had stopped, but the ground was covered in a white layer of ice and the temperature must have plummeted to well below zero.

Tom made a spur of the moment decision that was to change everything.

He lifted the wet, unconscious girl as best he could, wrestled his keys out of his pocket, unlocked the front door and struggled inside out of the cold, the girl in his arms.

Once inside, Tom pushed the door closed with his foot and hit the light switch with the back of his head. The darkness of the small living room was banished by the sudden glare of the overhead lights. The flat was sparsely furnished, but was both tidy and clean. Tom had learned the hard way that living amongst clutter and chaos did little to help his state of mind. What did they say, 'Tidy home, tidy mind'? He wholeheartedly agreed.

He carried the girl over to the sofa and gently laid her down before turning to the nearby storage heater to whack the temperature dial up to maximum. Tom then grabbed the USB charging lead that hung over the arm of the sofa and jammed it into the socket on his phone. He needed to get some juice into it before calling for an ambulance.

Tom considered going next door to see if he could use their landline, but discounted the idea. It would probably take ages to rouse his smackhead neighbours and he didn't want to leave the girl alone. Hopefully it would only take a minute to get his Samsung powered up again.

As Tom sat watching the display on his phone, willing it to suck in enough electricity to allow him to turn it on, the girl stirred next to him. Her movement made him jump as if it had been himself that he had plugged into the national grid rather than his phone.

The girl's eyelids started to flutter and her fingers twitched against the leather cover of the book she held. Tom watched her as she started to mumble quietly under her breath.

She looked like she was in her late teens or early twenties and had long, dark hair which curled around a face that was nothing short of striking. High cheekbones and fine features gave her an elfin look that would not be out of place on the front of some poncey fashion magazine. Her slim body was wrapped in a sleeveless dress made of a strange green material that flowed around her form. It was certainly not something that you would want to be wearing on a wintery February night in London.

When Tom looked at her arms, there were no sign of track marks and the girl's complexion didn't suggest that she was, as the bus driver had suggested, a 'bloody junkie'. So, what the hell was she doing out dressed like this? Her feet were bleeding and her legs were covered in cuts as if she had run full tilt through a hawthorn hedge.

"Come on you piece of junk," he said impatiently, pushing the power button on his phone. It had not accumulated enough power to boot up yet and refused to start.

Tom turned his attention to the book. It was the size of a normal hard-backed novel and was bound with a leather thong to hold it closed and looked very old. Its cover was intricately carved with swirls and flames and there was some sort of stone inlaid into the cover. He couldn't make out exactly what colour the stone was. It was catching the light in such a way that its surface seemed to churn like smoke from a fire. Was the book some kind of bible? Was the girl part of some weird religious cult?

He leaned over her and made to take the book from her grasp to examine it more closely. Just as he was about to touch the cracked leather cover, the girl's eyes snapped open.

She took a sharp intake of breath and, seeing Tom's hand reaching for the book, leapt up from the sofa.

"NA!" she screamed. "LIS ASLA REL SE!"

"Whoa, hold on there," said Tom as he stood back, holding his arms up in front of him, the fingers on his good hand spread in a passive gesture. "I'm not going to hurt you."

The girl tensed up like a coiled spring and looked frantically around at her unfamiliar surroundings.

"Lora im sa? Lora a Gask?" she blurted.

Tom didn't have a clue what she was saying and didn't even recognise the language.

"You're ok. You're safe."

She looked at Tom, confusion written all over her face. Her eyes darted around the room, flitting over Tom's furniture, flat screen TV, framed photos and bookshelves before coming back to rest on him.

"LORA IM SA? LOSA AL TAIR?"

"Look, I don't understand what you're saying, but you are safe here," Tom said gently.

The girl looked this way and that as if looking for a way to escape. She saw the front door to the flat and made a move towards it.

"No," said Tom, "I need to get you an ambulance." He took a step towards her.

"LIS ASLA REL SE!" she said firmly.

Before making another move, the girl suddenly stopped in her tracks as if listening to something. She looked down at the book in her hands and then her eyes flicked back to stare at him, a fire suddenly lit within them.

Tom took another step towards her.

"I need to get some help for you. I won't hurt you. You're safe."

With an intake of breath and eyes burning with strange fiery sparks, she spoke a single word in a loud, clear voice. A voice that was not hers.

"ASLA!"

The girl didn't move, but Tom was struck violently as if he had been punched in the chest. Hard. He fell backwards into a heap on the floor, but thankfully narrowly avoided anything too hard or pointy. What the hell?

She opened her eyes and looked in surprise at Tom as he stared up at her, gasping to catch his breath. She frowned and quickly turned towards the front door; the book held out before her like a weapon.

The girl ran to the door and pulled at it forcefully. The door rattled violently as she tried to force it open, but it stayed firmly shut. She yanked at the door handle and the inner locking lever, but Tom hadn't had chance to disable the deadlock since they came in which meant that it wouldn't open unless the key was used.

"It's locked. You can't get out unless I use my key. Come on, I need to get you checked out."

She turned and glared at Tom.

"Breval… tel… prenit!" she said slowly and deliberately, her eyes not leaving his.

"Calm down. I don't know what you're saying. What just hit me?".

"BREVAL. TEL. PRENIT!" she screamed, moving closer and closer, her body tensing up as if to spring at him.

For once in his life, Tom had absolutely no idea what to do. The girl's sparkling eyes seemed to bore into the depths of his very being. She moved towards him and paused to look down at the book. The stone on its cover blazed with a fiery light and Tom began to hear a strange whispering sound. He could hear voices, lots of voices and they all seemed to be whispering words that he could not quite make out. The girl suddenly stepped forwards and placed her small hand against Tom's face.

As her palm touched his cheek, light filled Tom's head and he was suddenly blinded by a barrage of chaotic, flashing images and sounds.

Men armed with swords. Screams. Battle. A tall, bearded man dressed in leather armour. A beautiful woman dressed in blue. She was crying and had blood on her hands. A tower. A girl running. A middle-aged man with grey hair wearing a silver crown. Screams. Blood. Falling. Darkness. The Book. Whispers. Grey faces watching him. Touching him. Hurting him. Soothing him.

The images abruptly faded and, as Tom's vision came back into focus, he could see the girl staring at him. Her eyes were no longer sparkling like fireflies in a jar, but were instead a deep green colour. A smile slowly spread across her pretty face.

"What the hell was that?" exclaimed Tom as he backed away from her.

"The Book," she replied in her own voice, the strange booming voice now gone. "It channelled the power of the Souls to touch you. It has changed you."

CHAPTER 4

West London, England

Tom watched the girl, fearing another attack, but her whole demeanour had changed, the aggression now completely gone. He flinched as she moved her hand towards him, but this time, instead of grabbing him, she gently put her hand against his cheek. There were no violent visions this time and as she touched him, Tom heard gentle whispering and a warmth and calmness flowed through him.

He suddenly realised that she had understood what he had said and, more importantly, he could understand what she had said in reply.

"I can understand what you're saying!" he exclaimed.

"Yes" she replied, "the Book has given me the knowledge to speak your language and you mine."

This was getting weirder and weirder.

"Who are you?" he spluttered.

The girl paused as if deciding what to say next. Tom heard the faint whispering at the very edge of his hearing again and glanced around. His heart skipped a beat as he wondered if there was somebody else in the flat, but there was no-one other than the two of them. He looked back at her as she pulled away from him. She sat down slowly.

"My name is Lalitha. I am the second-born of King Lestri Santra of Zakastra. Where am I?"

"This is London, England of course," offered Tom, "I don't understand! Zakastra? Where is that?"

Lalitha looked around once more at the unfamiliar sights around her.

London? She had never heard of it. She felt the pulsing energy of the Book rush through her and the voice spoke in her head.

"Teach him." It commanded.

Lalitha took a long breath and stared into Tom's eyes.

"My father was ruler of the realm of Zakastra, but a usurper called Gask murdered him and has stolen the throne. Gask and his allies made to capture me and the only way I had to escape him was to jump from the top of the cliffs at the edge of the Western Sea. I chose to die to keep the Book from him, but instead it saved us both. As I fell, it used me to summon the power of the Souls and that power brought me here. I do not know where this London is, but I think I am far from home now."

"Power of the Souls?" Tom exclaimed. "Kings and usurpers? What are you talking about?"

"The Book showed you a vision. It has touched you. Your ears may not believe what I am telling you, but your heart knows that what I say is true. You feel it in your soul."

Tom was lost for words. What was going on here? Was Zakastra somewhere in eastern Europe? He had never heard of it. The strange thing was that Tom could not shake the feeling that he should trust her. How could that be? Something within him was telling him that this girl needed his help.

Tom needed a drink. He went to the sideboard and picked up a bottle of Jack Daniels and two glasses. He poured two big measures and passed one to Lalitha before quickly tipping most of the contents of his glass down his throat, savouring the burn of the whisky. She sniffed at hers before tentatively taking a sip. Her face instantly screwed up and she hastily spat the liquid back into the glass. She put the glass on the coffee table and pushed it away from her, the sharp taste of the whisky still causing her face to contort in displeasure.

Not even noticing her reaction, Tom sat down, dropped his head into his hands and rubbed his eyes, trying to get his thoughts straight. After a few moments, he turned his attention back to the girl who was watching him intently.

"What were the images you showed me?"

"I showed you nothing," she replied. "It was the Book."

"OK, so what did your Book show me?"

"It opened a pathway to the power of Souls that it contains. They showed you a vision of the atrocities that have taken place in my land and they have touched your living soul to make you believe. Now you believe, you can keep us safe."

"What exactly is this book?" Tom asked.

Lalitha thought for a moment.

"The Book is sacred. Throughout the ages, it has endured on its altar in the tower at Krassak, collecting the immortal souls of countless kings, queens, mystics and magi. These souls live on within the stone that is embedded in the Book. This stone is called the Soulstone. The learnings, knowledge and power of each collected Soul is used to strengthen the Book and allows the Chosen to protect the realm."

"The Book selects its Chosen from the royal children who are presented to it when they are new-born. A Ceremony of Binding is carried out when a Chosen comes of age which binds their soul to the Book. When the Chosen eventually falls and death comes, their body is left behind and their spirit enters the Soulstone to become one with the Book. To keep the Souls of our ancestors safe, we must keep the Book safe."

Tom listened to the words she said, but found it difficult to take in.

"So, you're saying that this book of yours is magic?"

"Not magic. The Book protects its Chosen using the knowledge and power of the Souls that dwell within the Soulstone. If a Chosen successfully completes the Ceremony of Binding, the Book will allow them to use words of summoning to channel the power themselves, but until the ceremony is undertaken, the Book controls all. Even when Bound, a Chosen cannot access all the power and knowledge within. The Book would not allow it."

"I heard you shouting spells or something just before you hit me," He said.

"I did not utter the words of summoning and I did not hit you," countered Lalitha. "The Book used me as a vessel because it felt threatened. It uses the power within to protect itself if it senses any kind of threat. It spoke the words of summoning and it struck you because it thought you were a threat."

Tom snorted, "It thought I was a threat?"

"When I awoke here, I thought you meant to try to take the Book from me. It sensed my fear and struck out because it thought you meant it harm. It was only when I touched you that the Book read your soul and sensed that you could be trusted. That was why it showed you the vision."

"So, does that make *ME* one of these Chosen Ones?" Tom asked nervously.

The girl snorted with derision. "Of course not! You are not of royal Zakastran blood. I am of the royal line and I am Chosen, but I have not yet been Bound to the Book. I cannot yet channel the power of the Souls, but the Book can work through my body to protect us both. My father was Chosen, as was my older brother Relfa, but there are no others to my knowledge. The Book has not chosen any new-borns since I was presented to it as a child."

Tom poured himself another drink. This was just all too surreal. He gestured with the bottle towards Lalitha. She shook her head.

"Why did the Book bring you here?"

"I do not think that the Book had time to choose a destination. I was falling towards the rocks and it had to quickly open a gateway to save us just before we hit them. That we arrived here I think was pure chance."

Tom took another large gulp of the whisky. Was he losing his mind?

"The guy that you were running from. He wants the Book for himself?"

"Yes, Gask wishes to claim the Book. He wishes to destroy our whole way of life. He is an enemy of the realm and will stop at nothing to turn the people to his own way of thinking."

Tom thought back to the vision he had seen.

"Did your father have a silver crown?" he asked.

"Yes," Lalitha gasped. "Did the Book show him to you?"

"In the vision I had, I saw a grey-haired man with a silver crown looking down from a tower. He had blood on his hands. I also saw a big man with a black beard dressed in black leather armour."

"Gask! He murdered my father!" she spat.

"Why didn't the Book protect your father if it is so powerful and he was Chosen?"

"I do not know. When I found him, my father was lying dead on the floor and Gask was standing over his body. My brother Relfa knelt nearby wailing. He was covered in blood and my mother was holding him. The Book lay unguarded where my father had dropped it and to keep it from Gask, I snatched it and tried to run. My mother saw me and grabbed at me as I hurried from the room and then... then something else happened."

She shook her head as if trying to dislodge the memory from her mind.

"There was danger all around," she stammered. "There was blood everywhere and I ran... I just ran. I found my way to the secret tunnels that extend out beyond the city walls and I used them to get away."

Tom paused, trying to take this all in.

"In my vision I saw a beautiful dark-haired woman with striking green eyes like yours. She was crying. Could that have been your mother?"

"Yes," said Lalitha bitterly, her eyes suddenly brimming with tears.

"What happened to her when you ran?"

"I cannot talk of it," said Lalitha angrily, the tears starting to run down her face, "but all that happened is because of Gask."

Tom considered what she had told him.

"Do you think Gask killed your brother too?"

"I do not know," she sniffed, "but he was covered in blood. I think he is likely dead."

Tom was shocked and waited until Lalitha had composed herself again before speaking.

"I am so sorry, Lalitha. What are you going to do?"

"I need to return home to regain the throne and punish Gask for what he has done," she said wiping her cheeks with the back of her hands. "Under his rule, the realm is doomed to chaos."

"Can the Book not magic you straight there and just take him out?"

"The Book's control of the Souls diminishes the further away it is taken from its altar at Krassak. It does not have enough power here to open a gateway to take me home. Here, its power is weakened. If it were not, you may well be dead now. In my land, the summoning command that it aimed at you could have killed you. The Book needs to return to my land to become strong again, but it will not regain its full power until it is placed back on its altar at Krassak. I have to take the Book back there and use its power to help me destroy Gask and his allies."

"How can you do that if the Book is weakened here and can't get you home?" asked Tom.

"The Book knows what to do and you are going to help us to do it Thomas McAllister," Lalitha said.

Tom was taken aback. What was she asking him to do and how did she know his name?

"Me? Help you? How can I do anything to help you?"

Lalitha lifted her hand and touched his face again. The hair on the back of his neck and on his arms stood on end and his stomach lurched as if he had looked over a cliff edge into a bottomless chasm. The stone on the cover of the book burned brightly and a voice spoke in his head. A voice that hissed urgently at him.

"You will help us Thomas McAllister. Your fate is tied to our own. To deny your fate is to deny everything."

Tom flinched, shaking his head.

"You must help us," whispered Lalitha. She looked exhausted and she was struggling to keep her eyes open.

Tom stood up. He needed this to stop, even if just for a little while.

"This is too much Lalitha," he said. "I need to think this all through before my head bursts."

Lalitha tried to stand up as well, but her legs buckled underneath her and she fell back onto the sofa. She mumbled something incoherent as her eyes closed and she slumped onto her side.

Tom crouched beside her. She was breathing deeply and looked like she had fallen into a deep sleep. He carefully pushed his arms underneath her and lifted her up. She was small and didn't weigh very much. Even with his prosthetic arm, Tom managed to easily carry her to his bedroom. He laid her gently on the bed and pulled the duvet over her. He stood watching her sleep for several minutes before deciding that she was safe to be left on her own.

Tom walked back to the living room and picked up Lalitha's discarded JD and sipped at it as he debated whether or not to call that ambulance. After much soul-searching, Tom decided to leave things be and see what the morning brought. The girl didn't seem to be in any physical danger, she just looked exhausted.

He pulled a woollen throw from his armchair and plumped up the cushions as he sat down on the sofa. Tom finished off the whisky and took the glasses to the sink where he gave them a rinse and set them on the drainer. He took his prosthetic arm off and placed it carefully on the coffee table before taking a tube of cream from the kitchen drawer and awkwardly squeezing a little of the white paste into the palm of his hand. He winced as he worked the cream into the scarred tissue on the stump of his left arm. He hated having to do this, but it was something that had to be done. The last thing he needed was to develop sores and not be able to wear his prosthetic.

Once the cream had all gone, Tom turned the light off and went back to the sofa. He laid down, pulled the throw over himself and rested his head on a cushion. He watched the flash of headlights from passing cars as they illuminated the ceiling above the window and mulled through the events of the evening.

The whole thing felt surreal. Could this really be happening? If it hadn't been for the vision that he had seen and the voice he had heard in his head, Tom would think that Lalitha's story was utter insanity, but he had seen the vision and he had heard the voice. It was crazy, but Tom knew deep down that what Lalitha had told him was true.

What the hell had he got himself involved in?

CHAPTER 5

West London, England

Tom did not sleep well. He spent the night tossing and turning on the sofa and when he did manage to eventually drift off, dreams of strange voices, battles and blood filled his subconscious. He woke early and realised that sleep was not going to be possible now; his head was too full of the events of the previous night. Had that all really happened? He had to check to see if Lalitha was really asleep in his bed.

He got up and stretched out his tight body. He was too tall to spend a whole night trying to fit his frame onto that sofa! He picked his prosthetic up from the table where he had left it last night and pushed it back into place on his left arm. It ached like a sod this morning. Strange how a limb that wasn't even there any longer could hurt so much.

Tom turned a lamp on and walked to the bedroom. He quietly pushed the door open and carefully looked inside. Lalitha lay on the bed, breathing gently as she slept. She had cast the duvet off and lay on top of the bedclothes, the Book clasped in her left hand. Tom was not going to risk giving her a fright in case the Book attacked him again, so instead backed up and slowly pulled the door closed behind him.

"Shit!" He whispered to himself. "It's real."

What was he going to do? Was he really involved in a Tolkienesque quest to return Lalitha to a mythical throne somewhere? It was ridiculous wasn't it?

Tom went to the kitchen, turned the kettle on and poured himself a glass of water. He put two heaped teaspoons of instant coffee in a mug and popped a couple of ibuprofen to try to help with his phantom aches. The kettle clicked and he poured the hot water into the mug, the strong smell of coffee helping to make him feel more awake.

It was too quiet and to stop his mind racing, Tom went back to the sofa and used the remote to turn on the morning news. The BBC presenters were their usual chirpy selves as they linked into a report from the latest Middle Eastern warzone. A reporter came into view, all kitted out in helmet and flak jacket. She was taking cover behind a building whilst gunfire went off all around her. The sight and sounds brought vivid memories back of Helmand. Memories that Tom did not want to think about… especially now with everything else going on in his head. However, before Tom could switch the channel, the bedroom door was thrown open and Lalitha burst into the room looking alarmed. She quickly looked around the room as she tried to identify the unfamiliar noises and her eyes widened as she saw the TV.

"It's okay," assured Tom. "You're safe. You're safe. Don't try to blast anything!"

"What is that?" she exclaimed, pointing at the flat screen.

"It's just the television," he said, realising she may not have ever seen one before. "Amongst other things, it shows messages and pictures about events that are happening around the world."

The fear slowly left Lalitha's expression and she sat, mesmerised by the images she was seeing. She jumped visibly as gunfire cracked from the TV speakers.

"What is that?" she asked. "What are they doing?"

"It's a news report from a conflict in another country. Basically, they are killing each other. It is a war," he responded.

"A war?" Lalitha mused. "Where are their horses and swords and lances? What is that noise?"

"The noise you can hear is gunfire. We don't have swords or lances. We have guns and all sorts of other shit to kill each other with. We haven't used swords and lances for a long time. You wouldn't last five minutes here using a sword. They would be useless because somebody would just use a gun to shoot you dead before you got anywhere near them."

"Guns…" Lalitha repeated the words slowly. "Gunfire…"

"I don't think we should watch any more of this," said Tom making to turn the TV off.

"Wait!" she snapped. "What is a gun? How do you use them to kill your enemies?"

Tom didn't want to dwell on this subject and switched off the TV.

"Thomas McAllister," she insisted. "Explain to me what a gun is."

Tom sighed. "Soldiers use guns to shoot fast moving metal projectiles called bullets at the enemy. The bullets go through people. They kill them. That is gunfire."

"Like a bow and arrow?" Lalitha asked.

"Bullets are more destructive, they are much faster and can be fired from much further away, but yes, they are projectile weapons like arrows."

Lalitha started to frantically search around the room.

"Do you have guns and bullets here?"

"No. No, of course I don't. Only the army have them." Tom began to feel distinctly uneasy.

Lalitha was becoming very agitated.

"This is how you can help me!" she exclaimed. "You can get guns and bullets from your army and help me to fight Gask and return the Book to its altar at Krassak! You said their swords would be useless against us!"

"Whoa… hold on there!" said Tom. "I can't get guns for you. I'm not in the army. I used to be, but not any longer."

"Why did you leave your army?"

Tom held his robo-arm in front of her. "This is why. I lost my arm."

Lalitha studied Tom's polymer arm and hi-tech hand mechanism and shrugged as if she didn't know what he was showing her. He flexed his artificial fingers and they closed into a fist with a faint whirr.

"But your arm is there. What do you mean you lost it?"

Tom took a deep breath and pulled the prosthetic off, exposing what remained of his lower arm.

Lalitha gasped. "The arm is not real?"

"It was made for me by engineers. It works with what is left of my arm to give me some control. It lets me live my life."

"You lost your real arm in battle?"

"Yeah. I made a mistake and the enemy took my arm. I spent a long time recovering and my army didn't want me any longer."

Tom re-attached the prosthetic to his left arm and moved his fingers to make sure the sensors were detecting his muscle movements correctly.

Lalitha watched him thoughtfully for a few moments before talking again.

"You know where your army keeps their guns and bullets?"

"No," Tom lied, "I don't and even if I got them for you, you wouldn't know how to use them!"

"You could teach me," she said.

Tom shook his head. He needed to change the subject. He looked down and remembered the injuries that Lalitha had on her feet.

"Let me see your feet," he said.

She raised her bare feet towards him and he looked at the cuts and scrapes on them. Dirt was embedded within the cuts and they needed to be cleaned.

"Stay there," said Tom, "I'll be right back."

He went to the kitchen and grabbed the surgical spirit that he used to clean his prosthetic arm. He picked up a clean tea towel from the drawer and went back to where Lalitha sat.

"This will sting," he warned before pouring a small amount of spirit onto the cotton.

Lalitha winced, but made no noise as Tom gently cleaned her feet. It took several minutes, but after using half the bottle of spirit and getting another clean towel, Tom was confident that he had removed as much of the grit and dirt from her injuries as he could. He moved the coffee table nearer so she could rest her heels on the wooden surface.

"That should reduce the risk of the cuts getting infected," he told her. "Let the surgical spirit evaporate and I will put some dressings on them for you."

She nodded.

"Are you hungry?" Tom asked. Lalitha nodded again.

"Ok, I'll see what I can do."

Tom went to the kitchen and opened the fridge. There wasn't much in there and he wasn't sure what Lalitha would eat, but noticed the egg box and what was left of a loaf of thickly sliced Hovis. Egg Banjos it was then.

Soon the smell of cooking filled the flat and, ten minutes later, Tom presented his unexpected breakfast guest with a plate full of steaming fried egg sandwiches and a glass of water.

"Help yourself," he said.

Needing no second invitation, Lalitha picked up a sandwich and ate it hungrily. She smiled.

They ate and drank in silence for several minutes before Tom asked a question that had been troubling him.

"How did you know my name?"

"Thomas McAllister? The Book told me. When it touched you, it learned much about you."

"I should have guessed, shouldn't I? What else did it learn about me."

"That you are a warrior. That you can be trusted and that you will help us get back to the tower at Zakastra."

"I hope the Book isn't mistaken then," Tom grimaced.

"It is not," Lalitha said.

The last of the breakfast was finished and Tom cleared the empty crockery away. When he returned, Lalitha was sat with her head bowed. She looked deep in thought.

"What are you going to do Lalitha? How are we going to get you home?"

Lalitha took a few moments before replying. Was the Book talking to her? He could hear that faint whispering sound, so he guessed that it was.

"The Book is weakened here, but if we can find an altar in your realm that is powerful enough, the Book might be able to use it to take us back."

"An altar? Like in a church?"

"What is a church? We need an altar that harnesses the energy of the land and concentrates its life-giving power into one focused point. When placed on such an altar, the Book can harness the energy and use it to intensify the Souls' power. This power can open a gateway and take us home."

"I don't think we have altars like that in our churches," Tom said. "Here they are just symbolic religious tables."

Lalitha looked confused.

"Show me one of your churches?" she said.

Tom reached for his phone. It had fully charged overnight and Tom powered it up. Once he was logged into the device, Tom pulled up his web browser and typed a search into Google. He clicked on the first result and turned the phone to show Lalitha the photograph he had found of the inside of a typical British church. She gasped at the sight of the electronic image and grabbed the phone to examine it more closely.

"What is this?" she asked as she turned the Samsung over in her hands.

"It is a mobile phone… Errr… a communication device? It also lets me access a library of data online… like this image."

Lalitha looked carefully at the small screen and shook her head.

"The image that your picture box shows us does not look like an altar to me."

"It is what our altars look like," Tom answered.

"That is not what we need," she declared, dropping the phone on the coffee table. "Do you have ink and velum that I can draw with?"

Tom fetched an unopened bank statement and a biro. Lalitha examined the pen with interest before starting to scribble on the envelope. She drew a rectangular shape in the middle of the paper, then around it in a circle she drew a series of arches and pillars.

"An altar!" she declared, pointing at her drawing.

Tom looked at the drawing, picked up his phone, quickly ran another image search and then passed the phone back to her.

"What about this?" he asked.

Lalitha looked at the image of Stonehenge on the screen and smiled for the first time.

"Yes. That is an altar. We need to go there, but we need to do something else first."

"What's that?"

"We need to get guns and bullets to use against the enemy."

"I told you, I can't do that," he sighed.

"You must!" she said, starting to get angry.

"Lalitha," Tom insisted, "I really want to help you get home, but I can't get you guns. It is just impossible."

Lalitha was about to protest when a loud knock came from the front door. Startled, they both turned sharply towards the sound. Whoever was outside knocked again, even more loudly.

Lalitha clutched the Book tightly and the Soulstone started to pulse with light.

"Don't panic," Tom said. "It's probably nothing. Just let me check, okay?"

Tom went to the door and opened it up to reveal Danny standing in the cold early morning rain.

"Danny… What are you doing here?"

"Thanks Boss. Nice to see you too! Thought I'd call in on my way home to see if you're okay. I know the team get-togethers mess with your head sometimes, so I thought I'd call by and check on you. C'mon, let me in, I've been up all-night chasing around for Alexey bloody Petrov. It's cats and dogs out here. Jeez, is that egg banjos I can smell?"

Danny bowled in past Tom, brushing drops of rain out of his hair as he walked into the living room.

"Danny, it's not a great time…" Tom protested.

"Why, what's going… Ah… Shit!" Danny spluttered, suddenly seeing Lalitha sat on the sofa staring at him, a fearful look on her face.

Tom rushed to stand in-between Danny and Lalitha, fearful of what she might try to do.

"It's okay, Lalitha, this is Danny. He is a friend."

"Sorry Boss. I… errr… didn't realise you had company." Danny said. A smile slowly spread across his face as he took in Lalitha's attractive face and short dress. "Who are you then? The Boss has been keepin' you quiet, hasn't he?"

Tom took a deep breath. He had to say something, but Danny was going to think that he had lost his mind.

"It's not what you think. This is Lalitha. I pulled her out of the road last night. She got hurt while she was running away from a guy that had just murdered her father. We were trying to work out how to get her home again when you came barging in."

Danny looked at Lalitha and then back at Tom.

"What have you got yourself involved in here, Boss?"

"I know this is going to sound mental Danny, but Lalitha is not from here. She comes from somewhere a long way away and she's a princess. After she escaped from her father's killer, she was brought here by… errr… a magic book…"

Danny snorted in disbelief. "Have you been sniffing glue or something? What the fuck are you on about?"

Danny was looking at him as if he had lost his mind, but Tom pressed on.

"I know it sounds crazy Danny, but it's true. That's the book there in her hands. It is important and it must be protected. The book brought her here and she needs me to help her. She has to get back home and stop the maniac that murdered her father. It's true. Really."

"You must believe your friend," Lalitha said firmly. "He speaks the truth."

"What was that?" Danny exclaimed. "I can't understand a word she's saying. What language is that?"

"I told you, Danny, she's not from here."

"Man, you've really lost the plot this time," blurted Danny. "This chick is a looker for sure, but I think she must've spiked you with something. Have you checked your wallet this morning?"

Danny threw a disgusted look in Lalitha's direction. In response, Lalitha stood up and walked towards him. She stopped in front of him and looked up into his face. As he watched her with undisguised suspicion, she reached up to touch him. Danny tried to grab her arm to stop her, but as he did so, she lithely dodged his move and quickly placed her palm on his forehead. As their skin touched, Danny jerked and fell backwards as if she had hit him with a Taser. His eyes rolled up into his head and he collapsed onto the floor.

"What did you do?" accused Tom. He could hear the whispering voices again and noticed that the Book's stone was burning with orange fire between her fingers.

Lalitha glanced at him, the fireflies ablaze in her eyes. Slowly the green of her irises returned and she breathed heavily.

"The Book touched him. He has seen a vision as you did and the Book has enabled him to understand my language."

"I didn't pass out when it did its thing on me. What else has it done to him?"

Between them, they pulled Danny's limp form onto the sofa and propped his head on one of Tom's tartan cushions. Tom stood over him, nervously watching him breathe until, after a minute or two, Danny awoke with a jolt. He blinked rapidly and sat up, his gaze moving between Tom and Lalitha.

"You okay?" asked Tom.

Danny sat rubbing his head where Lalitha had touched him. He was looking at her with a strange expression on his face. He was calm. Calmer than Tom had been after his vision.

"Boss, I saw things. In my head. Places I've never been. People I've never met. A voice spoke to me and showed me a whole heap of freaky shit. I saw blood. Lots of it. Flames. Bodies burning. Some creepy lookin' tower and her. I saw her. Runnin'. Horses chasin' her. She was cryin' and her hands were covered in blood. A voice told me that my fate is bound with hers."

Danny paused, slowly massaging his face with his hands. He looked bewildered. Lalitha interrupted him excitedly.

"What else did you see? Did you see my father?"

Danny looked at her and rubbed his eyes.

"I can understand what you're saying now," he stammered.

"The Book has taught you to hear my words," Lalitha nodded. "What else did you see?"

"After I saw you and the blood, things went dark and then weird lights started to drift in front of my eyes like sparks from a fire. Then I was flyin'. I could see a rocky island out in the ocean. There was a temple or somethin' there and a voice was calling me. An old man dressed in a cloak and holdin' a staff was standing at the gate beckonin' to me. He was mumbling about a ceremony or somethin'. Boss? I feel weird as fuck!"

Lalitha suddenly went very quiet and she stared intently at Danny, a strange expression on her face.

"There is something more, something else has happened, but I am not sure what it is. What you saw sounds like... but that cannot be."

The Book tingled in her hands as if it had been suddenly charged with static electricity and lights danced within its stone. The voice spoke in Lalitha's head.

"He is Chosen."

Lalitha gasped and turned to Tom, "I do not understand how… or why, but Daniel Adams has been chosen!"

Tom stared at his friend and struggled to comprehend the implications of what he was hearing.

"What? Chosen as in CHOSEN? I thought you said you had to be royalty to be Chosen and he's hardly a new-born? He's not even from your land, he was born in Southwark for crying out loud!"

Lalitha appeared to be stunned at this turn of events.

"I do not know how this is possible. It has been centuries since a Chosen One was not of the royal house," she said. "Not since before the days of the Magi Wars has this happened… but, we must trust the Book. It sees what we do not."

Danny looked dazed, but his voice was strong and his eyes clear. "Boss. What the hell is going on?"

Lalitha took Danny's hand and placed it on the Book. The stone burst into life, His body began to tremble and his eyes began to burn as Lalitha's had. Inside his head, the Book spoke in its strange booming voice.

"You are Chosen." It pronounced. *"You must go to the Isle of Gessan and complete the Ceremony of Binding. Once this is done, return us to the Tower of Krassak to restore our power."*

Danny breathed in sharply and his eyes cleared.

"Danny?" Tom asked apprehensively. "What happened?"

"It spoke to me again. The Book. That voice. Jesus, Boss, we've gotta get her home, Boss, and we've gotta go with her. We have to help her. That Book has done something to me… I can feel it."

"It has chosen you," Lalitha smiled. "It is a great honour. Only members of the royal family are chosen normally. It must have sensed something in you."

"Danny, are you okay?" Tom asked.

"Yeah, Boss. I'm fine. This is all just freakin' me out a bit."

"Daniel Adams?" interrupted Lalitha, "can you get us guns and bullets?"

Danny looked at her, a confused look on his face.

"Course I can," he said, "but what do we need them for?"

"We need them to destroy my father's murderer."

CHAPTER 6

West London, England

Danny sat talking quietly with Lalitha as Tom used the last of his eggs to make another batch of banjos for Danny. Despite being up all-night doing God knows what, Danny did not seem to be at all tired. He looked up thoughtfully as he tucked into his breakfast.

"Boss," he said, "we've gotta do this. We need to ring the guys. I think I know where we can get the guns from, but we're not gonna be able to do it on our own. We need backup."

"No chance," asserted Tom. "There's no way we're dragging the others into this thing, whatever it is, and I'm not sure we should even be thinking about trying to get guns either."

"Listen to me," said Danny. "The Book has spoken to both of us. Unless we've both gone completely mad, we know that we've gotta do this. We have no choice. You heard the voices as strongly as I did. It's fuckin' real Boss! If we're serious about helpin' Lalitha get the Book back to its altar and takin' out this Gask guy in the process, we're gonna need some heavy-duty firepower. I think I know where we can get it, but we're gonna need the team back together if we're gonna stand a chance of pulling it off."

"Come on, Danny… as if this isn't crazy enough already, do you really think we'll be able to just sneak into some highly defended army garrison, break into their armoury, steal a heap of weaponry and leg it without being caught, arrested or shot?"

Danny grinned, "Nah. Screw that! I've got a much easier way of getting' it. A couple of months back, an army truck disappeared in between trainin' exercises on the south coast. It was chock-full of brand-new kit that the special forces and marines were gonna be trainin' with and then takin' out to Syria, but some low life scumbags heard about the shipment and nicked it. They found the truck the next mornin' out in woodland near Basingstoke. The useless monkeys that were supposed to have been guardin' it were in the back all tied up and the guns had gone."

"I never heard anything about it in the news?" said Tom.

"You wouldn't, would you? The military wouldn't want a balls-up like that becomin' public knowledge."

"So how did they do it?"

"No idea," laughed Danny, "but the interestin' thing is that I know where it ended up!"

"Where?"

"In a container, hidden in a warehouse in East London. Alexey's boss, a nasty piece of work called Kirill Kosnetsov, organised the whole thing and has the container ready to ship out to the highest bidder."

"How do you know all about this, Danny? You weren't involved, were you?" asked Tom.

"Me? No way! They don't pay me enough for that kind of risk. While I was workin' for Alexey a couple of nights ago, he had me deliver a package to Kosnetsov's goons in the old London Docklands near City Airport. I don't know what the package was, dodgy cash probably, but the point is I overheard a couple of them braggin' about a big score they'd made a while back. They were half pissed and didn't even notice that I was there. Unprofessional pricks! They were rabbitin' on about how they had nicked a shit-ton of guns from the army and were gonna make a fortune from floggin' them on to whoever offered them the most cash."

"Where is the container then?"

"That's the thing. It was right there. I saw it with my own eyes!"

"So, what's in it? What did they steal?"

"Well, I don't actually know that, but it's gotta be the good stuff hasn't it, if it was supposed to be for the spec ops lads?"

Tom looked sceptical.

"It's a bit bloody risky isn't it? What kind of security do they have?"

"There were about eight guys there that I saw. All tooled up, but only with crappy Skorpion machine pistols and you can't hit a barn door with those peashooters."

"So, eight guys? All armed?" said Tom, shaking his head. "In case you've not noticed there are just two of us and we're armed with what? Oh yeah, a good line in bullshit and a prosthetic arm!"

"Which is why we need the lads to help us!" sighed Danny.

Lalitha had been watching the exchange, but now spoke up.

"You have friends that could help us get the guns?" she asked.

"Yeah," said Danny at exactly the same time as Tom said, "No!"

Tom looked at Lalitha.

"Lalitha, could you get the Book to show the Russians a vision and then they just hand the guns over? We wouldn't need to involve anyone else that way."

"Think about it, Boss." Danny replied, "if one of the goons saw Lalitha put her hand on one of their mates and made him keel over, there's a fair chance that the muppets might just shoot her right there and then."

"I cannot use the Book in that way yet, Thomas McAllister," Lalitha added. "The Book would try to protect me if someone was attacking me, but I cannot wield the power myself until I am bound to the Book. That only happened to Daniel Adams because the Book chose him and delved deep into his soul. I believe that the Book should be able to protect me from guns and bullets, but it is weakened in this realm so I do not know for sure."

"Boss, come on," Danny groaned. "If the Book can't do anything to help, we need to get the old team back together. Who else would you trust to back us up?"

"But Danny, they're out! They're safe in civvy street. Away from the guns. Away from the death and blood and shit!"

"And they're bored shitless, Boss. They're living mindless borin' lives doin' meaningless shit to make a livin'. For Christ's sake, Cod stacks bloody supermarket shelves all night and all he ever does in his spare time is play on his bloody Xbox or get pissed with me. Some days he doesn't even talk to anyone at all! Slaphead is elbow deep in grease gettin' paid sod all for tryin' to get some old dear's banger through an MOT, and Moonshine gets grief all day long goin' door-to-door tryin' to sell burglar alarms to obnoxious racist dickheads who just want to stare at her tits!"

Danny took a breath and carried on before Tom could get a word in.

"This is the chance to do somethin' real Boss. Never mind just the Book, we can actually help people here. We can help Lalitha to stop the guy that killed her father and that sounds like it would help all the people in her country. We'd be making a proper difference for a change and not be hampered by the politics that made Helmand such a cluster-fuck!"

"But Danny, we'd be putting the guys in danger again after all this time."

"I know, but I reckon they'd snap your arm off if you said you needed them. If we don't do this, it seems to me that the lives of a lot of people in Lalitha's world will go to shit."

Tom was seriously conflicted. He knew that if he truly believed Lalitha's story, then what Danny was saying was true, but could he take the responsibility of putting them all in harm's way again? Look what had happened the last time they had operated as a team.

"I'm gonna ring them, Boss." He announced. "We can talk to them and if they want in, then fantastic. If they don't, then fair enough. What do you reckon?"

Tom took a deep breath. In his heart he knew that Danny was right. If they were going to do this and raid a Russian Mafia warehouse, then they needed help and he couldn't think where else they would find it.

"Okay, Danny, but I'll ring them."

CHAPTER 7

West London, England

Tom had been lucky. Because it was a Saturday, neither Alex nor Sam were working so he got through straight away. They were both surprised to hear from him so soon after seeing him, but when Tom explained that he and Danny needed their help, they both said they would be there as quickly as they could. Jimmy had not yet finished his night shift when he answered the call, but when he heard that everyone was coming round to discuss something serious, his response was instantaneous.

"No probs, Boss. I'll just bunk off work right now. Gimme a few minutes and I'll be there."

By the time they started to arrive at Tom's flat, the rain clouds had cleared and the winter sun was starting to peek up over the rooftops. Sam and Jimmy appeared first. Tom didn't fill them in, but kept them occupied with a cuppa and the last few digestives that he found in the back of the cupboard. Alex had the furthest to travel and it was another ten minutes before she knocked on Tom's door.

Danny let her in and she traded the customary insults with the guys as she came into the living room. However, as soon as Alex saw Lalitha the smile fell from her face.

"Boss, what's this all about and who's the girl here? The entertainment?"

Tom looked at the three new arrivals.

"This is Lalitha and she really needs our help. You're going to have to trust me. This is going to sound weird, but she is going to touch you and then you'll understand why I've got you here."

Danny nodded his agreement.

"The Boss is right. It sounds bat-shit I know, but you'll get it once she's touched you."

Alex, Sam and Jimmy all gaped at each other.

Sam gave Lalitha an appraising stare. "She can touch me any time she likes." He joked.

Alex shook her head firmly. "No way is she coming anywhere near me until I know what this is all about Boss."

Tom looked her in the eye, "Do you trust me, Alex?"

"Of course I do, you know that."

"Then just let her touch your face. It will just make explaining everything much easier."

"If this is a joke, Boss, it isn't all that funny," Alex said, watching Lalitha approaching them.

"Things will become clearer once I touch you," Lalitha said quietly.

"I don't even know what you're saying," Alex replied curtly. "Where are you even from?"

"You will understand once Lalitha has touched you," Tom assured her.

Alex didn't say anything further but gave Lalitha a sullen glance. Sam stepped forwards.

"Come on then. I don't know what this bollocks is all about, but let's get on with it. Touch me anywhere you like luv."

Jimmy and Alex looked at each other and slowly moved to Sam's side.

Tom nodded to Lalitha and saw her eyes ignite with the familiar sparkling pinpoints of flame. She gently touched Sam, Jimmy and Alex in turn and a few moments later, the three friends were all squeezed together on the sofa, dazed expressions on their faces. They had all been shown visions of Lalitha's parents, Findo Gask and the violence that had taken place in her land. Blood. Flames. Death. They could also now clearly understand the language that Lalitha spoke.

Tom and Danny sat on the coffee table facing them and carefully explained what Lalitha had told them and what the Book needed them to do.

Sam was the first to speak. "So, Lalitha, here has a magic book that has to be protected. Her father, the king, was murdered and we have to take her home and get the guy that did it?"

Tom nodded. "That's the gist of it. To get this done, we also need to steal ourselves some weapons and Fester has a line on where we can get them. His Russian mates have a shipment of military-grade kit that he thinks we can help ourselves to. It's a bit risky, but he thinks it can be done."

"Oh, this bollocks just gets better and better," sighed Alex. "Are you guys for real?"

Jimmy had been quiet since they had arrived, but now piped up. "Boss, after what I've experienced in the last few minutes and how it makes me feel, I think we need to help her. As I see it, we can help Lalitha and her people, or we can pretend that we didn't just experience those visions, leave her to it and get back to our shit lives. I think that we're going to need weapons to do this and if Fester thinks it's a go-er, I've got no problem nicking kit from a bunch of Russian mobsters, as long as we do it the right way."

Alex did not look at all happy.

"Can you all hear yourselves?" She spluttered. "Some pretty white girl appears from nowhere and you're all falling over each other to believe some, quite frankly, crazy story about magic and battles and evil murderers. Next thing you'll be telling us that her second name is Targaryen and she rides dragons!"

Jimmy grinned, but Danny did not see the funny side.

"Moony, come on!" he said. "Can you not feel that what she showed you is true? You saw the vision, didn't you?"

"I saw something, and I agree it feels pretty real," Alex admitted, "but I don't really understand how that can be. For all we know, this kid is Paul McKenna's baby sister and she's done a hypnotism job on us all. Before you know it, we'll be dancing like bloody chickens whenever we see a KFC advert on the telly."

Tom intervened before things degenerated into one of Alex and Danny's usual heated arguments.

"Come on you two," he said. "Alex, it's your call. If you don't want to help us, then nobody is forcing you to. It's fine. Honestly."

Alex looked at him, her face betraying her disapproval.

"Are you really buying into this, Boss?" she asked. "Are you going to potentially risk your life to help a girl that you found on the street literally less than twelve hours ago?" she asked.

"Yes, I am. I can't really explain it, but I just know that I have to help if I can," he replied.

"I can try to get the Book to explain more if you let me touch you again," Lalitha offered, moving towards Alex.

"Keep your fucking hands off me, Tinkerbell!" Alex warned, her hands coming up in a defensive stance.

Tom quickly moved in-between the two women.

"Really, Alex. If you don't want in, then just say so. It's not a problem."

Alex looked around the faces in the room.

"So, who is actually going to volunteer for this madness then?"

Danny nodded, Jimmy put up his hand, Sam sighed and put his hand up too.

Alex stood, deep in thought and then spoke.

"Okay so here it is. I think this is total bullshit and I can't believe that we're even considering going up against the Russian mob, but if you guys need me, I'll help. We're still a team yeah? Just know that I'm not doing it for Tinkerbell here, I'm doing it for the team. I'm doing it for you, Boss. Someone has to keep you safe and these idiots have proved in the past that they're pretty shit at that job!"

Tom smiled. He was relieved that she had agreed to join them, no matter how reluctant she was.

"Thanks, Alex," he grinned. "We'd be lost without you. You're the sensible one!"

"Well, I'll remind you that you said that when this all goes completely tits-up and we're sitting in a police cell somewhere or we're tied to chairs watching some Russian psycho pull our fingernails out!" Alex replied as she sat down on the floor at the edge of the group.

"Fester," said Tom, turning to Danny, "what do we do next? Is getting this kit from the Russians going to be as easy as you make out?"

"Give me a couple of days," Danny replied. "Hopefully Alexey will send me back there with another package and I can try to recce the warehouse out a bit better. Once we've got an idea what we're lookin' at, we can come up with a plan to get in and out without too much aggro."

"Okay," nodded Tom. "Just remember that, whatever happens, we don't want to spend the rest of our lives looking over our shoulders for Russian hitmen. We need to be able to get in and out without them knowing it was us. Lalitha, assuming that we manage to get the Danny's weapons, do we need to do anything to prepare for the Book to do its thing when we get to the Stonehenge altar?"

"No," she replied. "We can do nothing until we are there. We will not know if the Book is able to create the gateway until we have placed it on the altar. If it cannot draw enough power the gateway will not open…"

"… and we'll be left sitting in the middle of a major tourist attraction in Wiltshire with a heap of stolen army weapons and the Russian mafia hot on our heels," finished Sam. "Should be fun!"

"The Book won't let us down," said Danny. "Don't worry about what's gonna happen at the Henge. Let's get the kit from the Russians first."

"So, what, we meet up back here on Monday night? 19:00?" asked Tom. "If Danny has managed to suss the Russians' warehouse out and if we can put a workable plan together, we could aim to make our move on Tuesday night?"

They all nodded. Alex didn't look happy about it, but she would go along with it. For the time being at least.

Danny stood and looked as if he was going to leave, but then changed his mind and turned back to Tom.

"Can I kip on your bed for a bit Boss?" he asked. "I've been up all night. I'm knackered and I need to get some shut eye. I would go home but, y'know, I kinda want to stay close to Lalitha. Just in case."

"Yeah, no problem, Danny. Help yourself you know where it is."

Danny disappeared, yawning, into the bedroom. As he closed the door behind him, Sam and Alex started making their way towards the front door.

"Alex!" Tom called.

Alex looked back as she pulled her coat on.

"When you come back on Monday, could you bring some clothes for Lalitha? I know your stuff will be a bit big for her, but she should be able to make do. If she goes out like that again she's going to end up with hyperthermia."

Alex scowled, but nodded. "Yeah, whatever, Boss."

"Fun breakfast, Boss! We must do this again sometime." Sam quipped as he opened the door to leave. "Seriously though, if this is all as real as it feels and you need me with you, I'm definitely in. You know that right?"

"Thanks, Sam. I know this all sounds crazy when you say it out loud, but it just feels so real you know? There's nothing we can do right now so get on home. Let's see what Fester comes up with before we do anything else. I'll let you know before Monday if he comes up with anything new. Give me a bell if you need to talk or if you change your mind about getting involved in all this craziness."

"I'm not gonna change my mind Boss, but keep in touch okay?" said Sam as he headed out into the morning sunshine.

"I'll see you too," muttered Alex. There was no peck on the cheek this time as she strode off towards her car.

"Take care, Alex," Tom called after her. "Same is true for you as well. Call me if you need to."

"Okay Boss. I'm in, but I can't see this ending well."

Tom couldn't think of anything else to say to Alex to make this all sound any less crazy, so he watched her quietly as she unlocked the driver's door of her VW Golf, jumped in and quickly drove off without uttering another word.

Tom knew that this was all a lot to take in and Alex was obviously more skeptical than the rest of them. He didn't blame her. It all sounded like the plot of a movie, and if it hadn't been for the vividness of his vision and the voices he had heard, Tom would be far from convinced that any of Lalitha's story was true.

Back in the flat, Jimmy was sat next to Lalitha asking her question after question about what he had seen in his vision. Tom watched as Lalitha moved closer and began to tell Jimmy about her father and his conquests in the south. Jimmy's face was bright red and he was captivated by Lalitha. The sound of her voice and the closeness of her body cast a spell over the young man.

Tom sat down nearby and listened to the stories Lalitha was telling. He closed his eyes and let the sound of her voice wash over him. It was not long before Tom's head lolled forwards and he fell asleep where he sat.

CHAPTER 8

West London, England

When Tom awoke it was late in the morning. Jimmy had gone out to get provisions, as Tom's fridge was now looking depressingly empty and there was no way that they could feed the four of them on what was in there.

Danny was awake and was deep in conversation with Lalitha. The two of them sat together talking about the binding ceremony and what it entailed.

"Once the magi fully open our spirits to the Book, we will feel the fallen Souls flow through us. Once Bound, we will be able to use words of summoning to channel their power into the physical world. Through the ceremony, we pledge our mortal bodies to serve and protect the Book until we too fall and become one with the Souls inside it. Our spirits will live on forever in union with the great minds, champions and rulers of our past."

Danny was spellbound, hanging on every word that Lalitha uttered. He watched her lips as she spoke and his face was filled with wonder.

Tom coughed which seemed to break the spell between them.

"What would happen if you didn't go through with this Ceremony of Binding?" he asked.

"If the ceremony is not completed then we would never be able to channel the power of the Souls and when we die, our spirits would not enter the book, they would simply drift away and be wasted," replied Lalitha.

"But do you really want to spend your whole life committed to serving and protecting a Book?"

"What the Book wants and what I want are the same thing. To restore its strength and use the power of the Souls to bring order back to the realm. My father's spirit now resides within the Book. By protecting the Book, I am protecting the immortal Soul of my father and all that came before him."

"But what about Danny? Why would he want his spirit to be Bound?"

"Once Bound, Danny will stand by my side and have the ability to wield the kind of power that he has never even dreamt of. He will live as a prince in my land. Wealth and power will both be his."

Danny grinned, "Boss, who wouldn't want that? I've struggled to make do my whole life. Rather than spendin' the rest of my life doin' odd jobs for criminals and bouncin' pissheads out of nightclubs, I can be a prince. A prince! Me!"

Tom shrugged. He couldn't really think of a counter argument to that one.

"You're sure?"

"I am," nodded Danny.

At that moment the front door opened and Jimmy entered, laden down with shopping bags.

"Sorry, Boss, I borrowed some cash out of your wallet. I hope you don't mind. I got a shitload of stuff in as I know you struggle to carry shopping bags. I saw your arm drop off once when you tried to pick a bag up."

"Thanks for reminding me!" Tom groaned.

Tom remembered the event all too well. He had gone to a physio session at the hospital and had gone straight out afterwards to *The Drum* with the team. When they had started to wrap things up at the end of the evening, Tom had tried to pick his sports bag up with his robo-arm. Unfortunately, the handle of the bag had become entangled in the chair leg and rather than picking the bag up, Tom had pulled his arm off and helplessly watched it fall out of his sleeve onto the floor. The team had found it hysterically funny, which was bad enough, but much worse was the fact that other nearby customers also noticed. They stared at him, nudging each other and pointing at him. One of the morons even tried to film it on their phone. It had taken quite some time before that incident stopped bothering him in the dead hours of the night when he couldn't sleep.

Jimmy looked a little disappointed to see Lalitha and Danny sitting so close together and so, seeing that he wouldn't be able to sit back down next to her, busied himself helping Tom unload the shopping bags.

Once everything was packed away, the two of them managed to knock together a pretty good chilli-con-carne. Lalitha was not convinced that the spicy food was particularly appetising, but she ate it anyway. She was now wearing one of Tom's old jumpers and a pair of joggers. They were way too big, but helped to both keep her warm and stop Jimmy staring every time she moved and her dress exposed too much thigh.

They talked away the afternoon, recounting stories of their time in Helmand to Lalitha and listening to her describe the people and places in her country. The great cities of the realm, the mountain ranges that bisected Zakastra, the great lake in the west and the expanse of the northern forests.

Before they knew it, the sun had set and the outside world returned to its winter darkness. Danny picked up his jacket, grabbed a handful of biscuits and crammed them into his pockets.

"I've gotta shimmy," he announced. "I'm gonna go see Alexey and see if he wants me to go to the east end again. I'll tell him I'm goin' over there to see a mate, so I can take somethin' over for him if he wants me to. If he goes for it, I can recce the warehouse while I'm there."

"Just be careful, Danny," Tom warned, "don't push your luck. If they get suspicious, things could get messy."

"Trust me," grinned Danny as he made his way out of the door.

"Keep in touch…" yelled Tom, but Danny was gone.

Tom, Lalitha and Jimmy decided to pass the evening watching TV. The flashing images on the screen fascinated Lalitha and seemed to distract her from everything that had happened over the past twenty-four hours. However, rather than allowing Tom and Jimmy to wind down, the TV led to Lalitha asking a myriad of questions about absolutely everything she saw on-screen. After an hour or so, Tom switched channels to BBC One because he couldn't take having to explain any more commercials to Lalitha. It had been relentless. Trying to explain cars, insurance policies, pizza delivery, washing machines, online gambling, cosmetics, electric toothbrushes and much more to someone who had never seen any of these things was exhausting. The straw that really broke the camel's back was when the Lil-Lets advert came on the screen. Jimmy almost spat his beer out when Lalitha asked what they were and Tom mumbled something non-committal before rapidly changing the channel.

Strictly Come Dancing on the BBC had been a godsend. Lalitha was transfixed by the dancing couples and both Tom and Jimmy were grateful to not have to do so much explaining. Tom watched Lalitha as much as he did the TV screen. She smiled as the figures span and leapt around the dancefloor, their brightly coloured costumes holding her rapt attention. As the show was reaching its climax, Tom's mobile rang. It was

Danny. He swiped the green icon and put the call on speaker.

"Danny, you okay?" he asked.

"All good, Boss!" Danny's voice boomed through the speaker. Lalitha jumped, looking around as if expecting to see Danny in the room. Realising his mistake, Tom took the call off speaker and moved to the kitchen while Jimmy tried to explain the mechanics of mobile telephonics and hands-free speakers.

"We're on!" Danny said breathlessly. "Alexey has got some shit goin' on with the Albanians so he's sent a couple of his trusted goons over to one of their brothels in Soho to do some deal or other. It's left him short-handed, so when I told him I was goin' over to Stratford to see a mate and asked him if he needed me to take anythin' over that side of the city, he went for it. I've got a package to drop in at the warehouse. I'm headin' over there now. It'll take me an hour or so to get there, but I'll recce what I can and report back as soon as possible, yeah?"

"Okay, Danny. Just watch your back. These people are dangerous."

Danny laughed confidently. "They're not as dangerous as us though are they, Boss? Speak in a bit."

The line clicked and went dead. It was just a waiting game now. Tom returned to the sofa where Jimmy's description of mobile phones had left Lalitha shaking her head in disbelief.

"Your world has wonders that my people would not believe," she said.

Tom laughed, "The same could be said for yours, Lalitha. There are as many horrors as there are wonders here though. Believe me."

The next two hours seemed like a lifetime. They tried to watch a movie, but only Lalitha paid much attention to it. Tom had opted for *Saving Private Ryan*. He thought it would give Lalitha a flavour of how horrific the wars in this world could be and how dangerous the guns that she craved were, but she took the violence in her stride. Only occasionally did she divert her attention from the screen to ask who was on which side, or how a particular weapon worked. She was especially interested in the Sherman tanks.

"No," Tom said before she had chance to ask about them. "Before you ask, we definitely can't get you a tank!"

Lalitha pulled a face.

Eventually the phone rang, but it was Sam rather than Danny. Tom answered the call and put it on speaker.

"Hey Boss, any news from Fester?" the tinny voice asked.

Lalitha hardly reacted this time, already becoming used to the alien technology.

"He should be in the East End now," said Tom. "Petrov took the bait and sent him over there with another package. He's going to try and do a better recce while he's there. You okay, Sam?"

Tom's phone suddenly started to beep. He had another incoming call. It was Danny.

"Sorry mate, Fester's trying to get through. Talk to you as soon as I can."

Tom terminated the line to Sam and quickly accepted Danny's call before it went to voicemail.

"Danny! What's happening?"

"Boss, forget about Tuesday. Let everyone know, we're goin' in tomorrow night."

CHAPTER 9

West London, England

The fact-finding mission at the Docklands warehouse had, in Danny's own opinion, proved to be a great success. He had dropped the latest package in to the upstairs office at the warehouse and had managed to strike up a conversation with two of the heavies guarding the building. It turned out that the Russians had initiated a turf war with the Albanian mob and there was a big move happening on Sunday night. Kirill Koznetsov, the boss of Russian operations in London, had decided that the Albanian expansion was taking too much business from his own operation, so the opposition needed to be reined back in. There had been a meeting on Albanian turf the previous night to try and arrange a peaceful settlement, but the meeting had gone badly and violence was now inevitable.

The guards at the warehouse were only too happy to tell Danny that the Albanians were going to get their 'asses kicked'. Koznetsov was assembling a team of heavies at the warehouse on Sunday. Sometime later that evening, the hit squad was to pay a visit to the home of the Albanian boss Dren Bardhi to, in Koznetsov's words, 'cut the head from the snake'. The house near Epson was strongly protected, but Koznetsov's plan was to overwhelm the defenders with superior numbers and shoot anything that moved. Once the Albanian leadership was taken care of, Koznetsov could take advantage of the ensuing chaos to reclaim the business they had lost and expand Russian operations into their enemy's territory.

The good news for Danny and the team was that this meant there would be fewer guards at the warehouse on Sunday night, and the ones that were there would be distracted by the events taking place at Bardhi's mansion. Danny could not find out what time the hit on the Albanian was scheduled for, but he figured that if they staked the warehouse out, they would see the departure of the Russian hit squad and then have an easier run at the container.

It was late afternoon by the time the whole team was assembled at Tom's flat. Jimmy and Alex had spent the morning on a shopping trip, visiting all the outdoor pursuit and army surplus shops in the area. Alex's credit card had taken quite a bashing, but they had managed to obtain almost everything they needed. Water bottles, protein bars, dehydrated food packs, combat knives, improvised survival kits, bivvy bags, a set of heavy-duty bolt cutters and, at Alex's insistence, a pack of six toilet rolls were piled in a big heap on Tom's bed. Five German army surplus Bergens had also been purchased to pack all the equipment into. Alex had even had the presence of mind to purchase a solar charger so that Tom could still recharge his electronic arm when its power cells ran low.

"You lot owe me a fortune," she complained as they divvied up all the newly purchased kit and packed it away into the Bergens. "I'm going to be busy on eBay if this whole thing turns out to be a wild goose chase."

Once everyone was back in the living room, Danny briefed them on what he had found. He spread a crude map of the warehouse that he had scribbled onto a couple of sheets of A4 paper on the coffee table. It showed the warehouse's main entrance, CCTV cameras at the front of the building and the location of the guards he had seen whilst he was there the night before. Most importantly, it showed the location of the precious container inside the warehouse.

"What about the back of the building, Danny? Is there a way in there?" asked Sam.

"I could only check it out from outside the perimeter fence and it didn't look like there was another way in to me. It's just the main door at the front. I couldn't wander round too much while I was in there. It would have looked too suspicious and the goons would have asked questions." He responded.

"Okay," interjected Tom, "so, we go in the front. Was there any internal CCTV?"

"I saw one dome camera inside the main door, but nothin' other than that."

"Can we disable the cameras?" asked Jimmy.

Danny sucked air through his teeth. "Probably not. They're almost certainly Wi-Fi cameras connected back to a central server somewhere, so unless Moonshine has got some of her jammin' kit handy, we're a bit screwed when it comes to disablin' them."

"He's right Boss," said Alex. "It's the same principle as the kit I sell to people. I could jam the Wi-Fi signal if I had my old army bag of tricks, but I don't have access to anything like that now. We could cut the comms lines going into the building to try and disable the network connection to the cameras. The only problem then is that, if these guys are not total cowboys and they've got 4G connectivity, cutting the phone lines won't make any difference. The signal will get through using the mobile 4G network rather than the land line. It's a pretty safe bet to say that we'll be electronically eyeballed whatever we try to do to the security cameras."

"Which is why I got you all these," announced Danny pulling four black woollen balaclavas out of his bag.

Sam pulled his on immediately and stuck his tongue out at Jimmy through the mouth hole.

Jimmy groaned. "Shit, Boss, I'm allergic to wool. I'm gonna go all red and itchy!"

"Better than the Russians seeing your face. That would not be a good thing!" Sam retorted. Jimmy reluctantly agreed.

"So, how do we get in without getting the shit kicked out of us by the Russian mafia?" asked Alex.

Tom picked up the pen from the table and used it to point at the map.

"I've talked it through with Fester and we think that the best bet is to just drive straight in the front gate here. Fester nicked us a transit van and has changed the plates on it so we don't get pulled over by the cops if they check the plates for some reason. He'll drive it up to the warehouse gates and we'll all be hidden in the back. Because Fester has been there before, we're hoping that the goons guarding the gate will recognise him and let him in."

"What if they check the back of the van?" Alex asked.

"Let's just hope that they don't," Tom said. "We're banking on them recognising Danny and just letting him in. Assuming we get through the gate, we then move into the warehouse and subdue the three guys in there. We use bolt cutters to break the lock on the container, open it up, take what we want and get out of there."

Danny then continued, "I've left a big Nissan Pathfinder parked in a dark corner out at Clacket Lane services this mornin'. We get there in the tranny van, switch everythin' to the Nissan and motor on down the M3 to Stonehenge. Once we get there it's over to Lalitha and the Book."

"Using the power of your altar, the Book will open a gateway to my homeland and we will use it to travel back to Zakastra," added Lalitha.

"This is all a bit worryingly half-arsed don't you think Boss?" said Alex. "This is only going to work if the guards at the gate let us in, if they don't search the back of the van, if there are only three guards inside, if we can subdue the three guards without them either raising the alarm or letting loose with a gun, if we can get out again and if, once we get to the Henge, Tinkerbell there can actually manage to wave her wand and magic us off to Never-Never Land. That is a fuck-load of ifs!"

"We could do with more time and more detailed information I agree, but if we're going to do this, tonight seems to be the best opportunity," Tom replied. "There are going to be fewer goons there which improves our odds. We could wait and do more reconnaissance, but Danny is confident that we can do this tonight."

"Yep," confirmed Danny. "Waitin' will only make it more dangerous."

"Where did you get a Nissan Pathfinder from Fester?" asked Jimmy. "I had a go in one once. That's a nice motor!"

Sam coughed and held his hand up.

"It was in our place for a service so I, er, borrowed it. It's even got a roof-box so we can pile all the Bergens in there."

Jimmy and Sam exchanged high-fives and Tom couldn't help but smile. The old team dynamics were still there.

"What if they start shooting from the get-go, what do we do then?" asked Alex.

"We use these," grinned Danny reaching into his bag again. Out of the depths of his holdall he pulled two old and battered looking Browning Hi-Power pistols.

"Jesus, Fester!" exclaimed Sam. "Did you nick them from the *Antiques Roadshow*?"

"I borrowed them from my uncle," replied Danny. "He kept them as a souvenir from the Falklands War back in the day. He was there with the 36 Engineer Regiment and managed to smuggle them out when he came home."

"Oh my God, we are so going to end up in a police cell," Alex groaned.

Sam picked up the first of the pistols, ejected the magazine and worked the slide to make sure the chamber was empty. He examined the magazine to find six rounds in there. Using his thumb, he ejected the bullets from the mag and inspected each of them carefully.

"These rounds are ancient mate!" he declared. "You sure they're gonna work if we need them to?"

"They'll be fine," said Danny. "Trust me!"

Sam raised his eyebrows at Danny and reached for the other handgun. This one was in a similar battered condition and held five rounds in its magazine.

"So, two old handguns with eleven rounds between them," stated Tom. "Not great, but better than nothing… assuming they work of course and don't jam the first time we go to fire them."

"We could test-fire a couple of them somewhere," suggested Jimmy, "but that would leave us with even fewer rounds."

"We might not even need them," said Danny, "and if things do go pear-shaped, all we need to do is pop a couple of goons and take their weapons!"

"Yeah, Danny," scoffed Alex, "just as easy as that. You're talking about shooting civvies here."

"They don't count," grinned Danny. "They're the scumbags who feed drugs to children and steal young girls from Eastern Europe to pimp out to fat old businessmen in the city. They deserve what they get."

Alex shrugged. He did have a point.

Lalitha was fascinated by the handguns and quietly reached past Tom to pick up the nearest Browning. Tom gently caught her wrist and stopped her.

"No, Lalitha," he said softly. "Don't touch those things. They're dangerous."

Lalitha scowled, but did as he asked.

Jimmy suddenly looked up thoughtfully. "There are only four masks here Fester. I'm guessing that you don't need one because the Russians already know who you are. If we do this, they're going to know it was you. They're gonna come after you, aren't they?"

Danny nodded. "Yep, you're right mate, but once the Book has done its thing at the Henge, we'll be in Zakastra and we won't have to worry about the Russians any longer."

Everyone went quiet as they thought about the distinct possibility that they were about to travel to another world. Tom broke the silence with a cough.

"Right. It's just gone five o'clock now," he announced. "How about we get something to eat, then head out? It's going to take us at least an hour and a half to get there. You know what Sunday evening traffic is like around London. Sunday night is the new Monday morning."

The team agreed and Jimmy hastily cooked up a huge pile of bacon sandwiches. Everyone bolted theirs down and Lalitha declared that they were much better than the chilli they had eaten the day before. It apparently tasted less of 'fire'.

Once they were all finished, Lalitha went to Tom's bedroom to hastily change into the clothes and boots that Alex had brought for her. Lalitha emerged wearing jeans and a fleecy jumper with one of Alex's old black puffer jackets over the top. Once she had pulled on a pair of lace-up boots and fastened them tightly, the team bundled out of Tom's flat and climbed into the van that Danny had parked outside. Danny, Tom and Lalitha climbed into the front of the vehicle, leaving the others to load the Bergens into the back of the van and climb in after them.

The drive to East London was slow, but the traffic thankfully hadn't built up too badly. To start with, Lalitha asked questions about everything she saw through the windscreen and Tom began to wish that he'd put her in the back with Alex, Sam and Jimmy. Soon though, she seemed to become overwhelmed by the cacophony of sights and sounds and sat quietly, her eyes gazing out through the windscreen. Once on the M25, with their van surrounded by vehicles returning to the city in droves from their weekend travels, Lalitha sat with her face buried in her hands, the noise and smell of the traffic proving too much for her.

"Don't worry," Tom reassured her. "Not too much further to go."

Eventually, they arrived at the docklands and Danny pulled the van into a side street around the corner from their destination. Tom climbed out and walked round to the rear doors. Opening them he gestured to Jimmy.

"Okay, Jimmy. Out you get. Nip down there and set yourself up around that corner," he said, pointing to the turning a couple of hundred metres down on the right. "The perimeter fence there is the southern edge of our warehouse. Find a position there somewhere out of sight. We're going to move down the road out of the way so that we don't get spotted. As soon as you see the Russians leaving, WhatsApp us and we'll drive round and pick you up, okay?"

"Roger that!" Responded Jimmy as he hopped down out of the van and set off walking down the road.

Tom climbed back into the van and Danny drove them away from the warehouse, taking a left turn and pulling into the car park of a huge discount carpet store. It was a waiting game now. If Jimmy didn't see the Russians leave, then they were going to have a problem. Thankfully, that did not happen. At 20:35, Tom's phone pinged with a WhatsApp message from Jimmy. Tom quickly tapped the notification on his phone and read the message aloud.

"Three goon-filled Range Rovers just exited target. Good to go! *Smiley face. Big kiss.*"

"We're on!" hissed Danny.

CHAPTER 10

London Docklands

Danny drove the transit out of the car park and back towards where they had dropped Jimmy. The headlights of the van cut through the dark, and Jimmy suddenly jumped out of a doorway, waving for them to slow down. Danny wound his window down and Jimmy leaned in.

"They've gone. Three Range Rovers loaded down with muscle. If we're going to do this, we should do it now."

Tom exited the van and gestured to Lalitha to follow him.

"We need to get in the back with Alex, Sam and Jimmy until we get past the guards," he explained. "Once we are in the warehouse compound Lalitha, you stay in the back of the van…"

"But, I can help you," she interrupted.

"Stay in the van," he repeated. "These guys have guns and I don't want to risk you getting shot."

"The Book will protect me," she complained.

"We don't know for sure that it can though, do we? Just stay in the van, okay? I mean it, Lalitha!"

Lalitha did not look happy about it, but climbed into the back of the transit without saying anything else. Jimmy and Tom joined her and they closed the doors behind them. Tom banged on the cab and sat down on the floor as Danny revved the engine and drove towards their target.

Alex looked at Tom.

"Here we go again then, Boss. In the back of a vehicle about to get shot at. I hope you're right about all this."

Tom gave her a tight smile. "So do I Alex. So do I!"

They felt the van turn right into a side street and then left as Danny drove up to the warehouse gates. As the van slowed to a stop, they could all hear the voice of one of the guards outside. He had a deep voice with a thick Russian accent.

"We not expecting you tonight. What you want?" the guard asked menacingly.

"Alexey sent me," said Danny. "I've got a package that he told me to bring over."

Danny held up the jiffy bag that they had stuffed with chopped up pieces of newspaper earlier this afternoon. He prayed that the guard wouldn't ask to check the contents. If he looked inside, they were screwed. Danny couldn't help but notice the machine pistol that was badly concealed inside the man's coat.

"Give to me," demanded the guard. "I will keep safe until Koznetsov returns."

"No chance mate," snapped Danny. "I was told to leave this package in Mr Koznetsov's office and that's what I'm gonna do, okay? If you don't like it, I'll just drive away with it and tell Alexey that some jumped up security dickhead wouldn't let me in. What do you think Koznetsov will do when he hears that you sent me away without makin' his drop? What's your name mate?"

The gateman bristled, but obviously did not want to risk getting on the bad side of Koznetsov.

"No matter what my name is," he relented. "Take package to office. Be quick."

"Thanks," smiled Danny. "I appreciate it mate. I just want to get this drop done then I can piss off home."

The guard grunted, waved to his comrade and together they swung open the gates to the warehouse yard. Danny gave them a cheery wave as he drove past them, but they did not wave back. He drove around the shipping crates and cars that were parked in the yard, swung round in front of the main warehouse door and reversed their vehicle so that the back of the van was close to the wicket gate in the big metal doors. Danny walked to the rear of the van and tried the wicket gate handle. It was unlocked. He checked to make sure that the goons out at the main gate couldn't see what he was doing before he opened the van doors and leaned in.

"I'm going to leave the van doors open, but don't get out until I've checked inside ok? Matey at the gate will probably have radioed the goons inside to say I'm here... and put your masks on."

Danny pulled the Browning out of his jacket and worked the slide to feed a bullet into the chamber.

Jimmy and Sam pulled their masks on. Alex tied her long curly hair back and pulled her mask over her head before turning to help Tom with his.

"Do I need a hood?" Lalitha asked.

"No," Tom replied, "because, like I said, you're staying here."

Lalitha scowled at him, but did not argue.

Tom's heart was beating like a hammer. He pulled the second Browning out of his pocket and handed it to Sam.

"Sam, you take this. You're better with handguns than me."

"No probs, Boss," he said cocking the pistol and taking off the safety.

Alex looked at them both.

"I never thought we'd be doing shit like this again," she muttered.

Sam grinned wolfishly. "Missed it haven't you?" he said.

Alex waved a single middle finger in Sam's direction and watched as Danny stepped through the little door into the darkness of the warehouse, leaving it ajar behind him. They heard a scuffle and then Danny's head poked out and gave them a thumbs-up sign.

Everyone except Lalitha climbed out of the van and stepped through into the warehouse. The inside of the building was not well lit, but Tom knew that this would work in their favour. On the floor by the door was the prone form of a man and as Danny met them, he dragged the unconscious body behind a nearby crate. He turned and handed a Skorpion machine pistol to Jimmy.

"There you go, Coddy. A little present from Mother Russia for you." He whispered. "Its owner is taking a little nap."

Jimmy grinned and checked that the weapon was loaded and cocked.

Danny put his finger to his lips and gestured towards the left-hand side of the building. He pointed at his eyes and held up two fingers. Tom nodded. There were two guards patrolling in that direction. Danny held up another finger and pointed up the metal stairway to the office above. There was another goon up there. The container was to the right of them, which meant that they should be able to reach it unchallenged. Getting it open without alerting the goons was going to be a problem though.

They slowly crept in single file down the right-hand wall, Danny taking point and Jimmy bringing up the rear, covering their backs with his Skorpion. They were about halfway down the wall when Danny held up his fist in a stop signal.

All five of them froze as a guard came out of the shadows to the right and walked towards the other two Russians. Thankfully, his eyes were facing forwards and he did not notice the figures stood in the shadow of the wall as he walked towards his comrades. So much for there only being three guards in the warehouse. The new guard said something in Russian and the other two goons laughed. One pulled out a packet of cigarettes, offered it around and they all sparked up. Tom could hear them as they noisily sucked in the smoke from their cheap Winston cigarettes.

Tom was worried. There were more guards in here than they had expected and the team were exposed. If one of the Russians looked this way, they would be in trouble. Alex was right, they had not done anything like enough planning before embarking on this raid.

Danny moved his hand in a 'down' movement and the other four crouched down, trying to get as low into the shadows of the wall as they could. Danny stealthily carried on alone along the wall, moving slowly and silently until he was hidden behind the container. A couple of seconds later there was a clattering noise to the far left of the warehouse. Danny had thrown something in that direction. The guards instantly looked up and all three of them were suddenly alert.

"Jesus Danny! What are you doing?" Tom whispered under his breath.

The Russians all raised their weapons and slowly headed towards the far corner of the building where the noise had come from, their eyes scanning for targets.

It was at that point that things went to shit!

The goon that had been up in the office walked out onto the stairs to see what was going on. He had received a radio message from the front gate to tell him to expect a delivery, but the courier had not appeared yet. He looked down at the doors to try and see where the courier was and then scanned the length of the warehouse to check on his fellow Russians. As he did so, he spotted Tom's team crouched by the wall.

"You!" he shouted in Russian. "Stop!"

The three guards on the floor turned to look back towards the shouting and as they did so, Danny came around the end of the container. There were several loud bangs from Danny's Browning and all three of the Russians dropped to the floor. The office goon started to move down the stairs, raised his pistol and fired two shots in Danny's direction. It was the last thing he did. Jimmy raised the Skorpion and fired a burst of gunfire at him at the same time as Sam fired two of the five rounds from his Browning. Most of the bullets hit their mark and the guard tumbled down the remaining stairs, ending up in a bloody heap on the concrete floor.

"Shit!" Tom swore. "Alex. Sam. Get over to those Russians and get their weapons. I'm going for the container. Jimmy, get back and cover the door. The other two goons from the gate will be here before you know it."

Alex and Sam both raced over to the downed guards and took their machine pistols, checking their bodies to make sure that they would pose no further threat. Jimmy ran back towards the main doors but stopped halfway there, turning around to shout back to Tom.

"Boss, Lalitha's in the building!"

Tom squinted towards the front of the warehouse and saw Lalitha standing there, the Book held in her hands.

"For Christ's sake!" he swore. "Jimmy, send Lalitha back to us. Quickly! Sam, get over there with Jimmy and secure the door!"

Jimmy sprinted to where Lalitha was standing, Sam close on his heels. Tom could not hear what they said to her, but saw Jimmy pointing in his direction. Lalitha started to run towards Tom as the soldiers took cover behind the crate where Danny had hidden the unconscious guard.

Lalitha arrived at Tom's side, her face white and her hands shaking. Together they ran the few remaining metres to the container where Danny was waiting for them.

"Danny," Tom hissed, "What the fuck was that? This was supposed to be a simple raid, not gunfight at the fucking OK Corral!"

"Sorry, Boss," shrugged Danny. "I didn't have a choice once that goon appeared from the office and eyeballed us. It was that or risk one of us gettin' hit."

Tom shook his head in frustration.

"Come on, let's get what we came for and get the hell out of here before the whole bloody Russian mafia lands on us!"

Tom reached into the small backpack he had brought from home and pulled out a heavy-duty set of bolt cutters and a large Maglite torch. He handed the bolt cutters to Danny who quickly positioned the blades around the shank of the lock and squeezed. The cutters sliced through the metal and the padlock fell to the floor with a clatter.

Alex and Lalitha both arrived at the container as they swung the doors open and looked inside. Tom turned his torch on and shone it into the darkness of the container. Stacked up neatly inside were a large number of green wooden crates of varying shapes and sizes.

Danny pulled a head-torch from his pocket and stretched the elastic over his head before turning it on. Using the head-mounted light to work by, he used the bolt cutters to cut the locks on two of the larger crates, then lifted the first lid to see what was inside. His torch illuminated the contents of the crate and his eyes almost popped out of his head.

"Jackpot!" he exclaimed.

Tom looked over his shoulder. Inside the crate were four fully kitted-out Colt C8 CQB carbines.

"Get all these crates open!" Tom instructed.

As Danny started to cut the locks on the remaining crates, there was a sudden rattle of gunfire from the warehouse door. The goons from the gate had arrived. Sam and Jimmy fired at the wicket gate as it squeaked open and one of the Russians went down. The other was returning fire. Jimmy and Sam ducked hastily as bullets ploughed into the crate they were hiding behind, and splinters flew in all directions. Sam fired round the side of the crate in the direction of the assailant, but more bullets rattled in from outside.

Inside the container, Danny continued to open crates. It was like an Aladdin's cave of weaponry. More Colt C8's, Benelli M4 combat shotguns, Glock 17 semi-automatic pistols, STANAG magazines, L109A1 HE fragmentation grenades, flash-bangs, M18 Claymore mines plus boxes and boxes of 9mm and 5.56mm ammunition.

"Holy crap!" said Alex. "You could start a war with this lot!"

"That's the plan!" said Danny as he picked up one of the pistols.

"Danny, do those Glocks have the internal lock on them?"

Danny looked at the bottom of the handgrip and there was no keyhole to be seen.

"Nope, we're good," he reported.

"Good," Alex nodded.

"Come on." Tom yelled. "Let's get this stuff to the van."

At the front door, Jimmy and Sam were still exchanging shots with the remaining guard outside. There was a sudden lull in incoming fire and Sam lunged for the door as Jimmy fired a quick burst of covering fire over his head. Sam dived through the wicket gate as the big Russian finished reloading his pistol and fired in his direction. As the guard moved out of cover to get a better aim at Sam, Jimmy used the last of his ammunition to shoot him squarely in the chest, hurling him backwards onto the ground.

Sam whistled back to the team in the container and as Tom looked up yelled, "All clear, Boss."

Tom and Danny slung C8 carbines over their shoulders and went to pick up a big box of ammunition each. Tom struggled with a heavy box one handed and carefully used his artificial arm to help lift the ammunition up off the floor.

"You two get the Glocks, flash-bangs and a few claymores. Forget about the shotguns, we won't be able to carry everything," he said to Alex and Danny. "Lalitha, come with me."

Loaded down with the rifles and ammunition box, Tom walked out of the container towards the warehouse door. As he did so, gunfire ricocheted noisily off the metal beside him. Two more Russians had snuck into the warehouse from a concealed back door at the rear of the building. They were shooting their weapons at the container from behind a stack of nearby oil drums.

The sudden onslaught of gunfire caused Tom to stumble and, as he did so, the box of ammunition fell from his grip and bullets spilled out all over the floor. Tom took a step backwards and lost his balance as his foot came down on the loose bullets. He cursed as he fell onto his back on the container floor. Jimmy was out of ammo at the front door, but Sam moved towards the new assailants, firing single shots in their direction to keep them pinned down. Suddenly he too was out of bullets and sprinted the remaining distance to the relative safety of the container. Alex hooked her hand around the edge of the container door and fired a quick burst in the general direction of the new threat before helping Tom back to his feet.

Tom looked around at their faces. It had been a long time since any of them had been in a combat situation and none of them looked happy to be re-living the experience now. None of them except Danny. He was grinning like the Cheshire Cat. He reached into the small crate behind him, lifted out a frag grenade, pulled the pin and threw it around the container door towards the Russians. There was a massive explosion as both the grenade and oil drums went up. Shrapnel rained down on the container and the warehouse lit up as flames leapt up from the wreckage and licked against the ceiling. The incoming gunfire stopped abruptly.

Danny waited a few more seconds and then looked out.

"Clear!" he said.

"Fester, you prick!" Alex spat. "What kind of recce did you do exactly? Three guards? No back door? What the hell were you thinking?"

Danny ignored her and headed towards the front doors.

"I'm gonna get the van in here and we can load up," he said as he stalked off.

Tom put his hand on Alex's shoulder "Come on, let's get this over with before things get any worse."

There was a small gasp from behind them and Tom turned to see Lalitha sat on the floor at the back of the container, her arms around her head. She was trembling.

Tom went over and put his arm around her shaking shoulders.

"Come on," he whispered, "let's get you out of here."

Jimmy and Danny had got the main warehouse doors open and were quickly reversing the van back towards the container. As they screeched to a halt, Tom helped Lalitha into the cab before turning to help the others load what they needed into the back of the van.

"What are we taking, Boss?" asked Jimmy.

Tom thought about what to take, doing quick mental calculations on what they would need and what they could practically carry.

"A C8 each, a Glock each, 13 mags each for the C8's, 4 mags each for the Glocks, 2 claymores each, 4 frags and 4 flash-bangs each and as much ammo as we can carry. What do you think Sam?"

"Sounds good to me," he replied. "You sure you don't want the shotguns?"

"Too heavy," answered Tom. "We've got to carry this lot don't forget. Throw everything in the back of the van and we can load the mags on the way. Any ammo left over we will leave in the van when we switch cars. Don't worry about all the ammo I dropped on the floor; we don't have time to mess about with the loose stuff. There are plenty of full boxes in there anyway."

Between them they picked out what they needed from the crates in the container and quickly loaded it into the back of the van. In the distance they could already hear the faint sound of sirens.

"Crap!" cursed Jimmy, "I think the cops are on their way. Let's get out of here!"

Tom and Danny rushed round to the front of the van and climbed in. As Danny turned the ignition and gunned the engine, Sam, Alex and Jimmy clambered into the back and slammed the doors closed behind them. With a squeal of tyres, Danny hit the accelerator and raced out through the gates and away from the burning building.

CHAPTER 11

On the Road to Stonehenge

The drive to the car-swap was quiet and uneventful. Danny, Lalitha and Tom in the front of the van didn't talk much. The adrenaline rush of the warehouse gunfight had worn off and the come down had left them feeling drained and numb.

In the back, Alex, Sam and Jimmy were frantically loading magazines from the boxes of ammunition they had stolen. The back of the van was dark and they were having to work by torchlight. Dropped bullets clattered and rolled round the floor.

"That was all kinds of fucked up," said Alex.

"Yeah," agreed Sam, "trust Fester to not think it all through and land us in the middle of a firefight. If those Russians work out it was us, we're totally in the shit."

"Well, they're gonna know that Fester was involved, so basically, we're all screwed."

"At least we got the kit," Jimmy piped up as he pushed bullets into the thirty-round Stanag magazine in his hand, "If this whole other world thing of Lalitha's really is kosher, then this lot will come in handy."

Alex snorted, "Let's just see what happens when we get to Stonehenge."

The M25 was surprisingly empty of traffic and it didn't take long before Danny was pulling the van into the car park at Clacket Lane services. Before transferring to the Pathfinder, the team went in pairs to use the facilities and Tom bought a carrier bag full of sandwiches and snacks from WH Smith for them all to share.

Danny reversed the transit van into a space next to the big Pathfinder and the kit was transferred into the new vehicle. Sam pulled up one of the third-row seats at the back of the big SUV so that everyone would have somewhere to sit on the journey to Wiltshire. Some of the Bergens were piled next to the back seat and the others went into the roof box. The C8 carbines also went up there out of sight. As Tom pointed out, if the traffic cops pulled them over for some reason, it was probably best that they didn't have a pile of automatic military rifles on show in the back of the car.

There were still some boxes of ammunition in the van and bullets strewn across the floor in the back. They had taken far more ammunition than they needed, so were just going to have to leave it in the transit. Danny did one last check in the back of the transit before slamming and locking the doors. He turned and threw the keys into the bushes at the edge of the car park.

Moving to the new getaway vehicle, they all climbed into their seats. Danny took driving duty again, with Tom in the front passenger seat, Sam, Lalitha and Jimmy in the second row, and Alex by herself at the back. Tom was not a great passenger and didn't really enjoy Danny's driving, but his prosthetic arm meant that he could not take the controls. If for some reason the arm sensors didn't function, or it became unattached while he was driving, the consequences would not be good. It was another part of everyday life that the IED had taken from him.

"Lalitha, could the Book not have helped us when the shooting started back there?" Jimmy asked out of the blue. It had obviously been bothering him. "I thought it was supposed to protect you?"

"She didn't need the Book, Cod-Boy, she had me and I kicked their asses!" quipped Danny.

The quip elicited a number of graphic responses from the team before Lalitha answered Jimmy's question.

"The Book is still weakened, so its ability to protect me is lessened here," she said quietly. "It could be that the men with guns were too far away from us for the Book to be able to reach them. I do not really know."

"Don't worry, Lalitha," Jimmy said, "I'm sure things will be okay when we get to Stonehenge."

The team quietly considered this as the dark Surrey countryside flashed by. Sam's head was nodding and it was not long before he was gently snoring. It had always been the same, no matter what the situation, Sam could always manage a nap. He called it his superpower.

"If the Russians had all this military-grade weaponry," Jimmy piped up again, "Why were they using those crappy Skorpions? They would have made mincemeat out of us if they'd been using the C8's instead."

"They would be worth more brand-new rather than used," answered Danny, "and that's a shit-ton of money we're talkin' about. Bad guys everywhere would be queuin' up to buy them. Plus, if a courier like me saw one of those goons with a pistol, they wouldn't think too much about it, but a goon with a fully kitted-out, military-grade Colt C8 would have created a bit too much interest."

"Good job the goons had big mouths and enjoyed blabbing to you about the whole stolen shipment then wasn't it Fester?" chirped Alex from the back.

"The sun shines on the righteous," Danny laughed.

"Seriously though Fester, you do know that the warehouse was a complete cluster-fuck, don't you?" added Alex. "We were sitting ducks in there and the Russians are going to have everyone they know looking for us now."

"You worry too much," Danny retorted. "Did we get what we needed? Yes, we did. Did any of us get hurt? No, we did not. Stop bleatin' Alex. We got the guns and we got out. Job done!"

"Prick!" Alex grumbled.

The Pathfinder travelled on in silence for a while and before long, Danny pulled off the M25 and onto the M3 towards Basingstoke.

Jimmy gazed out of his window as the lights from distant farms and villages passed by in the darkness. "What will the Book do when we get to Stonehenge Lalitha?" he asked.

Lalitha rubbed her eyes and considered her answer before speaking.

"I do not know exactly," she said.

"Well, that's a weight off my mind then," muttered Alex.

"We must place the Book on the altar inside the circle. Then the Book either has enough power to open a gateway or it does not."

"How do you know that the Book will do anything at all?" asked Jimmy. "What if it doesn't try to open a gateway?"

"It will. The Book always works in its own best interest and its own best interest is to open the gateway, return home and regain its full power," Lalitha said, her voice betraying her frustration at Jimmy's lack of faith. "You must trust in the Book, James Lang and you must trust in me. The Book knows that it is stronger in my world, so that is where it will take us."

Jimmy lapsed into silence, embarrassed that he had annoyed Lalitha.

"Enough questions. Try to get some sleep," urged Tom from the front. "We don't know when we'll next get the chance."

Most of the team dozed away the rest of the journey, only rousing themselves when they felt the Pathfinder slowing down to a standstill at the side of the road. It was just after midnight.

There was Stonehenge, standing up the rise to their right. The clouds had rolled away and the moon was shining down on the tall stones, the grassy hillside sparkling with frost.

"Rise and shine campers!" announced Danny. "We're here."

CHAPTER 12

Stonehenge

Tom looked around, searching for the best way to approach the stone monument.

"What's the plan Boss?" asked Sam. "Do we hump the gear up to the stones from here?"

"Screw that!" announced Danny. He put the big four-wheel drive into gear, gave the engine some gas and turned off the road towards the Henge. The heavy vehicle quickly accelerated, and with a series of bumps and horrendous scratching sounds, drove straight through the barbed wire fence. Danny drove the Pathfinder up the field, a trail of wire and wooden posts dragging behind it, and kept going until he was right up at the great stones.

"Close enough?" grinned Danny.

The team leapt out of the Pathfinder and started to unload all their equipment into a pile by the stone monument. Danny left the Pathfinder's headlights on main beam and the halogen bulbs lit up the area in front of the vehicle.

"Sam," said Tom, "Do a quick weapons check and make sure everything is split evenly across the packs. Use the smaller backpack I used in the warehouse to put food, water and a survival kit in for Lalitha. She won't be taking any of the weapons."

Sam nodded and started about his task, inspecting the C8's and cycling the actions to make sure that everything was working properly.

"Jimmy. Alex," Tom said. "Set up a perimeter and watch the roads to the south and west. Danny. Lalitha. Let's go and look at the Henge."

While Jimmy and Alex took positions outside the great stone circle, Tom, Danny and Lalitha walked through one of the stone arches into the middle of the Henge. Tom was actually surprised at the size of the monument. It was big, but weirdly nowhere near as big as he had expected. They walked around the stones, looking at each of them, half expecting something to happen whenever Lalitha touched one. Inside the ring there were several large stones lying horizontally on the ground. Lalitha walked to the largest of them and laid her hand on it.

"This is the altar," she said.

"But, it's not even in the middle of the circle," noticed Danny. "Are you sure?"

"I am sure." Lalitha replied.

Tom was just about to ask what to do next when Sam ran up, a worried look on his face.

"Boss," he panted, "I think we have a problem. I was checking out the scopes and lasers on the C8's and I found these."

He opened his hand to show them five small cylindrical devices, each with a flashing red LED inside it.

"They're GPS trackers. They were fixed to the scope on each of the rifles."

This was not good news.

"Whoever put them there knows where we are," mused Tom aloud. "It must be the Russians. If it was the British military, they would have sent a team to the docklands to get their kit back ages ago."

"If it is the Russians," said Danny, "they could be here at any time. We had a head start, but then we stopped and pissed about at the motorway services for about twenty minutes. The Russians wouldn't have had to do that so they could've made up a lot of ground."

"We've got to move fast," declared Tom. "Sam, was the kit all okay otherwise?"

"Yes Boss. It all looks good to go. I've loaded mags into the Glocks and C8s and have spread the spare mags, frags, flash-bangs and claymores across the Bergens. They're heavy, but manageable."

"Thanks. Bring all the Bergens in here and stack them by Lalitha there. You better pass out the guns. We might be getting company before very long."

Sam ran back towards the Pathfinder, stuffed pistols into each of his pockets and picked up the rifles by their straps before moving round the team handing everyone apart from Lalitha a pistol and a rifle each. Once everyone was armed, he and Danny slung their rifles onto their backs and started to move the Bergens next to the altar stone.

Danny looked back at Lalitha.

"Okay Tinkerbell. Over to you."

Lalitha frowned. "Why do you call me Tinkerbell?"

Danny smiled. "It's your new callsign. You can thank Moony later."

Lalitha shrugged and turned back to the altar stone.

"I can feel the energy in there," she said, "The Book needs to draw it from the stones before it is strong enough to channel the Souls to open a gateway."

She placed the Book onto the altar stone and placed her hand on top of it. Instantly, they all heard the whispering start. Quietly at first, but gradually starting to rise. The Soulstone blazed with an intense orange light as the whispers grew louder. Lalitha closed her eyes and her breathing slowed down.

As Tom watched Lalitha's chest rising and falling, Jimmy ran into the Henge and gestured towards the road to the South.

"Boss, three big SUVs have just pulled up at the side of the road. Either some passing motorists are interested in what we're doing, or our Russian mates have found us."

"They must have diverted from the Albanian hit once they heard what had happened at the warehouse," said Tom. "We were lucky that they didn't catch up with us on the road."

He rushed to the edge of the stone circle and looked toward the road they had driven along a few minutes earlier. The three cars that had pulled over at the roadside suddenly started to move. They bumped up the kerb, drove through the hole in the fence that the Pathfinder had made and started moving quickly up the slope. The two lead cars headed straight for stones, but the third vehicle veered off and made for the paved tourist path that ran up the western side of the Henge.

"Shit! They're trying to outflank us." Tom grunted. "Jimmy, pull the guys back inside the circle and take up a defensive position near the Pathfinder. Kill its headlights so we're not lighting the whole place up for them. If they start shooting, shoot back."

"Will do," said Jimmy before running off towards the Pathfinder.

Sam and Danny arrived with the last of the Bergens. They dropped them next to the altar stone with the others and then pulled the cocking levers on their rifles to chamber a round, ready to fire. They turned to Tom, waiting for instructions.

"Danny. You stop here with me. Sam, get Alex and set up in cover with Jimmy at the south of the circle near the Pathfinder. Don't go outside the outer ring of stones. If they make a move in your direction, warn them off. If they start shooting, return fire, but set your C8's to semi-auto. We need to conserve ammo because where we're going, we won't get any more."

They both nodded their agreement. Sam scurried off in Alex's direction and Danny crouched beside one of the large upright stones to the west of the altar, quickly training his rifle on the car that was flanking their position.

Tom moved to a stone near Danny's and looked back at Lalitha. She was standing next to the altar stone with her eyes closed. The whispering had become louder and the hairs on Tom's neck stood straight up. He could hear the crackle of static electricity from his clothes as he moved. He was worried about her standing there like that. She would be a sitting duck if the fireworks started.

"Lalitha," he hissed, "get down."

Lalitha either didn't hear him or chose to ignore him.

The two cars to the south had stopped twenty metres short of the Pathfinder. The doors of the big vehicles swung wide and goons poured out of them, taking positions by their cars. They were waiting for something.

Jimmy whistled to get Tom's attention and yelled over "They're holding position, Boss."

Tom gave him a thumbs up. He could see Alex and Sam both set up near Jimmy's position, their rifles pointed at the waiting Russians.

He turned back to see the third vehicle, a black Range Rover, pull up on the paved path to the west of the circle. The doors opened and the occupants climbed out.

"Jesus!" Hissed Danny. "That's Kirill Koznetsov himself."

They watched as Koznetsov's men all drew their weapons and crouched, ready to fire. Koznetsov reached into his jacket and pulled out a huge Cuban cigar. He flicked a Zippo to life and shielded the cigar from the wind as he lit it. The big man exhaled a huge plume of smoke and then looked over, directly at Tom.

"I do not know who you think you are," he shouted, "but you have killed several of my men and stolen from me. What you took is worth a great deal of money to me and I want it back."

He paused to draw deeply on his cigar before he continued.

"If you surrender to me now and return my property, I will make sure you die quickly. If you do not surrender, I will not be so generous. Not only will you die slowly and painfully, but I will make sure that the same fate is brought down on all your families."

Tom stole another glance at Lalitha. Her long dark hair was sparkling with electricity and the voices were not whispering any longer, they were chanting loudly inside his head.

Koznetsov flicked ash from his cigar and looked around at his men.

"My men outnumber you greatly," he called in his thick Russian accent. "How long do you think you will last against us? You have nowhere to go."

Danny looked at Tom and winked.

"Fuck it!" Danny muttered before raising his C8, leaning around the side of the stone and shooting a single round of NATO 5.66mm straight through Koznetsov's face. The Russian dropped like a stone and his men opened up with everything they had.

Danny quickly rolled back into cover as bullets began to crash into the pillar he was hiding behind. He covered his eyes as fragments blasted from the stone hit his face. Tom went to raise his C8 but for some reason the fingers on his robo-arm would not close around the fore-grip of the weapon. He looked down at his wrist to see a red flashing LED. Not now! His electronic arm had run out of battery. Why had he not charged it in the car on the way here? Idiot!

Tom quickly slung the rifle back over his shoulder and pulled the Glock from the waistband of his trousers with his right hand. He aimed carefully and squeezed the trigger. One of the Russians taking cover next to the Range Rover ducked as the bullet punctured the car's bonnet.

To the south of the circle, all hell had broken loose. The Russians had all taken cover and were pummelling the Pathfinder with gunfire. The big Nissan would not be driving anywhere again. Jimmy crouched behind the engine block as bullets pierced the vehicle's bodywork as if it were made of paper. Sam and Alex both carefully returned fire from their positions behind the stones of the Henge. Two more Russians were thrown backwards as the high velocity rounds hit them.

Tom fired three more rounds at the Range Rover before hastily ducking back behind his stone. He quickly checked on Lalitha. Bullets were ricocheting from the stones around her and Tom started to panic that she would be hit. She was too exposed there. He prepared to move cover to get nearer to Lalitha, but another burst of incoming gunfire forced him back down behind the stones.

"Danny," Tom yelled, "We need to get Lalitha out of the line of fire."

Danny glanced back at the altar stone and nodded at Tom. He was about to make a run for her when suddenly, the remaining three Russians from the Range Rover decided to charge their position. Danny fired and took down one of them while Tom took down another with a well-aimed shot from the Glock. The third assailant reached one of the outer stones and dived behind it. They heard him shout something in

Russian, but neither of them knew what it was. The Russians to the south did.

All the surviving Russians from the two cars at the south fired their automatic weapons at the stone circle in unison. A barrage of concentrated fire hit the stones all around Jimmy, Alex and Sam and they had no option but to stay low behind their cover. Whilst their lines of vision were compromised, a small group of Russians broke from the main pack and sprinted off around the perimeter of the Henge.

The gunfire eased as the attackers reloaded their weapons and Sam took the opportunity to shoot several rounds at the two black vehicles. As he did so, he noticed the break-away group of Russians running around the Henge to the east. He quickly raised his C8 and fired at them, but his shots went wide of their targets.

"Boss," yelled Sam, "there's a group of four flanking to the east."

Tom looked up to see Russians running around the outside of the circle. He couldn't risk taking a shot at the runners because Lalitha was in-between him and them. The shot was too dangerous. His prosthetic arm was just dead weight now and his right arm was shaking, making aiming more difficult. It also didn't help that the voices shrieking in his head were almost deafening him.

"No shot. No shot," Tom shouted as the four goons disappeared behind another of the ancient stones.

Hearing Tom's cry, Danny rolled out of his cover and, from his new vantage point, fired at the last of the Russians from the lone Range Rover. Danny's bullet struck him in the throat and he was down.

Seeing that all the goons from their side were now neutralised, Danny started to stand up, desperate to get to Lalitha, but he realised that he was too far away. The voices in his head were disorientating him and he looked dazed.

Alex, Sam and Jimmy had managed to reduce the number of Russian attackers further with some well-aimed shooting, but they still couldn't move from where they were.

Tom looked up and saw the four break-away goons run from their cover and race towards the inner circle, their weapons raised. He dived sideways to allow him to take a shot without endangering Lalitha and pulled the trigger five times, but the shots missed all four of the approaching attackers.

They were all too late. The Russians were going to get to Lalitha!

The incoming goons aimed their weapons and pulled their triggers. A barrage of gunfire blasted in Lalitha's direction and all Tom could do was lie on the cold ground and watch it happen in slow motion.

Then something strange happened. The voices in Tom's head reached a crescendo and rather than piercing Lalitha's small body, the bullets simply disappeared in small flashes of light. The Russians stopped dead in their tracks. They looked at each other in confusion as Lalitha slowly turned to stare in their direction, the fires blazing brightly in her eyes. As the goons brought up their weapons to fire a second salvo, Lalitha smiled menacingly as she lifted her right arm and pointed at them.

"SCALTO!" she boomed in the other-worldly voice of the Book.

The Russians instantly exploded in a mist of blood and gore.

Still keeping her left hand on the Book, Lalitha closed her eyes and breathed in as if tasting the air.

"Gather your soldiers to me now", the voice commanded.

"We can't," yelled Tom, "they're pinned down."

"Gather them now." The voice repeated. *"The time draws close."*

"Jimmy, Alex, Sam… fall back to this position. Now!" Tom shouted.

The three teammates at the south of the circle started to edge backwards. Seeing their retreat, two of the goons ran forwards after them.

As Alex made it to Lalitha's side, she turned back to see that two Russians had made it to the edge of the circle and they had their guns pointed at them. She started to raise her rifle, but it was too late, they had already opened fire. Alex screwed her eyes tightly closed and braced herself, expecting to feel the bullets tear through her flesh. Instead, all Alex felt were tiny sparks of heat on her skin as the bullets that should have ripped into both herself and Lalitha disappeared in small bursts of orange fire. As Alex gasped in shock, she heard a voice from beside her boom out a single word.

"SCALTO!"

The bodies of the Russians that had fired at them exploded with a wet popping noise, turning the stones and the frosty grass around them bright crimson.

Bewildered at what they had just seen, the remaining Russians stopped shooting and looked at each other as they tried to process what they had witnessed. One second their comrades had been about to shoot the two women and the next they had burst like a pair of over-filled water balloons. What weapon could do that?

"Put your fucking guns down!" Alex screamed furiously. "The next one of you to shoot ends up like your friends here, so just don't fucking do it okay!"

Alex kept her rifle pointing in the direction of the surviving goons, but there were no further shots. She glanced at Lalitha, whose body was glowing with a faint orange aura, and realised that all the doubts she had been having about the young woman's whole crazy story were gone. The air felt charged with electricity and the altar stone itself was giving off a low humming noise.

"Lalitha," Alex said, "Thank you. I was wrong about you."

Lalitha looked at Alex, but there was no emotion on her face. Her eyes were ablaze with an unearthly fire. Lalitha spoke again in the voice of the Book.

"The time is here. Take up your weapons and join hands."

The five teammates looked at each other realising that this really, really was happening.

"Come on," said Tom, "Load up".

They picked up their Bergens and helped each other to get their arms through the straps and the heavy loads on their backs. Alex picked up Lalitha's smaller backpack and looped one of the handles over her arm.

"Join hands," said Danny.

Everyone joined hands and they all looked expectantly at Lalitha.

"DESSAT!" the Book's voice boomed.

The Russians still standing to the south of Stonehenge witnessed a blinding flash of light and a huge thunderclap. They looked up at the sky, but there was not a cloud to be seen. After a few moments one of the surviving goons carefully made his way towards the centre of the monument, his weapon raised and ready, but there was no-one there. The inner circle of the Henge was completely empty.

CHAPTER 13

Zakastra

Tom opened his eyes. He was lying on his back looking up at a large stone ceiling that had faint etchings on its surface. The etchings looked like they had weathered over many years, but their design was still visible. Tom could make out a series of star constellations, but he did not see any that he recognised. Sunlight shone down from above through a gaping hole in the ceiling and through it, Tom could see blue sky and small white clouds high above. A light breeze blew through his hair carrying with it the smell of the sea.

He took a deep breath and rolled his head to the side. He could see other figures lying on the grass next to him. Lalitha, Danny, Jimmy, Sam and Alex. They were all there.

Tom suddenly realised that he was seriously uncomfortable and tried to sit up. For a moment he could not work out why sitting up was so difficult, but then he remembered the heavy Bergen on his back. He rolled onto his side, pulled his arms out of the shoulder straps and rolled onto his front. He slowly raised himself into a kneeling position and looked around.

They were lying inside the ruin of a large round building. Stone pillars encircled them and it looked like the circle had once been enclosed by thick exterior walls. Most of the walls had long since either fallen or been pulled down and Tom could see much of the surrounding area from where he knelt. The ceiling was mostly still supported by the ancient looking columns of stone and in the centre of the great room there was a stone altar. Lalitha lay next to it, the Book still in her hands.

Through the many gaps in the walls, Tom could see that they were on the slopes of a large hill. He could see the ocean and also the ruins of a city stretching out below them. Beyond the city he could make out rolling green hills and valleys in the distance. They were definitely not at Stonehenge any longer.

Tom felt a little dizzy and nauseous so did not try to stand until the feeling started to pass and his head began to clear. He ran through the memories of the previous night and rubbed his eyes with his right hand, appalled at how close they had come to being killed by the Russians. Tom recalled how his left arm had run out of charge in the middle of the firefight at Stonehenge, and he was suddenly overwhelmed with feelings of shame and resentment. He had dropped a box of ammo when under pressure at the warehouse because of a poor grip with his prosthetic hand and when the team had needed him to be on his game, he had let his arm run flat and had not been able to use his rifle.

Should he even be here helping Lalitha and the team when he couldn't be depended on, or would they actually be better off without him?

He stood up slowly and moved around the unconscious bodies of his friends, making sure that they were all uninjured and breathing ok. Things had got so crazy at the Henge before Lalitha and the Book opened the gateway, that Tom couldn't remember for sure if anyone had been hit by Russian gunfire or not. Thankfully it looked like nobody had been hurt, so Tom left them all alone, allowing them to wake in their own time.

Tom picked up his Bergen with his good arm and half-carried, half-dragged it out of the building and into the bright sunshine. He could smell the salt from the sea below and caught the faint odour of sulphur on the breeze. As he turned around, he could see the flattened summit of the hill that the city had been constructed on a mile or two to the west.

There was an expanse of grass by the side of the altar building and Tom set his Bergen down here before sitting down next to it. He undid the lid of his pack and opened it to find the solar charger that Alex had bought for him on her shopping trip with Jimmy. He pulled the heavy unit out and checked its charge. Thankfully, all the power LED indicators lit up green when he held the on/off button down.

Tom opened the unit's storage compartment and pulled out the micro-USB charging lead before removing his arm. He sucked air through his teeth sharply as the prosthetic came away; it was always an unpleasant feeling pulling the closely fitting arm from his stump. Once it was off, Tom used his fingernail to pop open the arm's charging point cover and then plugged the charger's lead in. Tom watched until he saw the power LED on his prosthetic start to flash green to confirm that it was charging properly, before folding out the solar panels that connected to the main unit. The more of the sunshine's energy that he managed to collect into the charger's batteries for use later on, the better.

Tom carefully examined his arm for damage and wiped the dust and dirt from its surface using the sleeve of his jacket. He had to make sure that his prosthetic was kept in fully working order or he would be even more of a hindrance to the team. There would be no callouts from the manufacturer's engineering team here. If the arm failed here, so did he.

Tom pulled out a tube of E45 and applied the cream carefully to his stump. As he screwed the lid back on the tube, Tom jumped as a voice spoke from behind him.

"Hey Boss, you okay?" asked Alex.

"I'm good. You?" He answered, hurriedly pulling his sleeve down to hide his left arm from Alex.

"Boss, come on. Don't be mental. I've seen your arm loads of times. It's nothing to be ashamed of," she said quietly, sympathy in her eyes.

Sympathy. That's exactly what he didn't want.

"It's fine Alex. I just need to get some power into my arm. I let the damn thing run flat last night and nearly got you and Lalitha killed."

"You didn't nearly get us killed at all. From where I was standing, Lalitha seemed to be doing a pretty good job of looking after us. Did you see what she did to those Russian goons. There was blood and shit flying everywhere… and to think I didn't really believe her crazy stories…" she trailed off.

"Alex, I couldn't use my rifle because my left arm was just dead bloody weight. I couldn't defend you properly. Before that in the container, I spilled ammo everywhere because I couldn't even lift a box up without dropping the damn thing. You guys need to be able to depend on me. You shouldn't be hampered by me all the time because I fucked up and let a simple IED blow my bloody arm off. I'm not sure I should have come here."

"Tom," Alex said, as she crouched beside him and put her hand on his shoulder, "we would be lost without you. You're the one that holds us all together. You're the one that always takes charge and knows what to do. You made one mistake out of all the shouts we went on. Just one mistake!"

"But that one mistake took everything away from me, Alex!"

"It did and that is a tragedy, but that IED didn't kill you. You've been through some dark days, but you got through them and you're still here. So, your new arm isn't 100%?

I know that and I know it's hard for you, but it doesn't change who you are or what you mean to this team. You're one of the strongest people I know and definitely the best CO that I ever worked with. Women of my colour have a hard time in the forces, but you were always at my side to back me up. You cared about your team and you didn't lose your shit when everything went fubar. Can you say the same about Danny, or Sam, or Jimmy? You are here because, without you, this team would just be a bunch of crazy headless chickens running around blindly pecking at each other."

Tom put his hand on Alex's and managed to flash her a quick smile.

"Thanks, Alex," said Tom, "I can think of a whole heap of times that it was you that held this team together rather than me. Especially after I screwed up and wasn't with the team any longer. You got a new CO, but it was you that kept the lads going."

Alex leaned closer to him and started to say something, but as she did Danny appeared beside them.

"Holy shit you two," he yelled. "We did it! We got through the gateway."

Alex quickly removed her hand from Tom's shoulder and gave Danny a withering look.

"No shit, Sherlock!"

At that moment, Sam also appeared from the ruins of the circular building. He rubbed his face and looked around at their unfamiliar surroundings, seeing the sea stretch out to the distant horizon below them.

"Well, Toto, I've a feeling we're not in Wiltshire any more?" he said groggily.

Danny rushed over and hugged Sam, enveloping his bald head in a bear hug before planting a noisy wet kiss on top of it.

"Slaphead! Mate! We did it! We're on the other side!"

"Get off me, you dickhead," said Sam, pushing him away playfully.

Danny raced back inside and reappeared dragging a semi-conscious Jimmy with him.

"What's happening? What's happening?" Jimmy yelled, confused and disorientated.

"Fester! Jesus, you are a nightmare!" sighed Alex. "Leave him alone for Christ's sake."

Danny was way too hyper to take any notice of Alex and rubbed his knuckles roughly on Jimmy's close-cropped head.

"Rise and shine Cod-boy. We're in Zakastra. We did it!"

Jimmy pushed Danny's hands away and bent over, putting his hands on his knees to help keep his balance.

"Ooooo… I really don't feel that great," he said before disappearing behind a nearby wall to throw up.

Alex tossed her water bottle over.

"Drink some water, Jimmy, you'll feel better in a minute."

"Thanks, Moony," smiled Jimmy wiping his face on his sleeve.

The tension of the previous night gradually began to subside and the relief that Zakastra was a real place rather than just a young girl's infectious delusion was palpable.

Jimmy suddenly noticed that Lalitha was not with them. The smile instantly fell from his face and he started to panic.

"Where's Lalitha?" he blurted. "Is she okay?"

"I've checked her already and she's fine," Tom reassured him. "She's back inside next to the altar. She is breathing okay and she isn't injured. She went through a lot last night and having that much power flow through you can't have been a walk in the park. She'll wake up soon, don't worry."

"She'll be okay in a few minutes, Coddy," added Danny. "The Book is protectin' her and it's much stronger here. After the freaky shit she pulled on those goons last night, I'm not surprised she needs a bit more kip than us. Did you see all that explodin' body stuff? Jesus!"

"I'll go and check on her anyway," Jimmy said as he passed Alex's water bottle back to her and disappeared into the building.

Something suddenly occurred to Danny.

"I'm the same as her you know. I'm chosen. I'm gonna be able to do that shit too!"

He pointed at Sam and made a pistol with his fingers.

"Zap," he said, pulling the trigger on his imaginary weapon. "One word from me and the bad guys will be explodin' meat sacks."

Alex looked at Tom and raised her eyebrows.

"And give me one good reason why that shouldn't scare the living crap out of me?" she groaned.

"What time is it?" asked Sam. "I think my watch is busted."

Tom looked at the timepiece on his wrist.

"I think mine is broken too Sam. According to this it's a bit after four o'clock in the morning."

"Same," declared Alex.

They all looked up to the sky where the sun blazed down at them from high overhead.

"I don't think time is the same here Boss," said Danny. "After all, we left

Stonehenge just after midnight in the dead of winter and its warm and sunny here. No wonder Lalitha appeared at your place in the little skimpy number that she had on."

As they stood wondering about the time and season differences between their home and this new world, Jimmy re-appeared holding Lalitha up as she walked unsteadily beside him.

"She's awake," Jimmy announced unnecessarily.

"Hey, Lalitha. How do you feel? Are you okay?" Tom asked.

She looked over at him and smiled weakly.

"I am well, Thomas McAllister," she said. "I just need to rest for a while to regain my strength. The Book had to channel a great amount of energy through me to open the gateway last night and it has left me feeling a little depleted."

Jimmy retrieved his water bottle from his pack and passed it to Lalitha.

"Have a drink of water. It will help."

"Thank you," she smiled.

She leaned her head back and drank from the plastic container, the sun sparkling through her hair. As she swallowed the liquid, she gazed around at the team and their wider surroundings. Her eyes moved to look out over the sea before she turned to look at the ruins stretching away down the hillside.

They all heard the now familiar whispering voices coming from the Book and Lalitha smiled as she turned to address them all.

"Thanks to the Book, we have come through the gateway and are now in my realm, Zakastra. However, we are far to the south of where we need to be. Once we are rested, we should make ready to travel. We have a long road ahead of us."

CHAPTER 14

The Ruins of Melnor

While Lalitha regained her strength, the team ate a breakfast of protein bars and the remains of the sandwiches that Tom had bought from the motorway services. They were a bit squashed after being rammed hurriedly into their packs, but they tasted okay.

Everything felt surreal, but the years of training kicked in and the team soon started to prep their kit for moving out. The Bergens were all carefully repacked, with important items like the Glock pistols and spare magazines stored into side pockets where they could be easily and quickly accessed. The weather was warm now, very unlike the cold February night that they had left behind, so their winter jackets and sweaters were all rolled up and packed away.

Sam helped to stow Tom's kit while his arm was finishing its top-up charge.

"Boss," Sam said, "once you're finished with it, I'll take the solar charger for you if you want. That thing adds a fair bit of weight to your pack."

"I'm fine thanks," Tom smiled. "This is here for my benefit, so it's not fair that you should have to carry it. I'll be fine. Honestly."

Sam grinned. "Okay, but if you need me to, I can take it later on."

"Thanks," nodded Tom. Things would have to get bad before he let the team carry his kit for him.

"Where do you think we are, Boss?" Sam asked.

"Zakastra," Tom replied.

"Yeah, I know that, but where is Zakastra exactly? Is it somewhere hidden away in our world, or are we in another dimension or something?"

"I don't know, where's Lalitha?"

Lalitha was sat on the grass nearby with her back against part of the altar room wall.

She was talking quietly with Danny.

"Lalitha," Tom asked. "where is Zakastra?"

"What do you mean?" she replied.

"In relation to our world, where we just came from, where is Zakastra? Are we on another planet or in another dimension?"

Lalitha thought about this, brushing her hair out of her face as the warm breeze blew it across her eyes.

"I do not know, Thomas McAllister. All I know is that the Book can open a gateway between this place and your place. Does it matter where these places are in relation to each other?"

Tom thought about this question for a moment. Did it matter? Perhaps not.

"Okay, do you know where we are in Zakastra? I'm guessing that this is not your capital?"

"Of course, this is not Krassak," said Lalitha. "We are far to the south of there."

"Why didn't the Book take us straight to the capital then?" asked Sam.

"To go directly to the altar at Krassak would be too dangerous," shrugged Lalitha. "We do not know what the situation at Krassak is now. We could have appeared in the midst of a trap, unprepared and outnumbered. That would have been foolish. It knew of the existence of this altar in the south and brought us here where it is safe."

Tom nodded. Lalitha's answer seemed to make sense.

As he thought through what Lalitha had told him, Tom noticed Alex return from scouting the area around them. He raised his eyebrows as she flopped down on the grass and re-packed her valuable toilet roll back in her pack.

"All good?"

"Yep. All clear out there, Boss," Alex reported. "There's no sign of any people in any of these ruins that I could see."

"No people live here," Lalitha declared. "We sit amongst the ruins of the ancient city of Melnor. This city was destroyed many years ago as a result of a war that started here. Nobody has lived here since those times as the land is said to be cursed."

"That sounds kind of ominous," Alex commented.

"There is no threat here that I know of Alexandra Aluko," said Lalitha. "The curse is a myth. We are safe here. The nearest inhabited town is close by to the north and that is where we will travel to. The town is called Serat. It is not visible from here, but we should reach it today if we start walking soon. We will be able to find horses there and I need to find messengers willing to take word of my return to my allies in the north."

"Horses?" exclaimed Alex. "For some reason I wasn't expecting you to have horses. I thought it would be all griffins and dragons and magical flying monkeys or something."

"Where will the messengers have to go to find your friends?" asked Jimmy. "Are they close by too?"

"No, they are not. The road from Serat to where my allies are will be long. Even if I can dispatch messengers from Serat quickly, we will not be able to meet them until much further along our journey."

"And where will our journey take us?" Tom inquired.

"From Serat, we will make for the eastern port of Brentar. From there we will find a ship to take us to the island of Gessan. Gessan is where the last of the magi can be found and is where the Ceremony of Binding must be carried out."

"That must be the island I saw in my vision. The old bloke in the cloak that waved to me was there," Danny exclaimed. "Once we get there and we've done the ceremony, we'll be able to channel the Souls to help us."

Lalitha nodded in agreement. "Daniel Adams is correct. Once we are Bound, we can return to the mainland and meet with my allies. They will be able to help us to formulate a plan to allow us to reach the capital and stop Gask's evil."

Jimmy had another question.

"Lalitha, how far is the ride from Serat to where we can find a ship?"

Lalitha did some calculations in her head before answering. "I would say that Brentar is nearly eighteen days travel from Serat on horseback James Lang."

Jimmy looked worried. "Boss, I've never been on a horse before. I'm not great with animals."

Alex laughed. "Come on, Coddy! Horses are fine and if it means that we don't have to hump these hulking heavy Bergens across the countryside, then I'm all for it."

Jimmy did not look convinced. Neither was Tom. How would his arm cope with riding a horse? Not well, he suspected.

"Riding a horse is easy," Alex continued. "One of my posh schoolmates had horses and I spent a whole summer holiday at her place learning how to ride. It's like riding a bike, once you've got the hang of it, it just becomes second nature. I'll help you, Jimmy, don't worry."

"I agree with Codboy," Sam groaned. "Riding horses sounds painful. Will you help with my sore bits once we get to Brentar Moony?"

"In your dreams, Slaphead," she laughed in reply.

"I actually think I would rather eat a horse than ride one," Sam joked.

"Samuel Franklin!" Lalitha gasped. "How can you say such a thing? Horses are precious and valuable beasts."

Sam held his hands up and grinned. "Sorry, Tinkerbell, I was only joking. I've never eaten horse… well, not that I know of."

Lalitha calmed down a little, but gave Sam another disapproving look.

"Why do you call me, Tinkerbell?"

"It's your new nickname. You can thank Moony for that one."

"What is a nickname?" Lalitha asked.

"It is a term of endearment," answered Alex. "A nickname is something we call each other within the team. Nobody else uses them. Just us. It's personal."

Lalitha looked puzzled.

"Tom is the Boss because he was our commanding officer. Danny is Fester because Fester Adams was a character in one of his favourite TV shows and Adams is also Danny's second name."

"Plus, Fester was the ugly psychotic one… bit like Danny here," added Sam.

"Sam is Slaphead because of his being so follically-challenged and Jimmy is Cod or Codboy because of his addiction to shoot-em-up video games." Alex grinned.

"Don't forget yourself there, Moony," chirped Danny. "Alex is called Moonshine because she managed to repeatedly drink everyone in Camp Bastian under the table. She distilled her own illicit potato vodka, which was like rocket fuel, but tasted like utter shit. Even Sam ended up unconscious in a pool of his own puke after one night on that stuff."

"I put a lot of hours into that still," complained Alex, "and the stuff wasn't that bad. You lot are just lightweights who can't take your drink."

"Moonshine's vodka was also really good at getting the oil off your hands after servicing all the guns," chipped in Jimmy. "Unless you had cuts on your fingers, then it stung like hell."

Lalitha still looked confused. "Why am I Tinkerbell?"

Alex laughed. "Tinkerbell is a magic fairy in a kid's story and it seemed kind of apt. She's a good-guy though, I could have been a lot harsher."

"Don't worry about it, Lalitha," Tom said smiling. "You'll get used to it."

Lalitha still didn't look too happy about her new name and was about to ask another question when a quiet beeping noise near Tom's Bergen grabbed everyone's attention.

"That's my arm all charged up again," Tom muttered, embarrassed that everyone was looking at his prosthetic. "Give me a minute and I'll be good to go."

Tom unplugged the charging cable from his prosthetic arm and packed it away. Making sure that his back was turned to the group, he pulled his sleeve up and re-attached the electronic arm. He wiggled it into place and flexed the muscles in his arm to make sure that the electronic sensors were in contact with his skin, before rolling his sleeve back down again.

"We should make a move," he announced. "Let's get everything together and get to this Serat place. Hopefully we can find somewhere to sleep there. I don't want to sleep in these ruins, there's something about them that puts my teeth on edge and I keep catching a nasty rotten egg smell."

The group broke up as everyone returned to their Bergens and started to load up, each helping another on with their heavy packs.

"How heavy are these packs Slapper?" asked Jimmy.

"Including all the mags and everything, about twenty kilos or so I reckon," Sam replied. "Plus the C8. Plus the Glocks. It's all pretty bloody heavy kit. Perhaps horses aren't such a bad plan after all. Humping all that weight on our backs for miles on end definitely does not fill me with a huge amount of joy."

"Hmmm…" Jimmy muttered. "Bloody horses though mate? I don't like horses."

Tom wedged the solar charger into the top of his pack and plugged in the external panel-pack. Once the lid of the Bergen was shut, he clipped the fold-out solar panel in place using the mini karabiners attached to the outside of the Bergen. By doing this, the unit would continue to charge its internal batteries as they walked. Tom made sure that the charger panel was securely attached and then turned to Danny.

"Fester, can you give me a hand on with this pack? My arm can't lift that kind of weight."

"No probs, Boss," said Danny as he lifted the heavy pack and held it up while Tom threaded first his left arm and then his right arm through the shoulder straps. Tom took the weight and shrugged his shoulders a few times to get the pack in a comfortable position before fastening the waist belt with an audible click. Once he was happy that the pack was as comfortable as it was going to get, Tom checked his C8 rifle and slung it over his shoulder.

"Ok, everyone set?" he asked, looking around the group.

Everyone was ready to go, so Tom looked at Lalitha and gestured her forwards.

"Come on then, Tinkerbell. Lead the way."

CHAPTER 15

On the Way to Serat

The walk down the hill through the ruins of Melnor was relatively easy as there was a network of well-worn pathways that snaked down the hillside through the tumbled down buildings. Flowers and plants had taken over occupation of the decrepit houses to the point that some of the buildings had almost completely disappeared under wild grasses and shrubs. Occasionally small creatures could be heard scuttling around and an abundance of inquisitive birds hopped around, busily pecking at the mossy stones.

Tom noticed a number of large black rocks and boulders that looked almost glassy in their appearance. It was as if they had been subjected to a great heat. The moss didn't seem to grow on these rocks and they stood out like strange monuments to the crumbling city.

Tom walked beside Lalitha as they made their way down the ancient, cobbled pathways. He occasionally swore sharply as he skidded on the loose pebbles and the unfamiliar weight of his pack tried to pull him over backwards. Lalitha was much more sure-footed, partly because of her younger age and nimble feet, but also because she was carrying a light rucksack which only weighed a fraction of those being carried by the team. Even though there was plenty of spare room in her pack, she insisted on carrying the Book in her hand as they walked.

"What is this place Lalitha?"

Lalitha looked around at the ruins they were walking through and sighed.

"Many many years ago, the city of Melnor was one of the largest cities in the south. The altar that we arrived at was built by the same ancient order of magi that built the Tower at Krassak. In those days in addition to the Great Book, there was a Lesser Book, and the altar here at Melnor was created to be its home."

"Is that the Great Book," asked Tom, pointing at Lalitha's hands.

"Yes, this is the Great Book."

"So, what happened to cause all this?" Tom asked, looking at the abandoned city around him.

"It is a long story. There was dissent in the order and the magi splintered into two factions: the loyalists in the north and the rebel magi here in the south. The rebels fell under the leadership of a militant magus called Berellon, who declared that the royal family were not worthy to wield the power of the Great Book and that, henceforth, only magi should be allowed to be Bound to it. He proclaimed that the royal line was tainted and corrupt."

Lalitha had a disgusted look on her face and paused before continuing her story.

"Melnor was the seat of Berellon's rebellion. He took control of the altar here and used the Lesser Book to strengthen his treacherous forces. The Lesser Book could also gather Souls, but was younger and less powerful than the Great Book at Krassak. Berellon was a gifted magus and even though his Book was less powerful, he posed a significant risk to the north. His ultimate goal was to possess both the Books of Power. If he had succeeded, the loyalist magi order and the royal family would have been defenceless against him. Berellon would have destroyed them both forever."

"What happened?"

"The magi war raged for almost a year and the loss of life was significant. After many battles, Berellon and his followers gained the upper hand, but became over-confident and overstretched themselves as they advanced northwards. My ancestor, King Athrun, laid in wait for Berellon outside the city of Derralt and the rebel army was led into a trap set by the loyalist magi. It was a massacre. King Athrun, together with magi loyal to the crown decimated the rebel army. Berellon was captured and beheaded as a traitor and his magi followers were crucified on the city walls. Fearing that a similar uprising could happen in the future, King Athrun used the power of the Great Book at Krassak to destroy its lesser sibling and the whole city of Melnor was obliterated. The Book caused the hill above us to explode and the fireballs that it rained down destroyed almost everything. King Athrun returned to Krassak, safe in the knowledge that, now there was only one Book of Power in the world, there would be no further threat from the south."

"That explains the bad smell," Tom mumbled to himself. "We're walking on a volcano. The Book made the volcano erupt and it wiped out the whole city."

The brutality of the conflict sounded horrendous, but Tom knew all too well the atrocities that could be perpetrated by both sides in a war.

"Once the war was over, the people no longer trusted the magi and even though the surviving members of the order were loyal to the crown, several were killed by vigilante mobs in the cities. King Athrun knew that magi were vital to the future generations of the monarchy as they were the only ones able to conduct the Ceremony of Binding and only by being Bound could the royal family continue to wield the power of the Souls. Athrun realised that if too many magi were lost, there would be no more ceremonies and the power of the royal family would be irretrievably diminished. To protect the last of their order, King Athrun moved the great magi library from Krassak to the island of Gessan, where a new library was built. The remaining magi exiled themselves there with their archives, away from the eyes of the realm. Over the years that followed, life in the realm returned to normal and the magi slowly faded into legend, a myth whispered around the fire late at night to scare the children. Only the royal family and privileged members of the court know that the remnants of the magi order still exist at Gessan."

"And that is where we're going. To see the magi at Gessan." Tom nodded.

"Yes."

"Will they support you over Gask and his allies?"

"The magi at Gessan are loyal to the crown and will help us as long as we have the Book in our possession. If anyone were to try to land uninvited on Gessan without the Book, the magi would turn them away. Forcefully. Only travellers with the Book in their possession are allowed to make landfall… unless invited to do so by the magi."

"Does Gask know that the magi still exist on Gessan?"

"He may. Before he took up arms against us, Gask was a member of the royal court and became all too familiar with my family. The traitors in our midst have almost certainly told him of our secrets."

"Do you think he'll try to stop us getting to the magi?"

Lalitha smiled, "Even if he does know of their existence, Gask does not know that I am even still alive. He watched me fall from the cliffs into the sea. They will have searched for me, but will have found nothing so he must believe that both myself and the Book are lost. Once we reach Gessan and I am Bound, he will learn otherwise. I will then have the ability to channel the power of the Souls to wreak my vengeance on the usurper."

"Danny will be Bound too, so there will be two of you that could use the Book against him."

"Yes," Lalitha nodded. "Daniel Adams will also have the power to fight Gask, but he will only get that honour if I deem it necessary."

Tom wholeheartedly agreed with that sentiment. Danny was often a loose cannon and the thought of him shooting from the hip with such a powerful weapon was frightening.

"What happens if Gask learns where you are before we reach Gessan?" Tom asked. "We're going to be travelling through at least one town and if someone recognises you, we could have a problem."

"You are correct," agreed Lalitha. "We will need to take care that I am not recognised and I will have to conceal the meaning of the messages that I send to my allies in case they fall into enemy hands. Disguising myself may not be as difficult as you might think though Thomas McAllister. Normally I would be part of a mounted ceremonial royal procession with members of the king's royal guard and many servants. I would not be travelling on foot or be accompanied by a group of such outlandish companions."

"Fair point," nodded Tom.

Tom glanced over his shoulder to check on the others behind him. Danny was deep in conversation with Jimmy about what wonders they might expect to see in this new land and what life could be like for them once he was Bound and, in effect, part of the Zakastran royal family.

Alex and Sam at the rear of the party were quieter and Tom was pleased to see that both of them were alert and on their guard. They were in an unknown world and none of them realised yet the kind of threats that this island could throw at them.

It took them quite some time to walk through the ruined city of Melnor, but before too long, the broken-down buildings became sparser and the countryside opened up into pleasant grasslands and rolling hills. The atmosphere felt less oppressive here and the air smelled fresher.

At the edge of the city, they were confronted with a wide, shallow river. The water was clear and fresh and fish could be seen swimming in-between the rocks, their scales glinting as they caught the light. The team took the opportunity to wash their faces in the cool water and filled their water bottles.

"You'd never do this at home," laughed Danny. "You'd catch somethin' grim if you drank the water from the rivers where we live."

Because the water was shallow, the crossing was easy. If their packs had not been so heavy, boots and socks would have been removed, but nobody wanted to risk standing on a sharp stone with their bare feet while carrying a twenty-kilo pack. The warm weather would dry them out soon enough, so they ploughed straight through in their boots.

Lalitha had to be especially careful with her feet as they had not yet fully recovered from her barefooted escape through the woods outside Krassak. The boots that Alex had given her were two sizes too big for her, but they had padded them out with extra socks as best they could.

To stop her feet getting wet, Jimmy made two journeys through the water. The first to take his pack to the other side of the river and the second to carry Lalitha.

Alex shook her head as she watched her young friend's effort to help Lalitha stay dry.

"Jesus," she sighed, "that boy has got it bad, hasn't he?"

Once across the river, they could not see a path on the other side of the river and everyone turned to look at Lalitha.

"Which way, Tinkerbell?" asked Danny.

Lalitha pointed up the hillside.

"When we reach the top of this hill, we should see Serat. It lies in the next valley to the north."

They pushed on up the slope. With no path to follow, the going was much harder and slower. The ground became steeper and the weight of their Bergens made it increasingly hard for the ex-soldiers to stay on their feet. Lalitha was soon quite a distance ahead of them.

"Are you sure we can't load her up with some of the ammo Boss?" Alex suggested as she caught her breath with Tom. "Look at her leaping up the slope like a bloody gazelle. I don't think the old boots I gave her have ever moved so fast."

Tom laughed and looked back at the rest of the group. Sam was breathing heavily as he caught up with them and further back down the slope, Danny was making his way up the incline with Jimmy following on behind. Danny turned to encourage the younger man up the hillside as only he could.

"Come on, Coddy, you lanky beanpole," joked Danny. "If you'd actually done some sort of exercise since leavin' the forces rather than sittin' on your lazy arse playin' video games all day, you might not be so out of shape. Man, you look like you're about to have a coronary."

"Leave him alone, Fester. He's doing okay," scolded Alex. "You *are* doing okay aren't you, Cod?"

"Yeah… I'm… doing… just… fine…" gasped Jimmy as he climbed up to meet them. "Where's... Lalitha?"

"Oh, she bounded on ahead," smiled Alex. "Catch your breath for a sec and we'll go catch her up."

Jimmy propped himself on Danny and took a drink from his water bottle.

"Come on then," Jimmy panted. "Let's catch up with Lalitha."

The five friends pushed on up the slope and after what seemed like forever, arrived at the top of the hill. Lalitha looked at them disapprovingly.

"You are very slow," she scolded. "You need to be quicker. The day is passing quickly and we need to get to Serat."

"Don't worry yourself, Tinkerbell," replied Alex. "We'll find our yomping feet again soon enough. It's just a bit of a shock to the system is all."

Lalitha turned and pointed down into the next valley. Another river could be seen winding its way through trees and grassland until it reached a small town in the far distance.

"That is Serat. Let us continue on our way."

"At least there's no more uphill," breathed Jimmy thankfully.

CHAPTER 16

On the Way to Serat

The group descended through the grassy slopes into this new valley and soon arrived at the southern bank of the river they had seen. This river was much deeper than the one outside Melnor and Tom was glad they wouldn't have to try and wade through it with their heavy Bergens. If he lost his footing and had to try and swim one-armed with this pack on his back, he didn't rate his chances of not drowning very highly.

The weather was a little cooler walking along the riverbank as the trail they followed was shaded by willow trees growing near the water's edge. The breeze made a gentle rustling noise as the branches swayed backwards and forwards. Large dragonflies buzzed around them before quickly darting away into the rushes.

Birdsong could be heard in the trees and small brightly coloured birds flew across their path before disappearing swiftly into the undergrowth. It was difficult to keep in mind that they were not on a Sunday morning hike in the Peak District, but were instead starting out on a long journey into the complete unknown.

Jimmy had been walking with Danny, but quickly made his way to the front of the group. He had obviously thought of more questions to ask Lalitha and was keen to walk with her while she answered them. Tom listened in interestedly as they talked.

"Lalitha, how big is the realm of Zakastra?" Jimmy asked.

"Zakastra is an island realm. To ride from Melnor at the southern tip of the island to the far north would take about 50 days, unless you possessed spare horses and could push them hard. My father's army could have done it in 40 days, but they had strong war horses. To ride from the Western Sea to the eastern coast at Brentar would take around 15 days."

"So, if Zakastra is an island?" Jimmy interjected. "Are there any other lands across the seas?"

"There are other lands that we know of far to the east, but we do not send ships there any longer. Those distant lands are many weeks' voyage away and are inhabited by barbarians. We have tried to trade with them in the past, but these dealings have never gone well. The barbarians are not to be trusted. They have sent raiding parties to our shores in the past, but my father always made sure that these raiders were dealt with severely. He did not want any survivors to return to their home and encourage others to come here. No barbarians have been seen for some years now."

Jimmy went quiet. He had used up his questions, but continued to walk close by Lalitha's side anyway.

After a couple of hours walking, they rounded a bend in the river and the small town of Serat stood in front of them.

Jimmy asked Danny to delve into one of the pockets in his pack and then presented Lalitha with a green polyester buff.

"Pull this up over your face," he said. "It will help the disguise."

Lalitha tied her long hair back into a ponytail, before pulling the buff down over her head. Once round her neck, she lifted the front of the stretchy material up until it covered her nose and mouth. Her distinctive green eyes were still visible, but the buff would definitely help to disguise the rest of her face.

They left the riverbank and made towards the town, walking through several small fields carefully planted with rows of vegetables. The workers in the fields stopped what they were doing to stare warily at the passing strangers.

Tom nodded at them as they passed by, but received no response at all.

The figures were all dressed very simply in rough shirts and trousers made from linen or cotton. They were wearing leather sandals of some kind, but it was hard to see properly as their feet were caked in mud from the fields. Crude wooden tools were clasped in their dirty weathered hands. As one of the workers watched Tom cautiously, he could not help but notice the black teeth hiding behind the man's chapped lips.

"Serfs," declared Lalitha. "They work the land and harvest the crops."

"Looks like they're just outta Belsen to me," said Danny. "What have they done to deserve this?"

Lalitha frowned. "I do not know what Belsen is, but you make it sound like a bad place. This is not a bad place. These people are serfs. They belong to the town Elders and they are given food and shelter in exchange for the work they do. This is the only life they have ever known and they accept it willingly. Do not attempt to talk to them

Daniel Adams, they know their place and they will not answer you if you speak to them."

"Will we be able to understand the language the people here speak if they do talk to us?" Tom asked.

"Yes," Lalitha nodded, "the Book taught you our language so you will understand everyone else as easily as you can my own words."

"That should make life a bit easier then," Tom replied.

The team carried on towards the town buildings, each of them slightly taken aback by what they were seeing. It really began to hit home that they were in a land very different from their own.

They left the fields and stepped onto a rough thoroughfare that wound its way in between the nearby houses. The buildings themselves looked like something out of a medieval re-enactment. They were mainly low, single story dwellings made with timber frames and what looked like crude wattle-and-daub panels. The roofs were made of thick reed thatch, presumably sourced from the nearby river.

Lalitha led the team past the first few houses and carried on further into the town. As they walked by, the townsfolk stopped to stare at them. The locals were dressed more smartly than the workers in the fields and their attire was much more robustly made. Clothes seemed to be predominantly green or brown in colour with leather embellishments and patches. Both men and women wore short jackets over linen shirts and trousers tucked into long leather boots. There didn't seem to be any evidence of dresses or skirts on any of the women that they could see.

Many of the locals stopped to stare at them as they passed. The team's clothes and equipment were causing a lot of interest.

"Are you guys feeling as out of place here as I am?" Alex muttered under her breath.

"Yep," Danny nodded. "We seem to be causin' a bit of a stir."

Nobody approached the group as they walked further down the main thoroughfare and several of the doors banged shut as they passed. Lalitha brought them to a halt as they reached a larger two-story building with a sign hanging outside it. The sign squealed unpleasantly as it swung on its metal hinges and as Tom looked up at it, he noticed the rough outline of a carrion bird painted onto the woodwork.

"This is the town's inn," said Lalitha. "We can find lodgings here and I can find directions to where we can obtain some horses. Wait outside while I go in and talk to the innkeeper."

Lalitha disappeared through the inn door and the team stood, quietly examining their surroundings.

A crowd of young children were congregating nearby and they giggled and nudged each other as they watched the strangers with their unfamiliar clothes and equipment.

Chickens were running and scratching around their feet, pecking their beaks occasionally at whatever looked interesting in the dusty earth at the edges of the road. Sam pushed one of them away with his foot as it started to peck inquisitively at his boot laces.

"Has it occurred to anyone that we may have jumped in time rather than through dimensions?" asked Sam. "This looks like some dark age movie set. I keep expecting Sean Bean to walk around the corner."

"I don't know," Tom mused. "We could have, but unless I was asleep more than I remember in school, I don't recall anything about magic books and magi wars in my history lessons. Did you?"

"Nope," Sam agreed, "but then this whole thing is all just a bit freaky-shit isn't it?"

Tom nodded his agreement.

One of the urchins watching them was being egged on by the group and suddenly threw a small pebble at them. It hit Danny on the chest and he looked up at the children in mock rage, pulled a scary face and moved suddenly towards them with a loud pretend growl. The children shrieked and scattered in all directions.

"Little shits," chuckled Danny.

They watched as a horse-drawn cart rattled its way towards them. The cart was loaded down with reeds and the driver eyed them suspiciously as he trundled by.

Lalitha burst out of the inn door and stalked over to them. She did not look happy.

"They have rooms available here, but the innkeeper wants us to pay coin for them now. He told me where I can obtain horses, but they too will want payment before we can take them. We don't have any silver to pay him with."

Tom exchanged glances with the team.

"And that was a surprise to you?" He said incredulously. "I did wonder how we were going to pay for all this."

Lalitha looked angry, but lowered her voice before replying. "I am a member of the royal family. I do not carry coin."

"So, we either need to get cash from somewhere," said Sam, "or we need to steal everything that we need."

"We are not stealing from these people Sam." Alex declared looking at the townsfolk around them. "Look at them, they don't have anything."

Danny stood thinking for a moment and then turned to Lalitha.

"You say there are town Elders that own the serfs and run this place?" he asked.

"Yes," nodded Lalitha. "There will be a number of town elders who own all the farmland around here and run the towns affairs. They administer taxes and uphold the laws."

"Okay. Jimmy, help me off with this thing," he said gesturing at his Bergen.

Once Danny's pack was off, he handed his rifle to Sam and looked back at Alex.

"Okay, Moony, lose the C8 and the Bergen and come with me, we're goin' back in there."

Alex looked puzzled, but shed her pack and followed Danny back into the inn. Several minutes passed before they both emerged again.

They re-joined the group, but did not attempt to take either their rifles or Bergens back.

"Hang on to them a bit longer for us," Danny said cryptically. "We won't be long, we're just off to make a house call."

Before anyone could ask what was going on, both he and Alex strode off down the road.

CHAPTER 17

Serat

It was about half an hour later when Danny and Alex returned to the inn. The sun had disappeared behind the hills now and it would not be very long until night began to fall.

"Where've you two been?" demanded Sam. "We've been standing out here like piffy on a rock bun while the locals gawp at us."

Danny put his hand into his pocket and pulled out a sheet of paper.

"We've got ourselves a get out of jail free card," he grinned waving the paper at them.

"What does that mean?" asked Lalitha.

"It means that we can get what we need now without havin' to find money." Danny explained, "We asked the landlord of the inn where the most important town Elder lives and then we went to pay him a little visit. The guy was pretty nervous about openin' the door to us, but once we were inside, we had a bit of a chat and he ended up writin' us a letter of credit for everythin' we need."

"What? Jesus Fester!" snapped Tom. "Did you expose Lalitha?"

"Trust me Boss. Course I didn't," Danny grinned. "We carefully sounded him out and the Elder hasn't heard anythin' about what's happened in the capital. Serat is apparently a long way away from Krassak and they don't have the luxury of email or the *News at Ten*. It will be weeks before word of the king's death reaches this backwater."

"So, what did you tell him?" asked Tom.

"We said that we were special soldiers from the king's royal guard on a mission to secure the southern stone altar. We told him that there had been rumours that somethin' suspicious was happenin' in the ruins at Melnor and that we had been sent to

94

investigate. I convinced him that we had found nothin' of interest in the ruined city, but that an unexpected lightnin' storm this mornin' spooked our horses and they bolted. We had to walk here and now we need his help to secure food, somewhere to sleep and horses to get us on our way."

"He was sceptical at first," Alex continued, "but apparently a couple of the townsfolk did indeed see lightning in the sky in Melnor's direction this morning which must have been when the gateway opened. We assured the Elder that the King would look favourably on him if he helped us return to Krassak. Neither of us look like locals do we, with the colour of our skin, so the Elder totally bought the story that we were soldiers from the capital. He almost wet himself when we mentioned the King. Apparently, there was some trouble down here a while back and the King threatened to make an example of anyone who was not loyal to the crown."

"What it boiled down to in the end," added Danny, "was that the Elder is more scared of what the King might do to him if he thinks he's been disloyal than he is of parting with the money to buy six horses and a stay in the local inn."

"We promised that he would be handsomely rewarded for helping us once we returned to the capital," grinned Alex.

Tom looked worried. "What if he sends someone north to check your story and Gask hears about it?"

"I don't think he will Boss," said Alex. "We put the fear of God into him and Danny really banged on about how secret our mission is. He told the Elder that if anyone were to hear about us passing through Serat, the King would know that it was him that had betrayed us and he would know exactly who to point the bloody royal sword of blame at."

"So, we're good?"

"I think we're good Boss. Even if the Elder does talk at some point, there's nothing to make Gask think that this is anything to do with Lalitha. He will just assume that the Elder was a victim of a band of strangely dressed con-men."

"I thought you felt bad about ripping these people off Moony?" accused Sam.

Alex shook her head and pointed around her. "I said we can't steal from the ordinary people here. I didn't say anything about taking it from some wealthy Elder dickhead who uses slaves to tend his fields and line his pockets."

"That Elder's gonna be pissed once he eventually realises that he's not getting his money back," Jimmy said.

"He might well be," agreed Danny, "but we didn't tell him how long it would be before he would get his money. The capital is a long way from here so it will be at least a couple of months before he starts to suspect somethin'. By then, word of Gask's coup will have reached him and he will know that he's not gonna get his money anyway."

Tom was impressed. Danny could be a loose cannon sometimes, but occasionally his unique way of thinking came up trumps.

Alex and Danny retrieved their packs and rifles from Sam, and the team made their way into the inn. Danny took the Elder's note and went to talk to the landlord. Within a couple of minutes, he was back.

"We've got three rooms upstairs. Two on the left at the top and one on the right. There are no room keys or anythin', just bolt the door once you're in there. I told the landlord that we'd like some food in our rooms and he was okay with that. He's goin' to bring somethin' up for us as soon as he can."

"He was happy with the Elder's note?" asked Tom.

"Yep. He said that the letter was fine and he would go to the Elder tomorrow and collect what was owed. I told him to add a bit to the bill for good measure and all of a sudden, he was my best mate. He's gonna get his wife to put some cured hams, bread and fruit together for us to take with us tomorrow. Should help to keep us goin' for a few days."

"Nice work, Danny," Tom grinned. He was relieved that Danny's plan seemed to be working out and his flair for bullshit had actually helped their situation rather than getting them into trouble which was what normally happened.

The team carried their Bergens up the wooden stairs and piled them into a heap in the largest of the three rooms.

"Leave all the kit in here for now so we can keep an eye on it," Tom instructed. "We'll all eat in here together so that we can talk freely. Alex, after we've eaten, you go out with Danny and see about these horses. You are now promoted to our team equine expert. We need to have the horses ready for an early start in the morning. Okay?"

"Okay, Boss, leave it to us. Does my promotion come with a pay bump?"

Tom smiled. "No."

They soon heard the footsteps on the stairs and as Sam opened the door, the smell of meat and vegetable broth drifted in. The landlord carried a large pot, full to the brim with steaming broth and his wife followed with bowls and a basket of bread rolls. With a beaming smile, they rushed back downstairs and returned with jugs of cloudy looking beer and some mugs. Tom thanked the coupe as they left and bolted the door behind him.

"The food smells great," Sam observed, "but don't drink too much of that cloudy stuff. I guarantee that'll give you the squits and I'm worried enough about sitting on a horse tomorrow as it is. If I drink that I won't be sitting on a horse, I'll be shitting on a horse."

Alex threw a bread roll at Sam and laughed as it bounced off his bald head. "Don't you dare do that to a horse Slaphead. That's animal cruelty!"

They tucked into the food, but only Danny risked the cloudy ale. Everyone else chose to drink water instead.

They managed to eat about a third of the food and Jimmy started to wrap up the left-over bread using a roll of plastic food bags that he had found in Tom's kitchen.

"What?" he said defensively as he saw Sam watching him. "I thought we could keep these for tomorrow. These zip-loc plastic bags come in useful for all sorts of things so I brought some along. You can store food in them, carry water in them and even crap in them if you need to. Very handy these things!"

Alex pulled a face. "The less I know about your toilet habits, the better!"

"Right, you two. See if you can get the horses sorted for tomorrow morning," said Tom.

Alex and Danny picked up their C8's, unlocked the door and clumped off down the stairs.

"Jimmy, once you've finished what you are doing, can you and Sam split the Bergens across the three rooms? Alex and Lalitha can stay in this room, Sam and I will have the one next door, and you and Danny can take the room on the other side of the staircase."

"Oh, I thought I could share with Lalitha," Jimmy complained.

"Well you thought wrong then. You're with Fester."

The packs were distributed across the three rooms and the team settled back as they waited for Danny and Alex to return. It had gone dark by the time Alex knocked on Tom's door and Sam got up from his bed to let her in.

"All sorted Boss. The stable owner wasn't there, but his son was. He wasn't massively happy about helping out, but he said they would do it once Danny showed him the Elder's letter and rattled him by mentioning the King's name a couple of times. He told us to come back first thing in the morning and his Dad would be there to sort us out. We told him that they could charge whatever they liked for the horses which seemed to cheer him up a bit. He's also going to talk to the saddler tonight to get the horsey stuff that we need. He seemed to have a good idea of what the saddler could let us have in time for the morning. Fingers crossed; we should be ready to roll early tomorrow. Danny asked the landlord to give us a nudge in the morning so we don't all sleep in."

"Not much chance of that anyway," said Tom looking back at the hard, straw mattress on his bed.

CHAPTER 18

Serat

The birds were chirping and squawking noisily outside the bedroom windows as the sun rose, but nobody was too concerned about it as most of them had been awake for quite some time. The beds had been seriously uncomfortable and Tom was sure that there were some sort of creatures living in the straw mattresses. He tried not to think about it as he lay there, but his skin had become hyper-sensitive and every slight itch and prickle from the straw made him toss and turn. He was convinced that something was biting him or running over his skin. At last he could take it no more.

"Sam, you awake?"

"Yep, the bloody birds woke me up with their noise."

"You mean that you managed to sleep okay before that on these bloody uncomfortable things?"

"Yeah, what's wrong with them? They were a bit itchy, but I've slept on way worse."

"Sam, you never cease to amaze me. Come on, let's make a start, I can't lie here any longer."

The two men climbed out of bed and pulled on their clothes. Both had opted to make the journey in long-sleeved cotton shirts and khaki cargo pants with deep side pockets on the legs. After the weather had surprised them with its warmth yesterday, the army surplus sweaters and spare T-shirts that they had brought with them were packed with the winter jackets in the Bergens.

"Won't be needing them today," confirmed Sam as he stuffed the clothes to the bottom of his pack, "unless it's to pad my arse with once we get on these horses."

"We'll be fine once we get the hang of it," Tom assured him.

Tom unplugged his arm from his charger and checked the power status on the solar battery unit. It was still about eighty percent full, which was good news. He pushed the arm into place and buttoned the cuff of his shirt down over the top.

The men both slung their C8's over their shoulders and picked up their packs. Tom unlatched the bolt on their door and went to give the other two bedrooms a loud knock.

"You all ready to move out?" he called.

Alex opened the door next to them and gave them a huge yawn.

"Good night's sleep Boss?" Alex asked.

"Don't ask," Tom grumbled. "I think my mattress was alive with crawling insects or something."

"Didn't you sleep in your bivvy bag on top of the mattress? That's what we did and we didn't have any trouble with critters."

"Jesus Boss," chuckled Sam. "Why didn't we think of that?"

"Coz you're both a bit stupid obviously," Alex chuckled.

Her amusement did not abate in the slightest as Jimmy exited the third bedroom. His face and hands were covered in little red blotches and he was scratching at them furiously.

"What happened to you Coddy?" she laughed. "Something's had a good nibble on you through the night. It wasn't Fester was it?"

"Shut up, Moony," Jimmy snapped irritably. "I got eaten to bloody death in that bed last night. I ended up sleeping on the floor, but the little bastards must have got a taste for me coz they followed me and invited all their mates along."

Tears of laughter rolled down Alex's face as she watched Jimmy scratch at the red lumps on his forehead.

"It's not funny, Alex, this is torture," Jimmy moaned.

"Hold on a sec," Alex said trying unsuccessfully to disguise her amusement. She disappeared back into her room and appeared a few seconds later with a small tube of antihistamine insect bite cream that she passed to Jimmy.

"I thought we might need this so I brought some in my med kit."

"Moony, you are a life-saver," said Jimmy. "I didn't think of that, I just brought usual stuff; you know… matches, flints, snare wires. That kinda stuff."

"You boys would be lost without me," she smiled. "I once went to a talk by that SAS guy, Colin Armstrong, and he gave us all sorts of tips for what to put in our kits. Useful info. You boys were probably off doing something you thought was equally as useful… like getting pissed."

Jimmy enthusiastically rubbed the antihistamine cream into his skin as Danny appeared from their room carrying his pack and rifle.

"What's all the hilarity about out here?" he asked.

"Just itchy-boy there," Sam chuckled.

"Those beds were a bit rough last night, weren't they?" grimaced Danny scratching his head vigorously. "Can I nick some of that cream after you Coddy? I think I've got somethin' nestin' in my hair."

The landlord's head suddenly appeared around the corner at the foot of the stairs.

"I was just on my way to knock on your doors. There is bread and cheese downstairs if you want to eat before you leave. We have also prepared some food for your journey as you asked."

"Alex, can you give Lalitha a nudge and meet us downstairs?" Tom asked.

Alex headed back into her room, still chuckling to herself as the others made their way down the stairs and into the main bar. Bread and cheese had been piled high on plates on a table near the window and soon everyone was eating what they could, fuelling up for the day's travels. Jimmy filled everyone's water bottles from a large jug on the table and the barman arrived with hessian bags filled with fruit, meats and bread.

As Sam checked the contents of the sacks and nodded his approval, Danny took the barman aside and gestured to Lalitha to join them. They had a short, whispered conversation and the barman nodded his head as Lalitha wrote something on two sheets of paper and handed them to him.

"What was that all about?" asked Tom as the pair sat back down.

"We were sortin' out the messages that Lalitha needs to send north to let her allies know that we're on our way," said Danny. "The landlord knows a couple of young men in the village that can be trusted to take them. Lalitha coded the messages so that they won't compromise us if someone else gets their sticky mitts them."

"Good work, Fester. So, are we ready to make a move?"

Danny nodded as everyone finished the last of their breakfast and drained their water mugs. They thanked the landlord for his hospitality and the team picked up their kit and headed out into the street.

Even though it was early, there were already townsfolk going about their business. A heavily laden pony ambled past them, large bales of cloth strapped to its back. A small scrawny man walking by its side eyed the strangers warily as he continued on his way. The rhythmic clang of a blacksmith's hammer striking metal rang out from somewhere close by.

"The stables we found are next door to the Blacksmith's place, so just follow your ears," Danny said.

Making sure that they had not left any of their valuable equipment behind, everyone loaded up and headed off down the street towards the sound of the forge.

The stables were larger than Tom had expected. Two large wooden buildings stood adjacent to the Blacksmith's forge and the excited snorting of horses could clearly be heard coming from within them. To the side of the buildings, dusty fenced enclosures ran along their lengths and then stretched onwards towards the river. Standing by the nearest enclosure was a tall man with grey hair and an eye patch over one eye. He beckoned them over as he noticed them arrive.

"It is a fine morning, Masters," the man announced. "I am Bartrem. It was my son that you spoke with last night. I beg your pardon if the boy was not able to assist you. We are loyal servants of the crown and would not like anyone to say that we never did our part to support the King."

He made his point by giving the group a comical little bow before continuing.

"I have selected six of my finest horses for you. They are fed and watered and my boy has readied them with tack from the saddler. By good chance, the saddler is a friend of mine and was able to fulfil your requests at short notice."

Bartrem opened a gate in the fence and waved them through. Once everyone was inside, he closed the gate and led them all through the enclosure to a large open door in the nearest of the wooden buildings. He ushered them all inside and pulled the door closed behind them.

Out of the corner of his eye, Tom watched Sam slowly unsling his rifle and hold it casually in his hands. Tom raised his eyebrows in Sam's direction and did the same thing. It didn't hurt to be careful.

Alex and Lalitha rushed over to six large horses that were tethered loosely to a rail nearby. Three were large black mares, two chestnut-coloured mares and the last one was a striking grey stallion. Each horse looked well fed and in good condition.

"They are fine beasts," said Bartrem.

"They're beautiful," gasped Alex as she approached the nearest horse, one of the large chestnuts. The horse nickered gently and nudged Alex with its soft brown nuzzle.

"She's adorable," exclaimed Alex. "This one is mine."

Lalitha looked at the big grey and gently stroked his neck.

"You should have him," grinned Danny. "He looks kind of regal, doesn't he?"

Lalitha patted the horse's neck and smiled. "Thank you, Daniel Adams."

There were four horses left. Tom, Danny, Sam and Jimmy all exchanged uncertain glances, each waiting for one of the others to say something.

"So, which one do you want Boss?" asked Sam, breaking the silence.

"How should I know?" Tom replied, unsure of the difference between the animals in front of him. "The other brown one?"

Danny nodded and was about to say something else to Tom when Bartrem suddenly tugged at his sleeve.

"Begging your pardon Master. I need to see the letter of credit that my son said you possess. I fear that the Elder will not honour his word and I can hardly afford to lose the coin that these fine beasts would bring at market."

Danny handed over the Elder's letter and the stableman carefully examined the large red wax seal on the bottom of the paper with his good eye. After a few moments, he nodded in satisfaction and for the first time a smile appeared on his face.

"The seal upon this letter pledges that necessary coin will be paid to myself, the inn-keeper and the saddler. The Elders are not trustworthy men, but this paper bears their seal and is a binding contract."

"If he does try to wriggle out of payin' you," added Danny, "tell him that if he breaks the pledge he has made to us, we'll came back and demand to know why. Tell him that if he breaks his legal contract, the king's retribution will be swift and violent. Keep the letter and take it to the Elder. Tell him what he owes you and the others and make sure he pays you."

"I will take enjoyment from that Master," Bartrem grinned as he stashed the letter away within his shirt.

The horses were already tacked up with leather saddles, bridles and large saddlebags, one on each of the horse's flanks. There was also what looked like a leather rifle sleeve attached to the front of five of the saddles.

"How much weight do you think we can put in these saddlebags Alex?" Tom asked.

Alex looked at the large leather bags speculatively. "I'm not sure, but they're pretty big. I wouldn't want to overload them, so… what… eight or nine kilos in each?"

"Let's go for that and see what our one-eyed friend here thinks once we're loaded up," agreed Tom. "Put most of the kit in the saddlebags, but keep the really important stuff and some of the ammo in the Bergens."

Alex looked concerned at this plan.

"Boss, I'm not sure riding with a pack on is going to be the best plan. They're going to get uncomfortable pretty quickly."

Tom thought about this, but stuck to his guns. "I know next to nothing about horse riding, but if we get separated from the horses for some reason, I don't want all our ammo and kit disappearing off into the sunset. Keep the Glocks, the 9mm ammo, a couple of Stanag mags and the water in the Bergens. Everything else stash in the saddlebags."

Danny pointed at the rifle slings. "The saddler managed to knock these up for us overnight Boss. I showed him my C8 and it looks like he's made five slings so we can have the rifles handy if we need them while we're riding."

"Sometimes you are not as stupid as you look are you Fester?" grinned Sam.

"Great idea, Danny," Tom agreed.

As they loaded their kit into the saddlebags, Bartrem helped them to balance the weight across each of the bags.

"The horse needs balance," he advised. "Too much weight on one side and the beast will suffer."

After some minutes of moving food, weapons and ammunition between the saddlebags, the stable man was happy that they were correctly loaded. Bartrem opened the doors for them and the team led their horses out into the sunlight. Alex and Lalitha stepped up into the stirrups and used their right hands to steady themselves as they swung up into their saddles. They made it look depressingly effortless and immediately started to walk their horses around the enclosure.

The four men hesitated and looked at their horses in trepidation.

"Why do you wait Masters?" asked Bartrem, "Is something amiss with your mounts?"

"They don't know how to ride," called Alex, a mischievous glint in her eye.

The stable man shook his head and walked to Danny. He pulled Danny's sleeve and dragged him to his horse.

"Do not be feared Master," he instructed. "I will show you how to mount your animal."

Bartrem tapped Danny's right leg and pointed at the stirrup.

"Put your foot here, put your right hand on the beast's back and push up with your leg. When your right leg is straightened, swing over your left leg, sit in the saddle and put your left foot in the other stirrup. Be gentle mind, if you drop your weight on her too quick, your horse will be displeased. If she is to carry you any great distance, you do not want her to be displeased with you."

"Here we go then," breathed Danny. He put his right leg in the stirrup and his hand up on the leather of the saddle before pushing up with his leg and swinging smoothly into the saddle. Danny beamed and clapped his horse on the neck happily. "Good girl."

Sam went next and managed it almost as smoothly as Danny had.

Tom approached his horse nervously, but had taken some heart from the fact that everything was being done right-handed.

"You ok, Boss?" called Alex.

"I will be once I'm up there," he grimaced.

It proved to be a lot easier than Tom had feared. He swung up into the saddle on the first attempt and was soon sat astride his horse, a big smile on his face.

"Come on, Coddy," Alex shouted encouragingly.

Bartrem led Jimmy to his horse and showed him what to do before adding one last comment that did not do much to help Jimmy's confidence.

"Just mind this beast young Master, she is a spirited one."

"What the hell does that mean?" asked Jimmy anxiously.

"If you let her, she will think she is the master rather than you."

"Oh Jesus!" muttered Jimmy.

"Come on, Jimmy, you'll be fine," Tom called over.

Jimmy braced himself, put his right leg in the stirrup and started to push up before he had got a proper grip on the saddle. He lost his balance and started to swing round; at which point the horse took full advantage of Jimmy's mistake, turned quickly and bit him on the backside. Jimmy squawked and fell to the ground in a cloud of dust.

Judging from his reaction, this was possibly the funniest thing that Bartrem had ever seen in his whole life. The old man laughed so hard that he was in danger of joining Jimmy in the dirt.

"Try again young master," Bertram spluttered in-between great hoots of laughter. "Show her that you are in charge."

Alex was in fits of giggles and Danny was thoroughly enjoying the entertainment. Even Lalitha was smiling at his misfortune which cut Jimmy to his core. He had to do this!

Jimmy picked himself up and dusted himself down before looking worriedly at the horse. He was sure that the horse was smiling too.

Bartrem pointed to the stirrup again, a huge grin on his face. "This time Master, reach up to hold the saddle before you push with your leg. Swing up before she has chance to taste you again."

Jimmy took a deep breath, stepped into the stirrup, reached up to hold the saddle and pushed upwards. He swung his leg over the horse's back and he was up in the saddle.

"Well done, Jimmy," said Tom. "Ignore this lot, it's not as easy as it looks."

Jimmy sighed in relief and blushed as he saw Lalitha smiling at him.

"How do you steer these things?" asked Sam.

"Okay," said Alex. "It sounds a bit complicated, but it gets much easier once you get into the swing of things. To turn left, look where you want to go with your head rather than your eyes, pull slowly on the left-hand rein and move your right stirrup behind the cinch strap that goes under the belly. To turn right, do the opposite of everything I just said."

"What?" spluttered Sam.

"Look where you want to go with your head, pull the rein in the direction you want to go and press the opposite stirrup to the horse's side behind the cinch. Okay?"

"And how do you make it go?" asked Jimmy nervously.

"Pull both your stirrups back, squeeze them against the horse's flanks and release again quickly. Like, squeeze-release, squeeze-release, squeeze-release. While you're doing this, push forwards with your lower back and let the reins go loose. The horse will feel your momentum and start to walk."

Bartrem perched himself on the corner of the enclosure fence from where he could fully enjoy any more mishaps.

"How did you travel to these parts if you have no horsemanship?" asked Bartrem. "Surely you did not walk from Krassak?"

"We had a cart," Danny quickly bluffed. "Our two guides here rode horses and we followed in a carriage."

"Do you want a carriage?" the old man enquired with a twinkle in his eye. "I could likely find one willing to sell you theirs if you want one?"

Jimmy suddenly looked hopeful that he could sit comfortably in the back of a carriage rather than on the vengeful horse he had been given, but Lalitha quickly cut him off.

"These horses will suit our purpose Bartrem... as long as they are not highly strung beasts that are likely to bolt easily."

"They are good beasts," he shouted, "well trained. They will not bolt on you... well, unless they get spooked of course."

"Thanks for that," muttered Jimmy under his breath. "Very reassuring, I don't think!"

Alex and Lalitha walked their horses around the other riders.

"Come on boys," Alex chided. "Don't listen to Rumpelstiltskin over there. Give it a go. You'll pick it up quickly I promise. Boss, hold both reins in your right hand, that'll work just fine."

Tom, Sam and Danny tentatively did the squeeze-release thing with their legs, let the reins go slack and the horses did indeed start to walk slowly around the enclosure. They tried the steering instructions that Alex had given them and, after seeing it done a few more times, they all started to grasp how to communicate direction changes to their horses.

After some more encouragement from Alex, even Jimmy began to understand how it was done.

"How do you make them run?" asked Sam.

"Let's worry about the walking first shall we, Slaphead?" suggested Alex.

"Alex is right," said Tom. "If we can get the horses to walk okay, then that is fine by me. If we do get chased by anyone, we'll never be able to outrun them, will we?"

"True enough," said Alex, "if someone chases us, we'll just have to get off and shoot them."

"I hope that your journey is not a long one, Masters," chuckled Bartrem, "as it looks to me like it will be a slow one. What road will you travel?"

"We travel north," Lalitha answered, keen to not give away any details about their planned route.

"Everywhere is north of here, girl," laughed the old man. "Just be mindful on your way though. There has been rumour of misdeeds on the road to the mountains. I have heard it said that travellers have been robbed on their way to Lintar."

Tom wanted to ask Bartrem more about his warning, but Lalitha was getting increasingly eager to begin their journey and interrupted him before he could speak.

"Let us depart," she announced. "We are more than able to defend ourselves from common highwaymen old man."

"What do you think Boss?" asked Alex. "Shall we just set off and see how we go?"

Tom looked doubtful, but realised that Lalitha did not want to waste time here while he and the lads learned how to ride properly.

"Okay, let's set off and see what happens," Tom said. "Just one thing though Alex, despite what our friend Bartrem here tells us, what happens if the horses get spooked and they bolt?"

"Two choices," smiled Alex, "One. Try to stay on there until it runs out of steam, or two… jump for it."

"I can think of a third option," grumbled Jimmy. "Fall off and break my bloody neck!"

Still grinning from ear to ear, Bartrem opened the enclosure gate and Lalitha led them out into the street.

"Good luck, Masters," Bartrem called. Something suddenly occurred to him. He reached into the pocket of his smock and tossed a brush to Alex. "Here is something else you will need. Keep these beasts healthy and they will serve you well."

"Thank you, Bartrem," Alex nodded as she stuffed the brush into the saddlebag behind her. "I promise we'll look after them."

Bartrem closed the gate as the last of the riders went through and waved at them as they made their way along the main town thoroughfare. The horses walked along obediently and Lalitha led them to a track that headed off into the countryside to the north. Before very long, the town of Serat was out of sight behind them.

CHAPTER 19

On the Road to Lintar

The first day's riding was easy going as they rode along a series of dusty tracks that wound their way through the grassy countryside. Lalitha rode at the front of the group and the other horses seemed quite content to follow her lead.

"Looks like we didn't need to worry so much about the steering," commented Sam. "Our horses are quite happy to just plod along behind Lalitha."

The others agreed that this had made their first morning's riding easier than they had feared.

The land was relatively flat here, so any occasional travellers coming in the opposite direction could be seen from some distance away. Whenever anyone was spotted coming towards them, Lalitha had plenty of time in which to pull her buff up over her nose and mouth to disguise her identity. The strange attire of Lalitha and her companions earned some suspicious looks from the other travellers and nobody that they passed attempted to speak to them at all.

"Not a very talkative bunch, are they?" said Alex after a group of travellers on horseback passed them by without offering any kind of greeting.

Both Tom and Sam had noticed that all the men in the passing group had placed their hands on their swords as they rode by. Everyone seemed to be on edge, and Tom wondered if there was something to the warning that the old stableman had hinted at.

After several hours of riding, Lalitha pulled her horse off the track and into the shade of a grove of trees by a stream. She dismounted and led her horse to the water where it drank thirstily.

"We will rest here for a little while," she announced. "We can water the horses and stretch our legs before continuing."

Alex slid down from her mount and patted her horse on the shoulder.

"Come on girl, let's get you a drink."

Tom hoped Alex and Lalitha weren't watching him as he awkwardly dismounted. He kicked both feet from his stirrups, painfully dragged his left leg over the horse's back and held on to the saddle tightly while he lowered himself to the ground. He gritted his teeth and took a few tentative steps. He blew out his breath loudly as his lower back and buttocks let him know just how unhappy they were.

The others were in a similar condition.

"Holy shit," gasped Sam. "I feel like this horse has been riding me rather than the other way around!"

Jimmy gingerly began to lower himself down from his mount. Seeing this as a great opportunity, his horse turned its head and bit him on the right buttock again.

"Argh, you bastard!" squealed Jimmy as he fell the rest of the way to the ground. "This bloody horse has got it in for me. Can I swap with someone, Boss?"

"Suck it up, Coddy," laughed Alex. "She'll get tired of biting your skinny arse eventually. There's hardly any meat to get hold of anyway."

Tom would have laughed, but he was in too much discomfort to find anything really funny at the moment. He painfully led his horse to the stream and hooked the reins over the horse's head as it bent its head to drink.

"How are we doing?" he asked Lalitha.

She looked at him critically. "We make slow progress, but perhaps we will make better time once you all become more accustomed to the riding."

Tom watched as Alex made her way around the team to make sure they were all okay.

"If your arses really hurt," Alex said. "You might not be putting enough weight on your stirrups. You can't just sit there like you're in an armchair, you need to be putting about a third of your weight onto the stirrups. If you do that, your legs will work like shock-absorbers and it should help to take the pressure off your butt and your lower back. When you get back up in the saddle, I'll have a look at the length of your stirrups and make sure they're all set up at the right length for everyone."

"Jesus, Boss," complained Jimmy. "My arse is gonna be one big bruise by tonight."

Tom smiled. "You and me both, Jimmy. Grab something to eat and get your water bottles filled up. Once we've had a few minutes, we'll head on again."

"How far away is the next town?" Danny asked.

"Our destination is Brentar on the eastern coast," said Lalitha, "but we will reach the town of Lintar before then. If we can make better time, we should arrive at Lintar in about six days' time. In a few days' time, we will be able to see the Southern Mountains in the distance ahead of us. Lintar is in the foothills of those mountains."

"Six days to the next town?" moaned Danny. "I guess that means we are roughin' it at night until then? As if sittin' in that saddle isn't goin' to cripple me enough, I've gotta sleep on the ground too!"

"Did you think there was gonna be a Travelodge down the road Fester, you muppet?" quipped Sam.

Danny stuck two fingers up in his direction.

"Come on lads," Alex chided. "It will get better I promise. Your muscles will start to adapt after a day or two and the riding will get easier."

Neither Danny nor Jimmy looked convinced.

"At least the sun is shining and it isn't raining," added Tom.

"Don't tempt fate," warned Jimmy.

Once everyone had eaten and refilled their water bottles, they slowly remounted their horses and braced themselves for another few hours in the saddle. Alex made her way around the horses, checking their stirrups and making sure that nobody's cinch had loosened.

As she shortened Sam's stirrups for him, she noticed that he had pulled his sweater out of one of his saddlebags and was sitting on it.

"Isn't that a bit slippery?" Alex grinned.

"I don't care if it is," replied Sam. "If it means my backside takes less of a pounding, then it'll be just hunky-dory thanks."

Lalitha rode past them to the front of the group. "Let us go. We have several hours of light remaining and we need to travel as far as we can before nightfall. If you are unable to ride well in the daylight, then riding at night would definitely be unwise."

She gave her horse a quick flick of the reins, manoeuvred him back onto track and set off again northwards.

Alex mounted up and trotted her horse until it was alongside Lalitha. She then slowed to match the speed of the grey stallion as they walked further into the grasslands. Alex looked over at Lalitha as they rode.

"How are you doing, Lalitha? This must all be really hard on you. Everything that happened to your family, getting whisked away to our world with all its madness and then this journey and the uncertainty of what happens at the end of it."

Lalitha smiled weakly at Alex. "It feels like I am walking through a dream Alexandra

Aluko. My Father has always been the strength behind our family and without him I feel like I have lost a part of myself. My desire to avenge my father's death spurs me onwards and the knowledge that I will be able to feel his soul once I have completed the Ceremony of Binding at Gessan gives me great comfort."

"What kind of a man was he?" asked Alex.

Lalitha's smile deepened and her face seemed to relax as she thought of him.

"King Lestri Santra was a great man. He brought discipline, order and security to the realm. The south had become lawless and unruly under my grandfather's rule, but, once my father took the throne, he was keen to restore the rule of law. He travelled south with his army and carried the Book with him. Although the Book's potency was shackled by being away from its altar, my father had enough power at his hands to easily quell the subversive troublemakers there. Once the agitators had been dealt with, Town Elders were put in place to govern local wards and collect taxes for the crown. Elders were also given their own watchmen with which to maintain law and order. It was not long before the whole realm was at peace and the people flourished once again."

"Was Gask one of the subversives?"

"His father, Nestor Gaskkalt, was one of the most radical of them. He called together great gatherings of men in the town of Lintar and encouraged them to take up arms against the King. Thankfully, when my father rode south and routed the traitors, Nestor Gaskkalt was one of the first to be dealt with. In the years that followed, his only son Findo moved north and slowly wormed his way into the royal court using an assumed name 'Gask'. He was permitted to get too close to my family and he used his position of influence to spread vile doubt and dissent amongst the court."

"And that led to the coup against your father?"

"Yes. Gask twisted the minds of high-serving members of the court with his silver-edged tongue and gained himself allies within the army. He ingratiated himself with the queen and through her got close to my father. Gask bided his time and then struck his cowardly blow. My father was cruelly murdered and all I could do was take the Book and flee."

"What happened to the rest of your family?"

"I do not know for certain. My brother was covered in blood and after I grabbed the Book and tried to escape, my mother… my mother…"

Lalitha's voice cracked with emotion and she could not continue.

"Jesus, you have had a lot to deal with, girl!" Alex breathed.

"Once I am, Bound," Lalitha said angrily, "I will use the power of the Souls to kill Gask. He has to pay for what he has done. For killing my father and for… for what he did with the queen. If I do not stop him, he will continue to destroy my father's legacy. He will wipe away all traces of the royal family and his evil will spread across the land unchallenged."

"Lalitha, if we can help you stop him, then we will," Alex promised. "Do you still have friends in the royal court that can help us?"

"There are some that I can trust. I sent word to two of them from Serat. Cindal Ardum was the commander of the king's royal guard. He was my father's friend and protector and is fiercely loyal to my family. I have asked him to meet us at Prentak on the east coast. We can travel directly there from Gessan."

"The second is Castra Deman," Lalitha continued. "She is the head of one of the most powerful families in the realm. I sent a messenger to her family seat outside Derralt. She will welcome us and help us when we arrive there."

"Will that be enough to defeat Gask?" asked Alex worriedly.

"I hope so, Alexandra Aluko. If their support can get me to Krassak, then I believe that we can stop Gask. We have the Book."

"When we get you to the Tower, there might be a chance that your brother and your mother are still alive. They could be Gask's prisoners."

"He would have enjoyed having my mother all to himself," Lalitha spat, a vicious look on her face.

The conversation seemed to have caused Lalitha to withdraw into herself. Despite asking a couple more questions, Alex could get nothing else from her, so after a few minutes, she dropped back and pulled her horse in beside Tom.

"Hey, Boss. How are you getting on?"

"Not so bad thanks," Tom replied. "My backside is totally numb now, it's just my knees that are giving me jip."

"Yeah, that'll happen," grinned Alex, looking over her shoulder. The three horses at the rear plodded along behind them, their riders all looking sore and weary.

"Won't be too long before we stop lads," she called back encouragingly and tried her best to ignore the insults that they hurled back at her.

The sun was starting to dip towards the horizon as Lalitha steered her horse from the road and made her way through the long grass to a stand of trees a little way away.

"We will sleep here tonight away from the road and carry on at sunrise," Lalitha proclaimed.

"Thank God for that," sighed Sam as his horse came to a stop nearby.

Everyone dismounted, some more easily than others. The team unpacked what they needed from their saddlebags and laid everything on the ground with their Bergens.

Alex showed them how to remove the saddles and bridles from their horses and they each had a training course on how to brush their horse to remove dust and dirt from their hair. By the time they were finished, everyone was exhausted.

Alex took Tom to one side as the others prepared some of the food from the tavern at Serat.

"Boss, do you know the full story of what happened to Lalitha's family at the tower?"

"No, not all of it. Why?"

"I get the feeling that something else happened with her mother that she isn't telling us about. She is able to talk about Gask murdering her father, but she doesn't seem able to talk about what happened to her mother after that. I tried to comfort her and say that her mother may still be alive, but she just got even angrier and then totally clammed up. I think Gask might have done something really, really bad to the queen."

"What are you saying, Alex?" Tom asked worriedly.

"Well, Lalitha gets really emotional whenever she talks about her mother, but she hasn't said anything about Gask killing her. That makes me think that Gask must have done something else to the queen… something awful."

"Shit! Are you saying that you think Gask raped her mother? Right there in the Tower before Lalitha escaped? Jesus Alex, if that's true, there's no wonder she's so desperate to get him. If he'd done that to my family, I wouldn't rest until the bastard's head was on a pike either."

"Yeah, I know. I could be wrong, but there's definitely something about her mother that she can't bring herself to talk to me about. I'll see if she will open up if the opportunity arises again. It might help her if she can find the strength to talk about it. She's only a kid for Christ's sake and for her to have to go through all this is just fucked up."

Tom sighed deeply. "Let's leave it alone for now, Alex. We're going to be on the road for quite a while and she might tell you more as we travel north. Get some food and we'll keep an eye on her tonight."

Tom wandered back to the camp slowly shaking his head as he tried to imagine how Lalitha must feel. Alex stayed where she was and watched Lalitha as Jimmy brought her a hunk of cooked meat and a bread roll. Her instincts told her that Lalitha was really hurting and she felt sorry for the young woman. Her whole life had been ripped apart in just a matter of days.

Lalitha slowly started to respond to Jimmy's incessantly cheerful questioning and Alex relaxed a little once she saw her start to eat something. She made her way back to the group, accepted her share of the evening's rations from Sam and sat down to eat with the others.

The conversation soon degenerated into a 'who's got the worst riding injuries' competition. The guys all complained about their bruises and aches, but Jimmy easily won the contest with the two angry looking bite marks on his ass.

"That horse has got it in for me," Jimmy declared.

"I would have it in for you too if I had to carry your skinny arse halfway across the country," laughed Danny.

Lalitha remained quiet throughout the meal and did not really get involved with the banter. Before long she announced that she was tired and was going to try to sleep.

"We have another early start in the morning and a long day of riding." She advised. "We should all get some rest."

The team all agreed and everyone pulled on their woollen jumpers before sliding into their bivvy bags. It was a warm evening, but no doubt the temperature would fall away over the course of the night.

"I'll take first watch if you like," offered Alex. "You boys look more knackered than me."

"Thanks, Alex," said Tom with a grin. "Wake me in an hour and I'll take over."

Tom lay back on the ground and rested his head on his Bergen. He looked up at the night sky and marvelled at the number of stars that he could see. The heavens were alive with stars, but Tom did not recognise any of the constellations.

He thought about what Alex had told him and his stomach clenched when he considered what Lalitha had witnessed in the Tower.

Eventually he started to drift off to sleep, but as he began to doze off, he heard Jimmy's voice pipe up.

"Boss?" Jimmy whispered urgently. "Do they have spiders here?"

"No, Jimmy, of course they don't," Tom lied, before rolling onto his side and closing his eyes.

CHAPTER 20

On the Road to Lintar

The next four days melded into a blur of boredom and pain for Tom. The grasslands that they travelled through were featureless, and the endless swathes of long grass moved in the wind like ripples on water.

As the mountains to the north grew imperceptibly larger the distance to their foothills slowly decreased, Tom began to feel like his horse was actually a ship adrift in the sea and the mountains were an island that shimmered like a mirage on the horizon.

They rode through a small village that had been built in the middle of nowhere. It was a small cluster of houses marooned in an empty sea of grass. There was a small inn at the side of the road, but it looked anything other than welcoming. The timber-framed building looked run down, and a sign showing the picture of a star hung precariously from one hinge, the other having snapped off sometime in the past. One or two of the windows were broken and a horse rail stood empty outside. None of the team suggested stopping at the inn, so they pushed on through the village.

The few locals that they saw as they rode by swiftly disappeared inside their ramshackle houses and closed the doors hastily behind them. It seemed that the villagers were wary of strangers, especially ones that looked as peculiar as Tom and his team did.

As uneventful as the village was, it at least broke up the tedium of the endless swathes of grass. It wasn't long before Tom found himself nodding off in the saddle as they continued on through the featureless landscape.

Tom suddenly jerked awake as Alex pulled alongside him on her horse.

"You okay, Boss?"

"Yeah. Yeah. I'm just tired Alex. We've been on these horses for five days and these grasslands all look the same. It feels like we're never getting anywhere. Those bloody mountains still seem a long way away."

"You boys are doing really well. Nobody has fallen off yet and I think we're making good progress. Those mountains do look quite a bit bigger today."

"I'm not sure that Lalitha would agree with you. She's desperate for us to be able to ride faster."

Tom was right, Lalitha was becoming more irritable and was obviously frustrated at having to ride so slowly. Even Jimmy was careful about what he said around her in case she snapped at him.

"Did you manage to talk to her about, you know… her mother?"

"Not yet," Alex replied. I've nearly brought it up a couple of times, but either she was looking too pissed-off, or Jimmy would pitch up like a little lost puppy and start talking random crap again. I think I'm better waiting until she brings it up herself before I broach the subject again."

"Yeah, okay. I think that sounds like a good idea. By the way, I forgot to ask Sam this morning. How are we doing for food?"

Alex grimaced. "We'll be okay, but we might end up having a lean day before we get to Lintar. I think Lalitha was a bit optimistic when she said it was a six-day ride."

"Okay, well let's worry about that when it happens. You never know, we might suddenly find a burst of speed from somewhere."

"If you lot find a burst of speed, then something bad is happening," laughed Alex.

By the end of the day's riding, Alex still hadn't managed to talk to Lalitha about her mother, but at least the mountains were definitely much closer. Tom could see the craggy summits of the peaks as they jutted up into the late afternoon sky.

The next morning, after another night spent sleeping in the open, the team's spirits began to lift as the trail they were following gradually rose out of the monotonous grasslands. The countryside around them began to take on a completely different character as they left the grassy plains. They passed small patches of woodland, and rocky outcrops pushed their way up out of the greenery. They had arrived at the foothills of the Southern Mountains.

Lalitha seemed more at ease once their route started to rise up and down as it wound its way around streams and rocks. Her mood improved significantly as she realised that Lintar was probably only a day's ride away.

By lunchtime, the hills had risen around them and streams trickled from valleys and gullies on the left-hand side of the track. The horses splashed their way through the water as it ran through runnels in the track before flowing off to the east where a river meandered its way across the valley floor.

"Our route continues to climb through these foothills until we reach an upland lake on the shores of which is the town of Lintar," Lalitha told them. "We should arrive there tomorrow morning."

"That's good news," smiled Tom. "It'll be good to have a roof over our heads for a night at least."

"I need a shower as well. We must all smell like our horses," joked Alex.

"If you want to get your kit off and take a bath in one of these streams, feel free," Sam suggested.

"Yeah, Moony, you could give the locals a bit of a show and we could pass a cap around afterwards," laughed Danny. "It might buy us a couple of drinks when we get to Lintar. Look… These guys up ahead would probably be up for it."

Tom looked up the track in front of them and saw a pack of horsemen that had pulled out of a tributary valley further ahead. The horsemen had seen them and were riding slowly in their direction.

As the riders approached, Tom noticed that they all had scarves pulled up over their faces to protect them from the dust that their horses kicked up from the trail. The riders looked to be travelling with little or no baggage and Tom could see bows slung over their backs.

"Lalitha?" Tom asked warily, "any idea who these guys are?"

Lalitha studied the approaching group and Tom could sense rather than hear the whispering of the Book.

"Thomas McAllister, the Book is nervous about these men. I think we should stop here and let them pass."

"I think you're right. Everyone pull off the track and let these guys pass by," he instructed the team. "They're not giving me a warm fuzzy feeling."

Lalitha manoeuvred her horse from the track and the others followed closely behind. The team gathered their horses together and Tom noticed that the approaching group were arming themselves. Several of the riders now had their bows in their hands and their horses had sped up perceptibly.

Tom pulled his C8 from its leather sleeve and cocked the rifle's action. He heard similar metallic chak-chak noises from the team around him as everyone followed his lead.

"Okay, so as these guys pass by," said Tom, "just make sure…"

He never finished his sentence. Suddenly an arrow whistled past Tom's head and stuck into the ground a few metres in front of his horse. Tom looked at the arrow in confusion. It must have come from behind them. He spun round in his saddle to see another group of riders coming up quickly from the rear. They were caught in the middle of an ambush.

The riders to the front spurred their horses and, as they approached, several of them started to fire arrows.

"Boss?" Danny said as an arrow shot past him.

"Do it," Tom exclaimed.

Danny swiftly raised his rifle and fired two quick shots at the oncoming riders. The closest rider fell from his saddle and went under the hooves of the horses that were running closely behind him.

Firing his rifle also had another unintended consequence. It spooked the horses. Two of the team's horses reared and Sam and Tom were thrown from their mounts. They hit the ground hard but thankfully both managed to avoid falling on their rifles. Arrows were hitting the ground around them and Jimmy's horse screamed in pain as an arrow impaled his saddlebag and pierced the horse's flank. The horse bucked wildly and Jimmy quickly leapt from the saddle.

Lalitha's stallion panicked at the sudden loud noise and bolted away from the track. She hung on tightly to the saddle as her horse ran at full speed across the floor of the valley, towards the river to their right. Alex re-sleeved her rifle, fought to control her startled horse and then galloped off in pursuit of the fleeing grey horse.

Jimmy watched in shock as the two women raced off. An arrow suddenly hit his Bergen and stuck into something inside his pack. Jimmy spun round and crouched as he raised his rifle and squeezed off three shots in the direction that the arrow had come from.

Danny's horse was fighting him, so rather than trying to stay in the saddle and be a defenceless target for their attackers, he pulled his feet out of the stirrups and slid off the saddle to the ground as his horse bucked and ran. Danny flicked the selector switch on his C8 to full auto, raised the rifle and fired a prolonged burst of bullets at the riders up the track. They were less than fifty metres away now.

Several of the attackers were flung from their mounts and two of their horses crashed to the ground in a billowing cloud of dust. The remaining riders pulled their horses up sharply and leapt down. They looked confused by the loud reports from the guns, but it didn't stop them from continuing to fire arrows in the team's direction.

An arrow from behind them struck the dirt close to where Sam had fallen and he quickly climbed to his feet, shouldered his rifle and started to fire at the riders to the rear. Tom was still winded, but rolled to a kneeling position as he fought to breathe. He struggled to steady his shaking rifle and managed to fire off several rounds at their attackers.

The noise of the gunfire boomed and echoed around the valley as the ex-soldiers fired their weapons. One of the mounted men from the rear galloped his mount directly towards Jimmy and loosed off an arrow as he came. As Jimmy fired two rounds into the rider's body, the incoming arrow hit Jimmy's C8 and deflected off to the side, gouging a jagged line across his cheek as it went.

"Jesus," breathed Jimmy as he wiped blood from his face. "That was too close."

Five of the riders from the group behind them suddenly spurred their horses viciously and thundered off across the valley floor in pursuit of Lalitha and Alex.

Sam took careful aim through his scope and squeezed off a round. The leading rider was thrown sideways as the NATO round punched its way through his ribcage. As Sam moved his aim to take out the next rider, an incoming arrow streaked towards him and buried itself deep in his thigh.

"Shit! Boss, I'm hit," he yelled.

Tom glanced round as Sam fell to the ground.

"Jimmy. Danny. Cover us," Tom shouted.

Danny glanced back before re-concentrating his fire on the original group of riders up the valley who were now taking cover behind their fallen horses. Their numbers had been depleted, but he thought that there were at least five of them still alive over there.

Jimmy had thrown himself to the ground to make himself less of a target and was shooting towards the rear from a prone position. He picked his shots carefully and had soon taken down four of the attackers.

Tom grabbed at Sam's trousers and quickly used his knife to cut the trousers away from where the arrow had pierced his flesh. There was not too much blood running from the wound as the arrow itself was staunching the bleeding. Tom knew that the worst thing he could do would be to pull the arrow out right away. He threw his Bergen to the ground and pulled a field dressing and a bandage from his survival kit. He ripped open the packet with his teeth and pushed the dressing around the puncture wound before tying the bandage around Sam's leg to hold it tightly in place. Sam gritted his teeth and hissed, but did not cry out.

"Sam," Tom shouted as Danny fired another burst of gunfire from nearby, "You're gonna be fine. Just keep pressure around the arrow and try not to move. I've gotta help, Danny and Jimmy."

Sam nodded and flinched visibly as he pressed his hand around the arrow sticking out of his leg.

Happy that he could concentrate on the attackers again for now, Tom raised his rifle and fired two shots at the group in cover up the trail in front of them. He flinched as an arrow missed his right shoulder by only a few centimetres.

Danny turned his head. "Boss, keep those fuckers pinned down with coverin' fire okay?"

Tom nodded and squeezed off four more shots towards the group. As he did so, out the corner of his eye he saw Danny push a new mag into his rifle, take a deep breath and start to stand up.

"Danny, what the fu…"

Before he finished, Danny was on his feet and charging towards the attackers. Tom swore under his breath, aimed his C8 at the group and started to fire at anything that moved. One of the attackers was hit, a spray of blood blossoming from his chest. Another began to aim his bow, but he was too slow. Danny was on them.

Danny fired all thirty rounds from his clip into the four men crouching there. He carefully scanned the fallen bodies for new threats before relaxing slightly. He ejected his mag from his smoking rifle, pocketed the empty magazine and inserted a new one with a loud click.

"Clear!" He yelled after a moment or two.

Tom nodded and turned to assess the situation behind them. Jimmy was keeping them pinned down and it was hard to tell how many of the men were still alive.

"Jimmy," he yelled, "how many of them are back there?"

"I don't know for sure, Boss," he called back. "Two or three, I reckon."

"Okay, cover us, Jimmy. Danny… on me and calm the fuck down will you!"

Danny didn't say anything, but ran over to join Tom as he advanced on the attackers behind them. They moved slowly and smoothly, keeping their rifles shouldered and pointing at the carnage in front of them.

One attacker suddenly stood up and nocked an arrow. As he pulled the bowstring back, Jimmy's carefully aimed shot hit him in the torso and the man was thrown to the ground.

Tom and Danny paused and then continued their advance, careful not to get in between Jimmy and the targets. Two men jumped to their feet and fired their bows.

Danny and Tom both fired without hesitation and the two attackers fell to the ground. Tom lowered his rifle slightly and looked back at Jimmy.

"I think that's all of them, Boss," Jimmy called.

Tom took a deep breath and gave Jimmy a thumbs-up. As he did so, the archer that Danny had hit rolled over. He was still breathing and summoned up enough energy to hurl a wicked looking dagger directly at Tom's face.

Tom instinctively raised his left arm to protect his face and the dagger embedded itself deep into his prosthetic arm. Danny strode over and put two more rounds into the knifeman. Once happy that he was down for good, Danny walked around the other bodies making sure that there were no further surprises hidden there.

Tom stared at the dagger that was sticking out of his left arm and flexed his fingers. The arm still worked okay so he was hopeful that the weapon had only damaged the tough plastic frame of his forearm. He pulled the dagger out with his right hand and looked at the deep gouge it had made. For the first time that he could think of, having a plastic arm had actually been a godsend.

"Boss, what are we going to do about this arrow in Sam's leg?" Jimmy shouted over.

Tom rushed back to where Sam was lying. His face was ashen, but he was conscious.

"You okay?" Tom asked him.

"What kind of a stupid fucking question is that, Boss? I've got a bloody arrow sticking in me."

"Let go of it for a minute," said Tom.

As Sam gingerly removed his hand, Tom examined the dressing. The bandages were not too bloody, and Tom was relieved that the arrow had not hit an artery.

There was a sudden echo of gunfire from across the valley and everyone's heads snapped up to look in that direction.

"Where's Moony?" Sam grunted.

"I don't know," answered Tom, "but she knows what she's doing. I need to make sure you're okay before we try and go after them."

"Moony, can look after herself, but what about Lalitha? She's out there too," Jimmy exclaimed worriedly as he turned to squint in the direction that their horses had run.

"Jimmy, are you hit?" Tom asked worriedly. "You have an arrow in your back."

Jimmy tried to look over his shoulder, but couldn't see anything. Danny leant over and plucked the arrow out of his Bergen.

"You were lucky, Codboy. Something in your pack stopped this arrow. You could have been skewered."

Jimmy took the arrow and rolled it in his fingers as he thought about what could have happened. That was two lucky arrow escapes today.

Tom heard a whinnying nearby and looked up, hoping to see Lalitha and Alex, but it was not them. Several rider-less horses were standing close by and, mixed in with the attacker's horses, Tom could see four animals with large saddlebags. It was their horses. They had run away from all the shooting, but had not run very far and were pacing nervously near to the river about a hundred metres away.

"Those are our horses. Danny, you and Jimmy go and see if you can catch them. We're screwed without them."

"Will do, Boss," said Danny and the two men set off towards the horses.

As the two men set off to retrieve their horses, Tom pulled a sweater out of one of the Bergens and rolled it up to use as a pillow. He put the roll under Sam's head and then did a similar thing with a jacket, this time putting it under his injured leg to raise it up.

"Keep that leg up, Sam. Whatever you do, don't try and stand up."

Tom glanced up and noticed that Danny had managed to catch one of their horses by its reins. Jimmy was chasing his horse around in circles, but was not getting any closer to it. Danny climbed up onto the horse he had hold of and slowly walked it towards the other animals that watched him nervously with their big brown eyes. After a few failed attempts, he successfully managed to grab hold of the other two horses and tie their reins to the metal rings on his saddle.

Danny gently led the horses back to where Sam lay and handed Tom the reins of his horse. Tom gave his mount an encouraging pat on the shoulder and looked back towards the river to see that Jimmy had changed tactics and was now slowly approaching his horse with his hand outstretched rather than running around like a headless chicken. Slowly but surely, he got close enough to reach the dangling reins and he was soon leading his horse back towards them. The other horses continued to graze by the river, seemingly unconcerned that their masters had been killed.

Tom looked across the valley and squinted his eyes to see if he could see any movement. He had not heard any further gunshots and there was no sign of either the attackers, Lalitha or Alex.

Jimmy was out of breath as he arrived back with his horse.

"She got hit by an arrow," Jimmy panted. "That's why she threw me."

Sure enough, an arrow was sticking into the horse's left-hand saddlebag.

"Lift up the saddlebag Jimmy and see if you can find out what the damage is underneath," Tom suggested.

Danny held the horse's reins while Jimmy carefully gripped the saddlebag and slowly lifted it up. The arrow had pierced the tough leather and only the tip of the arrowhead had stuck into the horse's flank. The actual wound didn't look serious.

Jimmy pulled the arrow out of the saddlebag and threw it on the ground.

"You'll be okay girl," he smiled.

Jimmy's horse seemed to be relieved that the pain in its rump had stopped and it turned its head to look at him. Jimmy flinched, but rather than biting him, this time it nickered gently and nudged its muzzle into his chest. Jimmy smiled and stroked her head.

"There's still no sign of Lalitha or Alex," Tom said worriedly. "Danny. Now we've got the horses back, you come with me and we'll go and see what's happened to them. Jimmy, you stay here with Sam. He's not in any state to ride a horse."

"Will do, Boss," nodded Jimmy. "I'll look after Sam; you just go and make sure Moony and Lalitha are okay."

"Just go find them, Boss," Sam said through gritted teeth.

"If you need us," said Tom as he mounted his horse. "Fire three shots into the air and one of us will get back here as quickly as we can."

"Just go," Sam grunted.

Tom nodded. Danny climbed up onto his saddle and the two men set off across the valley as quickly as they dared.

CHAPTER 21

The Foothills of the Southern Mountains

Tom and Danny rode their horses through the river and cut across the valley floor to pick up any tracks they could find. The grass grew quite high here, but they soon started to see a trail where the greenery had been flattened and horses' hooves had churned the ground up. The tracks pointed towards the trees ahead of them and Tom urged his horse onwards.

Danny suddenly pulled up and cocked his head as if listening to something.

"Boss, I can hear the Book. It is whisperin', but I can't make out what it is sayin'. I think they must be in trouble."

Tom strained to hear the voices, but he could hear nothing.

"Come on, Danny, let's get to those trees. It looks like that's where the horses were making for."

Tom wound his reins round his left arm and pulled his Glock from where it had been tucked in the back of his belt. He wanted to be ready for whatever lay ahead in the woods and just hoped that his horse didn't jerk on the reins and pull his arm off.

They urged their horses along as they neared the woodland. They could see at least four individual sets of hoof prints and you didn't have to be an expert tracker to follow the trail. The riders had been travelling at speed and the dirt had really been kicked up as they raced by.

Danny drew his pistol as they entered the tree line and both riders slowed down as their eyes adapted to the shade. The tracks led on through the undergrowth and Tom and Danny moved forward cautiously, their senses alert for any threat.

After only a couple of minutes Tom found himself clear of the trees and was confronted with a cliff face that rose up in front of them. The ground here was very rocky and all signs of any hoof prints soon disappeared.

Tom dismounted and tied his horse's reins around the nearest tree. He pushed the Glock back into his waistband, pulled his C8 from its sleeve and slung it onto his back. He examined the rocks around him for clues, but couldn't see anything useful. Danny was doing the same thing, but was working his way over to the cliff face to the right.

"Boss, come over here," Danny called as he picked something up from the ground.

Tom rushed over and Danny held out his hand. In it were five shell casings. This is where the gunshots had come from.

"There's somethin' else over there," Danny said, pointing his finger at something in the ferns just inside the tree line.

They carefully walked towards the object and stopped when they realised that what they were looking at was the broken and bloodied body of one of the attackers. He had been shot.

"Boss, look!" Danny hissed pointing deeper into the trees further to their right. Through the undergrowth they could see two horses. Lalitha and Alex's horses. They were tethered to a tree and seemed unharmed. Alex's rifle was not in its sleeve and there was no sign of the two women close by.

"Where did they go?" asked Danny.

"They must have dumped the horses here and hidden somewhere nearby. Keep going to the right," Tom instructed.

The cliff face bent around a corner and as they moved round an outcrop, they saw that there was a wide fissure in the cliff. Would the women have hidden in here? In the darkness? Tom supposed that it was as good a hiding place as any.

Tom looked at Danny and nodded towards the fissure.

"What do you think?"

"I think it's worth a look, Boss."

Danny ran back to their horses and returned with their Maglites and some more ammo.

"Stuff this in your pockets, Boss. You left your Bergen back with Sammy so you'll need to wedge these somewhere."

Tom took the three mags and jammed them into the pockets of his combat trousers.

"Thanks, Danny," he said. "Listen, when we find them, just cool it. We don't know what we're walking into and we can't burst in there all John McClane, guns blazing."

"Yippee ki-yay, Boss," grinned Danny.

Tom raised his eyebrows and gave Danny a despairing look. He pushed his pistol into the back of his trousers, switched on the mag-lite torch and moved it to his left hand. He made sure that the grip of his prosthetic was tight against the shaft of the torch to ensure that he didn't drop it once they were inside the cave. Once he was satisfied that the torch was safe, he pulled out his Glock again and headed towards the fissure.

"Come on then," Tom beckoned. "Let's see where this rabbit hole leads."

Once inside, the light from the mouth of the fissure quickly started to fade and Tom soon needed his torch to be able to see where he was putting his feet. The floor of the fissure was dusty and smooth so thankfully there weren't too many trip hazards.

Danny shone his torch onto the ground in front of him and saw several sets of footprints and hoof prints going in both directions. He crouched down and looked more carefully as he moved forwards.

A few metres further on, Danny saw two sets of tracks that had been made by army boots. There was also a small patch of blood, the red contrasting sharply with the grey dust.

"They came this way," whispered Danny. "There are lots of other tracks here as well and I'm not sure what happened, someone is hurt. There is blood on the floor here."

"Keep moving," Tom whispered anxiously.

They moved deeper into the fissure and it gradually began to open out into a wide passageway. Through the darkness ahead, Tom could see some kind of faint, flickering light. As they drew nearer to the light, he also began to hear faint voices. Deep, guttural voices. There was laughing and then a woman's shriek echoed through the cave. Lalitha.

Tom was worried. There were more than three voices coming from inside the cave which meant that the three riders who had chased Lalitha and Alex had found some reinforcements from somewhere. Something was very wrong here.

Aware that they may be about to meet resistance, Tom and Danny turned their mag-lites off, jammed the pistols back in their belts and were about to unsling their C8's when Danny suddenly stopped and grabbed Tom's arm. Somebody was coming. They flattened themselves into the deep shadows at the side of the passage and held their breaths as the shuffle of boots came closer and closer. They could just about make out the vague outline of a figure moving towards them through the darkness. There was a loud hocking noise and the shadowy figure spat a large glob of phlegm into the dust.

The sound of laughter echoed down from the far end of the passage and the figure turned to look behind him. As he turned, Danny unsheathed his knife, crept up silently behind the figure, clamped his arm around the man's neck and plunged the knife into his back. Danny kept his grip on the man for several seconds until he felt him go limp and then laid the body down at the side of the passageway, re-sheathed his knife and unslung his C8.

The two men moved slowly forwards towards the sound of the voices and as they advanced, the flickering light in the cave becoming noticeably brighter. Large stalagmites rose from the floor in groups and Tom felt the cold splash of dripping water on his face as passed near to one of them. The passageway climbed slightly and then opened out into a huge chamber.

Tom and Danny quietly moved into a group of stalagmites to their left, crouched down and edged forwards until they could see into the cavern.

In the centre of the huge chamber, a large fire was burning and around it were sat at least twenty men, all dressed in the same attire as their attackers had been. Burning torches were placed in brackets positioned around the cavern walls which lit up the whole cave. Near the back wall was a corral filled with horses and next to it were parked three large wooden four-wheeled wagons. To the right of the fire was a large wooden cage and inside it, Tom could see a number of men, women and children. One of their captors walked past the cage and viciously kicked at the bars with his boot, laughing as the prisoners flinched away from him.

Danny nudged Tom and pointed. Next to the cage was a line of tall stalagmites and bound to these rocky columns Tom could see Alex and Lalitha. Alex's shirt was ripped and Tom could see blood on her face.

Danny went to stand up but Tom grabbed his arm and held him back.

"We hold fast and make sure we know how many of these guys there are before we do anything," he whispered.

Danny scowled but made no further move. "If they go anywhere near Alex or Lalitha, then I'm goin' down there," he hissed.

"You and me both," replied Tom grimly, "but we need to know what we're up against before we do anything."

The smell of roasting meat wafted towards Tom and he watched several of the men cut chunks out of some sort of large beast that was roasting over the fire. They laughed and pushed at each other as they ate. Tom noticed that one of the men had Alex's Bergen and was rummaging through its contents. The man straightened up and examined one of the items that he had found. It was a high explosive fragmentation grenade.

Tom quickly tapped Danny on the shoulder. "Forget waiting… We've got to move now. That guy has got a frag grenade in his hand. If he pulls the pin, he'll take Alex and Lalitha with him when it goes up. You flank round to the right and I'll stop here. Wait for my signal and when you see it, move in fast and hard. Your priority is to get Alex and Lalitha."

"Okay. What's the signal, Boss?"

"I don't know yet, but I'll make it obvious."

Danny nodded and quietly made his way back through the stalagmites, across the passageway and around to the right. Tom watched through the scope on his rifle and managed to track Danny's progress as he skirted around the fire. He found a position that he was happy with and Tom lost sight of him as he dropped down behind a boulder not far from the caged prisoners.

Tom turned his attention back to the men around the fire. A large figure stood up, kicked the man with the grenade and shouted something at him. Grenade-man cowered fearfully and quickly loaded all Alex's kit including the grenade back into the pack and pushed it towards his attacker, his head bowed. Tom decided that this tall, intimidating figure must be their leader and he was making sure the others knew who was in charge.

The big man strutted around the fire bellowing in a language Tom did not understand. The other men raised their fists, laughing and cheering noisily. Why were these guys so happy? His team had just taken out over ten of their men and yet this mob were celebrating like they'd won the lottery. Surely the returning riders had told them what had happened on the other side of the valley?

The leader kicked at Alex's pack and then swaggered away from the fire towards Lalitha. He clutched at his crotch, laughed lasciviously and shouted something at the group. This time Tom understood one of the words the man had shouted. This was not good. He had shouted a name… Lalitha.

Tom squinted through the scope at Lalitha and realised with a growing sense of dread that her buff was no longer covering her face. The leader had recognised her. These guys thought that they really had won the lottery. They had captured a princess.

Tom switched on the laser sight mount on the side of the weapon and put his hand in front of the barrel. Sure enough, a red dot shone brightly on the palm of his hand. He raised the rifle and aimed through the scope at the group below him.

The big man leaned towards Lalitha, stuck out his tongue and licked her face from jaw to forehead. His men roared their approval and stamped their feet enthusiastically. The leader turned to acknowledge their cheers and started to untie the front of his trousers suggestively. As he looked down, he suddenly noticed a bright red dot on his chest. He brushed at it thinking that it was some kind of bug, but the red dot stayed where it was. He took a couple of steps away from Lalitha and Tom shot him through the chest.

Danny took this as Tom's signal and rushed around the boulder he had been hiding behind. He raised his rifle and opened up on the group of men sitting around the fire.

Rather than shooting indiscriminately, Tom picked his targets carefully and squeezed the trigger again and again as the red dot of his laser settled on them. The men around the fire did not know which way to run. Some made for the passageway out of the cave, but Tom quickly cut them down. Others grabbed for their weapons, but were hit by Danny's hail of gunfire. One man picked up a long dagger and rushed at Danny while his back was turned, but Tom shot him through the side and he fell screaming into the fire.

Seeing that the number of targets had reduced dramatically, Danny drew his knife and rushed to Alex. He cut the ropes that bound her and quickly turned to free Lalitha.

As soon as Lalitha's hands were free, she grabbed the knife from Danny and ran to where the leader lay, gasping for air as blood pulsed out of his chest wound. She stood over him and stared into his eyes for a few seconds before she sat on his stomach and stabbed him over and over again, blood splattering over her hands and face.

"You can stop now, Lalitha," Alex said gently, putting her hand on the young woman's shoulder. "He's dead."

Lalitha slowly stood up and gazed down at the leader's corpse, her face devoid of emotion. Alex took the knife from her hand and pulled Lalitha down as an arrow whistled past them.

"Lalitha, stay here and stay down," Alex instructed as Danny passed her his Glock. Lalitha knelt down quietly and absently began to wipe the blood from her hands.

The remaining men had made it to the wagons. They had retrieved their bows and were shooting arrows in all directions. One of their number fell back as Tom's red dot hovered on his chest and a bullet smashed through him, but the surviving archers then turned their attention to where Tom was positioned. Tom hurriedly ducked down as arrows pinged off the stalagmites around him and took the opportunity to reload his rifle.

Whilst the arrows were directed towards Tom, Danny and Alex quickly ran around the fire towards the archers. The horses in the corral stamped and snorted, spooked by all the loud noise and Alex had an idea. She ran to the corral gate and threw it wide open. As the horses jostled to be free of the chaos around them, Alex fired three shots into the air, causing the horses to rear up and bolt away from her, towards the archers.

As the panicked horses smashed their way past the wooden wagons, the archers had no alternative but to stop shooting and run for safety. They didn't get far. Tom, Danny and Alex hit them with a hail of bullets and the archers were down.

The horses stampeded around the edge of the cavern until they reached the passageway that led outside. They turned into the passage and galloped towards freedom. As the thunder of their hooves faded into the distance, a blanket of silence fell over the cavern.

Tom stood up and walked down towards the fire, his C8 at the ready in case of an attack. Danny scouted round the fire in the opposite direction, making sure that all the bodies on the ground were no longer a threat.

Alex rushed back to where Lalitha knelt and wrapped her arms around the young woman's shaking body.

"It's okay now, sweetheart," she whispered. "You're safe."

Alex smiled tightly up at Tom over Lalitha's shoulder as he walked over to them.

"Thanks, Boss," she said. "Things weren't looking too great for a minute there."

"Are you two okay?" Danny asked breathlessly as he ran over.

"Yeah, we're okay," Alex said. "That big bastard beat me about for a bit and I thought he was going to do worse, but then one of his minions pulled Lalitha's buff off and bloody recognised her. The leader looked like he'd struck gold when he realised who she was. After that, they lost interest in me and he got himself all fired up to do God-knows-what to Lalitha just as you started shooting."

"I saw. Sorry it took us so long to catch up Alex. Sam got hit by an arrow and we had to patch him up before we came after you."

"Is he okay?" Alex asked worriedly.

"He's not bleeding too badly so I don't think it hit an artery, but it's not great. The arrow's still in there. Jimmy stopped with him just in case any more of these bandit psychos pitch up."

"Shit!" Alex swore. "Sorry you had to come after us, Boss. By the time Lalitha had managed to get her crazy horse under control, we were nearly at the trees and these tossers were not far behind. We rode into the woods thinking that we might lose them in there, but we came out of the other side almost straight away and there was a sodding great cliff in front of us. We went around the corner and saw the cave entrance but we couldn't get the horses to go in, so we left them in the trees and ran for it. I shot the first of the riders as they came out of the trees and that bought us enough time to make it in here. I was setting up ready to ambush the others in the dark, but we got jumped from behind. We didn't realise that we'd stumbled into some secret bloody bandit's lair."

"Why didn't the Book do anythin'?" asked Danny.

"Lalitha, dropped it," replied Alex. "When her horse bolted, she had to hang on for dear life. You know how Lalitha likes to hold onto that Book every hour of the day? Well, she couldn't keep hold of both the Book and her horse. It was bouncing her around all over the place as it ran and she dropped the Book somewhere back towards the road. She was desperate to go back for it as soon as we got to the trees, but the riders behind us were catching up fast, so we kept going. Without the Book I knew she was vulnerable and I didn't want to risk her getting hurt."

"Boss," Danny said, "we need to go back and find it."

"We will, Danny, just give us a minute, okay?"

Talk of the Book had brought Lalitha back to her senses.

"Did you see the Book as you rode here?" Lalitha asked.

"No, I'll go and look for it now," Danny said.

"Did it call to you?"

"Shit!" breathed Danny. "I did hear the Book whisperin', but I thought it was because you were in trouble. I'll go now."

Danny picked up his gear and was about to set off out of the cavern, but Lalitha caught his sleeve.

"I will come with you, Daniel Adams," Lalitha said. "We will find the Book together."

Lalitha picked up her backpack that had ended up near the wooden cage and together, she and Danny rushed towards the exit.

"Get back to Sam and Jimmy once you've found it and make sure they're ok," Tom called after them.

Danny's voice echoed back up the passageway. "Will do."

Alex walked towards the fire and retrieved her rifle and pack. She crouched down and checked the contents of her Bergen to make sure that nothing was missing. As she bent down, Alex realised that her shirt was hanging open where the bandit had ripped it. Noticing that Tom was still watching her, she hurriedly pulled four safety pins out of her survival kit and quickly pinned the front of her shirt together.

As Tom watched Alex, he remembered the wooden cage that stood to the right of the cavern.

"Alex, are you okay?" Tom asked.

"Yeah, I'm fine thanks, Boss. It looks like all my kit is still intact which is good."

Tom nodded and moved to stand in front of the big wooden cage. The prisoners inside looked terrified. They all crowded to the back of the cage and stared at Tom with wide eyes.

"Who are these people?" Tom muttered.

"We are travellers on our way from Brentar to the town of Verna on the western coast," a voice answered from inside the cage, "or we were until we were attacked by these men."

A man who looked to be in his early thirties walked to the front of the cage. He was short and looked like he hadn't eaten a decent meal for some time. His eyes were dark and sunken and his gaunt face was framed by long brown hair that was tied back into a ponytail. His clothes were filthy and the knees of his trousers had long since worn through.

"My name is Fellorn," the prisoner said gratefully, "we were travelling on the road from Lintar when we were attacked. They butchered the older members of our convoy and took all our belongings."

"How long have you been here?" Tom asked.

"It has been over twenty days now. Our women have been desecrated by these pigs and they have given us only their scraps to eat."

Tom took out his knife and sawed through the thick rope that held the cage door closed. He swung the door open and gestured to Fellorn and the other prisoners."

"You're free. Come out of there. If you can find anything in this camp that you need. Take it. These men can't hurt you any longer."

The prisoners staggered out of the cage and Fellorn clasped Tom's hand between his own.

"Thank you, sir. We had not dared hope that salvation would come. We thought this nightmare would endure until their leader found an Elder willing to pay enough coin for us. The older members of our party were not worth anything to these men so they were killed. I fear that those of that remained were destined to be sold into serfdom or harlotry."

Tom watched as the prisoners staggered out of their cage. They walked in the direction of the fire where they knew that the bandits had been roasting meat. The spit had been knocked over in the fighting, but this did not deter the prisoners in any way and they rushed over to it and hungrily ate chunks of meat that they ripped from the hot, dusty carcass.

Tom watched them for a few moments and then turned to Alex.

"While Fellorn and his friends here finish that off, let's see if we can find anything useful in this place. There must be more supplies in here somewhere."

Together they searched around the chamber and they soon found five trunks hidden out of the way in a natural alcove in the cavern wall. A torch positioned above the alcove burned brightly and Tom soon had the lids open.

Three large trunks were filled with food supplies. There were enough hessian sacks of bread, dried fruits and a variety of dried meats to keep Tom's team and Fellorn's group stocked up for some time.

The last two trunks were much smaller and each held a large number of small bags. Each small bag contained a fistful of small silver coins.

"Alex, look at this," called Tom. "I don't think we'll be having to talk Elders into giving us any credit notes again."

"Wow," Alex gasped. "These bastards have been busy, haven't they?"

Tom looked back at the prisoners at the fire. They were now busy depriving the bandits of their boots and whatever clothes they could find.

"Fellorn," Tom called, "come over here."

Fellorn was now wearing trousers and a tunic taken from one of the bandits. It had a bloody stain on the front and a hole where Danny's bullet had passed through, but he didn't seem to mind. He wiped meat juices from his beard as he approached and smiled at Tom.

"Yes sir? Can I help?"

"There are two trunks of coins like this," Tom said pointing at the nearest open treasure chest. "How about we take one and you take one?"

Fellorn's eyes nearly popped out of his head.

"Do you jest sir? It would take me years to earn this much coin!"

"I'm serious Fellorn. This is the very least that your people deserve after everything these men put you through."

Fellorn's eyes filled with tears and he waved some of his friends over.

"Look friends," he gasped excitedly. "The soldier here has given us enough coin to set ourselves up once we reach Verna."

Members of Fellorn's group came over and gawped open mouthed at the amount of money laid out in front of them. Several of the prisoners, both men and women, had tears streaming down their faces as they reached out to touch Tom and thank him.

As Tom gently pulled himself away from their grasp and moved out of the alcove, he saw Alex watching him, her eyes dewy.

"That was a good thing to do Tom."

"Well, there's load's there and it weighs a ton anyway," he smiled.

Alex wiped her eyes and looked back towards the corral.

"How about we see if those wagons are still useable?" she suggested. "If Sam has got a leg wound, he won't be able to ride a horse any time soon so we might be able to chuck him in there. Plus, we're going to need something to carry your treasure in."

"Good plan, let's go and take a look at them."

Only one of the wagons had been damaged by the stampeding horses. The other two looked to still be in good condition. All the harnesses for the wagons were piled up nearby alongside a range of saddles and bridles. Alex began to sort through the pile and had soon picked out two full sets of harnesses that could be used. All they had to do now was to track down a couple of horses to go with them.

Fellorn had been watching them with interest and suddenly piped up from behind them.

"These wagons were ours, but you are welcome to have one of them sir. Our horses were in the corral with the bandits' steeds, but they have now fled. I do not think they will have gone far and we should be able to catch them once they have calmed down."

Tom and Alex loaded one of the trunks of food and a coin chest onto the nearest of the wagons. They then lifted Alex's Bergen up there and carefully wedged their C8's in.

With help from Fellorn and his fellow prisoners, they pulled the wagon through the cavern, down the passageway and out into the sunlight. Everyone shielded their eyes from the bright sunshine and Fellorn's people wept again. It was the first time they had seen the sky for nearly three weeks and it took several minutes before they could open their eyes fully.

Alex retrieved her horse from the woods and trotted down the tree line to bring Tom's horse back to the fissure. As she rode back with Tom's horse in tow, several of the escaped horses followed them inquisitively.

By working slowly and carefully, Fellorn and his group soon had several of the horses saddled and had harnessed two of them, one for each wagon. They secured the shafts of the wagon they had pulled from the cavern to the best looking of the two horses and presented it to Tom.

"Take this horse and the wagon sir," said Fellorn with a beaming smile. "It is little payment for giving us back our lives."

"Thank you Fellorn," Tom replied, "I appreciate it. The wagon will allow us to transport one of our friends who was wounded by these bandits to a doctor."

"I hope that your friend recovers speedily," Fellorn smiled.

"Fellorn?" Tom said quietly so that no-one else could overhear them. "I need to talk to you about something."

"Yes sir?"

"The leader of the bandits in that cave seemed to think that he recognised one of my friends."

"Ah, yes," Fellorn replied, a twinkle in his eye. "The leader did mention the name Lalitha several times. The name seemed to excite him greatly."

Tom paused as he struggled to decide how much to reveal about Lalitha's identity, but Fellorn solved the problem for him.

"Do not worry sir. It is of no matter to us who your friend is. It may be that she is a woman of great importance or it may be that she is not. Whatever the truth is, nobody will hear that name from us. We owe you our lives and that is a debt that we will owe you always."

Tom smiled. "Thank you. If you could not say anything about our friend to anyone, that would really help us."

"Then that is settled," Fellorn laughed and clapped Tom on the arm.

As they spoke, a younger man had edged forwards until he stood nearby. The young man looked very serious and bowed his head as he waited quietly next to them. The young man was broad and strong looking with short blonde hair and a wispy beard. He had found himself some bandit clothes from inside the cave which looked a little too big for him and he had folded the arms of the tunic up over his wrists to stop them dangling off the end of his hands.

"Ah, yes," Fellorn exclaimed, noticing the young man. "This is Ramman sir. He was travelling with us, but no longer desires to journey to Verna. After everything that has happened to us on the road, he wishes to return home to Brentar. Do you travel in that direction?"

"Err… yes we do," said Tom.

"Is it possible that he could travel with you? I do not want to abandon him to travel on his own and he would certainly be an asset to your group. He is an excellent horseman and has no small experience as a carter."

"Well…" began Tom.

"I think it is a good idea Boss," interrupted Alex. "He can help me with the horses and he can drive a horse and cart. Can you?"

"But Alex, you know where our journey is taking us."

"Yes, I do, but he's only going to come with us to Brentar and no further. He wouldn't have to commit to helping our friend do what she has to after we reach Brentar. As long as we can trust him to keep his mouth shut after we're gone, I think he could be a great help. He knows these roads better than any of us and we're headed for the mountains."

Tom looked thoughtful. "Fellorn, will you stay here overnight before you go anywhere?"

"Yes sir, we will try to find more of our belongings and round up more of the horses before we travel any further. We also need to eat and regain some of our strength before moving on. Why do you ask?"

"We're going to take Ramman here with us to meet with our friends back at the road on the other side of the valley. If they agree that he can join us, then we will take him with us. If they don't agree, I will send him back to you. Does that sound fair?"

"Yes sir. It does."

"Okay then," Tom said. "Ramman, come on. You're coming to Brentar with us. How would you like to drive the cart?"

The young man smiled and climbed up onto the driver's seat of the wagon they had loaded.

"Thank you Master," he beamed.

"Don't call me Master," said Tom, "call me Tom."

The young man nodded. "Thank you, Master Tom."

Tom laughed and tuned back to Fellorn. "Will you be okay? There could be more bandits in these valleys. If there were any that were away from the cavern today, they could return."

"Do not fear sir, we will not let them take us again. There are many weapons back in the cave with which to protect ourselves if we need to."

"Good. Okay then, we need to get back to our wounded friend. Have a safe journey to Verna."

"Thank you, sir. I wish you safe travels also."

Tom surprised Fellorn by firmly shaking his hand. It was obviously a gesture that was unfamiliar to him, but he smiled and nodded his head.

"Take care, Fellorn," Alex smiled as she climbed up into her saddle. "Come on,

Boss, we need to get back to Sam."

Tom nodded and mounted his horse. As they set off, Tom turned to Ramman as the wagon's wheels began to rattle loudly on the rocky ground behind them.

"Come on, Ramman, let's go and find the others."

CHAPTER 22

In the Foothills of the Southern Mountains

By the time they arrived back at the road, Lalitha and Danny had already arrived back and their horses were grazing peacefully nearby, despite the fact that a pile of corpses stood close at hand.

Jimmy looked hot and bothered as he dragged the last of the dead bandits to a large grisly mound at the side of the road. A cloud of flies buzzed around the bodies, and overhead several large carrion birds were circling. A handful of the boldest of the birds had already started to rip flesh from one of the dead horses on the road and they hissed noisily at each other as they fought over the meat.

"Hey Boss," Jimmy panted. "I thought I'd get all the bodies together rather than having them spread around all over the place."

"What are you going to do with them?" Tom asked.

"I don't know… burn them?"

"Human bodies don't burn very well," Alex observed. "They're mainly water so, unless you've got a can of petrol stashed somewhere, you're not going to be able to get your bonfire going very easily mate."

"Oh. Shit. Guess I'll just have to leave them here then," Jimmy shrugged. "I haven't got a shovel so I couldn't bury them even if I did feel like digging a hole big enough to drop them all into. Which I don't."

"How's Sam?"

"He's okay, I think. The wound isn't bleeding so much and he was asleep last time I checked. I didn't want to try and move him in case I knocked the arrow and set if off bleeding again."

"Good decision," Tom nodded.

Alex dismounted and hurried over to where Sam lay. Danny and Lalitha sat next to him, both with worried looks on their faces. Thankfully they had found the Book on their way back and Lalitha had it in her lap. Sam was conscious again and smiled weakly as Alex crouched down beside him.

"Trust you to go and get skewered," she teased as she carefully examined his leg.

Alex gently touched the arrow's shaft and as she did, Sam's body stiffened and he gasped audibly.

"Lalitha, can the book do anything to help him?"

"Sorry, no," Lalitha said apologetically. "If it were going to act, it would have done so already. The Book does not feel threatened here so it will do nothing of its own volition."

"Great," Alex muttered sarcastically. "At least you found it okay though."

"Yes, it lay in the grass near to where Daniel Adams heard its voice. I am much relieved to have the Book back in my hands. If we had lost it, our quest would be impossible."

Sam moved position slightly and the resulting pain made him cry out.

"Hang on in there Sammy, just give me a sec," Alex smiled encouragingly as she stood up and pulled Tom a few metres away to talk to him.

"Boss, I don't know what we're going to do. I've never had to deal with an arrow injury. Gunshots and knives, yes, but arrows… no. We've got a real problem. He's stable as he is, but we can't move him because every time there is any movement on that arrow, he's in agony. Plus, when the thing moves, we run the risk of the arrowhead doing more damage to his leg."

"So, what do we do? We can't load him onto the wagon and take him to Lintar with that arrow sticking in his leg. The thing will be too rattly and the arrow is bound to get banged. The last thing he needs is for the damn thing to sever an artery before we can get him some help."

"Can we cut the arrow?" Alex asked.

"What with? A knife? That'll move the arrow around like crazy."

"Shit! The only other thing I've got is a wire saw from my survival kit, but that would be even worse."

"Can I help?" asked a voice and they turned to see Ramman standing behind them.

"Do you know anything about arrow injuries?" Tom asked.

"I think I know how to remove the arrow, but the bleeding will be bad."

Alex's face betrayed her nervousness, but if Ramman could get the arrow out safely, that would be a big help.

"If you can get the arrow out without making things worse, I can try to deal with the wound. That would make it more like a bullet wound and I know how to patch them up."

Tom looked torn. This was a big decision to make, but they had to do something. Staying here in the middle of nowhere was not going to solve anything. They couldn't cut the arrow shaft, and moving Sam with the arrow intact risked the arrowhead nicking an artery. That arrow had to come out.

"Okay Ramman. If you are sure, and I mean REALLY sure that you can get that arrow out, then let's do it."

They walked back over to Sam, and Ramman knelt down next to the injured man.

"Who's this?" Jimmy asked.

"This is Ramman," Tom replied. "He thinks he can help us."

"Can he get this fucking thing out of my leg?" Sam groaned.

"He's going to try, but it's not going to be easy."

"Just do it. I can't take much more of this. Every time I move it feels like my whole leg is on fire."

Tom looked sharply to Ramman. "Let's see if you can get it out, but be bloody careful okay?"

Alex grabbed hold of Sam's hand as Ramman slowly took hold of the arrow with two fingers and gently twisted the shaft slightly. Sam screamed in pain and squeezed Alex's hand tightly.

"What the fuck are you doing?" Sam screamed.

"Checking that the arrow is not embedded in bone," said Ramman quietly, "The arrow is not stuck in the bone, but because it does not twist freely, I can feel that it has barbs which is not good. If it were a straight bodkin arrow, I could just pull it out, but barbs will cause much more damage if they are pulled. I will need something to help me extract it."

"What do you need?" asked Tom.

Ramman looked around and saw the carrion birds as they fed on the dead horse.

"I need two wing feathers from one of those vultures," he said pointing at the birds.

"Alex, get your medical kit ready." Tom yelled as he ran towards his horse, "Once that arrow is out, you are going to have to take over quickly."

Tom pulled his rifle from its leather sleeve and moved as quickly as he dared towards the feasting birds. As he knelt down and took aim at the nearest vulture, he noticed that there were already a number of black feathers on the ground. They must have been dislodged with all the squabbling that the birds were doing. He wouldn't have to shoot one of the birds after all.

Tom lowered his rifle and ran towards the road, shouting and waving his arms above his head. As the vultures scattered with a series of loud, angry grunts Tom quickly picked up all the feathers he could find and rushed back to Ramman.

While he had been away, Danny had removed the bandages from around the arrow and the angry puckered wound was now exposed. Alex wiped the wound with an antiseptic wipe and looked up at Tom as he approached.

"Are these good, Ramman?" Tom asked, handing the feathers to the young carter.

Ramman nodded and pulled a knife from his belt. He used the blade to cut the shafts of two of the feathers near their tip so that they resembled blunt quills and then cleaned the two feathers with one of Alex's wipes.

Ramman looked straight at Sam and took a deep breath.

"I am sorry, Master. This is going to hurt… a lot."

"Go for it," hissed Sam through clenched teeth.

Ramman took a deep breath and slowly pushed the feathers into the wound, one on either side of the arrow shaft.

Sam screamed and his back arched with the sudden searing pain. Tom and Danny were forced to hold him still as Ramman gently probed downwards with the feathers, a look of great concentration on his face. After a few moments, the scowl on Ramman's face relaxed slightly.

"I have located the barbs. I can now pull the arrow out without it ripping the flesh as it comes. You must make ready to stop the bleeding."

Alex nodded. Sweat beaded her brow, but she had her kit ready and knew what had to be done.

Ramman took another breath and slowly pulled the arrow out. The feather shafts had covered the sharp tips of the barbs and stopped them snagging on the meat in Sam's leg as the arrow was withdrawn.

As the blood began to flow from the wound, Ramman moved back and Alex took over. She poured a little surgical spirit over the wound before ripping open one of the modular field-combat bandages she had pulled from her kit. Alex positioned the bandage's in-built pressure cup over the hole and wrapped the elasticated bandage around Sam's leg several times until she reached the plastic clip at its end. Once the clip was attached securely to the tightly bound bandage, Alex attached an additional safety pin for good measure. She then let out the breath she had been holding and sat back on her heels.

Sam, was sweating profusely and was in a huge amount of pain, but looked relived that the arrow was out.

"What now?" asked Danny.

"Now we wait and hope to Christ that the bleeding stops."

"What was that weird lookin' bandage Moony?"

"It was something the Yanks developed as a result of the Afghan war. I had a mate in the marines who used one to save a member of his team who had been shot. They seemed like a good idea so I bought a couple of them off the internet to keep in my kit."

"I'm glad you did," Tom said.

"How's it looking Moony?" Sam asked hoarsely.

"It's looking good for now Slaphead. You stay there for a bit. I'll stop with you and we'll see how it holds."

"So, what's our new pal's story?" Danny asked nodding in Ramman's direction.

"Ramman was locked in that cage in the cavern," Alex explained. "The others that we freed are going to push on with their journey, but Ramman wants to come with us to Brentar."

"I was going to see what everyone thought once we got back here," added Tom.

"He gets my vote," Sam said.

"Mine too," agreed Jimmy. "Where did you learn the feather trick from?"

"My uncle was a watchman on the city walls at Brentar. They were taught how to do this by their watch-master in case they were ever attacked by barbarians."

"Well, I'm glad your uncle passed his knowledge on to you," Danny grinned.

By now, the sun was starting to disappear behind the mountains and nightfall was not far away.

"Let's stay here tonight," Tom instructed. "We can see how Sam is in the morning and if he's up to it, we'll get him into the wagon and make for Lintar. I don't want to stay here longer than we have to. By the morning it's not going to be smelling great round here."

They looked towards the pile of bodies and the horse carcasses that were scattered around them.

"We also need to double up the watch tonight," Tom added.

"Why Boss?" asked Jimmy.

"One, because there might be more bandits, and two, because this amount of meat is going to attract predators and who knows what lives in these hills?"

Jimmy scanned the surrounding hills guardedly and made sure that his rifle was within easy reach.

CHAPTER 23

In the Foothills of the Southern Mountains

The team were up early the next morning and by the time the sun had risen over the hills, breakfast had been eaten and everyone's saddlebags had been loaded.

Some of the colour had returned to Sam's face and he managed to eat and drink something.

"What do you think Alex?" Tom asked. "Can we move Sam?"

"I've been checking the bandage through the night and he doesn't seem to be losing much blood. There's always the worry of internal bleeding, but I can't do anything about that here. If he's okay about it, I think we load him on the wagon and get him to the next town… Lintar was it? Hopefully we'll be able to find someone there who can help."

"Right. Let's do that."

Tom walked over to Sam and knelt down beside him.

"Sam, as long as you feel up to it, we're going to move you. If we lift you onto Ramman's wagon, we can get you to Lintar and get you looked at properly. Are you up for it?"

"Yes, Boss. It hurts like a bitch, but it's better without that arrow moving around in there."

After padding the wagon bed with jackets and sweaters, Jimmy, Danny and Ramman lifted Sam carefully into the back of the wagon and settled him in as comfortably as they could. Alex climbed into the back of the wagon with him, and the others passed up the saddlebags and saddles from Sam and Alex's horses. Once the two rider-less horses had been tied to the rear of the wagon, Ramman jumped up into the driver's seat and they were ready to set off.

Tom and the others swung up into their saddles and the caravan pulled back onto the road. They were on their way to Lintar again.

Alex kept a close watch on Sam as they travelled. The wagon had no suspension at all so every bump and porthole rattled the wooden vehicle and made the ride far from comfortable. The larger bumps caused Sam to gasp as he bounced against the wooden floor, but he didn't complain, other than occasionally clenching his teeth and giving Alex a pained look.

The team ate on the move and made reasonable time as they travelled up the valley. It was mid-afternoon when they came around a bend in the road and the valley sides opened out to reveal a huge lake. The sun sparkled off the surface of the deep blue water and across it they could see buildings and a network of jetties and walkways. It was the lakeside town of Lintar.

As they made their way around the lake, they could see a flotilla of small fishing boats out on the water. The wooden rowing boats were working in pairs, with long nets pulled between them. One fisherman was busy hauling in his net and they saw the flash of fish as he emptied them into the bottom of his boat.

On the shoreline, many nets were spread out to dry in the sunshine and as they drew near, the distinctive smell of fish started to reach them.

"Euugghhh," complained Jimmy, "I hate the smell of fish."

"You will not like Lintar then Master Jimmy," Ramman laughed.

Lintar was much bigger than Serat had been. The townsfolk here looked more affluent and they were obviously more used to strangers here, as the team drew many fewer hostile stares than they had in the south. Even so, Tom decided that they should hide their Bergens and rifles in the back of the wagon so as not to attract too much unwanted attention.

The buildings here were predominantly constructed from timber and the houses close to the lakeshore were raised on strong wooden stilts above the water. Many of the houses were painted in bright colours and the whole place felt a little bit like Iceland to Tom. They rode through several narrow streets and soon upon a large town square in which a market was in full swing. Stalls displaying all kinds of food, and wares were crammed together and the traders shouted over each other to try and attract valuable customers. There was a rich smell of different aromas as stallholders cooked local delicacies. Meats sizzled over charcoal pits, spiced soups and sauces bubbled away in pots and strange looking herbs hung in bunches at the front of some stalls.

Tom noticed that a number of soldiers were dotted around the edge of the market.

They were well armed and watched the crowds carefully in case there were any signs of trouble. He pointed out the soldiers to Ramman and he made sure to steer the wagon as far away from them as he could.

The noise and spectacle of the market were an assault to their senses, but Ramman especially seemed much happier to be back in the hustle and bustle of a town rather than out in the countryside. His experience with the bandits out on the road was obviously still weighing heavy in his mind.

"Do you know where we can find somewhere to eat and sleep Ramman?" Tom asked.

"There are a number of inns in Lintar," Ramman replied thoughtfully. "The best of them is called The Pike. It is expensive and I have never been inside, but I have heard it said that the rooms are very clean and comfortable."

"Do we have enough money to pay for rooms there?"

"We have enough coin to buy the whole inn and more!" Ramman laughed.

"Lead the way then," smiled Tom. "The Pike it is."

Ramman drove the wagon through the busy streets. People bustled about their business as they hurried to and from the market to either buy or sell. Children played noisily in the street while their mothers washed clothes in large wooden tubs or sat in the sun mending britches. Dogs yapped loudly and chickens ran amok amongst everyone's feet. Here and there, more heavily armed soldiers could be seen standing watch. Thankfully, most of the soldiers looked bored and did not seem overly interested in the new strangers. Tom wondered whether their presence signalled a heightened state of readiness, or whether they were stationed in the town as a matter of course to maintain order in the busy streets. Was this not where Gask's father had tried to raise a rebellion some years back? As the team moved on through the town, Tom relaxed a little and decided that the soldiers would probably not be an issue unless Lalitha dropped her disguise and one of them recognised her.

After making a couple more turns, Ramman brought the wagon to a stop outside an impressive two-story building. This was The Pike. The inn was painted a vivid blue and carvings of fish of all sizes had been expertly chiselled into the woodwork. A brightly painted sign depicting a huge fish with pointed teeth hung above a pair of ornate wooden doors which burst open abruptly as an officious looking little man rushed out towards them.

"You cannot park your wagon here," the man yelled at him. "Move along. Move along."

Tom urged his horse forwards alongside the wagon and leaned forward on his saddle as he looked down at the man.

"The wagon is mine," he said sternly. "Who are you?"

Somewhat taken aback, the little man suddenly noticed the four riders behind the wagon and puffed himself up as if to make himself look more important.

"I am Rendell and I am the owner of this establishment."

"Well, Rendell, I need seven rooms, food and someone to look after our horses. Also, I need a doctor to look at one of my men. He was wounded by bandits on the road here."

Rendell's eyes lit up at the prospect of this unexpected boost in business.

"It is market day, so I do not have seven rooms available, but I do have four rooms. They are good rooms and I am sure you will be comfortable in them."

"That sounds acceptable," Tom agreed. "Is there someone who can look after our horses?"

"Of course, sir, if you come inside with me, I will send someone around to take them to our stable."

"And can you arrange for a doctor to visit my man?"

"Yes sir, I know of a local physician who would be willing to attend him for a small fee. How badly is he injured?"

"A Bandit shot him in the leg with an arrow. We got it out, but the wound needs treating by a professional."

Rendell looked concerned. "We should inform the Elders, but if the king were to hear that the roads here are unsafe, he would undoubtedly send more soldiers here and nobody wants that. We have too many soldiers from the north in our city already."

Tom realised that they had obviously not heard of the king's death in Lintar yet.

"Let's not tell the Elders then," Tom nodded. "We have business in the north and I would rather avoid any unnecessary delays."

"Whatever you say," agreed Rendell. "The physician I know is good and should be able to help your man recover quickly."

"Thank you," Tom said.

"Boss, do the rooms have baths in them?" Alex called over.

"Bathing facilities can be arranged," Rendell nodded and the smile returned to his face. "We even offer hot water for a small fee."

"Boss, that's it. We're stopping here," said Alex decisively.

Tom climbed down and tied his reins to the wagon to prevent his horse from wandering off. Rendell ushered him through the doors and, once inside, scuttled behind the bar and pulled four keys out of a small wooden box.

"The rooms are four silvers each, plus five coppers for a hot bath in each room. A meal will be one silver each. Payable in advance of course."

Tom dropped a pouch of silver coins onto the bar and it hit the wood with a loud chink. Rendell licked his lips greedily as Tom counted out the correct number of silver coins.

"Is there anything else you would need sir? Perhaps some company for your gentlemen travellers?"

"Errr… No thanks," Tom replied, "but what about that doctor?"

"Ah yes, once your horses are safely in the stable, I will send the boy to fetch him."

Rendell handed the keys over and pointed to the stairs next to the door.

"Your rooms are numbers six, seven, eight, and nine, up the staircase and to the right. Six, seven and eight have two beds in each and room nine is a single room, best suited to one of the ladies in your party I would think. I will call my boy to take your horses now."

Rendell picked up a large hand bell and shook it vigorously. The bell clanged so loudly that Tom's ears were still ringing as he placed it back down on the bar.

A door to the rear of the room banged open and a boy ran in.

"Boy! Fetch the ostler and then help him to attend to this gentleman's horses" Rendell ordered. "Once that is done, run to fetch Siltan the physician. Go. Be quick now."

The boy raced off to find the ostler and Tom turned back towards the front door.

"Would you like assistance with your baggage sir?" Rendell called after him.

"No thanks," Tom called back over his shoulder, "we can manage."

He pushed his way out of the front doors and joined the rest of the team out on the street. Ramman had climbed down from his driver's seat and stood next to his horse.

"I will sleep in the stable with the horses Master," he announced. "There will be fresh straw enough for me there."

"Oh no you will not," argued Tom. "You are sharing a room with me… and stop calling me, Master!"

"Really? I can sleep inside?"

"Of course, you can," smiled Tom.

Ramman beamed from ear to ear.

Tom leaned over the side of the wagon and peered in at Alex and Sam.

"You two ok back there?"

"We will be once we get inside," Alex replied.

The boy suddenly appeared around the corner of the building and was accompanied by an older man who Tom assumed to be Rendell's ostler. The boy pointed at Tom and the two of them came over.

"The master tells me you have horses to stable sir?" the ostler said.

"We do. If you could take these two horses first, we will unload the wagon and then you can take that too."

The man nodded and untied the two saddle-less horses from the wagon. He passed the reins of one of them to the boy and they led the two horses off around the corner. Ramman followed them to the corner and watched them for a few moments.

"I was making sure that our horses got safely to the stables," he said as he walked back to the wagon.

Jimmy and Danny tied their horse's reins to the wagon, undid their cinches and lifted their saddlebags down ready to take to their room. Jimmy lifted Tom's saddlebags down for him and then climbed up into the back of the wagon where, with Alex's help he started to pass their baggage down. Ramman and Danny arranged the trunks, Bergens and saddlebags next to the tavern door as the ostler and the boy took another two horses round to the stable.

Danny wrapped the C8 rifles in their jackets and put them down carefully where he could keep his eye on them. Lalitha led her horse to the back of the wagon and Jimmy lifted the last saddlebag down. Lalitha had her buff pulled up over her face again and had put the Book inside her shirt so it wouldn't be seen.

"It will be nice to sleep in a bed tonight," she sighed.

"You have got a room to yourself," Tom said. "I thought you might like some alone time."

"Thank you," she replied gratefully. Tom couldn't see her mouth, but he could tell from the sparkle in her green eyes that she was smiling.

"Jimmy. Danny. Can you give Sam a lift inside? Once you've got him upstairs, the ostler can take the wagon round and we can shift all this kit off the street."

Between them all they managed to carefully slide Sam out of the wagon. Danny and Jimmy linked their arms around him and lifted him through the doors and up the stairs. They were soon back down and loading themselves up with the rifles and as many of the Bergens as they could carry.

"All the rooms have got two beds in them," Danny reported. "We put Sam in the nearest room to the stairs, just so we didn't carry him further than we needed to. He didn't say anythin', but his leg is obviously givin' him a lot of aggro."

"I'll share with Sam so I can keep an eye on it," Alex offered.

"Good idea," agreed Tom. "Danny, you and Jimmy take the room next to where you put Sam. Lalitha, you can have the single room and I'll share with Ramman in the other twin."

Tom stood guard over their equipment outside as Danny, Sam and Alex made several more trips with the Bergens and saddlebags. After one last trip up the inn stairs, they had all the equipment safely stored in the rooms.

Tom stayed outside until the ostler had taken all the horses and the wagon around to the stables. Tom and Ramman followed the ostler round the back of the inn to make sure that their mounts were being properly looked after. Once Ramman was satisfied that everything was in order, they headed inside the inn. Tom had another conversation with Rendell and then headed up the stairs to their rooms.

Tom discovered that everyone had reconvened in Sam and Alex's room. Tom squeezed onto one of the beds next to Alex and Lalitha, leaving Jimmy, Danny and Ramman to sit on the floor. Sam lay down on the other bed. Sam was pale and quiet, but seemed to be in good spirits. It was a bit of a crush as they all huddled together, but they all managed to fit in.

Tom leaned forwards and pulled one of the pouches of silver coins from his pocket.

"Rendell says that the market will be going for another couple of hours yet, so how about Danny and Jimmy go out to get some supplies? How long will our journey to Brentar take from here Lalitha?"

"About two weeks if we go as slowly as we have done up to now," she answered cuttingly.

Tom ignored the dig at their riding speed and looked back towards Danny and Jimmy.

"If it's going to be another two weeks on the road, we need to make sure that we have enough food to keep us going. I also thought that we should get some different clothes. Everywhere we go we stand out like sore thumbs. If we could dress more like the locals, then that would help us to keep a lower profile. What do you think?"

Everyone nodded their agreement.

"We'll head out now Boss and see what we can find," Danny suggested. "That market looked pretty interestin' and I wouldn't mind a look round."

"Just be careful okay? There are lots of soldiers around and we don't want to start any trouble."

"As if I would ever cause any trouble," Danny grinned. "Come on Coddy, let's go and do some shopping."

Armed with the pouch of silver coins, Danny and Jimmy headed out into the market.

A few minutes after they had left, there was a knock on the door. It was Rendell. With him was a man carrying a large wooden tub and behind them both stood two girls, each carrying a large pot of steaming water.

"Who would like to bathe first?" he asked.

CHAPTER 24

Lintar

By the time darkness fell in Lintar, the team was fully kitted out in brand new linen shirts, breeches and tunics. All their modern clothes were rolled up and stuffed into Sam's Bergen where it could be carried on the wagon. The two large trunks that they had taken from the cavern were filled with freshly cured and dried food. Meats, fish, fruit and vegetables were all wrapped in waxed paper bags and stored carefully away.

Everyone apart from Sam had taken a turn in the wooden tub and they all felt much better for being able to wash away the dust and grime from their journey. Tom had taken pity on the serving girls who had made a huge number of trips up and down the stairs with pots of hot water and then cold dirty bath water. He had surreptitiously given each of them a silver coin for their troubles and the girls had giggled wide eyed at the stranger's generosity.

The doctor had visited the tavern shortly after Danny and Jimmy had left for the market. For the princely sum of five silver coins, he had carefully examined Sam's leg. He was most intrigued by the combat bandage that Alex had used on the wound, but Tom had distracted him long enough for Alex to quickly hide it out of sight.

Much to Sam's horror, the doctor had stitched his wound together using a long, curved needle made out of bone and a foul-smelling balm had been smeared liberally over the injury. The doctor had re-dressed the wound with clean bandages to keep it clean and protect the stitches. Thankfully the wound had not bled too much and the doctor did not think that blood was building up under the skin. Sam had been lucky, although he didn't feel much like it by the time the doctor packed his bag and said his goodbyes. He promised to return the next day to check the stitches and change the dressings.

Whilst they were out, Danny had visited a tanner's stall at the market and had asked him to make some special items for delivery the next day. He wouldn't tell anyone what they were and the only clue that he gave them was it was something that would be useful. While Danny was making sketches and talking with the tanner, Jimmy had looked carefully around the tanner's stall and had bought a small leather bag that had intricate flowers carved into its surface. When they were back at the tavern, Jimmy had presented the bag to Lalitha.

"I thought that you could use this to keep the Book safe," he said sheepishly.

Lalitha opened the lid of the bag and slid the Book inside. It was an almost perfect fit. She closed the catch on the lid and hung the bag around her neck on its long leather strap.

"Thank you, James Lang. It is a very thoughtful gift," smiled Lalitha and gently touched Jimmy on the hand.

Jimmy blushed deeply and smiled.

"Rendell the owner says that we can eat downstairs if we like," Tom announced. "Does anyone want to go down there? Obviously Lalitha and Sam will have to stay up here, but the rest of us can go downstairs."

"I'll stay up here with Lalitha," said Jimmy. "We can keep Sam company."

"Okay. What about the rest of you?"

"Just so long as Fester doesn't get carried away and blab our secrets to everyone in the bar," smiled Alex.

"Who is Fester?" asked Ramman.

"We'll explain later," laughed Tom.

Tom, Alex, Danny and Ramman went downstairs and ate their dinner at a large wooden table in the main tavern bar. The meal they ate was the first hot food that they had eaten in almost a week and it tasted fantastic. Great slabs of steak were served with some sort of vegetables and a thick, fragrant gravy. The ale was much better than the weak cloudy stuff they had been served in Serat and they even had a pudding. Hot berries in a sweet, creamy sauce. Tom hoped that the guys upstairs had enjoyed the food that they had sent up there as much as he had.

"I think that might be one of the best steaks that I've ever eaten," declared Danny, "it's just a pity they didn't have chips on the menu."

"You'd eat chips with everything if you could Fester!" laughed Alex.

"Why do you use the name Fester for Master Danny?" asked Ramman. He had drunk quite a lot of the ale and he was much more at ease with the team now.

"It's a joke name that we just use within the team," said Alex. "We all have one. I am Moonshine and this is the Boss."

Ramman smiled broadly. "My friends call me Ram."

Danny pulled a dramatic face. "Hmmmm… Ram! I kinda like it. What do you think Moony?"

"Ram? It has got a ring to it. Boss?"

"Ram it is. Welcome to the team Ram!"

They all clicked ale mugs and took big swigs of the bitter tasting beer.

"So, Ram," said Danny, "what can we expect in the mountains?"

Ramman's smile broadened and he shrugged his shoulders before taking another drink.

"It depends on the weather Master Fester. If the rain falls, the journey will be hazardous and fraught with danger. If the sun shines, the journey will be hazardous and fraught with danger, but we will be dry."

He laughed a great booming laugh and drained his ale mug.

"I like the dry bit," laughed Alex, "not so much the hazardous and fraught with danger bit."

"The way to Brentar follows an old and ancient road that took generations to carve out of the mountainsides. Much of the road is cut into the rock itself and, once we get high into the mountains, the drop from the road to the valley floor is very great. If we can arrive at the Pass of Mauga without incident, then the journey down the other side is less difficult."

"Ram… mate… Did you just say the drop to the floor is very great?"

"Yes, Master Fester. The drop is very great indeed."

Danny looked nervously at Tom.

"Boss, you do remember that I have a problem with heights, don't you?"

Ramman laughed his booming laugh again.

"If you are feared of heights, Master Fester, you will need to wear a blindfold, I think. Let us hope that your horse is not equally feared."

Danny didn't think this was so funny any longer.

"Shit, Boss, is there not another way?"

"This is the easiest way Master Fester. There is another road that goes to the east, but that path is too steep for your horses and could only be travelled by foot. We could travel to the coast and try to find a boat to Brentar somewhere there, but our chances of success would be small. It would be much quicker to take the mountain road."

"Well that's just fan-fucking-tastic!" swore Danny grumpily.

Something had been niggling Tom since their arrival in Lintar and he decided to ask Ramman about it.

"Why are there so many soldiers in the town, Ram?"

Ramman cast his eyes around the bar and lowered his voice as he replied.

"There have been rumours of discontent down here. There were troubles here some years back and the king had to use force to subdue them. I have heard it said that people talk of rebellion again. The king does not wish to lose control of the south and so he has stationed soldiers in the towns and cities to be ready for any violence."

"Do you think it will happen?"

"I do not know, Master. I hope not. If the king thinks that the subversives here are stirring the pot, he will feel that he has to take action against them."

Tom looked at Danny and raised his eyebrows. What was going to happen down here when they learned that the king had been killed and that Gask had taken control of the capital. Rather than dwell on the subject, Tom decided it would be a safer bet to draw the evening to a close.

"I'm gonna call it a night lads," Tom announced. "Come on Ram, let's go and get some sleep. It sounds like we've got a hard road ahead of us tomorrow."

"Kayo."

"It's Okay, Ram, not Kayo."

"Okay, Master Tom," Ramman grinned.

As they left their table and made their way towards the stairs, Tom noticed a small man in a brown cloak staring at them. As their eyes met, the man quickly finished his drink and turned away. It was probably nothing, but all of Tom's instincts told him that they needed to be careful about what they said around these people, especially if there was an insurgent element at work in the town.

CHAPTER 25

Lintar

Early mornings in Lintar were very noisy with all the traders making their way to the town square to set up their stalls. The sun had been above the mountains for less than an hour when Tom decided that he had lain in bed for long enough.

As he swung his legs around and sat on the edge of the bed, Ramman opened his eyes blearily and then rubbed them slowly with his fingers.

"Morning, Ram. You okay this morning?"

"I think perhaps I had too much ale last night, Master Tom. My head is a little sore and my mouth is as dry as a harlot's…"

Ramman stopped dead as he noticed Tom's arm on the table next to the bed. It was plugged into the solar charger and the small green LED shone brightly. Ramman rubbed his eyes again and stared back at Tom's left arm.

"Master," he breathed, "what happened to your arm?"

"Don't worry, Ram. My arm was injured in an accident many years ago."

"But…" Ramman stuttered, pointing at Tom's prosthetic.

"I wear that on my injured arm to let me use it again. Watch."

Tom unplugged the charger, picked up his robotic arm and pushed it back into position. He twisted the prosthetic to get a slightly better fit and then lifted it and flexed his fingers.

"How is that possible?" gasped Ramman.

"Where I come from, we have skilled craftsmen. They made this for me."

Ramman's eyes widened and he sat up on the edge of his bed.

"You are not from Zakastra?"

"No, Ramman, we are from a place a long way from here?"

"From over the seas? Like the barbarians?"

"No, we come from another place."

Ramman slapped his thigh and a huge smile spread across his face.

"I knew it! I knew that you and the other masters were different. Your strange clothes and the weapons you used in the cavern… I have never seen anything like them before."

"You were right, Ram. We brought our weapons with us from our homeland."

"Are there more wonders like this where you come from?"

"Yes," Tom laughed. "There are."

"I would like to see your land, Master Tom. Will you take me there one day?"

"We'll see, Ramman, we have a long way to travel first."

Ramman was about to ask another question, but there was a sharp knock on the door.

Tom pulled his new linen shirt over his head and walked across the room to see who it was.

Rendell stood in the corridor with a well-built man wearing a long, weathered leather apron. The man was holding a bulging hessian sack in his hands.

"This is the tanner, sir. He says that he has a delivery for you."

This must be Danny's special order. Tom picked up his coin pouch from the table and opened it up.

"How much do we owe you?" Tom asked.

"Your companion already paid me sir," the tanner answered, handing the sack over. "I am simply here to deliver the order. I worked with my apprentice into the night to make sure that we had it ready for you before we set up our stall this morning."

"Thank you," Tom nodded as he put the sack down on the floor.

As he turned to leave, Tom took a silver coin from his pouch and pushed it into the tanner's hand.

"Take this. We appreciate the hard work that you and your apprentice have put in for us."

"Thank you, sir," the tanner beamed. "If you need anything else, you know where our stall is in the market."

"Why did you give him more coin?" asked Ramman as Tom closed the door. "He had already been paid. Did he cheat you? If he did, I will go after him and get your coin back."

Tom smiled. Tipping obviously wasn't a thing here.

"It's okay, Ram. I gave him the extra coin because if we have to ask the tanner for anything in the future, he will remember me and will gladly help us again."

"So, it is a bribe?"

Tom laughed. "I guess it is, Ram, yes."

"It seems to me that you simply wasted a silver coin," Ramman muttered, turning to pull his clothes on.

Once they were both dressed, Tom went next door to rouse Danny and Jimmy.

"Your order from the tanner arrived already," Tom announced as Jimmy let him into their room.

"Did you look inside?" Danny asked.

"Not yet."

Tom handed the sack to Danny who untied the drawstring and peered inside. With a huge grin on his face, Danny pulled a smart leather belt out of the sack. The belt featured a holster, a knife sheath and a small coin pouch.

"Ta-Daaaaa," Danny called as he handed the belt to Tom. "Don't say I never give you anythin'."

"Thanks, Danny," smiled Tom, "It's great. It'll make carrying the Glocks a lot easier. Will they fit in okay?"

"They should. I got the tanner to measure mine. He didn't have a clue what the pistol was, but I did a couple of drawings of a holster and he obviously understood what I was on about. We can wear them with our new Zakastran outfits and not look too weird."

The belts were sturdy and had a large silver buckle to fasten them. The tanner had even embellished the leather with small fish motifs. The holster had a soft lining and a simple press-stud fastening to hold the top flap shut and hold their pistols securely in place.

Danny passed an identical belt to Jimmy.

"Thanks, Fester," Jimmy said, grabbing his Glock from nearby and sliding it into the holster. The leather moulded itself perfectly around the pistol's polymer frame and the flap clicked shut over the grip.

"The tanner did a great job didn't he?"

Ramman appeared in the doorway and Danny rummaged in the bag. He pulled out another belt and gave it to Ramman. This belt had no holster, but did have a coin pouch and a knife sheath. The sheath had a long, sharp knife in it.

"For me, Master," cried Ramman, his eyes filling with tears.

"We couldn't leave you out Ram. We might have lost Sammy if it wasn't for you."

Ramman grabbed Danny and pulled him into a bear-hug.

"Ram, loosen off a bit mate, you're going to break a rib if you're not careful," Danny wheezed.

Ramman released Danny and hurriedly strapped his belt on over the top of his tunic. He pulled out the knife and checked the blade with his thumb. Nodding his head in appreciation he re-sheathed the knife and smiled at Danny.

"Thank you, Master Fester. It is a generous gift."

Danny gave him a wink and then busied himself visiting the other rooms and dropping off belts for the other team members.

Once everyone was up and dressed, Rendell delivered plates of hot eggs and meat to their rooms. The food smelled incredible and it did not take long for the team to clean their plates.

"What time is the quack comin' back to see Sam?" asked Danny.

"Later this afternoon I think," Alex replied. "He is out of town this morning so we're stuck until he gets back."

"If the doctor isn't coming until this afternoon, we should stay another night here," Tom suggested. "There is no point us heading off into the mountains just a few hours before it goes dark. It'll also give Sam another day to heal before we load him back into the wagon."

The team agreed and even Lalitha approved of the idea. The promise of a comfortable bed and another warm bath seemed to lessen her desire to get back on the road straight away.

The team spent the rest of the day relaxing. Alex and Tom visited the market and returned with bags of sweet nuts and pickles. They had also bought woollen fleeces to sleep under and lightweight scarves that they could use to protect themselves from both the sun and dust as they travelled. Lalitha was especially pleased with the scarf as it meant that she would not have to wear the tight polyester buff any longer.

Tom spent the next half hour showing them all how to tie their scarves around their heads in the style of the Berber tribesmen in Morocco. This style would keep their heads cool and also allow Lalitha to disguise her face quickly and easily as they rode if she needed to.

It was late in the afternoon when the physician called back to check on Sam's leg. He informed them that the stitches were holding and the wound looked like it was knitting together well. In his opinion, the stitches would have to be removed after about a week and it would take about two weeks for the wound to heal completely.

"Will he be able to travel tomorrow?" Lalitha asked.

The doctor pursed his lips and did not look very happy.

"Your friend will be unable to ride a horse for some time, but if you have a carriage or a wagon that he can be carried in, then that might be possible. Ideally, I would recommend that a patient such as this remain in bed for several more days, and would only think to move him if the situation were urgent."

Tom and Alex looked at each other, but Lalitha was quick to jump in.

"We have a wagon that we can use. Our friend can continue to travel in the back. We need to travel to Brentar as quickly as we can."

"A wagon is not ideal. Wagon travel into the mountains will be uncomfortable and dangerous, but if you really have to leave Lintar quickly then it will have to suffice. I will leave you a pot of salve to use on the injury to try and stave off infection, but you must keep the leg clean. If the arrow pushed small pieces of clothing into the wound then the risk of infection is significant."

Alex pulled a face. If infection set in while they were in the mountains, the ramifications could be severe.

"That is settled then," Lalitha announced. "We leave for Brentar in the morning."

"Can't we delay leaving for another few days?" asked Tom.

"No," snapped Lalitha. "Our journey has been slow thus far and we have stayed in Lintar too long already. We have a long journey ahead of us and we need to move quickly. We leave tomorrow."

"Sam?" Tom asked. "How do you feel about it?"

"I don't want to hold us up Boss. Stick me in the wagon. I'll be fine."

"Okay then, against my better judgement, we'll head into the mountains tomorrow morning."

The doctor handed a large pot of foul-smelling salve to Alex, and Tom paid him another five silver coins as he left.

"I wish you fair travels friends. Your journey through the mountains will be treacherous, but at least you travel in summer. If the winter snows were here, you would not even attempt to reach the Mauga Pass."

"Danny," Tom said, "can you go and have a chat with Rendell? We need all the horses tacked up and ready to go at first light. We need to get as far through those mountains in daylight as we can."

"Will do, Boss."

CHAPTER 26

Over the Southern Mountains

After an early breakfast, the team busied themselves loading everything into the wagon. The fleeces that Tom had bought now lined the floor and should make Sam's life a lot more comfortable. Alex no longer needed to keep so close a watch on him, so she loaded her saddlebags back onto her own horse.

They carefully carried Sam from his room and lifted him onto the carpet of fleeces in the back of the wagon before closing up the tailgate and fastening it shut with wooden pegs.

Ramman tied Sam's horse to the back of the wagon and Rendell waved them off as they set off for the mountains.

"Good journey, sirs," he shouted after them as they moved out into the busy street.

Ramman led the way with the wagon and they threaded their way through the narrow streets to the northern edge of the town. The last building they passed was a large guard house, and four soldiers with long pikes watched them suspiciously as they passed by. Tom nodded at them respectfully and they let the horses and wagon pass by unhindered. The fact that everyone was now wearing local clothing rather than their own clothes from home was going to make their lives a lot easier. The horses seemed happy to be out of the bustle of the busy streets and snorted excitedly as they followed the wide rock-strewn road that disappeared up into the hills ahead.

The next four days' travel was relatively easy. The road wound its way ever upwards through green valleys lined with trees and shrubs. The sun shone and a warm breeze blew from the south. There were plenty of places to set up camp each night with fresh running water and wood for their campfires. The road was fairly easy going and the team began to wonder what all the fuss had been about.

"Ram, mate," Danny called over as they set off on the fifth morning, "where is all this hazardous and fraught with danger stuff then?"

Ramman looked over his shoulder, but did not smile.

"Ask me that question again at this time tomorrow, Master Fester," he said.

Tom looked back at the road behind them as it snaked downwards though the valley. The lake at Lintar was still visible in the far distance, but the town itself was out of sight. They had climbed a long way already, but the mountains that flanked the road now towered over them. Their sides were steep and scree slopes littered with stones and boulders hemmed in each side of the valley making it feel quite claustrophobic. There were few trees here, and only course grasses managed to cling onto the harsh landscape.

Ramman drove the wagon through a wide river ford. The water was fast flowing and quite deep, but because the valley was still quite wide here, there was no problem getting through it. Once the wagon was through, Ramman reined his horse in and pulled to a stop.

"We should refill our water bottles here," he announced. "From this point onwards, the road becomes steeper and more treacherous. Master Tom, you and Mistress Lalitha should take the lead now. I will follow with the wagon and the others can follow behind."

"Why is that, Ram?" Tom called.

"Because the track is quite narrow in places and I may need help at the front and rear to get the wagon safely around some of the corners."

Danny did not like the sound of that particularly, but hey, how bad could it be?

After everyone had refilled their water bottles and mounted up, Lalitha and Tom took the lead and the horses began to climb their way up the track again.

The valley sides closed in the more they rode and the river, rather than running beside them, now ran in an ever-deepening cutting to their right. The water crashed and boomed as it rushed downwards through the tight rocky gully.

Danny began to look a little uncomfortable the higher they rose and the deeper the cutting beside them got. The road was now partially carved out of the slope on their left and Danny could see ancient scratches and grooves in the rock's surface where workmen's tools had been used to create the route through the mountains many years ago.

Their route continued to climb and it was not long before the whole road's width was hewn out of the rock face at their side. The cutting beside them had widened and the drop down to the white water below was almost twenty metres.

As the drop to their side deepened, the team began to ride their horses in single file. Everybody wanted to ride as far away from the edge of the road as they could. Lalitha took the lead, then Tom followed. The wagon was behind them, then Alex, Danny and Jimmy followed along at the rear of the group.

Danny had gone very quiet and gave only single word answers when anybody talked to him. Alex turned around in her saddle to try and distract him with conversation, but gave up quickly. Danny was trying his best to not look at the drop to his right and Alex could see the sweat on his brow.

There were occasional places in the road where it widened out to just over two carriage-widths. Ramman informed them that these were passing places in case they met any travellers coming in the opposite direction.

"If we meet travellers coming the other way with a wagon or carriage in between one of these passing places," Ramman informed them grimly, "we will have to unhitch the wagon and push it backwards until we reach one of these places. It is the law that uphill travellers must give way to those coming downhill."

"Let's hope we don't meet anyone then," muttered Sam.

The gorge to their right had really opened out now and the river below could hardly be heard any longer. Their route continued upwards and turned left away from the gorge, the road clinging to the side of the cliff face as it climbed.

Alex looked at Danny as the drop to their right got more and more extreme. He was shaking and muttering under his breath. Suddenly he stopped and started to breathe heavily.

"Danny, are you okay?" Alex asked.

"No Alex, I am really fuckin' not okay. That drop is doing my fuckin' head in and I keep thinkin' that this horse is goin' to throw me over the edge."

"You'll be fine Danny, the horse knows what it's doing, just close your eyes and trust it."

"Ramman," Alex called, "how much longer is the road like this?"

Ramman halted the wagon and turned around in his seat "We cannot sleep until we reach the top of the pass. There is nowhere to set up camp on this section of the road and there is a long way to go yet."

"Fuck, fuck, fuck," Danny groaned.

They pushed onwards for another couple of nerve shredding hours. The road climbed on and on up the walls of what was now a canyon, and the drop to the side of the road was well over two hundred metres deep. Danny was now shaking uncontrollably in his saddle.

"Danny, mate, you're starting to freak your horse out," Alex warned as she looked over her shoulder to check on him. "You need to pull yourself together because you're making things worse for yourself."

Danny couldn't bring himself to answer her. He was working himself up into too much of a state to talk.

At that moment, Ramman pulled the wagon to a halt just ahead of them.

"Master Tom," he yelled, "I need you to guide me around the next corner as part of the path has fallen away. It is very narrow and I do not want to put a wheel over the edge."

Sure enough, it looked like a sliver of rock at the edge of the road ahead had fallen into the chasm beside them and there did not look to be a lot of room for the wagon to get past.

Tom dismounted and passed the reins of his horse to Lalitha.

"Alex," he shouted, "can you watch the back wheels and make sure they don't get too close to the edge."

"Fuck me," gasped Danny, "I can't watch this shit."

As Danny clamped his shaking hands over his face, Tom and Alex slowly shouted instructions as Ramman carefully edged the wagon forwards.

"Come on, Ram… left a bit, come on again. Whoa… left a bit more. How are we looking Alex?"

"We're okay back here, Boss, just keep the wagon as tight as you can to the rock face Ram and you'll be good."

After several minutes of slowly inching their way around the corner, the road widened slightly and Ramman was confident that he could carry on without any assistance.

"Come on, Danny," Alex said as she went to remount her horse, "I'm pretty freaking scared myself, but we've got to keep going."

Danny looked at her, his eyes wide with fear. She had never seen him like this before, even in the worst firefights in Helmand.

Alex dropped back down from her saddle and walked back to Danny's horse.

"Let me take your reins, mate," she offered. "I'll tie them to the back of my saddle and you don't have to worry about them then, you can just keep your eyes closed and not have to worry about your horse."

Danny nodded his head and handed his reins down to her. Alex gently took the reins from his hands and tied them to one of the saddle rings at the back of her horse.

As soon as Alex had climbed back onto her horse, she checked behind her and could see that Danny had his eyes clamped shut and was clinging to his saddle as if his life depended on it. She flicked her reins and urged her horse on up the path, pulling Danny's mount along behind her.

As they came around the next corner they could see much further up the canyon. The road continued to wind gradually up the cliff face until it disappeared behind another mountain that stood in front of them.

At the front of the caravan, Tom looked up at the sky and noticed that the sun was not shining any longer. In fact, as he turned to look to the south, he could see a bank of dark angry clouds rolling towards them.

"Please don't let it rain," Tom muttered under his breath.

As he looked in front of him again, he could see one of the passing places ahead. That might be a good place to stop for a rest. They had been climbing this road for hours and it was taking its toll on both horses and riders.

"Let's stop in the next passing place," Tom called back to Ramman. "We can stretch our legs a bit before we go any further."

Once the road had widened, they all reined their horses in and got down to stretch their weary legs.

Danny stayed on his horse and kept his eyes tightly closed.

"Do you want some water?" Jimmy asked.

"Thanks mate, but can you just not talk to me right now."

Jimmy looked at Alex and they both raised their eyebrows and shrugged.

"There are some riders coming down the road," shouted Ramman. "We should wait here until they have gone past."

They stayed where they were for several minutes until four riders slowly walked their horses past the group. The riders nodded as they went by but none of them spoke. This road made everyone nervous.

Danny opened his eyes as the riders went by and really wished that he hadn't. As the riders passed him, their horses' hooves were only a handful of centimetres from edge of the road. One slight slip and they would plummet into the chasm.

Danny felt himself go dizzy, the pit of his stomach clenched and his shakes became even more violent. To stop his involuntary compulsion to keep looking at the valley floor way below them, Danny reached round behind him and groped around until he found what he needed. He quickly pulled his scarf from his saddlebag and tied it around his eyes.

The team started to move again and Tom suddenly felt drops of rain on his face.

"That's all we need," muttered Alex under her breath.

The sky got darker and the rain began to get heavier and heavier until it was hammering off the rock face beside them. Almost immediately, the road turned into a river as the water rushed by, dragging stones and dirt along with it.

Danny was now almost catatonic. Alex led his horse on through the rushing water, but even she was scared. It would take hardly anything for one of the horses to take a tumble and that would be the end of that.

Just as she thought it, Danny's horse stumbled on a rock hidden by the water and he screamed loudly.

"Alex. Stop. Stop. Stop. I can't fuckin' do this anymore."

Alex stopped her horse and looked back at him. As soon as his horse was stationary, Danny slowly climbed down from his saddle and crouched down with his back against the rock wall.

"Danny," Alex shouted, "I can't do a lot more to help you mate. I've got my hands full trying to keep these two horses under control. You're going to have to stand up and get yourself back on this horse."

"No fuckin' way!" he screamed. "Leave me. I'm not ridin' that horse any further up this fuckin' nightmare."

Jimmy caught up to where Danny lay and carefully climbed down from his saddle.

"You carry on Moony. I'll walk with Danny. We'll catch up with you when we can."

Alex watched as Jimmy helped Danny to stand. Danny was trembling from head to foot, but managed to start walking. As they moved, he kept his blindfold on, but made sure that his left hand was in contact with the rock face at all times.

Alex looked back up the road through the sheets of rain. She could just see the wagon ahead as it disappeared around a bend in the road. She would have to catch up with it and let the others know that the stragglers would catch them up as soon as they could.

Further ahead, Tom was getting increasingly nervous. He kept glancing up at the sky, nervously watching for any signs of lightning. If there was a thunderclap anywhere near them, the horses would freak out and probably tip everyone into the abyss. The rain was not easing up and the water rushing down the road was covering the horse's hooves.

Ramman was struggling to see where he was going and the horse tethered to the back of the wagon was getting very agitated. It could not see much of the road in front of it because of the proximity of the wagon and the sound of the rain hammering off the wooden vehicle was scaring it. The horse started to stamp its feet and neigh loudly as pebbles driven by cascading water bounced off its hooves.

"Ram, I don't think my horse is very happy back here," Sam shouted. "Can I do anything to help?"

"No Master," Ramman called back anxiously. "We must just carry on as quickly as we dare and get to the Pass."

Before Ramman had even finished his sentence, Sam's horse trod awkwardly on a large stone that was rolling down the road and lost its balance. The horse stumbled and fell. As it hit the rocky surface the horse panicked and started to thrash around as it tried to find its feet again. It managed to get its front legs back under itself, but as the horse tried to stand up, one of its back legs went over the edge.

The horse scrabbled with its hooves, but could find no purchase on the wet rock. Its other back leg went over the edge and it began to fall.

"Ramman!" Sam screamed. "My horse is down. It's going over the edge."

Ramman whipped his reins and shouted to get the carthorse to generate more power. They had to try and pull Sam's horse back onto the road before if plunged over the edge and took them with it.

The rein's tied to the back of the wagon pulled tight, but it wasn't enough, the horse was still struggling to get back up and was going further and further over the edge. The wagon began to skid sideways and one of the rear wheels inched closer and closer to the edge.

"BOSS!" Sam shouted at the top of his lungs. "We need help. Quick!"

Tom heard the desperation in Sam's voice and turned back to see the horse hanging over the lip of the road. He could see that its struggles were slowly pulling the wagon nearer and nearer to the edge. Despite Ramman's best efforts the carthorse did not have enough traction to halt their backwards slide.

Tom made the mistake of looking over the edge and his stomach lurched horribly. The rain was coming down so hard that he couldn't even see the valley floor any longer.

Lalitha had also seen the situation. As quickly as they dared, they turned their horses around and went back to where Ramman's carthorse was struggling to hold on. Tom leapt off his horse and ran over. He grabbed hold the straining horse's harness with his right hand and pulled with all his might. Lalitha dismounted and grabbed the harness with one hand and held one of her own horse's stirrups with the other.

"YAR!" She shouted at her horse to get it to pull and add its own strength to theirs.

Sam's horse was slipping further and further over the edge of the chasm and was screaming in fear. Its struggles to pull itself to safety were making the wagon shake violently and suddenly one of the wagon's back wheels was pulled over the edge.

The wagon lurched at an alarming angle and all the equipment in the back skidded quickly to the rear where it banged against the wooden tailgate. The shafts of the wagon lifted as the back was dragged down and Tom watched in horror as the carthorse began to lose more traction as the rising shafts lifted it in its harness. He pulled downwards with all his strength as he tried to counter-balance Sam's struggling horse as best he could. His grip on the harness was starting to slip and in desperation, he grabbed at the harness with his left hand. The carthorse jerked again and Tom's prosthetic was pulled away and fell to the ground where the water began to wash it down the road.

"My arm," he yelled. He let go of the harness and grabbed at his arm as it disappeared between the carthorse's hooves. Just as it was almost out of reach, Tom managed to catch hold of one of the robotic fingers and he seized his arm and jammed it safely inside his tunic.

The loss of Tom's weight and strength on the harness was disastrous and the wagon suddenly lurched backwards again. He seized the harness again and roared as he pulled with everything that he had. Lalitha screamed at her horse to pull and Ramman slapped the reins wildly on the cart-horse's back.

"PULL!" he roared.

The reins attached to the fallen horse had been tied to the tailgate and as the horse at the back twisted and fought, the hinges on the tailgate began to creak. Sam hung on to the wagon's sides as tightly as he could but another lurch from the fallen horse made him lose his grip and he skidded to the back of the wagon only just managing to regain his grip before being flung over the tailgate and into the darkness below.

"Hold on, Master Sam," Ramman cried, "hold on."

The horse was now dangling from its bridle with over half of its body hanging over the abyss. Its terrified movements were making the tailgate of the wagon bounce on its fastenings and Sam could see that the wooden pegs that held the tailgate shut were starting to bend and splinter. They couldn't hold on much longer.

"Master Sam!" Ramman cried again. "Jump to the road."

Sam tried to pull himself up, but the angle of the wagon was getting steeper and steeper and it was all he could do to stop himself being thrown over the back.

The bindings on one of the food trunks suddenly broke free and the heavy wooden box bounced down the wagon and disappeared over the tailgate.

Sam gripped the sides of the wagon with all his strength but he knew that this was it. He couldn't get to the road and the horse was going to pull them all over.

As he closed his eyes and started to say a silent prayer, Alex's face suddenly appeared over the side of the wagon.

"Hold the fuck on," she shrieked as she clung to wooden boards.

Alex fought to stay on her feet as she made her way around the back of the wagon. The terrified horse was thrashing its front legs and the wagon was shaking violently. One of the horse's hooves almost caught Alex on the knee as it kicked out and she had to pull her leg out of the way quickly. She looked down and her heart almost stopped as she saw how close the other back wheel was to the edge. If that one went over, the horse would fall and the wagon would go with it.

Alex quickly climbed up the wagon wheel and tried to reach over the side of the wagon as her feet slipped and slid on the wet wood. She almost lost her grip as the wagon lurched again, but her left foot got wedged in the spokes of the wheel and stopped her from falling.

"Alex, be careful for fuck's sake!" Sam yelled.

Alex glanced at him, her face a mask of determination. She gripped the wagon as tightly as she could with her left hand and pulled her knife free of its sheath. She gritted her teeth and stretched down to where the reins were tied to the tailgate. The reins vibrated and she nearly dropped her knife as the wagon shook again.

Alex glanced down and the fallen horse looked at her, desperation in its eyes.

"I'm sorry," she cried as, with tears welling up in her eyes, she sawed at the reins with her knife.

One of the reins snapped away and then with a loud twang, the second rein was gone and Sam's horse screamed as it fell into the depths of the canyon below.

Without the weight of the horse pulling them backwards, the wagon leapt forward and all four wheels crashed down on the road's surface. Alex threw herself clear and hit the safety of the wet road where she lay in a torrent of rushing water, her chest heaving and her breaths coming in ragged pants.

Sam leaned over the edge of the wagon and threw up noisily down the back wheel.

Tom and Lalitha grabbed the carthorse and pulled down on the harness to stop it moving.

Ramman looked back to check that Sam was okay and then breathed a huge sigh.

"Thank you, Mistress Alex," he called. "If it had not been for you, we would have been dragged over the edge."

"Thanks, Moony," Sam gasped. "Really. I thought I was gone. Are you okay?"

Alex sat up, looked up at Sam's worried face and wiped the tears from her cheeks.

"Yeah, I'm okay, Sam. I thought we were going over… and that poor fucking horse…"

Sam nodded, "I know Alex, I know, but if you hadn't cut if free, we'd all have fallen with it."

Alex took several deep breaths and then stood up. She let her trembling legs settle for a few seconds and then walked shakily back down the road to retrieve her own and Danny's horses. As she led them back towards the wagon, the downpour suddenly stopped and the water rushing down the road started to relent.

Tom and Lalitha held their horses' reins as they sat down heavily on the wet road. Tom pulled his prosthetic out of his tunic and inspected it for any damage. He couldn't see anything too serious other than a few scratches, but he would have to let it dry out a bit before reattaching it. Tom glowered as he berated himself for yet again nearly failing the team because of his disability. He felt sick to the core when he thought about what had nearly just happened.

Sam spat bile from his mouth and looked up as two figures rounded the bend behind them, one of them with a green scarf tied round his face and the other leading a weary-looking horse.

"Nice of you to wait for us," Jimmy called and then noticed the expressions on their faces. "What? What did we miss?"

CHAPTER 27

On the Road to Brentar

Once the group had recovered enough to carry on their journey up the mountain road, they pushed on and continued to slog onwards to the Pass of Mauga. Everybody wanted to get off this road as quickly as they could.

Danny was much happier now. Due to either the evaporation of all the rainwater or the dropping temperatures as they rose higher, clouds had formed in the valley around them. This meant that visibility had dropped significantly. The riders could only see the road out to fifty metres in front of them and to their right, the canyon was completely shrouded so they had no concept at all of the scale of the drop next to them.

Danny managed to convince himself that the canyon floor was rising up to meet them and the drop was nowhere near as bad now. He even got brave enough to take off his blindfold and get back on his horse.

Everyone else rode along in near silence. They brooded over the near disaster further back down the road and a disabling wave of depression began to fall on Tom.

It was heading towards early evening when the clouds abruptly parted and the team found themselves approaching a wide col between two of the largest peaks. Late afternoon sunshine hit the mountain tops and lit the mist that lay in the canyon below them with a golden light. As Tom looked back to the south it seemed as if he were looking out over an ocean of candyfloss.

As they carried on upwards, the riders realised that Danny's wishful thinking had actually been correct. There was no huge drop to the side of them any longer. The two mountains had come together and the road now rose gently towards the gap between them. They had reached the Pass of Mauga.

"Let's camp here for the night," Lalitha suggested. "The light will fade soon and we do not want to be travelling these roads in the dark."

Everyone wholeheartedly agreed and dismounted gratefully.

There was no wood around to light a fire with, so the team sat huddled together around the side of the wagon for shelter as they ate their rations. Everyone was still wet from the rain earlier and fleeces were pulled from the wagon to wrap themselves in. They lifted Sam down out of the wagon and Alex checked his leg while there was still some light in the sky to see by.

Tom sat by himself away from the group and examined his prosthetic. It had dried out a little and Tom decided to risk plugging the charger in. He watched the LED on his arm as he inserted the charging lead, but it did not flash green. He tried again, but with the same result. The charging port must still have water in it. Tom blew noisily into the USB socket and pushed a corner of his tunic into the hole to try and wipe out any water that was in there. He tried again and still the LED refused to flash.

"Fuck it," spat Tom and threw the prosthetic across the ground.

He squeezed his eyes closed, covered his face with his hand and sat breathing heavily until a touch on his shoulder made him jump.

"Tom, how are you doing?" Alex asked him gently.

Tom just shook his head and couldn't find any voice to answer her with.

Alex sat on the ground next to him and leaned in close.

"What's up?"

"You have to ask?" Tom snapped bitterly, his voice breaking with emotion. "I let us down yet again and if you hadn't got to the wagon when you did, we'd have lost Sam, Ramman, all the supplies and God knows what else. I'm no good to you Alex."

Alex put her arm around Tom's shoulder and hugged him tightly.

"It was a shitty day Tom and we all got pretty scared back there, but we're still here. We made it through."

"No thanks to me."

"That is not true. If you and Lalitha hadn't been there to hold onto the wagon, it may well have gone over the edge before I got anywhere near you."

"But that piece of crap let me down again," he spat, pointing at the prosthetic lying on the ground, "and this stump of an arm is no use to anyone."

"It is what it is Tom. We can't change the fact that you lost your arm in Helmand, but it doesn't define who you are. You are more than that… to the team… to me."

Tom looked at her and his eyes welled up.

"Alex, this team does not need me. I am a liability."

"No, you aren't Tom. You are the rock that this team is built around. It needs you. I need you."

Alex took Tom's hand in hers and held it tightly.

"Alex… How can you always have so much faith in me?"

"Because I love you, you fucking idiot!"

Tom's heart almost stopped.

"What?"

"I love you, Tom McAllister and I have done for years. You just never did anything to make me think that you thought the same way."

Tom stared at her and the tears ran down his face.

"Alex… I…"

Alex let go of his hand and put her finger on his lips.

"Shhh… Don't say anything."

She wrapped her arms around him and pulled him close as he sobbed uncontrollably into her shoulder.

After Tom's sobs had abated, he took several long breaths and rubbed his eyes as they released their embrace.

"Sorry, Alex."

Alex gave his hand a squeeze and then stood up to retrieve the prosthetic from where he had thrown it.

"You've got nothing to be sorry for Tom," she smiled. "I'm gonna go and give this arm of yours a clean."

Tom nodded and smiled weakly at her as she walked over to her Bergen, pulled a T-shirt out of it and started cleaning the inside of the prosthetic.

Tom sat alone for a few minutes longer and then went to check on Sam.

"Are you okay, Sam?" he asked as he climbed up into the wagon and sat down next to his old friend.

"I'm okay thanks mate. The leg hurts a bit more today, but it's not surprising I guess after being chucked around in the back of this thing today. Are you okay?"

"Not really. I… I just lost it a bit with Alex. It's been a rough day you know and that damn arm of mine let me down again."

"Yeah, well, Alex was a complete legend today. That girl is a marvel."

Tom smiled and went to say something, but stopped himself.

Sam noticed his friend's reticence. "Come on. What is it?"

"Sam… Alex said something to me and it came as a bit of a shock."

Sam grinned. "So, she told you eventually?"

"What?"

"I saw you both over there. She told you that she's in love with you, didn't she?"

"Yes, but how did you…"

"For fuck's sake Tom, for someone so clever you can be really dense sometimes. That girl has worshipped you for years."

"What?"

"You're surprised? Really? All those times in the unit when she was always near you, always backing you up and then after the accident she was there with you whenever she could be to help you through your treatments and appointments. Even in your darkest days when you pushed us all away, Alex was still there, checking on you and making sure that you were okay. She was devastated about what happened to you and how it affected you afterwards."

"But why did she never say anything?"

"Because she couldn't. When we were still in the Engineers, she couldn't say anything because you were her CO, and afterwards, well you weren't exactly very approachable for a while, Boss. But she stuck by you when most others would have left you to it."

Tom looked up and could see Alex watching him. She smiled and looked back down at what she was doing.

Tom sighed. "What do I do Sam? I haven't been with anyone for years… not since way before I lost my arm. I'd just be a burden to her."

"That's not really for you to decide is it? Alex loves you Tom and I think it's pretty bloody obvious that you love her too. She doesn't care about you losing your arm, she just cares about you. You're not a burden for Christ's sake and even if you were, she knows exactly what the score is. She went to enough of your sessions to know exactly what she's letting herself in for. Alex is one of the strongest women I have ever met and if she didn't want to do something, she wouldn't do it."

"But…"

"But what? We don't know what shit we're walking into here, Boss. We could have all ended up in the bottom of the canyon this morning and that would have been it; game over."

"But what if she…"

"Boss, stop with the what ifs! Life is short, so just don't waste it. Girls like Alex don't come along very often… Just let her know how you feel and worry about the other stuff later on. You know I'm right… just admit it to yourself and let her in."

Tom nodded and squeezed Sam's shoulder tightly.

"Thanks, Sam."

"You're welcome Boss… Listen… I know you think you screwed up today, but we're still kicking and that is all that matters. Fuck the rest of it. Be with Alex and just… be happy while you can."

Tom nodded and stood up. He had a lot to think about.

"You want something to eat?" he asked.

"Yeah, that would be great. Big Mac, fries and a thick shake please?"

Tom smiled and jumped down from the wagon to get Sam something from the remaining stores trunk.

"Master Tom," Ramman said as Tom opened the lid of the truck, "We lost one of the trunks when Master Sam's horse fell. We will have to be sparing with the food that we have left or we will run out before we get to Brentar."

"Is there a town or somewhere on the way where we could re-stock?"

"No, Master, there is nowhere that I know of before Brentar."

"Okay then, Ram, you are in charge of rationing the food okay?"

Ramman nodded and sat down next to the truck to work out how to manage what was left.

Tom handed a hunk of dried fish and some bread up to Sam and then sat down next to Alex. She was still busy cleaning the fingers on his prosthetic, but he leaned over and stopped her by taking her hand in his. He sighed deeply and looked into her eyes.

"Alex… I've been an idiot. I can't remember a time when I didn't care about you. You were the only thing that got me through after I lost my arm. If I hadn't had you, I don't think I would have made it. All the times you sat with me and held my hand, I was desperate to tell you how I felt, but I was just so scared that all you felt for me was pity. I had so much self-loathing that I couldn't understand why you kept coming to see me. I'm less than a man now Alex. I mess up and people stare at me like I'm a freak and I can't even get a proper job any longer. How could someone like you ever settle for a waste of skin like me?"

Alex's eyes filled and her voice cracked with emotion.

"Settle? There is no 'settle' Tom. I love you for who you are, for your strength, for your kindness, for your compassion. I came to visit you because I wanted to be with you, not because I pitied you. When I was away from you, all I could think of was being back at your side. Losing your arm was a tragedy, but it didn't change how I felt about you at all. You are not a lesser man; you are the man I love."

Tom's head dropped as tears ran down his face. Alex reached over and lifted his face towards her. She brushed the tears from his face with her thumbs and kissed him gently on the lips.

A cheer went up from next to the wagon and Tom looked around to see Danny, Jimmy and Sam all applauding enthusiastically.

"It's about time!" yelled Danny.

Alex stuck two fingers up at Danny and kissed Tom again.

The tone of the evening changed completely and the disaster that had almost befallen them earlier that day was pushed from their minds. They joked and laughed deep into the night telling stories of their days in the army, how many times they had survived near fatal encounters, and how Tom was such a dickhead for never realising how much Alex felt for him.

As the team settled down for the night, Tom and Alex pulled their bivvy bags close together and the last thing he felt as he rolled onto his side and pulled a fleece over them both was Alex's arm wrapping itself around him.

CHAPTER 28

Onwards to Brentar

The road back down the other side of the pass was much less steep and infinitely less frightening. The valley that they descended through was much wider and they could see in the distance that their route stayed much closer to the valley floor.

Lalitha and Danny took the lead now, with Ramman following them in the wagon. Tom and Alex rode together behind the wagon. Jimmy had decided to take a break from riding and was sitting in the back of the wagon with Sam. His horse was tied to the wagon and it walked along behind them, relived to be free of the weight of its saddle and rider.

Jimmy and Sam chatted between themselves and watched the countryside rattle by. By the time they stopped for the day, they had descended a long way. Looking back up at the dramatic mountains that caught the late afternoon sunshine above them gave no indication of how dangerous the road up there had been. They had passed several travellers heading up towards the pass that day and fully understood the grim look on the strangers' faces. None of the team had a desire to ever go over that road again.

"We cross another ridge tomorrow," Ramman told them once they had set up camp, "but it is nothing compared to that which we have travelled already."

"That's a relief," grinned Alex. "If I find out that you're lying to us Ram, you do know that I will have to shoot you?"

Ramman's eyes widened in panic.

"Don't worry Ram," laughed Tom. "She is teasing you."

Ramman smiled, but gave Alex a wary look as she winked at him.

A wide river ran near to their camp and large pools of cold, clear water could be seen. Jimmy took fishing line and hooks out of his survival kit and carefully baited the hooks with dried meat.

"I'm going to go and see if I can catch us some fresh dinner," Jimmy grinned as he and Lalitha headed for the nearest pool. "If we were at home, there would be trout in that river."

Tom watched as the two of them sat on a rock overlooking the pool and Jimmy showed Lalitha how to dangle the line in the best spot. After only a short time, Jimmy and Lalitha had eight shiny fish on the rock next to them.

Using the rock as a workbench, Jimmy used his knife to prepare the catch. By the time he was finished, his hands were covered in blood and fish guts.

"Nice catch Codboy," said Danny as he walked over to examine the fish, "but you really stink."

Jimmy jokingly went to put his hands on Danny's face and laughed as he recoiled in revulsion.

"Stay away from me with your filthy fish gut hands!" Danny yelled as he quickly backed away from him.

Jimmy laughed and moved towards Danny; his hands outstretched towards him.

"Ooooo… Fester hates fish guts," Jimmy laughed as he advanced towards him.

Lalitha looked bemused as Danny ran to stand by her side.

"Tell him, Lalitha. Tell him it's not funny."

"Come on, Fester," Jimmy chided, "It's only fish guts."

"Piss off, Jimmy… I'm warnin' you," Danny laughed as he took another step backwards.

"James Lang, that is vile," Lalitha said pulling a face.

Jimmy feinted a lunge at Danny and laughed as the older man took another step backwards… and fell into the pool with a huge splash.

Jimmy howled with laughter and moved to the edge of the rock so that he could better see Danny's splashing as he stood spluttering, chest deep in the cold water.

"Fester, you're all wet," laughed Jimmy as he looked down at him.

He was laughing so hard that he didn't notice Alex sneak up behind him.

"I think you need to wash your hands mate," Alex whispered in his ear before giving him a gentle nudge. The nudge was just enough to make Jimmy lose his balance and he fell, face first into the water.

"Moony, that was unfair," he coughed as his head rose back above the water's surface.

"You needed a bath anyway," Alex laughed as she undid her boot laces, kicked them off and jumped into the pool after them.

The three of them had a mock fight which ended up with Alex and Danny dunking Jimmy until he waved his hands in submission. The three of them waded to the shore laughing and spitting out river water.

Lalitha watched the three of them with a baffled look on her face.

"You are all children," she scolded which made the three wet soldiers laugh even harder.

Tom grinned as he saw the three bedraggled figures arrive back at the camp.

"What have you three been doing?" he laughed.

"Fishin'," laughed Danny holding up the line with Jimmy's fish dangling from it.

"Who caught who?" Tom grinned.

"Make yourself useful, Boss, and go and find some firewood to cook these on while we get dry," Alex laughed.

"Look," said Danny, "she's got him under the thumb already."

Alex gave Danny a playful slap across the back of the head, and Tom laughed as he headed off to search under the few windswept trees that he could see nearby. He felt much better this morning. The guilt and self-doubt were still there, but realising how Alex felt about him had changed things dramatically. Had he really not known how she felt, or had he just not been able to believe it until she actually said the words? Either way, he was glad that she had told him. He felt more hope and joy in his heart than he had in a very long time.

Tom gathered enough wood to get a decent fire burning and, before long, the fish were sizzling nicely. The team sat against the wagon as the sun started to dip below the horizon and they looked out over the darkening valley. Tom plugged his arm in to recharge and checked the power levels on the solar charger. Confident that he had more than enough power reserves, Tom leaned back against the wagon wheel and put his arm around Alex. She leaned into him and rested her head on his shoulder.

As soon as the fish was cooked, Danny worked his way around the group passing out the hot juicy meat. It smelled wonderful and tasted even better. Danny climbed up into the wagon and presented Sam with his share of the catch.

"Here you go Slapper. Freshly caught fish courtesy of Codboy."

Sam looked at the food and pushed it away.

"You ok?" Danny asked, raising his eyebrows. "It's not like you to refuse food."

"Sorry, Fester," Sam coughed, "I just don't feel so great. Is it hot? I'm sweating like a pig."

Danny looked at Sam and there were beads of sweat on his brow. Danny put his hand on Sam's forehead and his skin felt hot.

"Moony, can I borrow you for a minute?" Danny called.

Alex popped the last of her fish into her mouth, pushed herself up on Tom's shoulder and stuck her head over the side of the wagon.

"What's up, Fester?"

"Can you have a look at Slaphead? He says that he doesn't feel so good."

Alex frowned with concern, went around the back of the wagon and climbed up over the dropped tailgate.

"Let's have a look. How long have you been feeling rough Sam? You didn't say anything."

"It kinda came on gradually this afternoon, but I really don't feel so good now Moony. I'm burning up and my leg hurts worse today"

"Okay, let's check your dressings. Everything was okay when I checked it last night, but I'll put some more of the salve on it and see if that helps. Boss, can you throw me my first aid kit?"

Tom reached into Alex's Bergen and passed up her bag.

"Is Sam okay?"

"I'm just going to check his leg and make sure everything is good," Alex smiled.

Tom nodded. He saw Alex's smile, but he also saw the concern in her eyes. Something was not right.

Alex carefully unwound the bandage around Sam's thigh and pursed her lips as she examined the wound. The area around the stitches looked very red and as she gently touched the injury, Sam gasped and jerked.

"Sorry, Sam," Alex said, "I didn't mean to hurt you."

She turned quickly to Danny.

"Fester, could you go and get some water from the river? I need to give this wound a bit of a clean."

Danny nodded and jumped out of the wagon, taking one of Jimmy's plastic bags with him.

"Is it infected?" Sam asked her.

"It looks a bit angry Sammy, but it'll be fine. I'll give it a clean, put a bit of surgical spirit on it and slap some salve on. That should sort it out."

Tom looked at Alex as she smiled at Sam. As she glanced at Tom, her smile didn't fade, but Tom could tell by something in her expression that Sam's leg was not good.

Danny returned with the water bag and Alex tipped some on her hands to wash them and then dipped a clean bandage in it before gently wiping Sam's injury. Sam hissed and gritted his teeth, but did not complain.

Once the old salve had been cleaned away, Alex dabbed some surgical spirit around the stitches and applied some fresh salve and bandaged it all up again. She gave Sam a couple of painkillers to swallow and ruffled his hair as she climbed down to Tom's side.

Alex made a show of smiling as she repacked her first aid kit, but then pulled Tom by the arm and walked away from the wagon.

"It's not good is it?" asked Tom as soon as they were out of earshot.

Alex turned her back to the wagon and the smile fell from her face.

"No, it's not good. He has the early signs of an infection. If that gets worse, it could be serious."

"So, what do we do?"

"We're doing all we can. We need to keep him hydrated and that wound has to stay clean as possible. The problem is, we're not going to be able to get antibiotics here, so if it gets bad, I don't know what we'll do. I just hope that whatever is in that salve helps him, but to be honest I don't trust it a hundred percent."

"Okay, we're just going to have to do what we can and hope that it doesn't get any worse. Let's find out from Ramman how far away from Brentar we are."

They walked back to where Lalitha, Jimmy and Ramman were sitting.

"Ram, how many days do we have before we get to Brentar?" Tom asked.

Ramman looked around at their surroundings and sucked some fish juice from his fingers.

"Brentar is six or seven days from here, Master Tom."

"So, we're about half way from Lintar. Thanks Ram."

Tom turned and looked at Alex, concern written all over his face.

"Let's just hope Sam doesn't get any worse," he whispered to her. "How long do we have?"

"If it doesn't get any worse, then we should be fine. If the doctor's salve doesn't help and the wound starts to smell or we see green puss coming out of it, then without antibiotics, things are going to get bad… and bad quickly."

CHAPTER 29

On the Road to Brentar

The journey that day was tense as everyone realised that Sam's condition was worsening. His temperature had risen and he spent most of the day asleep. Alex travelled in the wagon with him and put her hand on his arm as he mumbled incoherently and tensed his body whenever they hit a particularly savage bump in the road.

The team had crossed the second ridge that Ramman had told them about and the journey down into the foothills of the mountain range was now straightforward. The road had widened and its surface was less bumpy which was good news for the passengers in the wagon.

They had made good progress by the time Ramman pulled them to a halt that afternoon.

"What do we do, Master Tom?" Ramman asked. "Do we press on, or should we make camp here?"

"Alex," Tom called, "how's Sam?"

"If we're stopping for a few minutes I'll check his leg now."

Nobody dismounted and a silence dropped over the group as Alex carefully removed Sam's bandages. Sam groaned as Alex pulled the last of the bandages away. As soon as the wound was exposed, Alex knew that they were in trouble. A clear liquid was oozing from the wound and her nose wrinkled as the smell of it reached her.

"Shit!" she swore under her breath.

"Alex?" Tom said, a feeling of dread rising though him.

"Tom, it's bad. The infection has really taken hold."

"Ramman, are you sure that we're still five or six days away from Brentar?"

"Yes, Master Tom, I am fairly sure that is right."

Tom turned back to Alex.

"Is that too long, Alex?"

She looked back at him anxiously.

"Yes. We don't have that kind of time."

"Then we're going to have to ride through the night," Tom decided. "It's the only thing we can do."

Alex nodded.

"The road from here is good, Master," Ramman said. "If we had been south of the pass then night travel would have been impossible, but from here… we could do it."

Tom looked at Jimmy and the young man nodded his agreement.

"We've gotta do it, Boss. We need to get Sam to Brentar as soon as we can."

Tom pulled his horse around the wagon and moved forwards to talk to Lalitha and Danny.

"Okay," he said to them. "Here's the thing. Sam's infection is bad. We're going to have to push on as quickly as we can until we get to Brentar. No overnight stops any longer. If we don't, I… I don't know if Sam will make it."

They both nodded.

"We've not travelled at night up to now so I am going to need you two at the front here to keep alert and scout the road for us. Let us know if there is anything that we need to know about okay?"

"Understood," Danny confirmed.

"You two lead on then and let's get Sam some help."

The caravan set off and as the sun went down, they continued onwards, desperate to get to Brentar in time to get Sam some help.

The next three days blurred into a waking nightmare for the team. They rode on and on, only taking short breaks to give the horses a brief rest. Everyone was exhausted, but no-one wanted to lose any time.

They took turns to ride in the wagon and rotated the horses around so that at least the animals could walk some of the way without their riders and heavy saddlebags.

As the early morning sun rose over the mountains, Ramman pulled the wagon to a halt, rubbing his eyes blearily. Tom jerked awake beside him on the bench at the front of the wagon.

"What is it? Is there a problem?"

"No, Master, I just needed to piss," he said as he jumped down from the wagon and ran to the side of the road.

THE FALLEN

Alex stirred in the back of the wagon and sat up.

"Why've we stopped?"

"Ram needed to take a leak." Tom replied. "How's Sam doing?"

"I'm really worried. His temperature is through the roof and he's not even mumbling any more. His leg smells bad Tom… really bad."

"I don't know what we're going to do when we get to Brentar. I'm guessing that they don't have a hospital there."

Alex leant forward and clasped her face in her hands.

"Master, I have an idea," Ramman declared as he pulled himself back up into his seat. "My parents' farm lies this side of Brentar. If we send riders ahead, they could go to the farm and arrange for a physician to meet us when we arrive there."

"That is a good idea, Ram. It would save us a lot of time."

"Let me go with Lalitha," Alex said. "We can ride much faster than you guys. How long would it take us to get to the farm, Ram?"

"The horses are tired, but yours and Master Tom's have been rested for the last few hours. If you ride them as quickly as they can manage, you could be at my parents' farm before midday today. I can draw you a map to show you the way."

Alex looked at Tom and nodded her head.

"We've got to do it, Tom. We'll go ahead and get things ready for you."

Tom didn't like the idea of Alex riding on without him, but he knew that this was the best option.

"Lalitha," he called, "did you hear all that?"

"Yes," she answered. "I will ride with Alexandra Aluko."

Ramman dug around in the stores chest and found some paper food wrapping that he could write on. Alex passed him a pen from her pack and Ramman hastily scribbled out a map.

"Follow this road until you can see Brentar ahead of you. As you near the city, you will see the gatehouse in front of you here," he instructed, pointing at his map. "Before you pass through the gate, follow a track to the left. The track goes through trees and bends to the right. You will see a small river and beyond that, stone-built farmsteads with barns and cattle. My parent's place is the fourth one on your left."

He marked the farms on the map and drew a big cross over his parents' farm.

"Tell my parents that I sent you. My father is called Sarratil and my mother is Lagna. Tell them how you saved Fellorn and the rest of us from the bandits in the south and that you need their help. They will know what to do."

Alex and Lalitha quickly saddled the two horses tied to the rear of the wagon and mounted up. As they prepared to set off. Alex pulled her horse alongside the wagon, leaned over and kissed Tom.

"See you later. We'll do everything we can to get things ready for you."

"Be careful okay?"

"I always am," she grinned "I love you, Tom McAllister."

"Love you too," he smiled as Alex kicked her heels, flicked her reins and her horse leapt away in a cloud of dust. Lalitha spun Tom's horse around and set off after her.

Jimmy tied his horse to the wagon and did the same with Lalitha's stallion, before settling down next to Sam. They didn't bother unsaddling the horses as they wanted to avoid everything that delayed their forward progress.

"Come on, Ram," Tom urged as he watched the two riders gallop off ahead, "let's keep going."

The sun shone down on them as they rode on through the morning. As the sun passed overhead, Tom and Jimmy rode again; Jimmy on his own horse and Tom on Lalitha's grey. Danny sat in the back and watched Sam worriedly as they bumped along towards Brentar.

The heat haze that had hung over the road gradually dissipated and late into the afternoon, they saw the city of Brentar in the distance. It seemed to take forever for the city to get closer, but eventually the team approached an imposing gatehouse set into the city walls. When they were some way from the great gateway, Ramman turned the wagon off the road and onto a rutted track that pulled off and followed the outside of the city walls.

The carthorse was pretty much on its last legs and Tom willed it to keep going just a little longer. The horse's breathing was laboured and it began to pant as they passed through a small copse of trees and then drove by one… two… three farms.

"This is it," exclaimed Ramman as they pulled off the track and towards a group of stone buildings. "My parent's farm."

As they rumbled up towards the farmstead, Alex rushed out of the door towards them.

"There is a doctor setting up inside," Alex said as she dashed up to the wagon. "He arrived just before you did."

"Where's Lalitha?" Tom asked looking around the yard.

"She's keeping a low profile with our horses. She's got her scarf on so nobody saw her face. Better safe than sorry I thought."

"Good plan," Tom agreed as he dismounted and tied his horse to the side of the wagon.

Ramman climbed from his driver's seat into the back of the wagon and helped Danny pass Sam's unconscious body down to Tom, Alex and Jimmy. Between them, they hurriedly carried him up to the farmstead.

"In here," said the man that Tom assumed to be Ramman's father, pointing at the doorway to the house.

They carried Sam inside and Ramman's father led them through to a bedroom where a well-dressed gentleman was arranging a collection of vials, pots and bottles on the wooden dresser.

"This is the doctor," Alex said as she followed them in, "Ramman's father sent word to the city and he came straight out."

The doctor nodded to the new arrivals and pointed to the bed.

"Take off his clothes and place him on the bed. I need to examine the wound."

Tom and Jimmy stripped Sam down to his boxers and laid him gently on the bed. Sam's body tensed as the doctor started to remove his bandages, but he did not wake up.

Once the wound was exposed, the doctor began to gently press it with his fingers. More clear liquid ran from around the stitches. He reached into his bag and withdrew a vicious looking scalpel with which he gently cut the stiches in Sam's leg. He pulled the stitches free with tweezers and dropped them into a bucket by his side. He then picked up a bottle from the dresser and poured yellow liquid over Sam's leg.

"Once this anaesthetic has taken effect, I need to carefully clean the wound and make sure that there is no foreign matter inside the flesh. I will then re-stitch the wound and apply a herbal salve of my own making to the infected area. This will help to reduce the swelling. Once that is done, I will bind maggots to the leg to remove the necrotic tissue. I have a medicine that the patient can take orally which will help to reduce his temperature and help his body to fight the infection in his blood."

At the mention of maggots, Jimmy went white and made quickly for the door. Danny did not want to see what the doctor was going to do to his friend either and swiftly followed him.

"I will do my best to save the patient's leg, but if I fail, it may become necessary to remove it," the doctor continued.

Alex met Tom's eyes as he took in this statement. Tom suddenly noticed a silver-bladed saw in the doctor's bag.

"You will not cut his leg off," Tom said in a firm voice. "No way."

Tom's head was in turmoil. It was happening again, but to someone else this time.

"Tom," Alex whispered, "Sam could die… It might have to be done."

"This can't happen," Tom stuttered.

Alex took Tom's hand in her own and pulled him towards the door.

"Come on," she coaxed, "let's leave the doctor to do what he can."

Tom started to protest, but Alex gently guided him out of the bedroom.

The last thing that Tom saw as the door swung shut was the doctor taking up his scalpel and starting to make small incisions into Sam's thigh.

CHAPTER 30

The Farmstead

Tom and Alex walked through the living area and made their way back outside where they found Danny and Jimmy sitting on a bench in the early evening sunshine. Danny looked up at Tom with a pained expression.

"Maggots, Boss? Are we in the dark ages here?"

"Maggots are sometimes used back home," Alex told him. "I don't know much about it, but I remember seeing something on the TV where they used them in a guy's infected wound. It worked a treat."

Jimmy looked less than convinced. "Well, it sounds bloody disgusting."

As Tom tried to come to terms with what was going on inside, Ramman walked over and introduced his parents.

"Master Tom, this is my father Sarratil and my mother Lagna," he said gesturing at the older couple standing next to him.

"I believe that we owe you a great debt for saving our son's life," Sarratil said. "We were worried about his travels to the south, but he assured us that it would be safe. It seems this was not the case."

Lagna stepped forwards and embraced Tom.

"He is our youngest son and is precious to us. I do not know how we can ever repay you."

"There is no debt to repay," Tom said. "If it were not for your son, the man inside your house would probably be dead already. He is a credit to you."

Ramman blushed and smiled as his father clapped him on the back.

"Your brothers will not be so keen to mock you for being young and inexperienced again. I am proud of you son."

As Lagna gave her son yet another hug, Lalitha appeared from a nearby barn, her lower face covered with her scarf. She walked over to the wagon and helped to untie one of the horses from the back of Ramman's wagon.

"Does your lady companion have a disfigurement?" Lagna asked, briefly letting go of Ramman. "She has not removed her scarf since she arrived and became anxious when I asked her about it."

"Errr… She is keen to keep her identity a secret," Tom said.

"She has a husband who was violent towards her and she is travelling with us in disguise," Alex added quickly.

"That is all too common these days," complained Lagna. "Men can be so cruel."

"We do not have enough beds to accommodate everyone in the house," Sarratil announced, "but you are welcome to use my barn if that is acceptable. It is dry and there is plenty of room for you and your horses."

"That is kind, thank you." said Tom. "We will gladly accept your offer. If we are close by in the barn, we can be near our friend when he wakes up."

Ramman unharnessed the wagon and together, they all led their horses to the barn. As they made their way across the yard, Alex heard Danny mumbling quietly to Lalitha.

"What're you two whispering about?" she called.

"I was just saying to Lalitha how I had been looking forward to a nice comfortable bed in Brentar, but we're back on the ground again," Danny grumbled.

"I don't care," yawned Jimmy, "I think I could sleep anywhere."

Lalitha did not speak and it seemed to Alex that something was wrong.

Alex sped her pace up until she was at Lalitha's side.

"You okay, Lalitha?" Alex asked.

"Did you hear the woman ask if I was disfigured? How dare she? I am of royal blood… and then you tell her that my husband beats me? I am not a weak woman to be beaten by a husband!"

"I know that, Lalitha. I am sorry. We were just trying to keep your identity a secret. If Gask finds out you're here…"

"Soon I will be Bound and then things will be different," Lalitha glowered as she stalked off to the back of the barn.

"Lalitha…" began Alex, but Tom put his hand on her arm.

"Leave her be for a few minutes. She'll be fine."

"Yeah, whatever," Alex shrugged. "Let's get these horses sorted then."

The team busied themselves removing the saddles from their horses and unloaded the wagon. They each gave their horses a much needed brush down and made sure that the long journey had not inflicted any damage to them. The horses were tired, but thankfully seemed uninjured.

Ramman walked into the barn with a platter of bread and cheese, together with a basket of what looked like apple pies.

"My mother sent me through with food for you all."

The team sat on sheaves of straw and most of them tucked into the food as they realised how hungry they were. Tom, however, could not bring himself to eat anything. He could not tear his mind from what could be happening at that moment in the farmhouse. He stood and paced around the barn picking at the seam of his tunic with his right hand.

"You need to rest and eat something," Alex told him. "The last few days have been exhausting and you can't do anything more to help Sam. You got him here and it's down to the doctor now."

"I just can't bear to think of him losing a leg," Tom said. "I wouldn't wish the nightmare that I went through on anyone, least of all Sam."

"I know, but it's not come to that yet. Let's worry about that if it happens. Sit down and eat something before you fall over."

Tom nodded, sat down next to her and nibbled on a piece of bread.

Lalitha stood up from where she had been sitting with Jimmy, Ramman and Danny. She looked towards Alex and walked over.

"I did not mean to be ungrateful to you Alexandra Aluko. I know that you have done much to keep me and my identity safe. The old woman's words just enflamed me."

"That's okay, Lalitha," Alex smiled. "These are good people. Ramman's people. I think we can trust them."

The young woman nodded and after a brief hesitation she turned her attention to Tom.

"I have spoken to Ramman and Daniel Adams. They are going to travel into Brentar in the morning and purchase more supplies for our journey. While they are in the city, Ramman is going to go to the harbour and make enquiries about a ship. If he can find an able captain, Ramman will ask him if we can purchase passage to Prentak. Once we are at sea, we can persuade the captain to divert our course to the isle of Gessan."

"I think that's a good idea, Lalitha, but it could be some time before Sam can travel. We could be looking at a couple of weeks before we can even think about moving him."

Lalitha scowled. "I cannot wait that long, Thomas McAllister. We need to reach Gessan as soon as we can and, if the messengers I sent from Serat are close to their destinations, my allies will soon be on their way to meet us at Prentak."

Tom was about to argue with her, but he suddenly noticed a figure in the barn's doorway. Lalitha also saw the figure and swiftly pulled her scarf back up. It was Sarratil.

"The doctor has done what he can and wishes to talk to you."

Everyone hurriedly put their food down and rushed back to the farmhouse. As they got there, the doctor was washing blood from his hands in a bowl of water. Tom instantly got a sinking feeling in his stomach and could not find his voice.

"How's our friend doing?" Alex asked nervously.

The doctor dried his hands and looked up at them.

"I think we might save his leg."

There was an audible sigh as everyone let out the breaths they had been holding.

"The infection was bad, but it seemed to be localised around the wound. I have lanced the inflammation and cleaned the wound out. There were some small shards of wood from the arrow buried beneath the skin and I think it was this that caused his body to react badly. I removed the splinters and treated the injury with my herbal salve."

"Did you use the maggots?" Jimmy asked, pulling a face.

"Yes, I have placed a net containing maggots against the wound and have bound it with bandages. I will need to return in a couple of days to change the bandages and apply new maggots. I will know for sure then if the leg is saved."

"How long will it be before he can travel?" Lalitha asked.

The doctor regarded the strange girl with the scarf covering half her face and scowled.

"Travel? He will not be able to travel for at least ten days… and that is my best estimate. The infection needs to clear and your man needs to regain his strength."

Lalitha seemed less than pleased at this news.

The doctor picked up his bag and walked towards his horse that had been tethered to a rail at the far end of the farmhouse.

Before he mounted his horse, Tom handed him ten silver coins.

"That is far too much coin sir," the doctor protested.

"You have earned it," Tom said. "We are indebted to you for helping our friend."

The doctor smiled. "Thank you, sir. Hopefully your friend will have a better night and I will see him again in two days."

After the doctor had gone, Tom and Alex went inside to check on Sam. He was still asleep, but he had fresh bandages on, and when Alex looked closer, the smell was nowhere near as bad.

"Thank God he didn't have to take the leg," Tom breathed.

Alex nodded her agreement. "Sam's made of strong stuff. We're going to have to talk tonight though. Did you see Lalitha's face? She's not happy about a two-week delay."

"I noticed, but what can we do? We can't move Sam, can we?"

Alex shook her head. "No, we can't."

They watched Sam sleep for a while and then decided that he looked comfortable so walked back to the barn. Once everyone was gathered there, Lalitha decided that it was time to make an announcement.

"We cannot wait for two weeks before moving on to Gessan. I propose that we leave Samuel Franklin here while we go on to Gessan. Ramman's family can look after him and he will recover well here with the doctor close by."

"So, we'd come back to Brentar and pick him up on the way back?" asked Danny.

"No, our journey from Gessan takes us further north to Prentak. That is where my father's friend Cindal Ardum will meet us. Once we have joined him, we head west. We will not return this way."

"So, you're saying that we leave him behind?" Jimmy said.

"Yes, James Lang. He will be safe here. He will not face the dangers ahead that we will."

Tom looked at Alex. What should they do? Lalitha was obviously keen to move on and they had to go with her. If she tried to go alone then what was the point of any of this?

"I've gotta go with Lalitha," Danny said. "We both have to complete the bindin' ceremony at Gessan, but you guys could stay here. You could try and catch us up once Sam is better."

"What if you hit more trouble, Danny?" Alex said. "As much as you think you are, you're not actually a one-man army."

"Sam's safe here, Boss," Jimmy piped up. "I want to go with Lalitha. You know what the visions showed us. She needs us more than Sam does now."

Tom did not know what to do. He didn't want to split the team in half as it would make everyone's journey much more hazardous, but Sam was too sick to make the journey any time soon. Was leaving Sam behind the best option?

"I can look after Master Sam," Ramman's voice said from the barn door. "Once he is well, we can travel a different path and try to meet you along your journey. I do not fully understand your quest or know your final destination, but I will help if I can."

Tom turned to look at the young man.

"Would you do that for us, Ramman? Where we are going could be dangerous and there's probably going to be more fighting. If you meet up with us once Sam is well, you could be putting yourself in danger."

"Masters, if it were not for you, I would likely be chained to a wagon on my way to work the fields of some Elder in the south. I owe you my life. You must carry on your journey wherever it leads and protect Mistress Lalitha. I will protect Sam and we will find you."

Lalitha smiled. "Our problem is resolved."

Tom was still not sure. There had to be another way.

CHAPTER 31

The Farmstead

Despite being exhausted, Tom had not slept well. He had risen early and walked through the nearby fields to try and blow the cobwebs away. The decision on whether to leave Sam here or persuade Lalitha to wait until he was able to travel was going around and around in his head. On one hand, Sam would be able to stay here to recover for as long as it took, but it meant leaving him behind. On the other, the team would be together, but they would lose almost two weeks; something that Lalitha was unwilling to accept.

As Tom slowly wandered back towards the barn, he saw Ramman and Danny getting ready to head to the city. If they found a ship willing to take them, Lalitha would be even more desperate to depart.

"Take care, Danny," he called as he got closer.

"Will do, Boss. We've got plenty of silver with us so we'll get all the supplies we need while we're there."

"If you find a ship, don't commit us to anything yet. I haven't decided what to do about Sam yet."

"Okay," Danny nodded.

Ramman had borrowed a carthorse from his father and had harnessed it to their wagon. The big beast stamped its feet, eager to be on its way. With a wave, Ramman flicked his reins and the wagon rumbled away down the track towards the city.

"We will return before mid-day," Ramman called over his shoulder.

As Tom watched the wagon disappear towards Brentar, Alex suddenly appeared behind him and put her arms around his waist.

"Where did you disappear to?" she asked.

"I just needed to think about what we do next. Do we leave Sam or wait until he's well enough to travel?"

"Let's see what Ram and Fester come back with. If there isn't a ship available, then that decision doesn't need to be made yet."

"True enough," Tom agreed.

They set off towards the farmhouse with the intention of checking on Sam's condition, but as they approached the door, Lagna bustled out towards them.

"I was coming to the barn to call you all for breakfast. It is porridge with sweet fruits," she said.

"I'll go and get the others," Tom offered as Alex followed Lagna back inside.

As he walked to the barn, Tom realised that Lalitha would not be able to eat porridge without removing her scarf. Ramman's parents would see her face. How bad would it be if Lalitha revealed herself? He was almost certain that they could trust the old couple, but there was still a risk involved.

"Lagna has invited us all in for breakfast," Tom announced as he entered the barn. "If we take her up on her invitation, you won't be able to eat unless you take your scarf off Lalitha. What do you think? It would mean showing them your face, but even if they did recognise you, I think we can trust them."

"Would they recognise you?" Jimmy asked. "These seem to be simple farming folk and we're a long way from Krassak. How would they ever have seen your face before?"

Lalitha looked torn, but her stomach rumbled loudly and she was still bristling about the 'disfigured' comment from the previous night.

"If you think it is safe, Thomas McAllister, then we will trust them."

The decision made, the three of them made their way back to the farmhouse. Tom nervously led them in through the open doorway and into the main room. Inside, there was a huge wooden table and around it were seated several figures. Alex was sitting at the end of the table and next to her were four young men who all bore a strong resemblance to Ramman. This must be the brothers.

They all looked up as Tom, Jimmy and Lalitha entered the room. Tom's heart skipped a beat as the brothers all looked at Lalitha's exposed face, but their expressions did not betray any shocked recognition. They didn't know who she was. Tom breathed a huge sigh and sat down next to Alex who gave his leg a squeeze under the table and raised her eyebrows.

"It is a shame to hide away such a pretty young face," Lagna said to Lalitha with a smile as she placed a bowl of porridge in front of her. "You are with friends here child.

No need to hide yourself. Your wicked husband will not learn of you from us."

"Thank you," Lalitha replied, forcing a smile onto her face.

The brothers all watched Lalitha with appraising eyes.

"How does my dullard baby brother come to be travelling with an attractive woman such as yourself?" asked the oldest of the four. "Perhaps you should take me with you instead."

"Daltran," Lagna scolded, "did I bring you up to have so few manners? Do not talk to the lady in this way."

Ramman's brother grinned lecherously at Lalitha as he shovelled heaped spoonfuls of porridge into his mouth. Lalitha bristled, but said nothing more.

"Where is your husband this morning?" Alex asked Lagna, trying to lighten the atmosphere.

"He has been out tending the cattle on the western pastures. He should be back before we finish eating."

The conversation around the table was very stilted. Daltran and his brothers ate in silence, occasionally glancing surreptitiously in Lalitha's direction. Jimmy scowled back at them, keen to deter their interest in her. Tom and Alex asked questions about the weather and the farm, but Lagna's answers were brief as she distractedly collected dishes and served mugs of hot tea.

"I checked on Sammy," Alex said quietly to Tom. "I think his temperature is down and he looks a lot more comfortable. I think he's going to be okay."

"Thank God for that," Tom smiled.

The table lapsed back into an awkward silence and Tom was relieved when he heard Sarratil approaching the door, whistling as he came. Sarratil's presence might make the situation feel a little less awkward and his work this morning might at least generate a bit more conversation.

Tom watched the door as Sarratil entered carrying a big bowl of eggs. He smiled at Tom and went to put the bowl down. As he moved towards them and glanced at the faces sat around the table, his eyes settled on Lalitha's exposed features.

The colour drained from Sarratil's face and the eggs crashed to the floor, smashing messily over his boots. Everyone jumped at the unexpected noise and eight pairs of eyes stared at Sarratil as he backed away from the table.

Sarratil's finger pointed at Lalitha and he stammered quietly.

"Lalitha!"

"Sarratil, you old fool," Lagna snapped. "Are you losing your senses? Look... The eggs have gone everywhere!"

Tom had a really bad feeling about what was about to happen.

"This is Lalitha Santra, second born to King Lestri Santra!"

"Do not be ridiculous Sarratil. What would our son be doing travelling with the daughter of the King," Lagna laughed "Princess Lalitha is renowned as a great beauty who wears fine dresses and travels in a silver carriage guarded by armoured royal guards. This girl is no great royal beauty. She dresses like a boy and rides with but a few poorly dressed companions... and she sleeps in our barn!"

She continued to chuckle to herself until she looked up and saw the expression on Lalitha's face. Lagna swallowed noisily and started to tremble.

"You cannot be that Lalitha can you, girl?" she asked with a shaking voice.

"Shit!" Tom whispered under his breath.

Lalitha rose from her chair and looked directly at Lagna.

"I am Princess Lalitha Santra, second-born to King Lestri Santra. You should mind your words old woman if you wish to keep your head on your shoulders."

Lagna made a small whimper and sank to her knees before leaning forward to place her forehead on the floor. Sarratil followed suit.

"Forgive us your royal highness," Sarratil moaned from where his face pressed to the floor amongst the debris of broken eggs. "We did not know it was you. Forgive my wife her unwise words."

"Bow before your princess," Lagna almost screamed at her sons.

With a clatter of chairs, the four young men threw themselves to the floor.

Tom, Alex and Jimmy looked at each other in shock. They knew that Lalitha was a member of the royal house, but they had not anticipated a reaction like this.

Lalitha looked down at the family as they prostrated themselves in front of her.

"I travel secretly to Krassak from the south. My identity must be kept secret from all. Do you understand?"

"Yes, your royal highness," they chorused.

"If you do not keep my secret, there will be dire consequences."

"We will say nothing of this your royal highness," Sarratil said as Lagna began to sob.

"Come on, Lalitha," said Tom. "These people are helping us, there's no need to scare them half to death."

Lalitha spun her head to glare at Tom.

"These are my subjects, Thomas McAllister and this woman dares talk to me like I am nothing?" she hissed. "Now they know who I am, they should show me the respect that my position dictates."

"But…" Tom started to say, but Alex kicked Tom under the table and shook her head almost imperceptibly.

"I swear that we will keep your secret, your royal highness," Sarratil pleaded. "Please forgive us and spare us the wrath of the king."

Lalitha walked slowly to the head of the table.

"Stand up," she commanded.

Sarratil climbed to his feet and stood with his head bowed, egg yolk dripping down his face and onto his tunic.

"Listen to me well. As soon as we find a ship in the harbour that can take us, we will leave this place. You will speak of our passing to no-one. If you endanger my journey in any way, you and your family will regret it. We will leave our injured companion with you and you will do whatever is needed to aid his recovery. Once he is able to travel, your son Ramman will accompany him and they will ride to the north to meet us."

"Of course. Of course," Sarratil blurted. "Your man will be well cared for here."

Lalitha stared into the scared man's eyes and then strode out of the house.

Silence fell over the room and it was several seconds before anyone spoke.

"I'll go after her," said Jimmy rushing to the door.

Lagna climbed to her feet, tears running down her face and her husband turned to embrace her.

"I am so sorry, Masters," she cried. "I did not mean to cause offence to the princess."

Tom was at a loss for words over what had just happened.

"She will be fine," Alex said reassuringly. "It has been a difficult journey and Lalitha has been under a lot of pressure. I'm sorry that she took that out on you Lagna. We will talk to her and everything will be fine."

"But our mission does need to be kept secret and you can't talk about us to anybody," Tom added.

"I promise that nothing will be said," Sarratil said.

Not knowing what else to do, Tom and Alex awkwardly thanked Lagna for the breakfast and headed back to the barn.

"We should have just stayed in the barn and Lalitha should have kept covered up. What was I thinking?" Tom muttered.

"You weren't to know that Sarratil would recognise her, Boss."

"It was just careless."

"Well, you've got one thing less to worry about anyway… There's no way we can stay here now after that. Lalitha got her way. We're going to have to leave Sam here and go with her to Gessan."

As they got back to the barn, Lalitha stood talking animatedly to Jimmy. Tom expected Lalitha to be angry and unapproachable, but surprisingly she seemed to be in a much better mood already.

"So, Thomas McAllister… there is no more debate. Sam will stay here and you will accompany me to Gessan at the first opportunity. The people here will not dare speak of me to anyone, so we can safely continue our journey."

Tom and Alex looked at each other as the same idea occurred to them both at the same time.

"Lalitha, did you know that Sarratil would recognise you?" Tom asked suspiciously.

"No, Thomas McAllister. I did not know that he would. I did visit Brentar with my father some years ago and we did parade through the city, but how was I to know that this simple farmer would have seen me?"

"But you realised that there might be a chance that he would recognise you?"

"I understood that there might be a chance, yes."

"And when Sarratil did know who you are, you took the opportunity to scare the shit out of him and his family."

"Yes. It will encourage them to keep our secret."

"That was out of order, Lalitha," said Alex. "These people took us in and helped us and you did that?"

"It protects all of us and means that we can continue our journey," Lalitha snapped.

"But I hadn't decided what to do yet!" Tom yelled.

"Exactly," Lalitha replied. "You could not decide what to do so I made the decision for you. We need to get to Prentak to meet Castra Deman as quickly as we can and this allows us to do that."

"She does have a point, Boss," Jimmy said. "Sam will be safe here. Let him get better while we ride on."

"Unbelievable!" Tom exclaimed shaking his head. "You played me Lalitha."

"I am sorry," she replied, "but you seemed unable to decide what to do. I simply made that decision for you."

"Okay, you win. We can't stay here now with the family scared half out of their wits. Lagna is petrified. The farm would go to shit because Sarratil would be too terrified to leave his wife on her own with us and who knows what Ramman's brothers would do? Jesus, Lalitha!"

Lalitha stared at Tom defiantly.

"The decision is made, Thomas McAllister. We make for Gessan as soon as we can."

Tom started to say something more, but Alex took his hand and started to pull him outside.

"Come on, Tom, let's go for a walk and everyone can calm down."

Tom glanced at Lalitha as they left the barn and saw the smile that spread across her face.

"She played us, Alex."

"I know and I don't like it any more than you do, but Jimmy is right. You can stop tearing yourself apart trying to decide what to do now. Sam can recover in his own time without feeling like he's holding us back. You know what he's like. Sam would've lied about how he felt and got us to travel to Gessan way earlier than he was ready for. If he can catch us up once he's up and about, then so be it, but if he can't then at least he will be safe."

"I know. I just hate abandoning him here."

"Yeah, we will have to leave him here, but we both trust Ramman to look after him, don't we?"

Tom nodded. "Yes… I suppose so."

"So that's it, we're going with her?"

"Yes… I suppose we are."

"Outplayed by a kid. You are losing your touch, Captain McAllister," Alex smiled and kissed him playfully on the cheek.

CHAPTER 32

The Farmstead

Tom avoided Lalitha for the rest of the morning. He was not quite ready to forgive her for how she had engineered the situation to her advantage. Sarratil and his wife avoided all of them, mainly confining their movements to the farmhouse.

To pass the time before Ramman and Danny got back from the city, Tom and Alex sat in the sunshine by the barn and tried to relax as best they could. Before long, both of them had dozed off.

Alex snapped awake as the sound of wagon wheels rattled towards her. She had slept with her head at a strange angle and massaged her stiff neck as she stood up and watched Ramman pull the wagon to a standstill.

Ramman and Danny climbed down from the driver's seat and Ramman rushed round to them.

"We have news from the city," he said breathlessly, "They say that the king is dead!"

Alex looked back at Tom as he rubbed the sleep from his eyes.

"The news was all over the market. There was a coup and the king was killed."

Danny walked over and shrugged his shoulders.

"Ram," Tom said, "we know about the king."

"How do you know? The news has only just reached Brentar."

"Tell him," Alex said, "he's going to find out in about two minutes anyway."

"Tell me what?" Ramman asked.

"Ram, we kept something from you. We know about the death of the king because Lalitha was there. Lalitha is his daughter."

Ramman's jaw dropped open.

"What? Mistress Lalitha is Princess Lalitha? From Krassak?"

"Yes. I'm sorry we didn't tell you earlier, but we had to keep her identity a secret. She was there when her father was killed."

"So that is why she hid her face whenever we met any other travellers. I did not think it was my place to ask why she did this."

"We need to keep Lalitha safe," said Alex. "The man that killed her father is searching for her as well."

"I did not know Mistress Lalitha's face so I did not know it was her. I will not say anything to anyone," Ramman promised, "not even my parents."

"You don't need to worry about that," Tom sighed. "Your parents already know."

"What? How?"

"Things got complicated at breakfast and your father recognised her."

"Jesus, I leave you for a few hours and everythin' goes pear-shaped," Danny exclaimed.

"Things got a bit heated," Alex said, "and I think your family got a bit of a scare Ramman."

"Are they hurt?" he asked worriedly.

"No, but Lalitha did warn them against talking about us to anyone… and the warning was quite harsh."

"I will make sure that they tell no-one," Ramman assured them.

"There's something else," Alex said. "We're going to leave Sam here to recover and carry on our journey with Lalitha. Did you mean what you said yesterday? About coming with Sam to catch us up once he's better?"

"I did, Mistress Alex. I will stay with Master Sam and make sure that he is well. Once he is able to travel, we can meet you. Where is it that you go?"

"We are going to Krassak," Tom said.

"Krassak?" Ramman gasped. "I have never been to the capital. I will gladly journey with Master Sam and try to find you there."

"Lalitha will be able to tell you more about our route, but we will do everything we can to meet you somewhere."

Ramman smiled and nodded. "I will do this for you. Master Sam is my friend and it will be my honour to journey with him. There is no life for me here. That is why I left with Fellorn all those weeks back."

Tom smiled and clasped Ramman's shoulder.

"Thank you, Ram. It makes me feel much better about leaving Sam if I know that you are looking after him."

"I will protect him with my life, Master."

At that moment, Ramman noticed his family. They were stood by the farmhouse door and watched the activity at the barn nervously.

"You'd better go and see your family," Alex suggested. "I think they are too scared to come over here."

Ramman nodded and rushed over to the house, where his mother embraced him warmly.

"What did you find in the city?" Tom asked, turning to Danny.

"Ramman left me at the harbour while he went and bought the supplies. I found a ship there owned by a guy called Namorn who has no cargo at the moment and is willin' to take us. I paid him five silver pieces to hold the ship ready and promised to give him thirty silver pieces when we get to Prentak. I thought we could persuade him to divert to Gessan once we've put to sea."

"What did Ramman do with the supplies?"

"He came back to the harbour with the supplies he bought and Namorn loaded it in his hold for us. I didn't think it would be worth bringin' it all back here to then have to lug it back to the harbour."

"Good plan. When can Namorn be ready to sail?"

"He's ready now," grinned Danny. "We can set off whenever we like."

"I think we've outstayed our welcome here Tom," Alex said. "How about we head off this afternoon?"

"Let me go and check on Sam and if he looks okay, then we'll start getting our stuff together and head out today."

"Okay," agreed Alex. "I'll go and tell the others."

Tom walked in the direction of the farmhouse, but as he got nearer, he heard raised voices coming from inside. Ramman's older brother was shouting loudly.

"How did you not know who she was, you brainless oaf? You travelled with these people for days and you never realised that she was born of that bastard family in Krassak? You are even more retarded than I thought you were."

"Do not speak to your brother in that way Daltran," Lagna yelled.

"Why not? This brother of mine has brains made of shit. Why does he defend the royal bitch? What have her or her degenerate father ever done for us?"

"Be wary how you talk about the king my son," warned Sarratil.

"Why? If he is dead then good riddance to the old bastard."

There was the noise of a scuffle and as Tom entered the room, he saw Ramman and his brother tussling beside the dining table. Chairs were pushed over and Daltran landed a punch to Ramman's jaw. The younger man reeled, but stayed on his feet. Ramman glared at his brother and launched himself at him.

The two men grappled with each other and crockery from the table flew in all directions. Daltran pushed Ramman roughly and head-butted him in the face. Blood streamed from Ramman's nose and he squeezed his eyes shut against the pain.

"You still fight like a child," Daltran mocked. "Perhaps you should let the spoiled royal brat that you ride with fight for you instead? Let me show her what a real Brentar man can do!"

"Stop this!" shouted Sarratil.

The older man tried to move in-between the pair, but he was too slow. Ramman dodged his father's grasp and punched Daltran in the throat. Daltran fell to the floor gagging, but Ramman did not stop. He rained blows down on his older brother's head with his fists and Daltran's face soon became a mask of blood and mucus. He threw his hands in front of his face to defend himself and Ramman paused his attack to scream at him.

"Do not dare to say such things about Lalitha," he roared.

Sarratil and Tom between them managed to grab hold of Ramman's shirt and pull him off his brother before he resumed his attack.

"Okay, Ram," said Tom firmly. "It's okay, I think you made your point."

"I am sick of his constant bullying and of the never-ending bile that spews from his foul mouth. He is the reason I left this farm before and I will gladly leave this place with Master Sam as soon as he is able to travel."

Tom looked down at the gasping, bloodied young man lying on the floor. Daltran spat blood onto the floor and scowled viciously at his brother.

"I will tell everyone I know that your bitch princess was here," Daltran muttered. "Let us see what happens then!"

Tom swiftly unsheathed his knife and held it to Daltran's throat. He brought his face down close to Daltran's and stared into his eyes. The young man went silent and stopped breathing.

"If I thought it wouldn't upset your mother there, I would slit your throat and let you bleed out right here and now, you twisted little fuck," Tom growled. "If I find out that you have told anyone about Lalitha, or if either Ramman or my friend in the bedroom over there come to any harm after I have gone, I will hear of it. If that happens Daltran, I will hunt you down and I will gut you like a pig. Do you understand me?"

Daltran nodded silently and Tom pushed the knife harder against his throat until the sharp edge began to draw blood. The front of Daltran's breeches were suddenly wet and the smell of urine hit Tom's nostrils.

"I said do… you… understand… me?"

"Yes, I understand," he whispered.

Tom slowly took the knife away from Daltran's throat and wiped the blade on the cowering man's tunic. He stood up slowly and re-sheathed his knife.

Daltran picked himself up off the floor and scurried out of the house. Tom watched him as he ran from the room and then turned back to Sarratil.

"Sarratil, you need to control you son. If he talks to anyone about us, I cannot be held responsible for the violence that Lalitha will rain down on you all."

"He will say or do nothing Master. I should have been harder on him for the way he torments his brothers. I apologise for his stupidity."

"So you should. Ramman is a credit to you, but that young idiot is most certainly not. Can I trust that my friend in there will be safe once we have gone?"

"Your friend is a guest in our house and no harm will befall him," Lagna said.

"Good, because if anything happens to him, I promise that you will see me again. I'm going to check on him now and then we are going to collect our things and leave for the city."

Tom went to the bedroom. As he opened the door and walked into the room, a weak voice asked him a question.

"What was all the rumpus out there Boss?"

"Sam! You're awake. How are you feeling?"

"Pretty beat up and absolutely knackered, but better than I was in the back of that bloody cart on the mountain. Where are we Boss?"

"We're at Ramman's parents farm just outside Brentar. We had to get you here to see a doctor. Your leg got infected and you passed out."

Sam looked quickly down at his leg.

"Is it okay? They're not gonna have to…"

"Don't worry mate. It's a lot better than it was. You're okay."

"That's a relief… So, what was going on out there?"

"Basically, Ramman's brother is a bastard. Looks like his father has indulged him for his whole life, so we just had to teach him a bit of humility. I put the fear of God into him, but it might be worth you keeping your Glock under your pillow, just in case the little shit thinks he can take advantage."

"Jesus! Don't worry, Boss, if he tries anything on me, he will know about it."

"Ramman's brother, Daltran, threatened to tell everyone that Lalitha was here. I think I managed to persuade him that it would not be in his best interests to do that, but I don't trust the vindictive little bastard. Keep your eye on him if you can."

"Does he know anything about what we're doing?"

"Yes, he does thanks to Lalitha. She was the cause of most of the drama today. She's pretty much forced our hand into what we do next. I'm sorry to have to do this, but we've got no choice mate. We're going to have to leave you here while your leg heals. We can't risk taking you with us and running the risk of your infection getting worse again."

"Don't worry about it, Boss. I know how keen Lalitha is to get back to Krassak and get the guy who murdered her father. What's your plan?"

"It's all a bit complicated, but the short version is that we're going to get to a ship that Fester found at the harbour in Brentar and get its captain to take us to Gessan. From there, Lalitha says that we have to sail to a city further north called Prentak where her allies will be waiting for us. Then we travel west to the capital and whatever shitstorm waits for us there. Once you've recovered enough to travel safely, you and Ramman can meet us on the road to Krassak somewhere if you're up for it. I feel bad leaving you here Sam, but I just don't see another way around it."

"I totally understand, Boss. Don't sweat it. The last thing I want to do is to hold you back and be a burden."

"You sure?"

"Totally. Assuming this leg of mine sorts itself out, we can try to catch you up before you manage to get yourselves into too much trouble in Krassak."

"Look, Sam I hate to spring this on you, but we're leaving this afternoon. Things got fairly intense here today and I think it would be better for you and Ram's family if we weren't around the farm any longer than is absolutely necessary. Fester's ship is waiting on standby at the harbour in the city, so we're going to get down there as soon as we can. You sure you're okay with that?"

"Yeah, really I am Boss. I get seasick anyway so I'm kinda glad to not have to get on a boat. You go and get packed up. I'll be fine here with Ramman. Just stick your head round my door before you go, yeah?"

"Will do. The lads will be glad to see you awake before we set off."

Tom started towards the door and then had another thought.

"Oh, and Sam?"

"Yes, Boss?"

"If you see maggots crawling out of your bandages… don't worry about it, okay?"

CHAPTER 33

The Farmstead

By the time Tom arrived back at the barn, the horses were tacked up and most of the equipment had been packed into the saddlebags. Alex looked up as he came back in through the door.

"How's Sam?" she asked.

"He's awake and looks a whole heap better. I told him that we were going to leave him here with Ramman and continue on for Gessan and he was okay with it."

"Really?"

"Yes, and to be honest, I get it. If things were the other way around and I was holding the rest of you up, I would be okay with staying behind too."

"I guess you're right. I would probably be the same. Is he going to try and catch us up?"

"Ramman and him are going to come after us as soon as they can. There was a fight in the farmhouse between Ramman and his oldest brother, and Ram is keen to get away from here as soon as he can."

"Is Ram okay?"

"Yeah, it got a bit nasty and I ended up having to get a bit rough with his brother Daltran. He threatened to tell everyone about Lalitha and I had to persuade him that doing that would not be good for his wellbeing."

Lalitha had heard the last of this conversation and headed over worriedly.

"Is Daltran a threat to our quest?" she asked.

"I think he understands what the consequences of opening his mouth would be, and I pushed Sarratil to make sure that he keeps his son under control."

"Good. As long as you are sure?"

"I'm sure enough to not want to do anything else to him if that is what you're suggesting."

Lalitha didn't look entirely satisfied, but nodded her agreement.

"Do you and Alex want to go and see Sam while I pack my kit up?" Tom asked. "You can give him a rough idea of where we're going so that he and Ramman know where to aim for when they come to find us."

"We'll go now," smiled Alex, "I want to see him before we leave."

Alex and Lalitha left to say their goodbyes to Sam and, once Tom had packed his saddlebags and stored his essentials back into his Bergen, he headed over to the farmhouse with Danny and Jimmy.

They all crammed into the little bedroom and said their farewells. Danny put Sam's Bergen by the side of his bed and laid his C8 on the floor beside it.

"We've shared out all the ammo and I've given your rifle a good clean. We've also put a couple of pouches of silver in your pack. When you've had enough lazin' around and decide to come and join in the fun and games, you should have everythin' you need," Danny winked.

"Thanks, Fester."

"Take care, Sam," Jimmy said with a worried look. "Catch up as soon as you can yeah?"

"Will do, Codboy. Don't let Fester get you into too much trouble."

"Get well, Samuel Franklin," Lalitha said, "I regret that we have to leave you here, but there is no other way. Keep safe the map I made for you. It will show you the route that we aim to take, and the places that we will travel through."

"Don't worry, Lalitha. I will definitely keep it safe. I hope things go well at Gessan."

"Sam," Alex said, "we're going to miss you mate. Get better soon and come find us, okay?"

"Course I will, Moony. Just make sure you look after the Boss."

Alex kissed Sam on the forehead and playfully gave him a gentle slap on the top of his head.

"Stay safe, Slaphead."

Sam nodded and his eyes met Tom's.

"I wish there were another way Sam, but we've gotta go."

"I know, Boss," Sam grinned. "Just stop with all the sentimental bollocks and go, will you?"

Tom nodded and smiled at his friend.

"Okay. Just take care and find us as soon as you can."

"You know I will. I'll swoop in and save the day, just you see."

Tom smiled and nodded.

"See you soon Sammy."

The team filed back out of the bedroom and made their way outside. Ramman was waiting for them.

"I will come with you to the harbour," he said, "but then I will return here to care for Master Sam."

"Thanks, Ramman," Tom said, giving his shoulder a squeeze.

Before they left, Tom sought out Sarratil and his wife. He found them feeding the chickens at the far side of the yard.

"Thank you for what you have done for us," he said to them. "This morning was not what I intended and I'm sorry things got so out of hand. I want you to take this."

He placed a pouch of silver coin into Sarratil's hand.

"No, sir," Sarratil protested. "We do not deserve this. My son Daltran has shamed us and my wife insulted the princess."

"Don't worry about that. You looked after us and thanks to you, our friend is still alive. This money is to say thank you and to pay for anything that Sam needs."

"There is too much here," Lagna said, and Sarratil tried to hand the pouch back.

Tom closed Sarratil's fingers around the pouch with his own and gently pushed his hand away.

"It is yours. Keep it."

"Thank you, sir," Sarratil said gratefully.

"Just bear what I said in mind though. Watch Daltran carefully. I do not make idle threats. If he does anything to endanger any of my friends, there will be consequences."

"Do not fear sir," Sarratil nodded. "My son will not step out of line again, I promise you."

Tom nodded and clapped the older man on the shoulder.

Tom turned his head at the sound of hooves and the team pulled up beside them. Alex led Tom's horse as he took the reins from her and climbed up into the saddle.

Ramman was riding one of his father's horses as there was no need to take the wagon with them into the city. As soon as Tom was sat in his saddle, the team turned and headed down the track towards the city.

They rode back along the track past the neighbouring farms and to the gatehouse on the main road. Ramman turned the cart to the left and led them through the great stone archway and into the hustle and bustle of the city of Brentar. Soldiers manned the gatehouse, but didn't seem too interested in Tom and the team.

The streets of the city soon became a chaotic mix of people, animals, carts and carriages all jostling amongst each other. Merchants' stalls lined the sides of the road and hawkers pushed in-between riders and carriages, peddling their wares to anyone who looked like they had a spare coin or two. Soldiers mingled amongst the crowds, watching for the pickpockets and troublemakers that plagued the city streets.

"Nuts, isn't it?" laughed Danny after several minutes of making only slow progress through the throngs. "Ram says it's like this all the time."

The noise was almost deafening. Goats bleating, horses whinnying and stamping their hooves on the road's cobblestones, chickens squawking, stall holders bellowing out the benefits of their wares plus the hubbub and tumult of hundreds of people all talking, shouting and laughing at once.

Lalitha had her scarf wrapped round her face and was gripping the leather bag that contained the Book tightly to her stomach. After the quiet of the road from Lintar, the noise of the city was jarring. Tom began to wonder if he should try to jam his own scarf into his ears to try and deaden the noise.

It took well over an hour to travel the short distance to the harbour that lay in the middle of the city. It would have been even longer had they brought the wagon, but at least they could thread their way through the chaos a little easier on horseback.

"I'm never going to complain about the M25 ever again," Alex joked as she narrowly avoided trampling an old man who led a pig on a length of rope.

The harbour was almost as busy as the city streets had been. Several tall ships were moored against the harbour wall and in-between them small fishing boats landed their baskets of freshly caught fish. Cargoes were being loaded and unloaded from the big ships, and the quayside was full of carts and men with trolleys, rushing backwards and forwards with barrels, crates, bales of cotton and all manner of other merchandise.

Ramman led them almost to the end of the harbour where a two-masted ship called *The Osprey* was tied up. The ship was constructed from a dark mahogany-coloured wood and Tom estimated it at about twenty-five metres in length. The prow of the ship faced them and Tom looked up its imposing figurehead. A naked woman's head and torso had been carefully carved out of the dark wood. Her arms took on the form of a great bird's wings that extended backwards alongside the sides of the ship and her legs ended in vicious looking talons rather than feet. The skilled woodcarver had made it look like the talons were piercing the ships bows as the harpy, if that is what she was, clung to the front of the vessel.

A swarthy looking man with long dark hair and a craggy weathered face leaned on the rail looking down at them as they pulled up next to the gangplank. He took a last long pull on his pipe and then tapped it out over the side of the ship, before spitting a gob of something horrible down into the water.

"I did not expect you to return so soon," he called down. "Wait there. I will come down."

"That's Namorn," Danny announced, "the Captain of *The Osprey*."

They watched as Namorn made his way to the gangplank and bounced down it to meet them. Namorn was a big man in every way. He was tall and well-muscled, but his tunic strained to contain his not inconsiderable waist. A long black beard fell from the man's face and brushed against his chest as he walked.

"Apologies, Namorn," said Danny, "Our circumstances changed and it turns out that we can travel sooner than I thought."

"No skin off my nose," Namorn muttered. "I would sooner be at sea than sitting in this harbour. This place smells of nothing but shit and fish."

"What a lovely turn of phrase our captain has," Alex whispered to Tom with a smile.

"When can we leave?" Tom asked. "Do we have to wait for the tide?"

"The tide is with us," Namorn asked. "We can leave as soon as your possessions are loaded on-board. The wind also blows from the land side this afternoon so, if we are careful, we can sail away from the dock."

"Okay," nodded Tom. "How do we get the horses onto the ship?"

"Horses?" answered Namorn shaking his head. "I already told your friend here that we cannot carry horses. Our hold is too small and even if there were space for the beasts, the hatch is too small to load them through."

"Ah... Sorry," Danny muttered, "I forgot to tell you about the horses. This is the only ship available and it can't take them. We'll have to buy more horses when we get to Prentak."

"Danny, what the hell?" exclaimed Alex.

"Sorry, Moony. I couldn't find a ship that could take them."

"They are just horses," Lalitha said. "We can obtain better mounts when we get to Prentak."

Alex flashed Lalitha a dirty look, but did not say anything.

"So, what do we do with the horses then?" Tom asked.

"Not my problem," Namorn grumbled.

"Danny?"

"I guess I didn't think that part through Boss."

"We can't just leave them here can we?" Alex snapped.

"I could take them for you," Ramman suggested, "but I have no coin to pay you with. I could sell them for you and give you the coin when we next meet."

"You don't have to pay us for them Ramman. We didn't even pay for them ourselves. If you can get them back to the farm, they are yours. Can you get them back there on your own?"

"No, Master, I could perhaps lead two of them, but not four. I can either get someone to help me, or stable some of them here temporarily. Do not worry about that, I can work something out."

Tom rummaged in the pouch on his belt, pulled out a few silver coins and gave them to Ramman.

"Take this and hire some help to take the horses back to your parent's farm. After that you can do what you want with them."

"Are you sure, Master?" Ramman asked.

"Yes. I trust you to look after them well, and you and Sam will need horses later on anyway."

"Thank you," Ramman smiled.

The team spent the next few minutes unfastening their saddles and saddlebags and carrying them up the gangway onto the ship.

Once everything was loaded aboard, the team tied the horses to metal rings mounted to a stone wall nearby and said goodbye to the mounts that had carried them over the mountains.

Jimmy gave his horse a pat on the shoulder and the horse gently butted him with her head.

"We were getting on okay as well," Jimmy said sadly.

Alex stroked her mare's nose as the horse nickered quietly.

"See ya girl. Don't worry, Ram here will take good care of you."

Ramman looked at his friends with sad eyes and the team huddled around him.

Alex gave the young man a big hug.

"Take care, Ram. Come and find us when you can."

"I will, mistress Alex. We will catch up with you as soon as Master Sam is able to travel."

"You look after my horse as well, okay?"

"I will," he smiled.

"Just watch, Sam," Tom warned as he embraced him, "he will probably try to lie to you about how well he is. Make sure he doesn't travel before he is ready."

"I will be careful, Master Tom, I promise."

Danny and Jimmy both hugged Ramman and slapped him affectionately on the back as they parted.

"See you soon, Ramman," Tom called as they walked up the gangway.

"See you soon, Master Tom, and thank you for everything you have done for me."

"You are more than welcome," Tom nodded.

The saddlebags and Bergens were piled neatly on the deck, and the team watched as two of Namorn's crewman pulled up the foresail until it flapped loosely in the wind. The ship's forward moorings were untied and the crew slowly tightened the lines to the foresail. The bow of the ship slowly swung out into the water and the ropes at the rear of the ship were slipped from the capstan on the quayside.

Namorn's crewmen raised the mainsail and heaved on the lines to trim it. The huge sails filled with wind, and *The Osprey* began to move away towards the harbour mouth. The team looked back and waved at Ramman as he watched them sail away.

Namorn somehow managed to guide his ship through the maze of other vessels in the harbour without hitting anything and they were soon out of the harbour and into the open sea.

"I hope Ramman's going to be okay," Alex said.

"He'll be fine," Tom replied.

As they stood at the rail watching Brentar slowly slip away, Tom pulled Alex towards him and pressed his face to her hair.

"Sam and Ramman will be back with us before you know it."

Lalitha was not thinking about what lay behind them, only about what lay ahead. She walked to the bow of the ship to gaze at the expanse of blue sea before them. She closed her eyes and clasped the Book within its bag and breathed in the salty sea air. She felt the sea spray from the waves as they crashed against *The Osprey's* bow, and smiled. They would soon be at Gessan and then everything would change.

CHAPTER 34

Aboard *The Osprey*

The Osprey was actually much more comfortable than Tom had been expecting. He had seen too many movies where the crew was all jammed together on a spider's web of hammocks and below deck was all grimy and smelly.

There was a crew of six on-board, not including Namorn. Namorn had a cabin at the rear and Lalitha claimed the cabin next to his. Tom and Alex were sharing a berth towards the front of the ship opposite the bosun, Allun's cabin. Danny and Jimmy took two of the crew's bunks after bribing two of the crewmen to give up their beds. The crewmen would sleep with the sails and spare ropes in the forepeak compartment. The cabins were all quite small, but were clean and snug. Each contained proper beds with rails on their sides to stop their occupants rolling out should the waters get choppy. Much to Tom's relief, there were no hammocks to be seen anywhere.

There was a small galley behind the hold and the team soon found themselves sitting in there around a large wooden table. The table had a lip running around the edge of it to stop the crockery from smashing on the floor as the ship rose and fell. Tom was thankful that there was nothing to eat on the galley table as they sat there. He was trying his hardest not to think about food. The offshore wind was stirring the sea up and the waves were causing *The Osprey* to roll in the choppy waters. The team were all struggling with the way the movement of the ship made them feel.

"It's a good job Sam didn't come with us," grimaced Jimmy as a particularly large wave caused the ship to rise before crashing down into the water again with a boom. "He would've bloody hated this!"

The others all looked at him. None of them were enjoying this overly. The motion of the ship was making all of them feel a little nauseous.

Namorn burst in through the galley doors and smiled broadly when he saw them all sitting around the table looking queasy.

"What is wrong with you lubberworts?" he laughed. "The sea hardly even moves today."

Nobody said anything and Namorn quickly reached into a nearby food locker and pulled out a fresh leg of meat. He cut off a big piece of fat and tied a length of twine around it.

"Here's how to stop yourself feeling seasick my friends," he declared with a wicked glint in his eye.

"Swallow a lump of fat like this and then use the twine to pull it back up again. Do this at least six times each. The fat lines your gullet and makes it as smooth as a doxy's tinderbox. You can all use the same bit of fat if you like."

The team all looked at each other in horror.

Namorn suddenly took the piece of fat and swallowed it with a loud gulp. He slowly began to pull at the twine that disappeared down his throat and started to make horrendous gagging noises as the lump of pork fat came back up into his mouth. He pulled it back out of his mouth and dangled it in front of Jimmy's face.

"You see how it is done?" he grinned.

Jimmy immediately started to retch. He barged his way past Namorn and scrambled up the companionway and flung himself towards the ship's rail. The rest of the team followed him, eager to get away from Namorn's string of pork fat. As they all got onto the deck, they could hear Namorn's booming laughter from below. Jimmy gripped the rail tightly and breathed deeply as he tried his hardest not to throw up over the side of the ship.

Namorn stomped up the steps behind them.

"Alternatively," he laughed, "you could all just stay on deck until you are accustomed to the motion of *The Osprey* before sitting down there where you can't see the horizon or feel the wind on your face."

He was still chuckling as he took control of the helm from his bosun.

After a few minutes in the fresh air, Jimmy began to feel better and everyone slowly started to get used to the motion of the ship.

By the time the sun began to sink over the horizon, the team all felt confident that they could walk around the deck without stumbling all over the place, or sit below deck without feeling too ill. Just so long as Namorn didn't repeat his pork fat party trick.

One of the crewmen doubled up as the ship's cook, and the little man busied himself cooking dinner over a small wood-fired stove at the back of the galley. He sang to himself quietly as he prepared a hot pork stew which bubbled away as the team gathered around the galley table. As soon as the dinner was served, everyone started to eat, gingerly at first, but then with more enthusiasm. The bowls of steaming meat and vegetables were good. Lalitha was careful to eat only when the cook was not looking and then pull the scarf back into place afterwards.

As they finished eating, Namorn reappeared and the cook passed him his own bowl of stew. Lalitha made sure that her scarf was in place, but Namorn didn't even give her a second look. He lowered himself onto the bench opposite Alex. It was quite a squeeze and Namorn's stomach pressed tightly against the edge of the table. He started to spoon down his food and glanced round at everyone as he ate.

"Where do the rest of the crew eat?" Jimmy asked.

"They would normally eat in here, but as all the space is taken up with you fine folk, Hultin here will take their food to them up on deck," Namorn answered in-between mouthfuls. "It is a fine evening and the men will be happy enough eating up top."

Namorn dripped stew down his beard and wiped it away with his sleeve.

"What takes you people to Prentak?" he asked.

Tom looked at Lalitha and raised his eyebrows. Lalitha nodded back at him.

"Actually, Namorn, now that you mention it, we need to talk to you about that. We need to make a detour on the way to Prentak."

"It will cost you more silver, but that should not be a problem," he shrugged. "Where do we divert to?"

"The Island of Gessan," Tom replied.

Namorn almost choked on his stew and spat half of what he had in his mouth back into his bowl.

"Gessan? Are you all tetched?" he blurted. "It is said that the island is haunted by the ghosts of those long dead and that phantoms drive ships trying to land there onto the rocks. The seas do unnatural things around that place. Winds change direction in an instant and whirlpools appear where they should not."

"We need to get there," Tom said.

"Why?"

"You don't need to know that... Just that we have to go there."

"I will not try to land *The Osprey* there."

"We will be able to land there safely," exclaimed Lalitha. "We are expected."

Namorn raised his eyebrows, but did not look happy. "I will not risk *The Osprey* by trying to land her at Gessan."

"How close can you get us?" Tom asked. "Could get us close enough to the island for us to take your rowboat and make landfall by ourselves?"

"I could, but my tender is worth much to me, plus if you all drown trying to get to that cursed island, who will pay me the silver you owe?"

"We could pay you the thirty silver for passage to Prentak now," Danny said, putting a coin pouch on the table. "Plus, if you lend us your rowboat and wait for us until we've done what we need to do on the island, we'll give you another thirty silver when we get to Prentak."

Namorn smiled broadly and looked Danny in the eye. "Forty silver now and forty when we arrive at Prentak."

"Thirty-five now and another thirty-five when we get to Prentak."

"Deal!" roared Namorn and banged his fists on the table. "We will celebrate our newfound friendship with drink!"

"Hultin," he roared. "Bring us glasses and a bottle of Medur."

The cook brought a large, brown earthenware bottle and six glasses, placed them on the table and grinned as he left the galley. Namorn used his blackened teeth to pull the cork from the bottle and then poured a huge measure of clear, strong smelling liquid into each glass.

Namorn pushed the glasses into the middle of the table, grabbed one of them and held it in the air.

"May your pintle never lose it vigour," he cried and swallowed the liquid in one gulp.

The team looked at each other and everyone picked up a glass. Tom sniffed carefully at his. It smelled sweet and very alcoholic.

"Bottoms up!" said Alex and tipped the glass back. The spirit burned at her throat and she coughed as it went down.

"Not too bad," she grinned.

Tom, Danny and Jimmy all downed their drinks as quickly as they could. All three of them pulled faces as the evil-tasting liquid set their tongues ablaze.

"Holy crap!" gasped Danny. "That is worse than Alex's moonshine!"

Lalitha looked suspiciously at her glass and put it back down on the table without even trying it.

"Ha, your mysterious woman friend here does not like my Medur. I am not surprised… it is too much for a woman to take."

Alex raised her eyebrows at Namorn, leant over, picked up Lalitha's glass and downed the contents.

"What was that you were saying about women, Namorn?" Alex said as she pushed the empty glass across the table at him. "Fill it up. Oh, and you're one behind me now."

Namorn laughed his booming laugh, poured himself another massive measure of spirit and drank it. He wiped his mouth and refilled all the glasses.

He lifted his glass again and stared at Alex.

"May your paps never droop!" he shouted and poured the drink down his throat.

Alex stared right back at him.

"May your belly never fall below your belt," she said before drinking the liquid down.

Tom, Danny and Jimmy all sipped gingerly at their glasses. Namorn was focused on Alex's face so while nobody was looking, all three of them tipped the rest of their glasses out under the table.

"Ha. I like you, woman," Namorn roared. "Another!"

Namorn filled all the glasses again and picked his up. Before he could think of another toast, Alex picked up her glass and drank the contents. She then rapidly did the same with Tom's glass, Jimmy's glass and Danny's glass.

"I've got a bit of a thirst on tonight," she said smiling at Namorn. "Come on, Namorn… drink up."

Namorn looked at Alex with an open mouth, but then drank his own glass down before filling three more glasses and drinking them all, one after the other. He now started to look a bit uncertain about the way things were going.

"You should slow down a little," he warned. "Medur is a strong old mariners' spirit. It is not wise to drink too much of it too swiftly."

Alex stretched over and picked up the bottle. She refilled her own glass and poured an equal measure into Namorn's. She knocked it back and set the glass gently back down on the table.

"You whine like a girl, Namorn. It's your turn I believe."

Namorn hesitated, but then drank down his latest measure of Medur.

"Where did you learn to drink woman?" he asked.

"In the army. I used to distil my own vodka from potatoes. It was not as sweet as this, but had a similar kick to it."

"In the army?" Namorn mused. "Since when do they let women to join the army? Were you a cook?"

Tom caught Danny's eye and they both grimaced.

"A cook?" Alex spluttered. "I was a specialised field technician, not a bloody cook you fat misogynist!"

"Ha," laughed Namorn. "you entertain me greatly you tetched warrior wench."

"Stop playing for time, Namorn," Alex chided. "Come on... Less talking, more drinking."

Alex refilled their glasses, quickly gulped hers down and stared at Namorn with a smile on her face.

"What are you waiting for big man?"

Namorn, belched loudly and hesitated before picking up his glass. He held the clear liquid in front of his eyes and gazed at it uncertainly.

"Down it," Alex grinned.

Namorn took a deep breath, tilted the glass to his lips and then swallowed the sweet spirit.

"Another?" Alex asked. "I'm having one so I think you should too."

She poured yet another glass and threw it back. Namorn was beginning to look visibly unwell. He raised his glass and slowly drank it down. His face had begun to take on a distinct green tinge.

"One last shot for the road?" Alex asked.

"I... am not shure that is shuch a good idea..."

"Come on, Namorn, you can't be outdone by a woman, can you?"

The bottle was almost empty, so Alex split the remaining liquor between two glasses. She picked hers up and cheerfully drank it down in one.

Namorn lifted his glass, but as it reached his mouth, he abruptly pulled himself to his feet and staggered out of the galley. They heard the distinct sound of retching as he struggled to get up the steps and to the ship's rail.

"Ha," laughed Danny. "I knew he was gonna regret that 'women can't drink' comment and as for accusing Alex of being a cook... well, that was just suicidal!"

Alex grinned and winked at him.

A few moments later, Namorn staggered back in and crashed back down on the bench, traces of vomit clearly visible in his beard.

"You are a very impresshive woman," he slurred. "Are you shpoken for?"

"Yes, I am," Alex laughed. "Talking of which... I think were done here so I'm going to call it a night."

Alex stood up, picked up Namorn's last glass of Medur and drank it down before turning to grab Tom by the hand. She pulled him to his feet and dragged him towards their cabin.

"Come in here, Thomas McAllister. There is something I have been wanting to do to you for a very long time."

As she flung the cabin door open, Alex undid her trousers and pulled them down slightly, exposing the top of her thong before pushing her butt back into Tom's crotch suggestively. He gaped mutely at her, and Alex laughed loudly, dragged him into the cabin and slammed the door closed behind them.

As Danny and Jimmy gaped at each other, Namorn's head hit the table with a loud bang and he started to snore loudly.

CHAPTER 35

Sailing to Gessan

They saw little of Namorn the next morning as he tried to sleep off the after-effects of the Medur. The crew busied themselves around the ship making sure that *The Osprey's* progress was as fast and efficient as they could make it. Sails were trimmed and Allun the bosun steered them onwards towards Gessan. Alex, however felt no after effects from the previous night's drinking and was very chirpy indeed despite her lack of sleep.

"I am traumatised after last night," Danny complained as they ate meat and bread for lunch on the deck of the ship. "I kept gettin' woken up and I couldn't work out of it was the waves makin' all that noise or if it was you two!"

Tom had sat in the sunshine near the bow of the ship with Alex all morning with a grin permanently fixed to his face. He could not believe the direction his life had taken in such a short time. Only a matter of weeks ago he had felt alone and depressed in a grotty flat in west London, and now here he was, in another land God-knows-where, fighting off bandits on his way to help a princess reclaim her throne from an evil villain… and on top of that it turns out that the woman that had meant everything to him for such a long time loved him and had done things to him last night that he didn't even realise were physically possible.

He looked at Alex and realised that she was watching him. His smile broadened even further and he pulled her close and kissed her.

"For Jesus' sake you two… you're puttin' me off my lunch," Danny moaned.

Tom and Alex both burst into a fit of the giggles.

They were still laughing when Namorn's head appeared above deck as he climbed slowly up the companionway from his cabin. He walked carefully to the ship's wheel and spoke to the Allun before making his way forwards to where the team were sitting.

He looked at Alex's smiling face with incredulity and rubbed his bloodshot eyes with the palms of his hands.

"Remind me to never… ever share my liquor with this woman again," he groaned. "Her capacity for strong drink is like none I have ever seen before. You have my utmost respect lady."

Alex stood and performed a mock curtsey for him. "Why, thank you, captain."

Namorn laughed and gave her a mock bow. "Anyway, I did not drag my carcass over here just to trade pleasantries with you dullswifts. I came to tell you that we make good speed and if the wind continues to blow as it does, we should arrive at Gessan shortly after mid-day tomorrow."

"Thanks, Namorn," Danny said.

"I will now return to my bed," announced Namorn with a grimace. "I do not suppose I could tempt you to join me lady?"

"I think not, Namorn," Alex laughed.

Namorn shrugged and shuffled back below deck, massaging his forehead as he went. Danny stood up and headed after him.

"I'm gonna go and check on Lalitha and Jimmy," he announced.

Lalitha had been in her cabin all day. Jimmy had gone down there earlier, but neither of them had re-appeared yet.

Tom leant back against the side of the ship and looked upwards. The sky was blue and the wind was filling the huge brown sails. He closed his eyes and listened to the seabirds calling in the distance. The only other noises he could hear were the crashing of waves against the prow of the ship and the muted singing of the cook below deck.

"What are you thinking?" asked Alex.

"I'm wondering how strong spirits just do not affect you in the same way as everyone else," Tom smiled.

"It must be my genetics coupled with a fast metabolism and years of practice," she grinned. "Seriously though, what're you really thinking about?"

Tom looked at her. "I'm thinking that I would rather this voyage were longer. I don't really want to get to where we're going. I just want to sit here in the sun with you."

Alex smiled. "That would be nice wouldn't it. I can't think of anything I'd like better, but unfortunately, we've got a job to do. Have you got any clues from Lalitha about what happens when we get to Gessan?."

"She hasn't said much about it at all. She told me that we should be able to land on the island safely because we have the Book with us, but what happens after that I have no idea. I'm not even sure that she knows."

"Not worth worrying about it now then. Let's just enjoy the sunshine and relax while we can."

Tom took her hand in his and rested his head back against the wooden side of the ship. He could feel the sea through the wood as *The Osprey* surged through the waves. He closed his eyes as he listened to the sea around them and the sun warmed his face. It would indeed be nice if the voyage were longer.

The rest of the day passed by in much the same way. Tom and Alex sat together talking and laughing while the crew busied themselves around the ship. The wind was still blowing consistently from the south-west and *The Osprey* made good time as it ran northwards with the wind.

By late afternoon, Lalitha, Jimmy and Danny had eventually reappeared and the whole team gathered in the galley to eat dinner. The cook had made another stew, but this time it featured chicken rather than pork. He left the large cooking pot full of food on the table for them and went above deck with a small bowl for Namorn who was at the helm.

"Are you ready for tomorrow, Lalitha?" Alex asked as she spooned stew into each of their bowls.

Lalitha nodded her head. "Everything will change when we get to Gessan. I am excited that I will eventually be Bound with the Book."

"What about you, Danny?" asked Alex.

"My life changes tomorrow Moony. I won't be a nobody from a council estate in Southwark any longer. I'll be powerful and important. I'll be a prince!"

"But you'll be committing yourself to the Book… no questions asked."

"C'mon, Alex? What have I got to lose?"

"Other than your immortal soul… errr… nothing I suppose."

Danny grinned. "Do you really believe all that stuff about your soul going to heaven or hell?"

"I don't really know what I believe, Danny," Alex replied, "I do know that I believe that we have a soul of some sort, but I have no idea what happens to it when we die. I'm just pretty sure that I wouldn't want my soul ending up in a magic book."

"It'll be fine, just you wait and see."

Lalitha looked at Danny and smiled. "Once you are Bound, you will stand by my side as we re-instate my family to its rightful place. I will command the power of the

Book and Gask and his followers will be defeated."

"I thought as much," said a voice at the galley door.

Namorn put his head around the doorway and stared at Lalitha. Her scarf dangled loosely around her neck and her face was in plain sight.

"No need to hide your face any more, Princess Lalitha."

Tom's hand went to the holster on his belt. He quietly unclipped the leather flap and rested his hand on his pistol's grip. Namorn moved towards them and frowned.

"You should have told me earlier who you were rather than carrying on with this cheap deception."

"Namorn… don't move any closer," Tom warned.

Namorn glanced at Tom and stopped his advance towards Lalitha.

"There is no need for concern," Namorn said. "I am not a threat to you, I simply wish to offer condolences to the princess," Namorn said. "I heard about the death of the king whilst we moored in Brentar. The rumours say that he was killed by a usurper. The son of Nestor Gaskkalt by all accounts."

"Findo Gask. He is a traitor," Lalitha spat. "He longs for power and murdered my father to get it. He would do the same to me if given another chance. How do you know me?"

Lalitha gripped her leather bag tightly and Tom heard the whispering start.

"Other than just hearing you reveal yourself?" he laughed. "Before I captained *The Osprey*, I worked as a crewman on many ships. One of those vessels was the Royal Lestri…. your father's flagship. When you sailed to Brentar to intimidate the people with your beautiful clothes and shiny armoured guards on your last trip to Prentak, I was on-board. I spent many days watching you as you stood with your father, all regal in your finery. Your eyes are not those which are easily forgotten Lady."

"I do not remember you, Namorn."

"You would have little reason to remember me, Lady. I was a lowly crewman and you would not have looked twice at me. I did not have my beard then and neither did I have so much padding around my guts. The past few years have been good to me."

"We need to keep our journey secret, Namorn," Alex said. "If Findo Gask finds out where Lalitha is, she will be in danger."

"I had no love of Nestor Gaskkalt and the unrest he created in Lintar in the past, but equally I am no great royalist. Many people despised the king for the way that he ruled over us, but I had no quarrel with him. Your father's laws were strict and punishments were harsh, but this suited me well enough. For a while, the sea's around

Zakastra were treacherous and vessels like *The Osprey* were not safe. Barbarians sailed here from the east and raided many ships for their cargoes, but when your father learned of the raids, he ended them by burning any barbarian ship that he encountered. The barbarian crews were burned alive with the ships. Harsh, but effective. The king sent messages to the barbarians over the eastern ocean and told them that any ships seen approaching the shores of Zakastra would be destroyed and their crews killed without exception. The raids soon stopped after that."

"My father made the seas around our realm safe to travel again."

"That he did my Lady… that he did."

"What is your intention, Namorn?" Lalitha asked.

Namorn shrugged. "I will take you to Gessan and then on to Prentak as I agreed. I have no desire to throw away easily earned silver."

"Can we trust you to keep Lalitha's identity secret?" asked Alex.

"You can. Nestor Gaskkalt was deluded and would have made a poor ruler. If his son is anything like his father, then the same will be true of him. If we have a weak indecisive king on the throne of Zakastra, I fear the barbarians will return and *The Osprey* will not be able to sail freely around these shores. I will keep your secret as long as is needed."

Tom breathed a sigh of relief and took his hand off his pistol.

"Thank you, Namorn, we appreciate your help."

"I simply help myself," Namorn grinned. "If Princess Lalitha's bid to claim the throne is successful, there will be no more need for secrecy. I can let it be known that I aided you all in your quest and that *The Osprey* was the ship that made it possible. My fame will allow me to raise my fees accordingly. However, if you fail and this Gask fellow takes power, I will need to keep the fact that I helped you very secret indeed."

Lalitha frowned. "You need not worry, Namorn. That will not happen."

"For your sake, let us hope that this proves true my friends," Namorn chuckled.

"Do you want to celebrate our alliance with a drink, Namorn," Alex teased.

"No Lady, I do not," chuckled Namorn. "I do not make the same mistake twice. I suggest that you all go to your bunks and sleep. I do not know what business you have on that cursed island, but if it is important to your quest, then you will all need to have your wits about you when you land there."

The team agreed and everyone gradually made their way to their cabins.

"What do you think tomorrow will bring?" Alex asked Tom as they settled down.

"I don't know," he replied. "I just hope that there are no nasty surprises in store."

CHAPTER 36

Sailing to Gessan

The weather the next morning was sunny and warm, but as Tom looked out over the bows of the ship, he could see a fog bank lying low over the water in the distance.

"That is where Gessan lies," Namorn informed him. "No matter how strong the wind, that mist never moves. Something other than nature holds it there."

"You're not making me feel all that happy about this, Namorn," Tom muttered.

"Nor should you be. That island is not a place to be taken lightly. There are captains who will take supplies to whoever lives on that rock, but they never talk about what they have seen there. I have no desire to discover what it is that takes place on that rock."

"Do not fear, Namorn. We will be allowed to land there. The order of holy men that live there are expecting me," Lalitha assured him.

Namorn sucked air through his teeth noisily and headed back to the ship's wheel. "I hope you are correct, my Lady… for all our sakes."

Nobody could relax for the rest of that morning and the team remained at the front of the ship watching as the fog bank ahead drew nearer and nearer. The Book had begun to whisper and the closer to Gessan they got, the more incessant the whispering became.

The team forced themselves to eat something, but it was hard to think straight with the whispering voices in their heads. As *The Osprey* approached the edge of the mist, Namorn ordered his crew to drop the sails and the ship slowed to a halt. The anchor was dropped with a deafening rattle of chains and the crewmen lowered the rowing boat that had been upside down on the deck down into the sea. A rope ladder was thrown over the side and they all climbed carefully down into the small boat that was being tossed around by the waves.

"Is this thing safe?" Danny asked as a wave caused the rowboat to crash against *The Osprey's* side.

"Be careful, friends," Namorn shouted down to them as he pulled the rope ladder back up. "We will stay at anchor for three days. After that we will assume you lost and will return to Brentar."

"Thanks, Namorn," Tom shouted back. "We'll see you as soon as we can."

Danny pushed them off and Alex and Jimmy unshipped the oars and began to row towards the fog bank. Lalitha sat in the bow of the boat and the mist began to envelope her. She turned to look back at *The Osprey* and Tom saw the fires ignite in her eyes. The whispering voices filled their ears and a bright glow began to emanate from Lalitha's bag.

Lalitha whipped round to stare into the haze in front of them and the Book's voice boomed from her lips.

"BREVAL!"

The mist began to pulse as if it had a life of its own and suddenly a tunnel of clear air appeared. Danny took the oars from Alex and he and Jimmy rowed as hard as they could to propel the boat through the swirling tunnel towards the daylight at the other end. As they got about halfway through it, a huge whirlpool suddenly opened up in front of them and the rowboat lurched as it was pulled towards it. Everyone grabbed hold of the boat's sides and held on as the whirlpool began to drag them in.

"Do somethin'!" Danny yelled.

Lalitha glared at him, her eyes a mass of dancing orange flame. The boat spun and pitched forwards dangerously towards the spinning chasm of water. As the boat began to tip down into the void, Tom stared down into the bottomless rotating cascade of water and the pit of his stomach churned. They were going in.

"TELLAS!" Lalitha suddenly yelled in the Book's voice.

The whirlpool immediately closed and the small boat was thrown upwards in a plume of water before it crashed back down onto the sea's surface. Freezing cold water flew everywhere and Tom rubbed his eyes, desperately trying to get the stinging saltwater out of them.

"Jesus," breathed Danny. "That was a bit too close for comfort!"

The boat carried the momentum the whirlpool had given it and the team found themselves floating slowly out of the fog. They could see the sky again and the warm sun shone down. In front of the boat there was a rocky island that jutted dramatically up out of the sea. On the peak of the island they could make out a large building with minarets and a large glass dome.

Danny and Jimmy put their oars back in the water and rowed the boat towards a stone jetty that they could see extending from the cliffs out into the water. Strangely, there were no waves this side of the fog and the boat slipped easily through the water until they touched the jetty with a gentle bump. Everyone suddenly heard the voice of the Book in their heads.

"The magi approach."

It was only then that Tom noticed that an old man in a hooded blue cloak stood on the jetty watching them. The man lowered his hood and stared carefully at Lalitha. He had a bald head and a short grey beard. His left hand was gripped tightly around a long silver staff.

"Welcome to Gessan," the old man announced as he reached down and offered Lalitha his hand.

Lalitha took the man's hand and stepped up on to the jetty. The stranger bowed his head and then turned to help Danny. He again bowed his head and then spun on his heel and walked quickly towards a set of steps that were cut into the cliff face.

"Follow me," he called.

"I guess we don't qualify for the helping hand then," Alex commented as Tom helped her up onto the jetty.

Tom stepped onto the stone landing after her and Jimmy followed them. They tied the boat's painter to a metal ring set into the rock and hurried to catch up with the others as they started to climb the steps. Jimmy almost fell off the jetty as they rushed along it. The ground still felt like it was moving after being on *The Osprey* for two days and Alex had to grab the back of his tunic as the young man struggled with his balance.

The stone staircase climbed up and up towards the building they had seen from the boat. By the time they reached a set of big iron gates at the top of the steps, their legs had got used to being back on dry land, but Tom's thighs burned with the effort of the climb. He had started to count the steps as they ascended to take his mind off the effort of the climb, but had lost count somewhere after two hundred and eighty.

The old man touched his staff to the gates and they swung open silently. The team followed him along a smooth path cut through the rock until they arrived at a huge studded wooden door. The man beat on the door with his staff and the door opened inwards, the hinges letting out a low moaning creak.

They walked inside. The entrance hall was dark and the walls were lined with torches that burned brightly, casting their flickering light around the ceiling. The high ceiling was supported by great stone arches which featured many gargoyle-like faces carved into the stone. The flickering torchlight made it look like the eerie faces were laughing at them.

Stood halfway down the hall was a group of men wearing long hooded cloaks identical to the one the old man wore. Each man stood quietly, their hoods pulled up and their heads bowed.

The old man walked towards the group but then turned to face Lalitha and the team. He brought the lower end of his staff down on the floor with a boom that echoed around the hall.

"Welcome to those that the Book has Chosen. Step forwards Chosen ones."

Lalitha confidently took a stride towards them and Danny, after a quick glance over his shoulder, stepped forwards to stand next to her.

"I am Rellik, head of the Order of Magi that reside within these halls. These are my brothers who guard our ancient library and serve the one Great Book."

Each member of the group standing behind Rellik beat the tips of their staffs on the stone floor.

"Those who are Chosen… make yourselves known to us."

Lalitha held her head up and spoke in a loud clear voice.

"I am Lalitha Santra of Krassak, daughter of King Lestri Santra. I am Chosen."

Taking her lead, Danny gathered his nerve and stood to attention as he spoke.

"I am Daniel Adams of… errr… Southwark and I am Chosen."

"Present the Book to us," Rellik commanded.

Lalitha opened up her leather bag and pulled out the Book. The Soulstone blazed brightly and Rellik walked towards her.

"Give me the Book, child," he said.

Lalitha hesitated, but then placed the Book into Rellik's open hands. As the Book touched his skin, Rellik took a sharp intake of breath and the whole hall was filled with the echoes of whispers.

"Is it just me, or is this all a bit too creepy?" Alex muttered under her breath.

Rellik looked up sharply and Alex clamped her mouth tightly shut and looked down at the floor.

"The Book has spoken to me," Rellik announced. "It demands that Lalitha Santra and Daniel Adams undergo the Ceremony of Binding in order to pledge their immortal souls and commit unwavering loyalty to it."

He held the Book up and the light from the Soulstone illuminated the hall.

"Do you who are Chosen willingly submit to the will of the Book and agree to undertake the Ceremony."

"I do," said Lalitha and Danny in unison.

Rellik drummed his staff on the floor again.

"So be it. You will be taken from here and prepared for the Ceremony of Binding. The Ceremony will be carried out as dawn breaks upon the new day. Until then, my brethren will take you and prepare you for what comes next."

Two of the hooded figures moved forwards and led Lalitha and Danny away through a side door. Rellik looked back at Tom, Alex and Jimmy.

"You will be taken to quarters within the east wing of the library where you must stay until it is time for the Ceremony to begin. Brother Treson will show you the way."

The old man gestured with his arm and another one of the hooded magi came forwards and stood in front of them. He lowered his hood and looked at each of them in turn. The pale skin of his bald head shone in the torchlight. He had a short, dark beard, but the main thing that caught Tom's attention were the man's eyes. They were a striking deep blue colour.

"My name is Treson, I will show you to your quarters."

He walked towards the back of the hall and the three remaining team members followed him obediently. Rellik watched closely as they filed past him, but said nothing more.

Treson opened one of the large double doors in front of them and ushered them through. The room that they walked into took their breath away.

Tom stood in awe as he looked up into the huge glass dome that soared above him. Walkways wound their way around the walls of the vast circular room and from these walkways led corridors that were lined with shelves neatly stacked with books. Thousands of books.

Statues of kings and magi were dotted around the perimeter of the room and huge tapestries hung on the walls depicting battles and great deeds of the past. Light flooded down from the immense glass dome above them illuminating intricate designs that had been carefully inlaid into the floor's surface.

"This is the Great Magi Library," Treson told him. "Gathered here are the histories of our realm and the teachings of all the great scholars and magi through the centuries."

They watched as figures in simple brown robes flitted around the walkways and shelves. Some placed books back in place while others collected books and scuttled away with them. Nobody spoke and the only thing that could be heard was the quiet slap of their sandals against the stone floor.

"The men that you see are our stewards. They bring books to us in our chambers when we need them and replace them after our work is done. Do not talk to them as they cannot answer. Their tongues are removed when they arrive here. If they were to ever leave this place, they must be unable to divulge any of the secrets of our Order."

Alex glanced at Tom, but didn't say anything. Jimmy just stared up at the cavernous dome and watched the clouds drift overhead through the huge glass panels.

"This is where our Order keep the histories of the realm and the secrets of our order," Treson announced. "Over the centuries, we have been entrusted with documenting the happenings within Zakastra. We gather information from a variety of sources and compile the books of history you see before you. Everything is catalogued and stored here within the library."

Tom looked around at the vast multitude of bookshelves and marvelled at the extent of the historical records that must reside here.

"We can learn much from what has preceded us," Treson continued. "We can make sense of the present by looking at what has happened in the past and by referring to the teachings of scholars and the magi of old. On occasion, we even consult the ancient prophecies in order to better understand present events and the outcomes that they may bring about."

"Prophecies?" asked Tom.

Treson blinked his eyes and hesitated as if he had said too much.

"And of course, the Great Magus himself presides over the Ceremony of Binding," he spluttered, eager to change the conversation. "Only he knows the secret incantations that are used to Bind the Souls of the Chosen to the Great Book. All the Chosen must travel here so that the Grand Magus can bestow the honour and glory of Binding upon them."

Several of the stewards were furtively looking at the strangers and Treson suddenly became keen to move on.

"We need to go," he announced hurriedly. "This way please."

Treson guided them across the open expanse of smooth stone under the dome and took them through another set of doors to the right. They followed a corridor lined with rooms and went up a flight of stairs. They passed another line of doors until Treson stopped and unlocked one of them with a small metal key.

"These are your quarters," he told them. "Food and water will be brought to you.

Please do not try to leave as it is forbidden for you to roam this place unattended."

"Don't worry," Tom assured him. "We won't go anywhere."

Treson nodded and, once the three of them were inside, closed the door behind them. They heard him put the key into the lock and there was an audible click as he locked the door shut.

"He's locked us in," exclaimed Jimmy.

"At least we won't be tempted to go and look around the place," shrugged Tom. "Not that I would want to go walkabout and see something that I shouldn't. I'm quite attached to my tongue."

"I really don't like this place," said Alex. "It feels like something out of a Stephen King movie. I half expected a guy with horns to jump out at us."

"I know what you mean," Jimmy nodded. "It is creepy as hell. Do you think Lalitha and Fester are going to be okay?"

"They're the guests of honour," Tom assured him. "I don't think we need to worry about them too much."

"Not until dawn tomorrow anyway," Alex said. "Who knows what happens then."

They looked around their quarters. There were three beds against the wall and a bathroom through an alcove. Alex took a quick look at the toilet and pulled a disgusted face. It consisted of a wooden seat with a lid that concealed a hole disappearing down to who-knows-where. Alex quickly dropped the lid back down and tried to not think about what she had just seen down there.

"Better than going behind a tree I guess," she muttered, "but not much."

There was a large window in the wall opposite the beds and the three of them stood looking outwards over the rocky coastline and down over the cliffs to the white cloud that enveloped the island.

"Which way is that? Is *The Osprey* out there somewhere?" asked Jimmy.

"I think it's that way, but it all looks pretty much the same doesn't it?" answered Tom.

"I'm thinking we might not have come here very well-prepared Boss," Alex said. "We left pretty much everything on the ship."

It was true, they had left their rifles, Bergens and most of their kit on *The Osprey* thinking that they were going to be on friendly ground when they got to Gessan. This didn't feel anything like friendly.

Tom patted the pistol in his belt holster and felt a little better that at least they had their handguns.

"According to Lalitha, these magi characters are on our side so we should have nothing to worry about," he said.

"If this is how treat their friends, I'm really glad we're not their enemies."

Alex flopped down onto one of the beds and put her hands behind her head.

"What're we going to do?"

"There's nothing we can do until tomorrow morning I guess," Tom replied.

"What do you think is happening to Lalitha and Danny?" Jimmy wondered aloud.

"I don't know Jimmy," Tom answered. "I really don't know."

The monotony of the day was only briefly interrupted when Treson brought them a large jug of water and food. After he set everything down on the windowsill, Treson headed straight back to the door.

"What is happening to our friends?" Jimmy demanded.

Treson paused and looked back at them.

"The Chosen are being prepared for the Ceremony tomorrow. They learn about what the Ceremony of Binding entails and also about how being Bound will change them. They begin to accept that they must leave their selfish ways behind and henceforth strive to work in the interests of the Book before their own. I must go now and attend to my other duties."

Treson rushed out of the room and locked the door behind him.

"Strive to work in the interests of the Book before their own?" echoed Alex. "I really don't like what Danny is getting himself into here."

Tom agreed. He had a bad feeling in the pit of his stomach that being Bound was not going to be as cushy as Danny believed.

They all settled back on their beds and tried to rest as best they could, but it was difficult to not worry about what sunrise would bring.

As the sun went down and the room fell into darkness, Treson appeared once again and brought a handful of candles with him. He placed the candles around the room and placed a new jug of water on the windowsill. He turned as he picked up the empty jug.

"I will wake you before sunrise so that you are able to witness the Ceremony."

CHAPTER 37

The Isle of Gessan

Tom had a restless night. Every time he fell asleep, he ended up dreaming about hooded figures chasing him and an old woman who kept trying to cut his tongue out. It was almost a relief when their door creaked open in the darkness and Treson walked in carrying a lantern.

"The Ceremony will begin soon. Prepare yourselves and I will return to get you shortly."

As he left, Tom, Alex and Jimmy dragged themselves out of bed and forced themselves to use the bathroom, horrible though the experience was. They drank some water and used what remained in the jug to have the briefest of candlelit washes. They gathered their things together and sat on their beds waiting for Treson to reappear.

It was not long before a key ratted in the lock and Treson swung their door open again.

"Follow me," he whispered.

They followed the light of Treson's lantern down the hallways and back into the main domed library. Instead of turning left towards the entrance hall, they turned to the right and passed through another set of strong wooden doors.

Tom, Alex and Jimmy found themselves outside, high above the sea on a semi-circular terrace that jutted out over the rocky cliffs. Across the middle of the terrace was a long stone table which stood about three feet from the floor. The table was covered in intricate lettering that looked like some kind of ancient Viking runes.

Tom started to worry that what he was looking at resembled what he imagined a sacrificial altar would look like.

Around the terrace's perimeter ran a stone parapet and about thirty magi were assembled along the low wall, their heads bowed.

Treson ushered Tom, Alex and Jimmy to the side of the doorway and hastily took his position with the other magi against the parapet.

Tom could see a light coming from back inside the library and Rellik appeared through the doorway. Danny and Lalitha followed closely behind him. Rellik held the Book above his head and the Soulstone burned with its intense orange light. The whisper of the souls was almost deafening. As they made their way towards the stone table, the wooden doors boomed closed, making Tom and Alex jump.

Neither Lalitha nor Danny looked in Tom's direction as they followed Rellik. They both wore plain brown robes and their bare feet made no sound as they walked over the cold stone terrace.

As Rellik reached the table he stopped and placed the Book carefully down on the centre of its stone surface. The whispering seemed to quieten slightly as Rellik turned to face the magi around the perimeter of the terrace.

"We are assembled here to witness the Binding of these two Chosen. They pledge their souls to the one Great Book and commit their lives to its interests and protection."

Rellik raised his arms and looked up to the sky.

"Assembled brothers of the ancient magi order, do you agree to witness the Binding of these Souls?"

"We do," the magi chanted in unison.

"Do you confirm that you pledge your allegiance to the one Great Book?"

"We do," they chanted again.

Rellik lowered his arms and turned back to the carved stone table. He placed his hands on either side of the Book and looked up at Lalitha and Danny.

"The Book has chosen these two souls and it is our duty to Bind them to it."

He fixed his eyes on Lalitha and placed his right hand on the Book. The Soulstone shone brightly through his fingers and the voices of the Souls increased in volume as if they were calling out to the two Chosen.

"Lalitha Santra, do you freely pledge your soul to the one Great Book?"

"I do," said Lalitha.

"Do you promise to forsake your own bodily interests in lieu of those of the Book?"

"I do," she replied.

"Do you commit to be guided by the One Great Book and the fallen that dwell forever in the Soulstone?"

"I do," Lalitha confirmed.

Rellik turned his gaze to Danny and asked the same questions again.

"Daniel Adams, do you freely pledge your soul to the one Great Book?"

"I do," Danny replied.

"Do you promise to forsake your own bodily interests in lieu of those of the Book?"

"I do," he said.

"Do you commit to be guided by the One Great Book and the fallen that dwell forever in the Soulstone?"

"I do," Danny said again.

Rellik bowed his head, took his hand from the Book and slowly walked around to the front of the table. The sun was just starting to appear over the clouds surrounding the island and Tom squinted as the bright rays of sunlight dazzled him.

The magi at each end of the assembly walked forwards and stood in front of each of the Chosen. Rellik raised his arms and the two magi quickly pulled the robes from Lalitha and Danny's bodies. Tom heard Jimmy gasp as the two figures stood naked in front of them.

"Chosen," Rellik commanded, "take your positions."

Danny and Lalitha both swung themselves up onto opposite ends of the stone table and lay down on their backs with their heads almost touching the Book. The Soulstone seemed to burn even more brightly and the whispering ramped up in volume again. Alex put her fingers in her ears to try and cut out some of the noise, but it didn't really help. Tom began to pray that his friend wasn't about to be sacrificed to the Book. Surely that was not going to happen was it?

Rellik leaned forwards and placed his hands on the foreheads of the two Chosen. He started to chant quietly. Tom could not make out any of the words that he muttered. These must be the secret incantations that Treson spoke about.

Tom tried to see Danny's face to make sure that he was okay, but Rellick's outstretched arms blocked his line of sight. He considered moving to get a better view, but discounted the idea quickly. He didn't want to risk getting in the way of the Ceremony and causing something to go wrong.

The other magi began to join in with the chanting and Tom realised that the same words were being repeated over and over again.

"Althea fel solis luri tel nimtul Soliston."

The chanting continued for several minutes. As the sun rose higher above the horizon, Rellik's voice became louder and louder until it was booming the incantations across the terrace and out over the cliffs below them. Tom could not understand any of the words and guessed that it was the language of the Book that Rellik was speaking. Whatever the language was, it didn't really matter now because the voices emanating from the Book itself had risen to such a volume that they drowned out everything else.

Alex reached for Tom and she gave him a worried glance as their hands clasped together tightly. The hairs on Tom's arms were all standing on end and he could feel crackles of static electricity against his skin.

As the sun broke free of the horizon and its full power shone over the terrace, Rellik's head suddenly snapped back and the voice of the Book boomed from his open mouth.

"AKTHA!"

Orange lightning leapt from the Soulstone into Rellik's chest and he roared as the energy ran down his arms and into the Chosen. Both Lalitha and Danny screamed and their backs arched up from the table. Rellik kept tight hold of each of their heads and the energy crackled and snapped loudly as it flowed between them.

Jimmy made to move towards Lalitha, but Alex grabbed him and held him back. Whatever was happening, it was too late to stop it now.

With a loud crackling noise, the lightning suddenly raced back up Rellik's arms and was pulled back into the Soulstone from his chest. The stone went dark and the whispering instantly stopped. Silence fell on the terrace.

Rellik took a deep breath and looked at each of the naked bodies lying on the table in front of them.

"The Ceremony of Binding is completed. Your Souls are now Bound to the Great Book. Consider well the pledges that have been made here this day. Leave this place and work to strengthen and protect the Great Book and the Fallen Souls that live on within the Soulstone."

Danny and Lalitha both looked dazed, but they managed to slowly sit up and swing their legs down to the floor. The magi rushed forwards with their robes and, once covered up, the two Chosen slowly followed Rellik back inside. The magi walked in a line behind them and all but one of them disappeared into the library. The last remaining magus, Treson, came over to the three friends, a big smile on his face.

"Do you not feel honoured?" he beamed. "There are few non-magi that have ever witnessed this ceremony."

"Errr, yes, I guess so," stuttered Tom who was just hugely relieved that the ceremony had not involved long curved knives and blood-loss.

Jimmy, however, was very much in shock after what he had just witnessed.

"Come on Jimmy," Alex said as she put her arm round him. "Let's go and see if we can talk to Lalitha and Danny, just to make sure that they're both okay."

Jimmy nodded mutely and they let Treson guide them inside. There was no sign of Danny or Lalitha, but Rellik saw them enter the huge room and made has way over.

"Companions of the Chosen," he smiled, "it is a great day. It has been many years since the last Chosen was Bound to the Great Book. King Lestri's first-born was chosen, but never travelled here to Gessan to complete the Ceremony of Binding. It gladdens me to see that his second-born recognises the duty that her family must fulfil."

"Has word reached you here that the king is dead?" Tom asked.

"Of course. I know most of what happens in this realm, Thomas McAllister. We received a message three days ago informing us of the king's death."

"Did you know that he was in danger?"

"We heard rumours of unrest in the capital, but there was nothing that we could do. It is many years since the magi have involved themselves directly in the dealings of Zakastra. We live a simple life on this island in exile with our books. We watch, we record and we learn. We do not interfere. It is best for us all that these ways continue. If we were to openly leave this island, the outcome could be dangerous for us all."

"How do you write your history books if you don't go to the mainland?" Jimmy asked.

"We have our ways," Rellik answered cryptically.

Seeing that Rellik was not going to say anything else on the matter, Alex jumped in quickly.

"Are our friends okay?" asked Alex. "Did the Ceremony hurt them?"

"No, they are well, Alexandra Aluko. It will take them a little while to recover from the exertions of the Ceremony, but then they will soon return and you can continue on your quest."

"Will they need to rest here overnight?"

"No, Lady, why should they need to rest overnight?" Rellik replied. "They are newly strengthened, not weakened. Immeasurable power flowed through them during the Ceremony and they just need a little time for the energy to dissipate from their physical bodies."

Wanting to answer no more questions, Rellik shepherded Tom, Alex and Jimmy through the library and back to the entrance hall where a table had been laid with food and drink.

"Eat and drink your fill before you leave us. As soon as the Chosen are ready, they will join you here. Treson will stay with you to ensure that you do not wander the halls alone."

Rellik abruptly spun on his heels and left the hall, tapping his staff on the floor as he went.

The door boomed closed, and Tom, Alex and Jimmy were left alone with Treson in the huge hall. A table laden with food had been set up halfway down the hall. There were wooden bowls filled with fruit, cold pastries, meats and some sort of chopped vegetables. None of them were particularly hungry, but as the wait for their friends dragged on, they stood and picked at some of the fruit.

"We grow our own fruit and vegetables in gardens on the roof above the sleeping quarters," Treson told them. "We also have pigs for meat and goats for milk. We are blessed that we need little contact with the outside world to continue to carry out our work here."

"Why do you keep yourselves apart from everyone on this island?" Alex asked. "Why all the secrecy?"

"Most of the people of Zakastra now believe the magi to be a thing of myth. Our presence on the mainland was curtailed long ago following the Magi War. The war was brutal and took a great toll on the realm. As a result of what happened, ordinary people no longer trusted our order, so the Grand Magus agreed that we should be exiled here; partly for our own protection and partly to protect the people from us. We now have little contact with anyone. Supplies are shipped here but a few times a year and the traders that deliver them to us are never allowed to set foot on the island. The only non-magi that are permitted to enter the library are our stewards and the Chosen who come here to be Bound."

"Other than ourselves?" Tom queried.

"Yes, your admittance was allowed as you accompanied the Chosen who were to be Bound. That circumstance arises very rarely indeed."

"How long is it since the last Binding Ceremony took place?" Tom asked.

"The last Ceremony was for King Lestri and was many years ago. Prince Relfa was supposed to be Bound, but as you know, that did not happen."

"Why was he never Bound?" Jimmy asked.

"Lalitha's brother Relfa is weak," sighed Treson. "The young fool lacked the courage to make the journey despite being Chosen. He became enamoured with the politics of the royal court and shunned his responsibility as a Chosen. King Lestri had arranged to bring Relfa here himself to complete the Ceremony of Binding, but alas the king was murdered before they could begin the journey. Relfa continually disappointed his father and it is a tragedy that the king could not have lived to see at least one of his children have the strength to carry out their duty."

"Treson," Alex interrupted, "you said that Relfa IS weak. He died with his father, didn't he?"

"No. He is not dead. Not according to our associates in Krassak. He was seen alive after the king's death."

"But Lalitha saw her brother covered in blood," Alex said. "If he isn't dead, what happened? Was he wounded? Is he a prisoner now?"

"Nobody seems to know the fate of Prince Relfa. I assume that the traitor who murdered the king has him locked in a dark dungeon somewhere. We have heard nothing to make us think that he was injured, but our associates were not in the tower when the king was killed, so I cannot tell you exactly what happened."

Alex glanced quickly at Tom and then started to toy with the fruit again.

"What about the king's wife Treson? Do you know what happened to her?"

"Tella Santra? What happened was treacherous and immoral. What Findo Gask did fills me with disgust."

"What happened, Treson?"

Treson opened his mouth to reply, but at that moment a door opened and Danny and Lalitha walked into the room. Both were dressed in their own clothes again and both of them looked well.

Treson rushed over to the two Chosen, and Alex's chance to find out more about Tella Santra's fate was lost. Instead she went with Tom and Jimmy as they all hurried over to greet their friends.

"Danny, are you okay?" she asked. "That ceremony was kinda freaky."

"I'm good, Alex. Better than good. I feel great," he laughed.

"Lalitha?"

"I too feel well, Alexandra Aluko. I feel like my body is full of power. It is exhilarating."

She clutched her leather bag and it was obvious to them all that the Book lay safely inside again.

"I'm famished," Danny announced as he saw the table laden with food. He rushed over and hungrily started to chew on the savoury pastries and cold meat.

Jimmy moved to Lalitha's side and his eyes welled up.

"Did they hurt you, Lalitha?"

"Of course not, James Lang. They filled me full of light. I feel unleashed… unbound… I feel powerful!"

"I was worried about you… I felt for you when they… well… when they took your… your robe…"

"You mean when you saw her naked?" laughed Danny from where he stood, his mouth half full of pork and pastry.

Jimmy blushed deeply.

"Leave him alone, Fester," Alex chided. "Tom had to hold Jimmy back. I thought he was going to attack the magi when they pulled her robe off."

"Why would you wish to attack the magi?" Lalitha asked sharply. "The Ceremony opened my soul to the Book. It was what I wanted. You were concerned because I was naked? Did my body offend you, James Lang?"

"Of course not… I mean… I'm sorry, Lalitha… I just… well I was scared."

"He doesn't understand, Lalitha," Danny said, "and he never will. The gift that we have been given is beyond his comprehension."

Danny took Lalitha's hand in his own and grinned at her.

"We are Bound."

Jimmy scowled darkly at Danny and stalked off to the other side of the hall where he sat down on the floor. He glowered back in their direction and angrily bit at his fingernails.

"Lalitha," Alex said, "the magi think that your brother is alive."

"Rellik told me," she replied. "He was seen alive, but his whereabouts are unknown. It could be that Gask has either imprisoned him or executed him later. I suspect that we will not find out until we reach Krassak."

"Can you not just ask the Book about him?"

"It does not work like that, Thomas McAllister. The Book does not always answer my questions, it simply tells me what it thinks I need to know. I have tried to consult the Souls about my brother, but they refuse to answer me. I do not know whether this is because they cannot determine whether he is alive or not, or if instead the Book does not feel obliged to let them answer my questions."

"If he is alive," asked Tom, "will he become the new king?"

"No. I have been Bound and my brother has not. That makes me the next in line to the throne. If he were to agree to be Bound then things might be different, but he has always refused to do so up to now and has always implied that he never wishes to rule.

He is too weak to be king."

"So, we work on the assumption that your brother is out of the picture and the plan stays as it was. We get you to Krassak and you take the throne once the Book is back on its altar."

"Yes," Lalitha nodded. "If my brother still lives after this, then we will work out what to do with him then."

Tom nodded and Lalitha turned to whisper to Danny. Treson watched the two carefully as they leaned their heads together to talk.

"I'm going to go and make sure Jimmy is okay," Alex said quietly to Tom and then headed over to where the young man was sitting. As she walked across the hall, Rellik appeared through a doorway and strode over to the newly Bound couple.

"My fellow magi tell me that you are recovered from the Ceremony and there have been no adverse effects. As this is the case, you may leave whenever you are ready your royal highness. I wish you luck with what lies ahead of you. It is imperative to both the Great Book and our order here on Gessan that your quest is successful. The people need a proper ruler. One born to power, not some common deceiver from the south who seeks to disrupt the proper way of things, or a weak cowering wretch who has neither the strength nor courage to do what needs to be done."

"Thank you, Rellik," smiled Lalitha. "I will return the Book to its seat of power and I will take my place upon my father's throne."

"That is good to hear. The Great Book is ultimately all that matters, but I would be glad to see you crowned as Queen. Keep the Book safe and keep it secret until you reach Krassak. Since the initial reports of the king's death, we have heard nothing from the capital. We do not know what your journey holds in store for you."

"I will keep the Book safe, Grand Magus. You can trust me."

"You can trust… us," added Danny firmly.

"You must both do what you have to in order to keep the Book safe."

"Rellik," Lalitha asked, "when I last saw Gask, he had a hooded stranger with him. The stranger made to take the Book from me and the Book did not react to protect itself. How can that be?"

Rellik looked troubled. "I do not know."

"Could it be that one of your magi has joined Gask? I thought that the magi confined themselves to this island."

Rellik licked his lips and his eyes could not meet Lalitha's.

"Your father dictated that the magi may not leave this island. We would be foolish to disobey the orders of the king."

"So, the man I saw was not a magus from Gessan."

"He was not."

"Rellik, I want you to put your hand on the Book and swear that what you say is the truth. I would not recommend lying to me."

Rellik watched Lalitha with a guarded expression as she drew the Book from her bag and held it out. Rellik placed his hand onto the leather cover and stared into Lalitha's eyes.

"I swear that the hooded stranger that you saw was not a magus from this island."

"He tells the truth," the Book whispered in Lalitha's head.

"Thank you, Rellik," she said out loud. "I apologise for having to test your word. What you say is true. The stranger I saw is not of this Order."

"Do not worry, your royal highness," breathed Rellik, a relieved look on his face. "I would do the same if our roles were reversed."

Lalitha nodded and turned to Tom.

"Very well. Let us make haste, Thomas McAllister. We should return to *The Osprey* and set sail for Prentak as quickly as we can."

Tom looked at the others, and everyone nodded their agreement.

Danny crammed as much food as he could fit into his pockets and pulled at Jimmy's tunic as he walked past him.

"Come on Coddy, you'll be keen to get back to your bunk and think about what you saw this mornin' won't you?"

Jimmy slapped Danny's hand away from him and stormed off towards the door.

"The sooner we get off this island, the happier I will be," Alex whispered as they walked towards the exit.

The magi pulled the large door open for them and the team headed for the staircase back down to the jetty. Danny looked back as they passed through the iron gates and Rellik held up his staff.

"Travel well Daniel Adams," Rellik called. "There will come a time when your commitment to the Book will be tested. Do not fail it."

Danny nodded his head and raised his hand in farewell. The magus gripped his staff, walked back inside the building and the door swung shut behind him.

The descent back down the steps was significantly easier than the climb up them had been. In only a few short minutes, they were back in the rowboat and heading towards the cloud bank that separated them from *The Osprey*.

Lalitha excitedly clutched her leather bag, and focused her mind. The sparks flared in her eyes and she uttered a single word.

"Breval!"

The command came in her own voice, rather than the voice of the Book, but the outcome was the same. A swirling tunnel opened through the mist and they saw *The Osprey* in the open sea beyond the fog bank.

Lalitha looked at Danny excitedly.

"It worked, Daniel Adams. I summoned the power of the Souls and they answered. The path opened through the mist. I can do it!"

Danny smiled. The Ceremony at Gessan had indeed changed everything.

CHAPTER 38

Back on The Osprey

Namorn seemed genuinely pleased to see them as the rowboat pulled up alongside *The Osprey*.

"Welcome back, my friends," he called down to them. "I am glad that the phantoms on that island did not kill you."

He threw the rope ladder down to them and two of the crewmen dropped ropes with hooks at the end that they hooked into rings at either end of the boat. Jimmy quickly scrambled up the ladder and climbed over the rail. Lalitha followed him and Alex went next. Namorn was keen to help Alex swing her leg over the rail and grinned a wide, black-toothed grin at her as she stood beside him on his deck.

"I am glad to see you back, Lady."

"Strangely, Namorn, I am glad to be back," Alex grinned.

Tom struggled to climb the rope ladder. His prosthetic was dangerously low on charge and he couldn't use that arm to pull up on anyway. Tom's only option was to slowly make his way up towards the rail, hooking his right arm through the ladder and carefully stepping up one rung at a time. As he was about halfway up, a particularly large wave caught *The Osprey* and the ship listed to the right. The ladder swung and Tom lost his footing. He grabbed desperately at the rope, but he couldn't get his feet back into the swinging ladder and he fell. As a reflex, he grabbed out with his left arm and gripped one of the rungs, but rather than slow his fall, all that happened was that his prosthetic was ripped off.

Tom landed back in the rowboat with a bang. He hadn't fallen far and nothing was broken, but it wasn't the physical hurt that Tom cared about. Namorn looked down to see what the commotion was and his eyes almost popped out of his head when he saw

Tom's left arm dangling from a rung halfway up the ladder. He looked down at Tom in the rowboat and back to the arm in horror.

"What has happened?" he shouted. "Your arm!"

Danny climbed nimbly up the ladder and freed Tom's prosthetic before carrying on up to the deck of *The Osprey*. As he climbed over the rail, he waved the arm under Namorn's face.

"What have you done, Namorn? Look, your ladder has pulled the Boss's arm off!"

Namorn's face was ashen and he gaped at the arm in Danny's hand.

"Ignore him, Namorn," Alex said despairingly. "Tom lost his arm in an accident years ago. That one is not real."

Tom's head appeared over the rail and Alex helped him to clamber over. Tom snatched his arm back from Danny and quickly went down below decks.

"Don't worry, Namorn, he'll be fine," Alex said as she followed Tom.

Danny chuckled at the look on Namorn's face and stood back to allow the crewmen to pull the rowboat up the side of the ship and over the rail. Once the rowboat was onboard, they turned it over and lashed it back down to the deck. Danny sat down on the deck next to the rail and proceeded to eat some of the food from Gessan that he had crammed in his pockets. Most of it had been crushed by the trip back in the boat, but it still tasted good.

Below deck, Alex went to their cabin and did her best to try to cheer Tom up, but it was not an easy job. Tom lay back on the bunk and covered his face with the crook of his right arm.

"Are you okay, Tom?" Alex asked him gently. "You didn't hurt yourself when you fell, did you?"

"I'm fine," he said quietly. "I just need a few minutes. Go and see how the others are doing and I'll come up in a while."

"You sure?"

"Yeah, really, Alex. I just need a minute or two."

Alex kissed him on the tip of his elbow and walked softly out of the cabin. She made her way back up onto the deck where Danny and Lalitha were looking back at the fog-shrouded island. As she joined them, there was a loud rattling from the front of the ship as the crew raised the anchor. The sails were raised and *The Osprey* slowly moved away.

"Is he alright?" asked Danny.

"Yeah, I think his pride is hurt more than anything," Alex sighed. "That damn arm sometimes causes as many problems as it solves. Day-to-day living when he is by himself is fine, but when something like that happens around other people, it hurts him. He feels ashamed that he can't do what everyone else can and the humiliation eats him up."

Danny nodded. "It's not easy, is it?"

"No, Fester, it most definitely is not."

Lalitha looked at them both thoughtfully and walked off towards the front of ship, holding her leather bag tightly in her left hand.

"How do you feel about the whole being Bound thing now Danny?" Alex asked once Lalitha was out of earshot.

"I felt full of power back on the island, but now I feel kinda back to normal again. It's a weird feelin'. I can feel that I've changed, but without the Book in my hands, I can't do anythin' with the ability I've been given. Lalitha keeps the thing clutched to her chest all the time and I can't get anywhere near it."

"So, the power only works if you're in contact with the Book?"

"Yeah, you have to be touchin' it in order to channel the power of the Souls. That's what Rellik told us."

"Ask her nicely… she might let you have a go," Alex grinned.

Danny grimaced. "I doubt it. I think I'm goin' to be playin' for the reserves for a while."

"Don't worry about it mate. I'm sure you two will suss out a way of working together."

"We'll see I guess."

Seabirds flew noisily overhead and they watched them as they flew westwards towards the mainland.

"Where did Jimmy scoot off to?" Alex asked.

"I think he's down in the cabin sulkin'."

"Don't be a git, Danny. You know he's got a thing for Lalitha. He was mortified when those magi whipped her robes off."

"I wish I could've seen his face," Danny laughed. "It must've been a picture."

"You are just cruel," Alex chided, slapping him on the shoulder.

"Seriously though Moony. I think I'm goin' to have to have a little man-to-man with that boy. He can't really think that he's in with a shout there can he? I mean… she's goin' to be the Queen before very long and he stacks supermarket shelves for livin'. It's not goin' to happen is it?"

"No, you're probably right, but I think I'd be better talking to him rather than you.

You're not renowned for your tact and diplomacy."

"Fair enough," Danny grinned.

"I'll just have to pick my moment carefully," Alex said thoughtfully.

Danny frowned and looked towards where Lalitha stood.

"I can hear the Book," he said.

Alex could just make out faint whispers on the periphery of her hearing, but Danny obviously heard it more clearly. Lalitha looked in their direction and the whispering stopped. They saw her take a deep breath as she started to walk towards them.

"I think I can do something to help Thomas McAllister," Lalitha announced. "Can I go to your cabin to talk to him?"

"Of course you can, Lalitha. Just give him a knock before you go in in case he has nodded off."

Lalitha smiled and headed off below decks.

"I wonder what that is all about?" Danny mused.

Lalitha walked through the galley and moved forwards through the ship until she reached Tom's cabin. She knocked gently on the door and heard Tom's voice call out from inside.

"Come in," he said.

Lalitha opened the door and walked in. The bed took up most of the floor in the cabin and the remaining space was taken up with Bergens, rifles and saddlebags. Tom sat up on the edge of the bed self-consciously. His arm lay on the saddlebags at the foot of the bed where it was plugged into the solar charger.

"Sorry, Lalitha, my arm was out of power and I had to put it on charge."

"You do not need to apologise to me. Your arm is the reason that I wanted to talk to you."

Tom's face fell.

"You don't think that I am able to help you any longer do you? Seeing me fall off that ladder has shown you what a liability I am."

Lalitha looked confused.

"That is far from the truth, Thomas McAllister. You have proven yourself to be a valuable ally. No, I think I can help you with your arm."

Tom frowned. "In what way?"

"Now that I am Bound, I can ask the Souls to help me. With your permission, I would like to try something."

"Okay," Tom said hesitantly.

"Is it possible to remove the power source from inside your arm?"

"Yes," he nodded.

"Show me."

Tom hesitated, unsure as to where this was going, but then picked up his arm, unplugged the charger and reached inside the socket that normally encompassed his stump. He popped open a compartment and after a few seconds of fiddling, extracted the long flat NiMh battery. He held the battery up to show Lalitha.

"This is the battery that powers the arm."

"Can you put your arm back on now?"

"I can, but it won't do anything without the battery."

"Do it anyway, Thomas McAllister."

Tom shrugged and inserted his arm back inside the prosthetic. It was significantly lighter without the weight of the battery inside, but none of the motor controls would function without the power source.

"Do you trust me, Thomas McAllister?"

"Errr… yes of course I do, Lalitha."

"Then close your eyes."

As Tom shut his eyes, the last thing he saw was Lalitha pulling the Book from its leather bag. The Soulstone was pulsing with orange light and the voices started their familiar unintelligible whispering.

Tom felt Lalitha take his arm in her hands and he could hear her breathing speed up. The bed started to tremble and Tom was not sure if Lalitha or the Book was the source of the vibration. The voices were getting louder, and Lalitha suddenly took a sharp intake of air and uttered a single word.

"Maldra!"

An intense heat began to build in Tom's left arm and it continued to get hotter and hotter until it became almost unbearable.

Up on deck Danny looked up sharply as he heard the voices in his head getting louder.

"Alex, something is happening down there. Lalitha is channelling the Souls."

There was a sudden scream from below them. It was Tom's voice.

Alex raced for the companionway with Danny close behind her. They both climbed down as quickly as they could and ran to the forward cabins, banging past the galley table as they went.

Alex burst through the door of their cabin and saw Lalitha and Tom sitting on the edge of the bed. Tom had tears streaming down his face and he was holding Lalitha in a tight embrace.

"Tom, what happened?" Alex blurted. "Are you okay?"

"My arm… Alex… my arm…"

Alex looked at the bed and saw the battery lying there.

"Has something happened to the battery? Did it overheat?"

Tom looked into her eyes and smiled. He raised his left arm and wiggled his fingers.

"Look! I can move my fingers!"

"I can see that."

"But Alex look… the battery isn't even in!"

Alex's eyes flicked to the battery on the bed and then shot back to Tom's tear-streaked face.

"Tom?"

"Alex, Lalitha's done something. She's made my prosthetic part of me. I… I can feel things through it!"

Tom gently pulled himself away from Lalitha, stood up and stumbled towards Alex. He raised his left arm and cupped Alex's face in his palm.

"I can feel you Alex…"

Tears welled up in Alex's eyes.

"How is that possible?"

"I channelled the Souls and used their power to join the arm to Thomas' body," Lalitha said. "The arm is not flesh, but it is now part of him and will carry the sensation of touch through it."

Alex's tears spilled down her cheeks. She hugged Tom tightly and looked at Lalitha over his shoulder.

"Lalitha, if this is real, you have no idea what a big deal this is. I… I cannot even put into words what this means."

Lalitha smiled, but looked tired all of a sudden. Her eyes were heavy and her posture was more slumped than usual.

"Are you okay?" Alex asked worriedly. "You look shattered."

"I did not realise how tiring it would be to channel the Souls in this way. I think I will need to rest for a while."

Jimmy had appeared at the door to see what all the commotion was, and as Lalitha stumbled towards the door, he pushed past Danny and put his arm around her.

"I'll help you to your cabin, Lalitha," he said eagerly.

"Do you want me to look after the Book while you sleep?" Danny offered.

"No, Daniel Adams. I will keep the Book by my side."

Danny shrugged his shoulders nonchalantly, but the look on his face betrayed his feigned indifference.

"Don't keep treating me like a lapdog, Lalitha," he muttered under his breath. "I am Bound too."

Danny briefly watched Jimmy as he helped Lalitha towards the rear of the ship, but then spun on his heel and walked in the opposite direction, mumbling to himself as he went.

Left alone in their cabin, Alex and Tom clung to each other. Tom could not believe that the nightmare could be over. Could it really be that he was whole again?

Tom pulled away from Alex and his face was alive with excitement as he tried different movements with his arm. He flexed his fingers, plucked the battery from the bed and gripped it tightly. He tossed the battery across onto the saddlebags on the other side of the room and rotated his wrist before pushing against the cabin door with his hand flat against the wooden surface. He could feel the texture of the wooden door through his fingertips and the sensation was exhilarating. He pushed hard with his fingers and door slammed shut with a loud bang.

"Alex, grab my hand," he said breathlessly as he spun to face her.

Alex took his left hand in hers and grinned. "Now what?"

Tom took a deep breath.

"Pull!"

"Are you sure?"

"I'm sure. Really. Pull me."

Alex pulled at Tom's arm, gently at first, but then with more force. Tom set his feet on the floor and leaned back as Alex gradually began to pull with all her weight. The arm stayed firmly attached and Tom managed to pull against Alex with more force than he had been able to use since before the accident. With a sudden burst of strength, he jerked Alex towards him and they both fell back onto the bed.

"Jesus Alex, she's really done it. I've got my arm back!"

"Let's see what you can do with it then," she grinned wickedly as she straddled him and planted a passionate kiss on his lips.

CHAPTER 39

Sailing to Prentak

The next three days passed in a blur. Tom was like a kid at Christmas who had received everything they had ever wanted on their wish list. He became an unofficial member of the crew and helped raise and lower the sails, repair a rope that had become frayed in the rigging, took turns steering the ship and even helped carry supplies from the hold to the galley when the cook needed more ingredients. He relished every job that meant he could use his new arm.

Alex smiled as she watched him rushing around the ship. It warmed her heart to see him so happy and so eager to involve himself in the running of *The Osprey*.

Namorn walked over to stand next to Alex.

"Has your man been sucking on Elrood leaves?" he asked with smile. "He acts like a man possessed."

"His arm is better since Lalitha helped him."

"Ah, yes the Princess and her magic book. To be honest, Lady, that Book scares me. It is said that her father used the power held inside such a Book to subdue the uprising in the south that Nestor Gaskkalt instigated. There were rumours of some brutal things being done down there."

"But the king stopped the uprising, didn't he?" she said. "It seems to me that the means justified the ends."

"You could be right, Lady. The king was capable of great violence, but it seemed to have the desired effect. He proved with the quelling of the Gaskkalt uprising and later on with the destruction of the barbarian ships that his violence could bring stability to the realm. If the methods proved successful, who am I to question them?"

"I think that the Book is capable of doing good things as well as bad things. Look at

Tom's arm… I haven't seen him looking so happy and positive for years."

"Aye, Lady, the young princess does seem to have helped your man. I just hope there is not a price to pay for it. I do not know what witchcraft that Book contains but I would rather not be beholden to it myself."

Alex's smile faded a little as she considered Namorn's words, but she soon forgot them as Tom came up to her and kissed her on the forehead.

"Will we get to Prentak tomorrow, Namorn?" Tom asked.

"Aye, we should arrive there by mid-morning. I will hopefully find a cargo to take back to Brentar that does not involve secret quests and disguised royal princesses. I am getting far too old for such intrigue."

Tom grinned and looked out to sea. The mainland was a dark smudge on the horizon, but would become easier to see the longer they sailed into the afternoon. Tomorrow morning, they would be close to the eastern coast of Zakastra as they approached the port of Prentak.

As Tom squinted out over the sea, he noticed something floating in the water nearby.

"What's that?" he asked.

Namorn pulled the spyglass from his belt and extended it before putting the end of it to his eye.

"It is but wreckage of some kind. Nothing you need worry about."

"Excellent," grinned Tom. "I'll be back in a minute, Alex."

He rushed off below deck and returned a couple of minutes later carrying his C8.

"I want to just see if I can shoot any better now my arm works properly," he smiled, "and that lump of wood out there looks like ideal target practice to me."

"Okay, just remember that we only have a finite amount of ammo," she reminded him.

Tom nodded and flashed her a smile.

"What is this contraption?" Namorn asked.

"It is a Colt C8 close quarter combat assault rifle," Tom replied.

He checked to make sure that the rifle's chamber was empty and then removed the magazine from the bottom of the weapon. He pushed the bullets down in the clip and gave it a tap on the ship's rail before inserting it back into the gun. Tom pulled the cocking lever and pushed the fire selector switch to semi-auto before steadying himself and taking a deep breath.

"It looks like it has a spyglass on it. What exactly does this Colt thing do?" Namorn asked.

"I'll show you," Tom said with a grin. "Put your fingers in your ears, Namorn."

"What? Why do I need to put my fingers in my ears?"

In one fluid move, Tom raised the rifle, squinted through its scope and fired two quick shots at the floating debris. The gun boomed and bucked in his hands, but Tom's left hand held firmly onto the rifle's foregrip and both bullets hit their mark. Chunks of wood exploded from the floating debris and two empty brass shell casings bounced noisily onto *The Osprey's* wooden deck.

"Scitte!" exclaimed Namorn as his ears rang from the proximity of the gunshots.

"Nice shooting, Boss," Alex grinned.

"You people are devils," laughed Namorn. "What other witchcraft do you have on my ship?"

Tom laughed and made his C8 safe before slinging it over his shoulder.

"That felt good," he chuckled. "I haven't felt that steady on a shot since… well, since before the accident. I could feel the rifle properly again."

Alex kissed him on the cheek.

Danny and Jimmy both came rushing over with worried looks on their faces.

"What's goin' on?" Danny asked.

"I just wanted to see how my aim was," Tom said, "so I used a bit of floating junk as target practice."

"Thank God for that. I thought you were shootin' at someone," Danny sighed.

"How was it?" Jimmy asked.

"Two out of two. Centre mass from a moving ship. That'll do for me."

Jimmy nodded his approval.

"Bout time you learned how to hit what you're aimin' at," joked Danny.

"Don't annoy me, Fester," laughed Tom. "You wouldn't believe how hard I can punch with my left hand now!"

"You people are all insane," Namorn mumbled and wandered back off below deck.

Lalitha looked over from where she sat in her usual place in the bow of the ship. It had taken her a couple of hours to recover after using the Book to fix Tom's arm and, since then, she had not tried to use the Power of the Souls again, despite Danny's almost constant cajoling for her to do so.

"Lalitha," Danny called over, "can I hold the Book?"

Lalitha stood and walked over to where they were gathered.

"It is not a toy, Daniel Adams. What do you intend?"

"I need to see if I can channel the Souls. You haven't let me try yet and I thought this might be a good time to see if I can do it."

"I am not sure if it is a good idea. You do not know what you are doing."

"So, show me."

"He might have a point, Lalitha," added Tom. "If Danny has to use the Book for some reason on our journey, then it is probably a good idea that he has at least some idea what to do."

Lalitha looked sceptical, but pulled the Book from her bag.

"I will keep hold of the Book as well in case something goes wrong, but I admit that it is probably time that you tried to channel the Souls."

Danny's eyes lit up.

Lalitha took his hand in hers.

"I will place your hand on the Book, Daniel Adams, and you will feel it's power start to flow into you. You must concentrate your focus on what you want the Souls to do for you. Be careful what you focus on. I do not want you to accidentally sink our ship. The Book will sense your intentions and if it permits your request, it will tell you the word of summoning that must be used to achieve your objective. Utter the word and the Souls will do your bidding."

"Okay," Danny said. "Let's do it!"

Lalitha placed Danny's hand on the Book alongside her own and the Soulstone leapt to life. Everyone could hear the whispering start and Danny shook slightly as the fiery sparks appeared in his eyes. He looked over the rail at the floating wooden debris and reached out with his free hand. He took a couple of long breaths and then in a clear voice said a single word.

"Brul!"

The floating wreckage suddenly shot up out of the water in a huge plume of spray. It flew several hundred metres up into the clear afternoon sky and hovered there momentarily before plummeting back down into the ocean with an enormous splash.

"Yes!" Danny shouted loudly. "I can do it!"

Lalitha smiled thinly and took his hand off the Book. As Danny's hand parted from the leather cover, his legs buckled and he almost fell.

"Enough frivolity," Lalitha said sharply. "You have proved that you have the capacity to call the Souls, so now I will put the Book away. You see now that calling the Souls takes much energy from your body."

"Lalitha, let me try it again. The rush of power was incredible."

"No, Daniel Adams. The Book should be treated with respect and reverence. It is not your plaything."

"But I just…"

"I said NO," Lalitha shouted at him. "This Book has been with my family for generations. I and I alone will determine when you are permitted to touch it."

He was about to argue with her, but Tom put his hand firmly on Danny's shoulder.

"Come on mate," Tom said softly. "You've proved that you can do it and to be honest you look like you're knackered from the effort. Let Lalitha put the Book away and you can practice later on."

"When though, Boss? When can I practice?"

"When I say you can," Lalitha said adamantly.

"Fuck this," Danny swore and strode past them to the bow of the ship where he sat facing away from them with his back against the mast.

"That went well then," Alex commented sarcastically.

"Daniel Adams is impatient for power and it concerns me," Lalitha said. "He needs to understand that the Book is primarily my responsibility and not his. He is peripheral."

Tom, Alex and Jimmy were at a loss as to how to respond without making things worse, so they said nothing.

Lalitha took their silence as agreement and nodded with satisfaction. At that moment, the cook's head appeared above the deck and he announced in a loud voice that dinner would soon be served in the galley.

CHAPTER 40

Aboard The Osprey

The last evening on *The Osprey* had not been very relaxing. Jimmy was still moping about what had happened at Gessan, Danny was obviously still brooding about Lalitha's tight control over the Book, and Lalitha herself was giving Danny a wide berth. Even Tom's newfound joy could not lift the mood in the galley as they ate. Namorn had steered clear of them, preferring to eat in his cabin and it was not late before everyone decided to go to their bunks.

All in all, Alex was relieved to see the coast of Zakastra so close off their port bow when she went up on deck the next morning.

Namorn was at the helm and she walked over to talk to him.

"Morning, Lady," he smiled. "Have your companions settled their differences yet?"

"Hopefully. Once we get ashore and they have less time to just sit and brood, things will get back to normal."

"Ah, yes. Being at sea can bring out the worst in people. The confines of a ship at sea can cause friction between those that are unaccustomed to it."

Alex watched the cliffs to their left as *The Osprey* sailed northwards with the wind. Flocks of seabirds swooped around the rocky outcrops, crying out with harsh voices. Namorn pointed out over the starboard rail.

"Look, Lady, a whale. That is an omen of great portent."

Alex watched as the enormous animal surfaced less than a hundred metres from *The Osprey* and blew a huge plume of spray into the air.

"Is it a good omen or a bad one?" she asked.

"I always think of them as a good omen. They bring good luck at sea as do cats and cormorants."

"What brings bad luck?"

Namorn raised his eyebrows and grinned at her.

"Women. If there is one thing more than any other that brings bad luck on-board, it is most certainly women!"

"You'll be glad that we'll be leaving you today then captain," she laughed.

"I will not miss your companions, but you my Lady are welcome back on-board *The Osprey* whenever you wish it."

"Thank you, Namorn."

They watched the whale as it moved slowly away from them and before long, they couldn't see the great beast any longer. As Alex looked back to the coast, she thought she could see buildings in the distance.

"Is that Prentak?"

"Yes, Lady, the port is not long away now. You should rouse your companions and eat something. You will soon have to gather your belongings ready for our arrival at Prentak."

Alex went to wake the rest of the team up and before long they were eating their last breakfast aboard *The Osprey*. Everyone ate on the deck so that they could watch the coastline as they sailed past. More ships could be seen in the distance, some were at anchor whilst others approached or departed the coastal city. Fishermen watched them pass from their launches. Some waved greetings while others just stood and watched the larger vessel sail by, smoke from their pipes billowing around them.

Tom was sorry that this part of the journey was coming to an end. They would soon be back on land and he had no idea what that would bring. They were supposed to be meeting one of Lalitha's allies here, but what if Lalitha's messenger had not made it. What if there was no-one to meet them?

Lalitha seemed to be having none of these doubts. She was keen to get to Prentak and was convinced that her father's friend would be waiting for them. Tom really hoped that she was right.

The team brought all their possessions up onto the deck and stacked them carefully where they would not get in the crew's way. Carrying everything was not going to be easy, but Tom was ecstatic that he could now help to lift and carry their kit. Alex watched him as he took the heavy saddlebags from Jimmy and lifted them up the companionway. He had a broad smile on his face as he took the weight easily with his new-found strength.

All the crewmen were at their stations and busied themselves lowering the fore and aft sails as *The Osprey* swung into Prentak harbour. A small sailing boat headed towards them and as it pulled alongside, Namorn leaned over the rail and had a shouted conversation with the pilot below. Nodding his head, Namorn walked to Allun who had the wheel and pointed towards the quayside. Allun corrected their course and made for a section of the quay where no ships were moored.

"The harbourmaster has a berth for us," Namorn told Tom. "We will soon have you ashore."

The crew slowly furled *The Osprey's* main sail and as they did, the ships speed reduced. The wind was blowing from the south, directly into the harbour mouth, so with a bit of careful steering *The Osprey* was soon gliding slowly towards their mooring at the quay. The main sail was furled completely and *The Osprey* slowed down as Namorn steered the ship towards the quayside. Once they had drifted close enough, crewmen leapt from the rail to the quayside and ropes were thrown down to them. The thick ropes were looped around metal capstans sunk into the surface of the stone quay and the crewmen tied the ropes off as *The Osprey* gently bumped to a halt.

Namorn unfastened the bolts on the gangplank gate and swung it open so that two of his men could extend the wooden plank down to the quayside. Namorn strode down it and stood on the stone flags below them. He was instantly surrounded by merchants and urchins trying to sell all kinds of wares. Namorn shooed most of them away, but held the arm of one of the men and had a brief conversation with him. The man nodded and hurried away as Namorn walked back up on deck.

"I do not know where you intend to go in the city, but you should not try to carry all this equipment by hand. I have spoken to one of the longshoremen and he has gone to fetch his wagon. He will take you to wherever it is that you need to go to in the city."

"Thank you, Namorn," Tom said.

"You do not need to thank me. I did not pay him or even negotiate a price for your journey. That is for you to arrange."

Tom smiled. "Talking of payment. Here is the rest of your money Namorn. We are grateful to you for getting us here... and for the detour that we sprung on you."

Tom handed Namorn a handful of silver coins and the big man grinned as he counted them.

"Ha. I only wish that I could make this amount of silver on all the trips I make between Brentar and Prentak."

There was a clatter of hooves on stone and the longshoreman pulled up alongside them in his wagon. The team carried their Bergens and saddlebags down the gangplank and loaded them into the wagon. The longshoreman didn't help them, he was too busy fending off the locals.

Namorn stood beside the wagon as they climbed aboard and gave them a wave. Lalitha had her scarf tied around her face once again and climbed up onto the seat at the front of the wagon. Everyone else would have to sit in the back with the Bergens. One urchin climbed up the far side of the wagon and looked interestedly in at the stacked Bergens, but the longshoreman shouted a very graphic threat at him and the boy hastily jumped back down.

"Farewell my friends. It has been… interesting," Namorn laughed.

They all shouted their thanks to him and Alex gave the big man a hug before climbing up with the others.

"Take care of yourself, Namorn."

"You too Lady and if you ever tire of your man there, you will always find a warm bed aboard *The Osprey*."

"I will bear that in mind," she laughed.

Everyone climbed up onto the wagon and, once they were ready, the longshoreman cracked his reins and the horse set off with a jerk. The team waved at Namorn as they rumbled through the crowds towards the harbour gates. The wagon was swiftly engulfed in the chaos of the city, and *The Osprey* and it's larger than life captain were soon out of sight.

"Where do we head for Masters?" the longshoreman asked.

"We go to the house of the Ardum family. It is in the west of the city near the great statue of King Lestri. Do you know it?"

"I do, Lady. Everybody knows the Ardum house, although the statue is no longer there."

"What do you mean?"

"Did you not know? The king is dead! A mob ripped down his effigy and smashed it with hammers. His head was dragged through the streets and thrown into the harbour."

"Why did they do this?"

"The taxes here are high and many struggle to pay them. After the crown takes its coin, many families have little left to live on. We see the Elders and their cronies living in luxury while the ordinary people have little to call their own. When it was known that the king had died, many decided to take the law into their own hands and show the Elders what they think of their authority."

"Taxes fund the army and keep the people safe from the barbarians in the east and agitators in the south. Elders use their allocated money from the capital to maintain roads and keep the harbours in good repair."

"The taxes also pay for the Elders' mansions, feasts and womanising. I do not know what happens in the capital as I have never been there, but little of the Prentak Elders' coin is used to help the people of this city."

Lalitha bristled with anger, but did not say anything more.

Tom listened carefully, worried that he would hear the Book start to whisper as Lalitha's temper surfaced, but all he could hear was the hubbub of the city streets and the clatter of the wagon wheels on the cobbled road.

CHAPTER 41

Prentak

The houses close to the harbour in Prentak were very similar to those that they had seen in Brentar. They were constructed with thick stone walls and had tiled roofs rather than thatch. The windows in the houses were glazed and everywhere looked to be well kept. The state of the buildings however did little to lessen the smell of the place.

"I'm guessing that they haven't invented a way to deal with their sewage yet," gagged Alex as she pulled her scarf up over her nose.

The longshoreman laughed, but the laugh contained little humour, "We will be taking a shortcut through the poorer district of Prentak. If the smell here offends your senses Lady, then you will like the next part of the drive less."

The wagon bumped down off the cobbles as the longshoreman turned down a dusty track that made its way between rows of smaller, more ramshackle buildings. As they progressed along the track, the smell worsened and Tom soon felt like he was tasting the air rather than smelling it. The stench was awful and Jimmy especially looked like he was struggling to keep his breakfast down. By now, all of them had their scarves tied tightly around their faces.

The people here were thin and badly dressed, some of them wearing nothing more than rags. They all had a beaten expression on their faces and even the children seemed to not have enough energy to pay much attention to the passing wagon. Flies swarmed everywhere, they crawled around the eyes of the people and, to Tom's revulsion, the people hardly even seemed to notice their presence. Scrawny chickens ran around in the dust, pecking at anything that looked even vaguely edible and occasionally a stringy goat or sheep could be seen tied up outside one of the buildings.

The houses that lined this dirt road had no glass in their windows and the roofs were patched up with pieces of cloth and wooden boards.

There was no sign of any soldiers anywhere. Perhaps the Elders did not care what happened in these slums.

"What is this place?" asked Tom.

"This is where the Elders of Prentak keep their serfs. It is a harsh life, but at least they are fed and they have shelter. Many disagree with how the Elders keep the serfs, but it is simply the way of things. They were just unlucky that fate saw them born of a serf mother."

Tom was appalled at the way these people were living; if you could call it living.

"What do the Prentak Elders do with these people?"

"They are used wherever they are needed. Some walk out beyond the city walls each day and work in the fields; planting, picking and tending the crops. Others work the shit-carts in the city. They clean the streets and take the shit to use in the fields. The women who look half-decent and still have their teeth, are put to work in the city whorehouses. The Elders keep most of the coin that they earn and once they have lost their looks, they return here and join the others in the fields."

"It has always been this way," Lalitha snapped. "The Elders may not all be perfect, but they keep order by maintaining the laws of the land with the help of the army. Without them, the cities and towns across the realm would fall into chaos. The serfs do necessary work and are looked after by their Elders. They are fed and given homes to live in. They work hard and are rewarded for their efforts accordingly."

Tom looked around at the poverty around him. This hardly seemed like any kind of reward.

Lalitha saw the look on Tom's face.

"Nobody forces these people to stay here, Thomas McAllister. They are free to seek another Elder to take them in whenever they like if they think they will receive more favourable terms elsewhere. Saying that, Elder's should not abuse their position and they should certainly not be selling their serf's bodies for profit. Corrupt Elders can be dealt with as easily as barbarians."

"Hopefully, whoever takes the throne from the late king will be able to look at practices like this and do something about them," Tom said deliberately.

Lalitha turned to look directly at Tom, but she didn't comment on what he had said.

The wagon rolled onwards and Tom closed his eyes to shut out the sights of the slums. The others had already taken a similar approach. Jimmy had even tied his scarf around his whole face rather than just covering his nose and mouth.

They continued in this way until they felt the wagon bump back up onto another cobbled roadway.

Tom opened his eyes to find that they had left the serf slums behind and the houses here were much grander. The longshoreman turned left at the next crossroads and headed towards a large stone plinth ahead of them. As they neared the plinth, Tom could see that there were lumps of stone strewn around the ground. He guessed that this had been the statue of King Lestri.

Lalitha shook her head in disgust, but said nothing. Thankfully, neither did the longshoreman.

The wagon carried on past the broken statue and after a few hundred metres pulled in towards a set of impressive iron gates. A figure clad in leather armour and clutching a long wicked looking pike appeared from the wooden guardhouse that stood beside the gates.

"What is your business here?" the guard shouted.

"I have passengers from the harbour who wished to be brought here," the longshoreman replied.

"I do not know you or your companions. Move along."

"I have business with your Master," Lalitha said sternly. "Is he here?"

"I cannot answer that. What business would the likes of you have with Lord Ardum?"

"The likes of me?" Lalitha blazed. "You will call for Lord Ardum now. If he learns that you have spoken to friends of his in such a disrespectful way, he will surely punish you severely."

The guard looked less certain about his previous position and made a quick decision to hedge his bets. He strode over to the gates and pulled a metal lever that stuck out of the wall at an angle. Somewhere inside the compound, Tom heard the clang of a bell. Within a matter of seconds, a boy appeared inside the gates. He was out of breath and had obviously run down to them when he heard the bell.

"Boy, fetch the Master. These people say that they are friends of his."

The boy disappeared again and Lalitha turned to Tom.

"Cindal Ardum must be here if the boy has gone to fetch him. That is good. He must have received my message."

They waited for some time as the guard continued to watch them warily, his hand never moving from the pike at his side.

Eventually, there was the sound of hooves and a mounted man appeared.

"Open the gates," he commanded.

The guard hurriedly unlocked the metal gates and swung them inwards. The rider dismounted and walked to the side of the wagon. Lalitha climbed down from the wagon and stood before the stranger.

The man was tall and well-built with thinning black hair and a well-groomed goatee beard. He wore a long green tunic and breeches with tall black leather riding boots. Around his waist was a thick leather belt and hanging from it was a sword with an intricately cast metal fob featuring a horse's head. He took one look at Lalitha's eyes and bowed his head.

"These are friends indeed. Welcome to you. I am relieved to see you're safe my Lady. Leave your baggage here and I will have my men bring it to the house. Come with me."

He held out his hand to Lalitha and she took it in her own.

"Lord Ardum. I am very glad to see you."

"And I you, my Lady."

Ardum gestured to the rest of the team in the wagon.

"Join us my friends. I would learn more about your exploits in comfort back up at the house."

"This sounds more like it," Danny muttered.

Tom gave him a nudge and passed Danny's rifle to him.

"Until we know for sure what's going on here, keep your C8 with you."

The same idea had occurred to Alex and she already had her rifle slung over her shoulder.

"This guy is obviously who Lalitha was expecting to see, but do we know that he is definitely on her side?" she asked.

"She thinks so, but I don't know for sure. That's why we stay on our guard until we know we've sussed the situation out."

The four friends walked through the gates and trotted to catch up with Lalitha and Ardum as they walked up the wide path towards the house.

The gardens around them were breath-taking. Thousands of roses grew in neat, sculptured rows alongside the path. Their fragrance was in stark contrast to the slums that they had ridden through, and Tom was relieved to be able to loosen the scarf from around his face. The path ran in a straight line up to the front steps of a large house. A house that became more imposing the closer that they got to it.

A set of stone steps led up to a wide terrace that was lined with statues of warriors and huge stone urns with colourful cascades of flowers flowing from them. The house itself was fronted with a row of six tall white pillars. Each pillar had been carved in such a way that their bases took the form of a life-sized galloping stallion that appeared to be leaping out of the very fabric of the building. The pillars rose from the horses' backs and extended upwards to join the roof of the house. Each of the glazed windows was framed by intricate stone carvings depicting vines and flowers. The workmanship was spectacular.

In the middle of the six pillars stood an enormous set of wooden doors. The doors were studded with iron and at their centre had been carved a huge coat of arms. Central to the design was a huge fist that clasped the blade of a massive sword which pointed down towards the ground. One half of the coat of arms was carved into each door, so as Lord Ardum pushed one of the doors open, the coat of arms split in two and half of the clasped sword swung inwards with him.

"Welcome to the Ardum family home," he announced.

The team walked inside and the interior of the building was like nothing they had seen before. Rather than being dark and gloomy like most of the places they had been to, this room was full of light. The entrance hall ran vertically to the roof of the house and sunlight cascaded in through a huge window that stood above the doors.

The floor was tiled with what looked like marble and a staircase rose directly in front of them before splitting off left and right to the floors above. In the middle of the floor stood a statue that depicted a soldier in armour, his sword drawn and ready for battle.

"Wow," gasped Danny.

Ardum pushed the door closed behind them and turned to Lalitha. He kneeled in front of her and lowered his head almost to his knee.

"Welcome, your Royal Highness."

"Thank you, Lord Ardum. Please stand."

Ardum rose back to his feet and looked at Lalitha's disguise.

"You can remove your scarf now. The need for subterfuge here is unnecessary. All my people can be trusted."

Lalitha unwound the scarf from around her face and smiled at her father's friend.

"I am relieved to see you alive and well Lalitha. After the king's death, we feared the worst. It was said that you had fallen into the western seas and perished, but I did not believe it. I knew that the Book would keep you safe."

"Thank you Lord Ardum. The Book did indeed save me. It took me to another place entirely where I met my companions here. The Book told me to trust them and its advice has proved true. Did you receive my message?"

"I received no message," Ardum said with a frown. "I came to Prentak to escape the chaos in the capital. Where did you send the message from?"

"A messenger was dispatched from Serat in the south. Perhaps you had already left Krassak by the time he arrived."

"That is indeed possible princess. The capital is a dangerous place now for supporters of King Lestri and I had to leave secretly before Gask's men found me. Hopefully he believes that I still hide within Krassak's walls. As your message never found me, it seems then that simple fate has brought us together here. How did you come to be in Serat?"

"It is a long story, but the Book transported us to the old altar in the ruins of Melnor. We made for Serat, then Lintar and then over the mountains to Brentar. We recently came to Prentak by ship, but we sailed via the isle of Gessan."

"Gessan? You have completed the Ceremony?"

"Yes," smiled Lalitha. "I can now channel the power of the Souls."

"That is welcome news indeed, Lalitha."

"There is more," said Lalitha gesturing towards Danny. "This is Daniel Adams. He has also been Chosen and he also took part in the Ceremony of Binding."

Ardum looked shocked.

"A non-royal was Chosen? And Bound? It has been many generations since the Book has allowed that to happen."

Ardum strode over and clasped Danny's shoulders.

"You are welcome in this house, Daniel Adams."

"Thank you, Lord Ardum. It's good to meet you," smiled Danny.

Gesturing towards the others, Lalitha introduced each of them and Ardum welcomed them all warmly.

"Come, let us go through to the drawing chamber where we can talk more comfortably."

CHAPTER 42

Prentak

Ardum led the way to the left of the entrance hall and they found themselves in a large, carpeted room with a number of ornately carved sofas dotted around it. Enormous windows looked out over the rose gardens and tapestries hung on the walls, each depicting soldiers on horseback or violent naval battles. An impressive marble fireplace dominated the room and above it hung a massive painting of an imposing man astride a warhorse. The man held a sword in his grasp and Tom realised that it was the sword that hung from Ardum's belt.

"That is my grandfather," Ardum said as he noticed Tom's interest. "He built this house and it is his sword that I bear. He was a great man and stood by the old king's side for many years."

Tom nodded, "Your house is magnificent, Lord Ardum."

Ardum beamed. "Thank you. I am glad that you like it. Let me get us some refreshments and you can tell me your stories."

Ardum picked up a bell from one of the low tables and rang it loudly.

A smartly dressed man appeared through a door at the other end of the room and bowed his head towards Ardum.

"Yes, Lord?"

"Askal, bring us some tea."

The man bowed his head again and hurried back out of the door.

"Now sit and tell me everything that has happened," Ardum said.

He pulled three of the sofas closer together and they all sat down. Lalitha told Ardum what she had witnessed in the tower, how she had fled through the tunnels under the city and had ended up at the Western Sea. Ardum looked grave as she told her story.

"I am sorry that I was not there with you and your father in the tower Lalitha. Gask's supporters were stirring up trouble in the lower city and I went down there with a company of royal guards to disperse them. I did not realise that Gask had gained access to the altar. It will be to my undying regret that I could not save the king."

"I do not hold you at all responsible for what happened. That is down to Gask himself and I will not rest until his head stands on a pike at the city gates."

Askal came back into the room carrying a tray laden with delicate cups and a large silver teapot. He poured six cups of the strong-smelling tea, bowed his head and left the room again.

"Drink," said Ardum pointing at the teacups.

The team sipped at the strong black tea and as they did so, Lalitha went on to tell how the Book had taken her to London. Ardum listened wide-eyed as Lalitha described the things she had seen there and the battles that they had fought with the Russians. He was especially interested in the team's weaponry.

Tom and Alex took up the story as they described the battle with the bandits south of Lintar and the rescue from their cavern.

"I am truly grateful for your help," Ardum said earnestly. "If the princess had been killed and the Book lost, our hope would be at an end."

Lastly, they told Ardum about the events on Gessan and how both Lalitha and Danny were now Bound to the Book.

"Your story is incredible," Ardum declared. "If I did not know you so well Lalitha and I could not see these warriors in front of me with their outlandish weapons, I would find it hard to believe."

"It is all true," Lalitha promised.

"I do not hesitate to believe you princess."

"Tell me, Lord, how are things in the capital. I am told that my brother is still alive."

"Krassak is in turmoil," Ardum sighed. "Word of the king's death soon became known and the word spreads that Gask is responsible. He has not yet appointed himself as king, but I fear that it is only a matter of time before he does. Prince Relfa has vanished and it is commonly believed that Gask has him imprisoned somewhere in the city. No body was found so it is assumed that he lives."

Lalitha scowled and her lips pursed in anger.

"Gask has much to answer for," she said fiercely. "Why has the bastard not declared himself king yet?"

"You were feared lost princess, but nobody could find a body, so the matter of succession is difficult. I believe that Gask is putting pressure on the royal court to appoint him as the next ruler, but some within the court remain loyal to your family and want to wait until your body is recovered from the sea. However, the more time that passes without a body being found, the stronger Gask's claim becomes. With Relfa's disappearance, your apparent death and the loss of the Great Book, the court is being presented with few options other than to crown Gask."

"But now I'm back."

"Indeed, princess. Now you are back."

"What do we do next, Lord Ardum?"

"We have to be wary. One of the first things that Gask did was to put his own men in positions of power within the royal guard. Soldiers like myself who remain loyal to the Lestri family were either arrested or ran. When I saw what was happening, I left my post in the Tower and retreated here to Prentak. It is only a matter of time before Gask comes for me. He knows that I am a threat to his rule and I believe that he only waits for the succession to be decided in his favour before he sends men to kill me."

"Let him try!" Lalitha growled.

"Ha. We will not give him that opportunity. I have assembled men of the royal guard and others from the army that wish to fight to preserve our way of life. They wait for us at Deman Castle outside Derralt. We will join with them there and move on Krassak. I fear that we will not have the numbers for a frontal assault, but if we use the secret tunnels below the city, we may be able to use the element of surprise to take the tower from within."

"How many men does Gask have?" Tom asked.

"Gask used his silver-tongued lies to beguile key commanders within the army. Between these commanders, he now controls the majority of the forces stationed in and around Krassak. We are looking at more than a thousand men either within the city walls or stationed in nearby garrisons. On top of that he has the royal guard. Once we had lost the king and I was forced to flee, the guard was leaderless. Many loyal royalists like myself fled the city, but there were many that stayed in Krassak. Gask took the opportunity to put one of his traitorous army generals in command and so what remains of the royal guard, almost two hundred men, now protects that bastard. It could be that some of these men are secretly still loyal to the royal family, but I cannot guarantee it."

"I cannot believe that members of the king's royal guard would side with that snake," Lalitha said.

"I agree my princess. They were my soldiers and now they side with that traitor. It makes me sick to the stomach. On top of that, Gask has a number of fanatical followers that journeyed from the southern cities to join him in the capital. They are spread across the city, but will be quick to respond to any calls for help."

"And how many men do we have on our side?" Tom asked.

"From the reports and messages that I have received, I estimate that we can muster around two hundred men. They would be mostly made up of the royal guards that left Krassak at the same time as myself, and forces that the Deman family can raise in Derralt."

"Jesus, those are not great odds," Tom breathed. "A frontal attack is out of the question, even with the weaponry we have with us. I agree with you, Lord Ardum. We have no option but to try to access the tower covertly from below and attack from the inside. If we can mount the strike without anyone getting wind of what we are doing, we might be able to pull it off with the numbers we have."

"If you can get me to the altar in the tower, I can use the Book to subdue whatever they throw at us," Lalitha said. "Their numbers will not be an issue then."

"It is the getting you to the altar part that could be the problem," Tom added. "I don't know how much damage you can do with the Book by summoning the power of the Souls whilst it is away from the altar Lalitha, but I'm guessing taking out twelve hundred men is going to be asking too much."

"Yes, Thomas McAllister. Even if Daniel Adams works with me, we would not be able to summon enough energy to do that much damage."

"Let's worry about Gask's forces when we get closer to Krassak," Danny suggested. "If we already know that our best shout is to sneak into the city through the secret tunnels that Lalitha knows, we can recce the lay of the land when we get near to the capital. What is our next step from here in Prentak?"

"We travel to Derralt to join with the forces that await us there," Ardum said. "I let it be known to all the loyal royal guard deserters that they should make for Castle Deman. I have a few men with me here, but the main force is gathering at the Deman family estate, out of the way of prying eyes. Once we have joined with them, we can make for the capital."

"Sounds good," Danny nodded. "What do you think, Boss?"

"It sounds like the best option. We're going to have to be careful though. If any of Gask's people see two hundred soldiers marching towards Krassak, we're going to have a problem."

"That is true," Ardum agreed. "We will need to move at night and scout our surroundings carefully."

"How long will it take us to get to Derralt?" Tom asked. "Bearing in mind that we are far from fast riders."

"If I were riding there myself it would take no more than seven days. You say you are not good horsemen?"

"It took us twelve days to ride from Lintar to the port of Brentar," Lalitha said, pulling a face. "To begin with, we couldn't even ride at night because of my companions' inexperience."

"That is indeed slow," groaned Ardum. "Riding at that pace, it would take us at least ten days to journey to Derralt."

A thoughtful look crossed Ardum's face.

"I have an idea. I have a carriage in my stables and a team of horses that are well used to being harnessed. If we use two horses to pull the carriage and lead two spare horses behind, we could alternate them and make relatively good time. To my reckoning, we could arrive at Derralt in about eight days if we took the carriage. What do you think?"

"I will ride with you on horseback Lord Ardum," said Lalitha, "but my companions would be better suited to carriage travel. Do you agree Thomas McAllister?"

Tom looked at the others and nodded his head.

"It sounds like a good option to me, especially if we can potentially save two days of travelling."

"I definitely agree," added Jimmy. "Horses are seriously uncomfortable and they don't seem to like me for some reason."

Ardum glanced at Lalitha and smiled.

"It is agreed then. Let us rest for the remainder of the day and we will depart for Derralt at first light tomorrow. I will arrange food for us now and you are free to make yourselves comfortable in my house."

"Thank you, Lord Ardum," Lalitha said.

Ardum picked up the bell from where he had left it and rang it loudly. After a few seconds, Askal hurried into the room.

"Askal, show our guests to suitable rooms and once they are comfortable arrange food for everyone. I am going to the stable to get the men to prepare the carriage for travelling. We leave for Derralt in the morning."

"Very well, Master."

"I will see you all for dinner in a little while," Ardum said as he headed for the door. "Askal will show you to your rooms. Princess, if you would accompany me, you can select your horse and we can talk further about your father."

Lalitha nodded in agreement and followed Ardum from the room. Once they had gone, Askal guided the team back through the entrance hall and up the stairs. They went to the right at the top of the staircase where it split in two and Askal guided them down a long corridor to rooms that overlooked the front of the house. Everyone was given a room of their own, apart from Tom and Alex who quietly informed Askal that they would like to share.

"I will have the men bring your baggage to your rooms," Askal said. "If you would like to bathe before dinner, I can show you to the bathhouse."

"Bathhouse? With warm water?" asked Alex excitedly.

"Of course, Lady. The water is heated by an underground wood furnace."

"Really? I can't tell you how good that sounds. Please... Lead the way," Alex smiled.

Askal led them downstairs and through another door that led towards the rear of the building. They walked down another set of stone steps and found themselves in a room containing a large sunken pool filled with gently steaming water. Windows set high in the wall let natural sunlight illuminate the room and marble floors ran around the perimeter of the pool.

Alex crouched down and dipped her hand into the water. It was more than warm, it was hot.

"Enjoy the baths," Askal said as he climbed back up the stairs. "There are towels and robes hanging on the wall over there. If you call me once you are ready, I will arrange for the food to be served."

"This is more like it," laughed Danny as he quickly stripped down to his underwear and jumped into the pool.

Everyone else raced to do the same and they were soon all immersed in the soothing hot water.

"How good is this?" laughed Danny.

"I'd almost forgotten what being clean feels like," Alex chuckled.

"It just seems wrong that there are houses like this when most of the city that we went through is such a slum," said Jimmy. "I bet the serfs don't have heated indoor pools."

"Trust you to put a downer on things," Danny groaned. "It's the same everywhere Codboy. The rich live in luxury and the poor live in squalor. That's the way of things...

You're just not used to seein' it in the UK. Go to somewhere like Mumbai and you'll see that our world isn't so different. Do you not remember Helmand?"

"Of course, I remember. It doesn't make it right though does it?" Jimmy replied.

"No, Jimmy you're right. It doesn't," Tom said.

"It doesn't," agreed Danny, "but that doesn't stop it happenin'. Where I grew up was nowhere near what we've seen today, but it wasn't exactly a bundle of laughs. Why do you think I was so keen to get Bound to the Book? It is my way of escapin' my shit life and movin' up in the world. I could even end up livin' in a pad like this."

"Perhaps once we've helped Lalitha become queen, she can do something to help the serfs?" Jimmy said hopefully.

"Perhaps so Jimmy," Alex nodded.

"Not if it jeopardises my new mansion," Danny grinned.

There was a sudden splash as Tom stood up and looked at his left arm in alarm.

"What is it?" asked Alex.

"I just realised that I jumped in here without thinking. Before Lalitha fixed my arm, there's no way I could have submerged my prosthetic in water."

"Is it okay?"

"Yes," said Tom as a smile slowly spread across his face. "It is. I can even feel the water on my fingers."

"That's fantastic!"

Alex swam over to Tom, pulled him back down into the water and kissed him passionately on the lips.

"We are still here don't forget," Danny teased.

Alex laughed and splashed water in his direction.

After almost an hour of being submerged in the pool, hunger began to get the better of them and they realised that they had not eaten since they had left *The Osprey* that morning.

"Come on," Danny yelled as he climbed out of the pool. "Let's go and find Askal. I'm starvin'."

Everyone took Danny's lead, dried themselves with the freshly scented towels and donned the cotton robes that Aksal had showed them. They picked up their clothes and boots and headed back upstairs.

Either Askal had been waiting for them all this time or he had heard them getting out of the pool because, as they walked into the entrance hall, he stood there watching them.

"I have laid out fresh clothes on your beds. Lord Ardum thought that you might feel better in new travelling clothes. If you would like to dress yourselves and return back here, I will arrange for dinner to be served."

CHAPTER 43

Prentak

Tom, Alex, Danny and Jimmy assembled back in the entrance hall about half an hour later. All of them felt better than they had done for days and they looked much smarter in the clothes that Lord Ardum had provided. They were all dressed in black. Black tunics and shirts with long trousers which they had tucked into the tops of their combat boots. The clothes were well made and fitted a lot better than their old garments. Best of all was the fact that the new clothes were made from a much higher quality material that was soft against their skin. It was a great improvement over the scratchy linen that Danny had bought from the market in Lintar.

Aksal nodded his approval and lead the team through the drawing chamber to a large dining hall that lay beyond. A long table ran down the length of the room and Tom guessed that you could have easily seated twenty people around it. The walls were adorned with a variety of spears, shields, swords, axes and other exotic looking weaponry.

"Wow," Danny said. "Look at all this stuff."

Lord Ardum and Lalitha were already seated at the head of the table. Lalitha was also dressed in new clothes, but hers was a long flowing dress made of a green silky material. She had her leather bag around her neck as usual, but in this setting, she looked much more regal. She had obviously bathed somewhere privately and her long hair shone as she turned her head to look at them.

"Welcome friends," Ardum called. "Be seated and we will eat."

Askal pulled elegant looking wooden chairs out from under the table for each of them and everyone sat down. Jimmy, as usual, made sure that he sat next to Lalitha. Another set of doors opened and a procession of servants began to fill the table with food. Large silver platters containing hot roast boar, beef steaks, whole roast quail-like birds, roasted fish and vegetables were placed in front of the team. Their mouths began to water in anticipation. Askal hurried around after the servants and distributed six large, stemmed glasses that were all filled with a rich, heavy red wine.

"Eat, friends," Ardum said gesturing at the feast in front of them.

The conversation for the next few minutes was scarce as everyone dived into the amazing looking food.

"I've got to stop," complained Alex after finishing a second plate of roasted boar and vegetables. "If I eat any more, I'm going to burst."

Ardum laughed loudly. "I am glad to be able to offer such a meal to you and your friends. It is an honour to have Princess Lalitha and her companions here in my home."

"Thank you Lord Ardum," Lalitha said. "Can your servants be trusted to keep our stay here a secret?"

"They can princess. My servants know all too well that if they displease me, they will soon find themselves living back in the stink of the city rather than in this fine house."

"Good. That eases my concerns."

"You appear to treat your servants more kindly than the Elders of the city do," Tom observed.

"That is true sir. But then my servants live in my house rather than in the slums. I would not want them to smell as rancid as those wretches in the city, or look as filthy and underfed. It would not reflect well on my standing as a Lord for people to visit my house and see my servants in such a condition. The serfs that belong to the Elders work mainly in the fields so they are expected to look and smell like shit. Here they are not."

"Does nobody say anything to the Elders?" Jimmy asked.

"About what?" Ardum replied.

"How badly the serfs are treated?"

"The serfs know no better and the ordinary city-folk understand that this is just the way of things."

"But perhaps things could change when Lalitha becomes queen?"

Ardum laughed loudly. "You would have her free the serfs from their bonds and treat them all like lords? Who would plant and harvest the crops then? Such ideas are nothing more than childish nonsense. You sound like those anarchists from the south."

Jimmy blushed and said nothing more. He looked around the table at the vast spread of food and felt a bit sick. They were sat here eating roasted quail and steak whilst the serfs in the city scrabbled around in the dust trying to find something to eat.

"I was just saying that things are hardly fair here are they," Jimmy mumbled.

"What has fair got to do with anything?" Ardum laughed. "This realm runs on power and wealth. Fairness does not come into it."

"Well perhaps it will when Lalitha is on the throne," Jimmy said stubbornly.

"We will see," Lalitha nodded.

"What do the people here in Prentak think of Gask?" Tom asked. "They seemed keen enough to pull down the king's statue. Are they on his side?"

"The people think that they know what they want, but they are usually misguided. As is always the way, when a leader falls, the common people take advantage of the situation and believe that this is the end of the laws and taxes that they object to. The result is always disorder and violence. Such mayhem is not good for anybody and a strong figurehead must be put in place to bring stability back to the cities. Without a strong arm to enforce the laws of the land, the realm faces chaos and economic ruin."

"And Gask?"

"The people here do not know Gask and, more importantly, they do not fear him. How can he hope to keep control if nobody fears the consequences of disobedience? The king may not have been popular in the provinces, but few dared to break his laws. They knew what would happen if they did."

"Gask must not be allowed to destroy everything that my father fought for," Lalitha said. "If we let him take the throne, he will inflict his twisted anarchistic ideals on the realm and it will end in ruin."

"Enough talk of Gask," Ardum demanded, "I wish to know more about your warrior friends here. Have you fought in many battles or is your land at peace?"

"Our world is a very violent place and wars rage all the time," Tom replied. "We fought in a country far from our own where opposing political and religious ideals led to different factions constantly fighting each other. Both sects believed that if they crushed their enemy, then they could force their own ideals on the losing side. One side in particular lead a long campaign of terror. They killed innocent civilians without any qualms and whole cities were decimated as the factions fought each other."

"You see?" exclaimed Ardum, banging his fist on the table, "This is what Gask intends! He has stirred up fanaticism within the people and the Royal Court, and now he seeks to stamp his beliefs on everyone else. Did you destroy many of the enemy forces?"

"Our forces were put in place to try and keep the factions apart and encourage them to negotiate a peaceful settlement. My team's role was to search for traps that the insurgents had laid to kill and demoralise the local population. If we found their traps, it was our job to dismantle them safely. We destroyed as many of them as we could, but there were always more than we could deal with."

"Were the peace negotiations successful?"

"Well, no not really. There are still skirmishes now, years later and the tensions that existed before are still there. The hatred between the different factions is too deeply rooted to be easily forgotten. Populist leaders and activists still stir up the tensions and it often ends in violence."

"There is no negotiating with such people. They only understand force, which is why what we do here is so important."

"So, you don't believe in ever trying to negotiate peace?" Alex asked.

"Negotiation has its place, but not when you are dealing with such fanatical beliefs. It was the same with the barbarians. Some of the court recommended that we seek to negotiate peace with them, but how could we trust them? They burned our ships and pillaged our coast without conscience. The king understood that the only way to deal with the barbarians was to bring swift and decisive violence down on them."

"That is exactly what we should've done in Helmand," Danny muttered. "What did all the pussy-footing around achieve? Far better if we had just gone in full-force and stomped the insurgents out altogether."

"But all that does is foster hatred in the next generation," argued Alex. "If you put one side down using extreme force, then the resentment and discontent just builds again in the defeated faction. Without there being a common goal towards peace, then the circle of violence will just continue round and round."

"Not if you completely wipe out the opposition," grinned Danny.

"There's a word for that Fester. It's called genocide."

"We will not negotiate with Gask," Lalitha declared. "His ideals are reason enough to stop him, but what he has done to my family demands justice. I want him dead."

The room fell quiet and the tension was palpable. Everybody had finished eating and an awkward silence descended on the group.

"Lord Ardum, when I escaped Gask at the western cliffs, he had a hooded stranger with him. The stranger made to take the Book from me which concerns me. I wondered if he was a rogue magus from Gessan, but Rellik assured me that this was not the case."

"I didn't trust that magus character," Jimmy said quietly. "The Book may have said that he was telling the truth, but did you see his face? He was hiding something."

"He could not lie to the Book James Lang. It would know. I trust what he told me to be the truth."

Jimmy raised his eyebrows, but didn't argue.

"I do not know who the stranger was," Ardum pondered. "Perhaps it was no more than a foolish ploy intended to trick you into willingly giving up the Book. I would not put such trickery beyond Gask and his followers."

Lalitha did not look completely satisfied by his answer, but there was no more to be gained by further questioning.

Ardum looked at the faces sat in front of him and pushed his chair back away from the table.

"If you will excuse me, I must attend to my men. We need to prepare for tomorrow's journey. Feel free to walk in the gardens or relax in the house. If you need anything, just let Askal know."

"Thank you Lord Ardum," Tom smiled.

Ardum nodded and strode out of the room.

"Fancy a walk round the gardens?" Tom asked Alex.

"Yeah, come on let's stretch our legs."

Tom and Alex left the others in the dining hall and walked back through the house and out into the rose gardens. Once they were out amongst the fragrance of the flowers with bees buzzing around and birds singing cheerfully, it was easy for them to forget where they were. They could quite easily be walking around a National Trust property in the home counties.

"What do you think of Ardum?" Alex asked.

"He seems okay, I guess. Some of his ideas are a bit old school, but he's army. You get what it says on the tin."

Alex smiled and nodded her head. "You're probably right."

She took his hand in her own and they wandered slowly around the gardens until they reached a stone bench in a secluded alcove. The sun shone down and a gentle breeze stirred the rose bushes as the couple sat down and enjoyed the warm sunshine on their skin.

CHAPTER 44

Leaving for Castle Deman

The rest of the evening passed by quickly. Askal had Lord Ardum's men take the team's saddlebags and anything that they did not want to keep by their sides. Everything was to be loaded on the carriage ready for their departure in the morning. The team kept their essential kit close by in their Bergens along with their rifles, but everything else was carried away.

The team sat around Ardum's dining table talking until late into the evening. Tom's eyes started to feel gritty and both Jimmy and Alex had started to yawn. With another journey about to start in the morning, Tom suggested that they should all get some sleep. They all retired to their rooms and Tom fell asleep almost as soon as his head hit the soft feather pillow.

The sun was only just rising over the city the next morning as Askal roused everyone. Alex stretched like a contented cat and slowly climbed out of bed.

"That was the best night's sleep that I have had in weeks," she smiled.

"It was comfortable wasn't it?" grinned Tom. "It's a good job that you won't have time to get used to this kind of luxury. We're on the road again today and will probably be sleeping on the ground tonight."

"At least you lot won't be moaning about saddle sores this time. We'll be in a carriage rather than on horseback."

"That should please, Jimmy, and Lalitha won't be able to moan about us being so slow."

Tom and Alex pulled the black clothes that Ardum had given them back on and loaded all their odds and ends into their packs. They each shouldered their Bergens and headed downstairs where Lalitha, Danny and Jimmy were all waiting for them. Lalitha had abandoned her green dress in favour of more practical riding gear.

"Ardum is assemblin' his guys out the front," Danny informed them. "We're gonna leave straight away before the city gets too busy and lots of people notice us."

"Good idea," agreed Tom. "Let's get out there then."

The team made their way through the entrance hall and out of the front doors. From the terrace, they could see the large black carriage standing on the driveway at the foot of the steps. Two massive horses were harnessed to the carriage at the front and two more were tied to the rear by their reins. An armed soldier sat in the driver's seat and Ardum stood nearby. As he saw the team come out on to the terrace, he gestured for them to come down.

"There is room inside for you, but your bags will have to go on the roof," he told them. "Askal has prepared food for you. It is inside the carriage so that you can eat as we travel. Lalitha, if you come with me, your horse is ready for you."

The soldier in the driver's seat climbed on top of the carriage and Tom handed the heavy Bergens up to him and watched as he tied the bags down with lengths of rope. Satisfied that their gear was safely stowed away, Tom opened the door of the carriage and climbed inside. The carriage bounced as Tom stepped in and he realised that the vehicle must have some sort of primitive suspension. That should make things more comfortable for the journey to Derralt.

The carriage sank further on its springs as Alex, Danny and Jimmy all climbed aboard. The carriage's passenger compartment had bench seats at the front and back, both of which had thick cushions on them. Also, on the rear seat was a hessian sack that Askal had prepared for them. It contained bread and meats and two large earthenware bottles. Tom undid the cork and sniffed at the contents.

"Wine?" Alex asked hopefully.

"Water," grinned Tom.

There was no glass in the carriage windows and Tom leaned out as he heard the sound of horses' hooves. He watched as Ardum and Lalitha led a line of horsemen towards them. There were twelve armed soldiers that would be riding with them to Derralt. Tom felt confident that, at the very least any bandits would think twice about taking them on.

"Are you ready to depart?" Ardum called down.

"Yes," Tom replied. "We're all loaded up and good to go."

Ardum turned in his saddle and looked at the men behind him.

"We ride for Derralt," he called and waved his arm forwards.

Danny lent back on the seat and smiled.

"This is more like it. I feel like royalty already."

Ardum and Lalitha set off at the head of the column and the carriage driver pulled into the middle of the soldiers so there were six riders behind them. The guards swung the front gates open and Ardum led the way out onto the cobbled street.

As soon as the carriage made it to the cobbled road, the smile faded from Danny's face. The carriage vibrated and rattled as the metal-edged wheels clattered over the stone cobbles.

"Holy crap," Danny exclaimed as a particularly large bump made his teeth bang together. "Is this thing gonna rattle like this all the way to Derralt?"

The streets were relatively quiet, but as they got nearer to the city gates, they could see a long line of serfs heading out towards the fields. Danny looked out at the procession of faces as the carriage drove past them. Most of the serfs did not look up or acknowledge that the carriage was even there, but one of the serfs looked at them angrily, picked up a stone from the road and threw it at the coach. It hit the carriage's window frame within a couple of centimetres of Danny's face and he flinched backwards as the stone banged off the woodwork.

Seeing what had happened, one of the mounted soldiers behind the carriage peeled off the column and rode towards the offending serf. The man shouted something at the soldier and gestured in the carriage's direction. Without hesitating, the soldier kicked the serf in face. The serf fell, blood gushing from his nose and lay unmoving on the ground.

"What happened?" Alex asked.

"Nothing to worry about," answered Danny. "Just our escort doin' its job."

The convoy rolled on through the city walls and the soldiers on duty watched them warily. They traded stares with Ardum's men, but nobody said anything, and the convoy was soon out of the city and on the dusty track to Derralt.

Now that the carriage had left the cobbled road, the ride in the carriage had become much more comfortable. The passengers inside the carriage watched the countryside pass by with interest, but it was not long before each of them started to feel sleepy. Alex rested her head on Tom's shoulder and was soon snoring gently.

The team spent the next seven days cooped up in the carriage. They made occasional stops to stretch their cramped legs and one night they managed to find an inn in a small town that had enough rooms to accommodate them. The soldiers slept in the stables with their horses, but the team at least managed to get a comfortable night in a real bed. The other nights were spent sleeping either in the carriage or back on the ground.

The journey began to take its toll on them. The countryside did not change very much as they travelled. Rolling green hills gave way to more rolling green hills, and sparse patches of woodland gave brief moments of interest as the landscape changed outside the carriage window. They passed through villages and hamlets, but none of the locals came anywhere near them. The sight of armed soldiers riding in their direction made most villagers hastily retreat inside their houses.

The team found the best way to combat the tedium of carriage travel was to doze or sleep. Even Jimmy began to wish that they were riding on horseback, just so they had something to do rather than spending long days sitting looking out of the window doing nothing.

Danny had taken to riding up with the driver for most of the day. He had befriended the soldier, Surrin, and had even talked him into letting him take the reins when the road permitted it. Their carriage passed a variety of travellers on the road. Some carrying wares from Prentak, some transporting products and animals to market and others who, like themselves, had business in other parts of the realm.

Few of the travellers that they passed spoke. Occasionally one would offer a brief word of greeting, but nothing more. All of them regarded the soldiers with a mixture of fear and distrust. Some travellers that they encountered even turned off the road and went in another direction when they saw the armed convoy coming.

With Danny riding up top, it was just Tom, Alex and Jimmy riding inside the carriage. Tom and Alex sat next to each other and Jimmy lay out along the bench seat opposite them. Alex decided that now was as good a time as any to have her little chat with Jimmy.

"Jimmy, are you awake?"

"Yeah, I was just resting my eyes Moony," he said and opened his eyes to look at her.

"I need to talk to you about Lalitha."

"What about her?" he asked.

"You're fond of her, aren't you?"

"Course I am. She's beautiful and smart and powerful. She's my friend."

"Just be careful, okay?"

"What do you mean?" Jimmy said with a confused look on his face.

"Look mate," Alex said, trying to choose her words carefully. "It's pretty obvious that you've got a thing for her, yeah? Just remember that she is probably going to end up being queen in the very near future."

Jimmy swung his legs down to the floor and sat up to face her.

"What're you trying to say Moony? That I'm not good enough for her?"

"It's not that I think that… but…"

"But you reckon that she thinks that?"

"Well… yeah Jimmy. I do."

"You think I don't know that? You think I'm stupid enough to believe that she'd choose me?"

"I… I'm sorry Jimmy."

"I've spent my life falling in love with women who wouldn't give me the time of day. I have a track record for it. I can't help how I feel though. I'd do anything for her Alex."

"I know Jimmy and I love you for it, but just don't go and get yourself hurt okay?"

"I'm fine Alex. She talks to me and she values what I have to say. When has a woman like her ever actually listened to me before? I know that someday she'll end up with a prince or something, but until then if she just sees me as a friend, then that's okay."

"But Jimmy…"

"Honestly Alex… just drop it," said Jimmy and turned to gaze out of the carriage window.

Tom had kept quiet during their conversation but chose this moment to squeeze Alex's hand. As Jimmy brooded and looked out at the passing scenery, Alex looked at Tom and he shook his head almost imperceptibly.

Alex raised her eyebrows and turned back to watch Jimmy as the young man lay back down on the bench and closed his eyes again. They would just have to leave Jimmy to work this one out for himself and pick up the pieces when it all went wrong. Which it would.

As they travelled into their eighth day, Lalitha had decided to take a break from riding her horse and had moved into the carriage with them, much to Jimmy's obvious delight. Alex realised that there was definitely no reasoning with him. He was too far gone for rational thought.

They had been travelling uphill for most of the morning, but the gradient was not too steep, so their speed had not reduced dramatically. Lalitha was telling them tales of the magi wars at Dellart when the carriage came to an abrupt halt in a patch of trees.

Jimmy hung his head out of the window and shouted up to where Danny sat with Surrin.

"What's happening, Fester?"

"I don't know," Danny called back. "Ardum has stopped. Nip up there and see what the problem is."

Jimmy open the carriage door and stepped down to the road. Up at the front of the column, Ardum waved to them and called over.

"Come and see friends."

Tom, Alex and Lalitha got out of the carriage and Danny climbed down to join them. They walked towards Ardum and as they got closer to the edge of the trees, they could see the reason that they had been travelling uphill most of the day. They had been climbing the shallow slope of an escarpment and they now stood at the top of the steep-sided scarp face.

In front of them, the land fell away sharply for several hundred metres. In the valley below they could see a wide river twisting its way across the plain and on its banks a couple of kilometres away stood a walled city. Towers and spires could be seen jutting up above the imposing city walls, and from this elevated angle, Tom could see many houses and buildings built around a network of roads that radiated out from the centre of the city like the spokes of a wheel. Smoke rose from chimney stacks and tiny figures could be seen moving around like ants in a nest. This was by far the biggest city that they had seen yet.

The city was surrounded by acres and acres of farms and fields. Arable crops grew in neat straight lines and animals could be seen grazing in open pastures. In the distance to the north was a thick forest that extended almost as far as they could see, but beyond it they could just make out a substantial body of water as sunlight reflected from its surface.

"Behold the great city of Derralt," Ardum announced.

"It almost doesn't look real from up here," mused Alex.

"Yeah, it looks like something out of a Disney movie," agreed Jimmy.

"Is that the sea in the distance?" asked Tom.

"No," replied Lalitha. "That is Lake Viran. The river that you see down there is the River Viran. Its source lies to the south in the mountains that we travelled through before we reached Brentar, and it feeds the great lake that you see in the distance. The sea is another two days' journey westwards."

"Is Derralt bigger than Krassak?" Jimmy asked.

"Krassak is bigger and much grander, as befitting a capital city," Ardum grinned. "Derralt is a hub for commerce as it stands at the exact centre of the realm. It is often said that all roads lead to Derralt."

"The city looks pretty well fortified," Alex said.

"The walls of Derralt have never been breached... even in the magi wars," Ardum said, "It was on these plains that King Athrun defeated the rebel magus Berellon, and on those walls that you see before you where he mounted the heads of Berellon and his fellow traitors."

The view down over Derralt and the plains surrounding it was captivating and everyone stood quietly taking it all in for several minutes before Jimmy broke the silence.

"Can we see Krassak from here?"

"No," Lalitha answered. "Krassak lies to the north of the forest you can see. The River Viran flows out at the northern end of the lake and passes Krassak before it empties into the Western Sea."

"So, where is the castle that we need to get to?" Tom enquired.

"Look to the left," Ardum smiled.

Tom turned to the left and looked along the ridge of the escarpment. About a kilometre away along another track stood an imposing looking fortress that overlooked Derralt and the lands below.

"That is Castle Deman, the home of Lady Castra Deman," Lalitha told them. "She was my father's greatest ally and is the head of the richest and most powerful family in the land, outside the royal family of course. I hope that my message got through to her here and that she is expecting our arrival."

"This is where I told all members of the royal guard (That are still loyal to the Royal Family) to make for," Ardum told them. "I am hopeful that a significant number of my comrades will be here waiting for us."

"Let us go and find out," Lalitha said. "I will ride with you at the head of the procession Lord Ardum."

The team hurried back to the carriage and climbed in as Ardum set off towards the castle with Lalitha at his side.

CHAPTER 45

Castle Deman

As the carriage followed the track along the ridge of the escarpment, the views down over the city were spectacular. The team were glued to the windows as they took in the panorama before them.

It took a little over ten minutes before Ardum halted his horse in front of a huge barbican built into the fortified walls of the castle. An ancient portcullis barred their way and there was no way around.

"Who goes there?" shouted a voice form the tower of the gatehouse.

"It is Lord Cindal Ardum and companions of his that your Lady will be eager to greet," Ardum called.

There was silence for quite some time and Tom began to think that they were not going to be welcome at the castle, before there was a sudden loud noise of clanking chains and the portcullis slowly rose to reveal two strong wooden gates. Ardum urged his horse forwards and as he approached the gates, they swung open to admit him.

Everyone followed Ardum's lead. They passed through walls that were over ten metres thick and emerged into an extensive courtyard that was thriving with activity. All around them were armed soldiers, horses and carts filled with armaments and provisions. Shelters had been erected everywhere and many fires burned with an accompanying aroma of roasting meat. Many of the soldiers turned to look at them and, on seeing Lord Ardum's face they quickly picked up their shields and began to beat their swords against them. The noise became louder and louder until Tom could hardly hear himself think.

It was at this point that Lalitha lowered the scarf from her face. The noise stopped abruptly and the soldiers began to fall to one knee and bow their heads. Lalitha smiled, took the Book from her leather bag and held it aloft. The Soulstone blazed to life and the soldiers looked up in awe. One man climbed to his feet and shouted at the top of his lungs.

"Hail Princess Lalitha; bearer of the Great Book."

The soldiers all rose and the noise of their cheering and shield-beating was deafening.

There was movement at the back of the crowd, and Alex nudged Tom and pointed as a group of figures made their way through the cheering men. A tall woman with short grey hair led three armoured men towards them, a determined look on her face. She wore a long white ermine-edged gown which would have been dragging in the dust of the courtyard if she had not been holding it up with her left hand. The soldiers fell back like the receding tide and a path opened up through the crowd.

Ardum and Lalitha climbed down from their horses and stood watching the approaching woman as she strode towards them and stopped directly in front of Lalitha. She had a serious look on her face and she stared into Lalitha's eyes.

Nothing was said for a few moments and then a smile slowly crept across the woman's face.

"Lalitha, it is good to see you child."

Lalitha launched herself at the woman and they clenched each other in a tight embrace.

"Lady Deman," Lalitha cried. "I cannot tell you how glad I am to see you."

"Come child, no need to be so formal. Call me Castra."

"Thank you… Castra."

"Lord Ardum," Castra said. "I am glad that you escaped the capital. I understand that it is you that I have to thank for having so many deserters from the king's royal guard arrive at my door?"

"Yes, my Lady," grinned Ardum. "I did make it known that any soldiers still loyal to the throne would be welcome here."

"So they are, I just hope you will be helping me find the coin to pay for all the meat I have had to buy in order to feed them all."

Ardum went quiet as he floundered to find the right response. Castra laughed out loud.

"Do not worry, Ardum. The day that I cannot afford to feed a few soldiers will be a sad day indeed."

Tom, Alex, Danny and Jimmy had climbed down from the carriage and stood watching the exchange.

"Did you receive my message, Lady Castra?" Lalitha asked.

"I did Lalitha. I must admit that some of the message was difficult to decipher, but I understood your need for secrecy. You did not speak your name in the message, but it was apparent to me that it was you who sent it. You spoke of warriors from another realm. Are these the warriors standing before us now?"

"They are. They are few, but they are strong. The Book led me to them and they have proven themselves to be both brave and loyal. One of them, Daniel Adams, was even Chosen by the Book."

"One of them is Chosen?" Castra exclaimed.

"Yes. Daniel Adams and his companions escorted me to Gessan and we completed the Ceremony of Binding. We can both now channel the power of the Souls through the Great Book."

"That is good news indeed princess. Introduce your companions to me."

Lalitha gestured to Danny and he led the team over to meet their host.

"Lady Castra Deman, this is the Chosen Daniel Adams and his companions Thomas McAllister, Alexandra Aluko and James Lang."

They all bowed their heads to the grey-haired figure.

"Welcome to you all," Castra smiled. "You have my gratitude for protecting Princess Lalitha and getting her back to us safely. She is our only hope of preserving our way of life here in Zakastra. If the usurper in the capital is allowed to establish himself on the throne, then our days are numbered."

"There is no need to thank us, Lady Deman," Tom said. "Lalitha has helped me more than I can tell you in the short time that I have known her."

"Nevertheless, we are in your debt for giving us hope that not all is lost. Come let us go inside and we can talk properly."

"What about all our equipment in the carriage?"

Castra turned to one of the armoured men standing at her shoulder.

"Lissan, arrange for my friends' possessions to be brought up to the keep."

"Of course, my Lady."

"Now friends, please accompany me and tell me of your travels."

Castra gestured with her hand and she led them towards the large stone keep in the centre of the courtyard. The structure towered above them and as they climbed a flight of steps to the main entrance, Tom craned his neck to look at the battlements far above him. The stonework was adorned with enormous statues of warriors and noblemen who all stared down menacingly at them. The figures were so lifelike that Tom could imagine them coming to life to repel any attackers that dared try to breach the keep.

As they reached the top of the steps, a soldier swung an iron-bound wooden door open and bowed his head as Lady Castra passed through it. Before he walked inside, Tom turned and looked back at the courtyard and all the soldiers within it. Most of the soldiers had returned to cooking, eating or sharpening their swords, but several of them still watched with awe-struck expressions as Lalitha disappeared inside the keep. They had an almost religious fervour in their eyes and Tom didn't doubt their loyalty to the young princess. Alex touched his hand and Tom smiled as he followed her inside.

The interior of the keep was nothing like Ardum's house at Prentak. The entrance hall was more like the library at Gessan. The room was huge, but there were few windows so it was quite dark inside. Candles burned in a multitude of wall sconces, and a massive wooden chandelier filled with more candles hung from the ceiling by a thick metal chain.

They followed Castra through another door that had its own guard and they found themselves in a banqueting hall with a large round table. A fire burned brightly in the fireplace and flagpoles lined the walls, each with a colourful banner hanging from it. The banners all featured the same coat of arms, which Tom realised was a stylised representation of Castle Deman.

"Sit," Castra said gesturing at the table. She clicked her fingers and a boy rushed over.

"Bring refreshments for my guests."

"Yes, my Lady," the boy bowed and hurried away.

Once everyone was sat down and servants had delivered flagons of some kind of beer and bowls of what Jimmy hoped were sausages, Castra shooed the servants away and sat down next to Lalitha.

"Tell me everything," she demanded.

It took over an hour to recount the details of their adventures since Lalitha had fled the tower at Krassak. Castra asked many questions and listened intently as the team gave her all the details that she sought. Once they had brought Castra up to date, she sat back in her chair and stroked her lips with her finger as she processed everything that she had heard.

"Your message caused great consternation in my hall Lalitha. Some doubted that it was you that had sent it and believed that Gask had sent the message himself to discover our intentions. Others agreed with me when I declared that I believed you to be alive still. It is no little relief to discover that I was right to trust my heart."

"I sent a second message to Lord Ardum in the capital, but he never received it," Lalitha told her. "It could be that the messenger arrived in Krassak too late to deliver the message before Ardum had to flee, but I must admit to being worried that the message was intercepted."

"There is little we can do about that now princess," Ardum said. "Your messenger rode from Serat in the south and there are many things that can happen to a lone traveller on the roads. Let us not worry about that which we can do nothing to cure."

"We have already sent scouts to the north to watch troop movements around the capital," Castra added. "We have had no word back of anything untoward happening there yet."

"Why has Gask not attacked you here already, Lady Deman?" Tom asked.

"He has control of the army, but his grip on the powerful families in the capital is still weak. Several of them still wait for proof that you are dead. Only then can the succession be ratified. If he were seen to attack the Deman family without any provocation before the succession is determined, some of his support would be threatened. That insect is too weak to risk the families rising against him; he would rather use his serpent tongue to beguile the fools than use direct force."

"Could we rely on any of the families in the capital to support us?"

"Once they know that Lalitha is alive, some will support you in principle, but few have the means to support you with soldiers. Gask has a large number of men in and around the city and up to now he has been unwilling to use them, though that may not be the case if he were to face armed opposition."

"So, we're on our own?"

"Indeed, we are, Thomas McAllister."

"Can we get inside the capital without raising the alarm?" Alex asked.

"Our forces must move through the forests that border the eastern shore of Lake Viran and they must travel at night," Castra replied. "If we are careful and stealthy, we may be able to approach Krassak unseen. It will be difficult and slow, but it is possible. Getting into the city once we get there will present more of a problem though."

"We think that we have a solution to that," Tom said. "Lalitha knows of a network of secret tunnels that run under the capital. If we can get to one of the entrances to the tunnels, we will use them to enter the tower from below."

"I didn't know about these tunnels," Castra said thoughtfully. "It seems that King Lestri kept more secrets than even I was aware of."

"I escaped from Krassak using these tunnels," Lalitha said, "so I can confirm that they do exist. My father showed me many of the concealed entrances and I know which of the entrances we can use to gain access to the capital."

"Time is of the essence," Ardum said gravely. "If we are to do this, we need to do it as soon as we can. The longer Gask has to entrench his position, the more difficult he will become to defeat. Also, the longer we stay here, the more chance there will be that Gask learns of our intentions and is forced to move against us. How soon could the men be ready to move out, Lady Castra?"

"They are ready right now. Everyone has been preparing for your arrival and preparations have been made to allow us to mobilise as soon as you are ready to depart. I would suggest that you use the rest of today's daylight to rest, and once the sun sets, you can use the cover of darkness to cross the plain. You should be able to conceal your forces within the forests before the sun rises again."

"Very well, my Lady," agreed Ardum. "That sounds like wise counsel. We do not want the whole population of Derralt to stand watching as our forces march across the plain before them. I will tell the men that we depart at sunset today and march under the cover of darkness."

"Lady Castra," Lalitha asked, "have you had any word about my brother Relfa?"

"No, child, I have not. He was seen being escorted through the Tower by Gask's soldiers after your father's death, but nothing has been seen of him since then. I do not know if he lives, or if Gask murdered him as well. Either way, there is nothing that milksop of a man would be capable of doing to aid us."

There was a loud knock at the door and the team's equipment was brought into the room. Once everything had been laid carefully on the floor, the soldiers went back outside, closing the door behind them.

"I have horses that you can take with you when you leave. I will arrange to have your saddlebags loaded onto them when the time comes."

"No more travellin' in the carriage then," mused Danny. "I'm not sure if I'm happy about that or not."

"I'll be much happier to be back on a horse," Alex said. "The carriage was just so boring. All we did was sleep."

"Do you wish to sleep now while you have the chance?" Castra asked. "I have rooms that you could use."

Tom looked around at the others. They had done nothing but doze and catnap for over a week in the carriage and, with the prospect of moving into more dangerous territory, Tom's mind was too busy thinking about what the next part of their journey held in store to sleep.

"Thank you, Lady Deman, but I think I would rather spend the time checking our equipment and preparing for our departure."

Everyone else nodded their agreement. Nobody rated their chances of being able to get to sleep very highly.

"Very well, you can use this room while our forces muster in the courtyard. If you need anything, ask one of the guards and they will bring you what you need."

"Are you travelling with us, Lady?" Lalitha asked.

"No, Lalitha. I will stay here. My strengths do not include wielding a sword. Once I hear that your quest has been successful, I will journey to the capital to assist you, but until then I think it best that I remain within the walls of Castle Deman."

"As you wish, Lady Castra."

"Lalitha, come with me and I will find you something more suitable to wear for what comes next."

Castra took Lalitha's hand and with a last smile back in the team's direction, she led her from the room and the doors swung shut behind her.

"Come on then," Tom announced. "Let's do a full weapons check and make sure we're ready for whatever tonight brings."

The contents of all the saddlebags and Bergens were emptied out onto the table and Danny made a note of what they needed to split between them.

"I've divvied up everythin' that we have and it's not lookin' too bad," Danny announced. "We've still got eleven spare rifle mags each and three mags each for the Glocks. We've not used any of the claymores or grenades so we're lookin' good."

"I think we should keep as much as we can in the Bergens," Tom decided. "Perhaps leave the flashbangs in the saddlebags. What do you think about the frag grenades and the claymores?"

"I think put them in the Bergens as well," Danny said. "When we got hit by the bandits on the road to Brentar, we saw how easy it was to get split up from the horses. If we run the risk of meeting resistance on the road, I would rather not have to watch my kit disappearin' off into the distance. The packs will be heavy, but they're lighter than they were when we started this whole thing back down south."

"I agree," nodded Alex.

"Okay, let's do that," Tom agreed. "Just check your survival kits as well. If we're short of anything like bandages, we can see what Castra can find for us."

Everyone re-packed their Bergens with the equipment that they had decided to carry in them and the rest was crammed into the saddlebags. Tom looked at the solar charger that he had carried all the way from Stonehenge and he put it back onto the table next to the NiMh battery for his arm.

"Leave them, Tom," Alex said. "You don't need either of them anymore. Its weight that you don't need to carry."

Tom thought about it for a moment and then nodded. Alex was right. Lalitha had fixed his arm and they didn't have anything else that needed to be charged. The days spent permanently worrying about running out of charge in his arm were over. Tom felt liberated at being able to escape his debilitating dependency on electricity.

Danny and Jimmy laid the Colt C8's and Glocks on the table and began to strip them all down. They cleaned dust from the mechanisms and then reassembled everything carefully, making sure that the rifles and pistols all worked smoothly.

Tom and Alex left them to it and moved their chairs so that they could sit in front of the fire. Even though it was sunny and warm outside, it was quite chilly inside the banqueting hall. Tom put his arm round Alex and pulled her close. There was something Tom had been thinking about and he knew that Alex wouldn't be happy about it.

"Alex," Tom said softly, "there is something I want you to think about."

"What's that then?" she asked with a smile.

"I want you to stay here with Lady Deman while we go to Krassak."

"What? No way!"

"Alex, listen to me. I don't know how things are going to go when we get to the capital. We're hugely outnumbered and even though Lalitha has the Book, I'm not a hundred percent convinced that we can pull this off. I want you to be safe."

"The only way I'm staying here is if you stay with me."

"I can't Alex. You know that I have to help Lalitha. Not just because of what the Book said, but because I owe her. Look what she's done for me…"

"I know that, Tom. I know you need to help her and I know more than anyone what she has done for you, but don't expect me to just wave you off and then sit here for days on end worrying about you and praying that you're still alive. That ain't gonna happen! You go… I go. Simple as that."

"But Alex…"

"There is no 'But Alex'. I have fought by your side for a long time Tom and this is no different to what we've been through time and time again. Yes, there is a risk, but I am just as capable of looking after myself as the others."

"I know that... I just... I can't lose you, Alex."

"And I can't even think about losing you either. All the more reason to make sure that we look after each other."

She leaned forward and kissed him tenderly.

"Come on, Tom. Let's just get to Krassak and get this done."

Tom smiled and nodded. He knew her well enough to know that arguing any further was a pointless exercise. Tom was glad that she would be with him, but at the same time if he even started to think about anything bad happening to her, his stomach clenched tightly and his head swam. He would just have to make sure that nothing bad happened.

More food was brought into the hall and as they ate, Lalitha appeared. She was now dressed in leather armour that hugged her body tightly. Her hair was tied back in a long ponytail and she wore a short sword on her belt. The Book was, as ever, hanging from her shoulder in its leather bag.

"Wow," Alex exclaimed, "you look every inch the warrior princess."

"Thank you, Alexandra Aluko," Lalitha smiled. "It is Lady Deman's armour from when she was younger. She thought it would protect me and also give the right impression to our men. She said that they need to see what they are fighting for."

"You look fantastic," Jimmy beamed. "They will be proud to fight for you."

"Daniel Adams?" Lalitha asked. "Will you be proud to fight for me?"

"Don't forget that I am Bound too, Lalitha," Danny answered. "I will be fightin' *with* you not *for* you."

A brief frown flashed across Lalitha's face, but it vanished again almost instantly. She was about to say something else to Danny, but was interrupted as the door opened. Ardum and Castra strode in followed by a number of armed soldiers.

"The sun begins to set, my friends," Ardum announced. "These men will take your saddlebags to your horses. Let us make haste and prepare for our departure."

The soldiers gathered up the team's saddlebags and marched away with them.

"I wish you luck in your quest," Castra said to them all. "You fight to protect our way of life and it is imperative that you succeed. Princess Lalitha, I look forward to meeting you again once you sit upon the throne, and crows devour the flesh from the usurper's corpse as it hangs upon Krassak's walls."

"Thank you, Lady Castra," Lalitha said. "I will eagerly anticipate your arrival in Krassak."

Castra embraced Lalitha warmly and kissed her on the cheek.

"Daniel Adams," Castra said, turning to Danny. "You are also Bound and your fate is tied closely to Lalitha's. Protect her and protect the Book. If either are lost, then so is our cause."

"I will, my Lady," Danny nodded.

"To the rest of you, I thank you again for bringing Lalitha to us and for giving us the opportunity to grasp victory from the jaws of defeat. Kill Gask and his fanatics and allow us to restore order to Zakastra."

Tom, Alex and Jimmy nodded.

"We will protect Lalitha and make sure that she takes her father's place on the throne," Jimmy said, a determined look upon his face.

"Very well," said Lord Ardum taking a deep breath. "It is time for us to depart."

Tom picked up his Bergen and put it on the table before crouching down and looping his arms through its straps. He then stood up and fastened the pack's belt around his waist. The others did the same and, once everyone was ready, they followed Ardum back through the keep and outside to the courtyard.

Many of the soldiers in the courtyard were mounted, but most were to travel on foot. The men stood in ordered ranks and as Lalitha emerged at the top of the steps, they all stood to attention and then began to noisily bang their weapons against their shields.

Ardum held up his arm and the noise subsided.

"We ride to Krassak," he called in a loud voice. "We take our rightful heir to reclaim her throne and vanquish the usurper that would steal our way of life from us."

The men cheered and beat their shields again.

"Prepare to ride," Ardum shouted and mounted his great black steed.

The team climbed up onto their horses and urged them forwards as Ardum and Lalitha rode through the ranks of cheering soldiers. Tom and the team fell in line behind Castra's commanders as they followed their princess out beyond the castle walls.

CHAPTER 46

On the Road to Krassak

The armed column moved quickly along the ridge line back towards the main road, and Tom looked down at Derralt as they rode. The city was shrouded in the darkness, but lights could be seen in windows and a haze of smoke lay over the rooftops. Fires had been lit around the city walls, but their light was way too far away for it to illuminate their progress.

The long line of mounted and foot soldiers made its way carefully down the road that wound its way down the scarp face. The loose dusty surface was treacherous underfoot in the dark, but everyone made it safely to the valley floor below.

The column moved as quietly as possible. Derralt's fortified walls were still quite a distance away, but care was still needed so that the population inside the city did not witness the passing of Lalitha's army. They managed to avoid moving too close to any of the outlying farms and Tom was soon relieved to see that they were approaching the open plain that stretched out to meet the forests to the north.

It took the army almost two hours to cross the plain, but the safety of the trees was close at hand now. Tom began to breathe more easily as the front of the column came within a few hundred metres of the tree line. Above them, the evening clouds had thinned out and the moon shone down over them, making the forests ahead much more visible.

Ardum slowed his horse down so that Tom could catch him up.

"Once we are within the forest, we will be able to relax a little," Ardum told him. "We will be able to hide within the cover of the trees and if we are careful, we will be able to travel up the eastern shore of Lake Viran without being detected."

Tom was about to reply, but his eyes were drawn by movement in front of them. A rider burst from the forest and galloped quickly towards them.

Ardum raised his arm to bring everyone to a halt and they watched as the rider rapidly closed the distance between them.

"I think that is one of our scouts from Castle Deman!" one of the commanders yelled as they watched the horse draw closer. "I recognise his mount."

The scout was still over a hundred metres away when they saw him suddenly twitch and crash down to the ground. His horse, now rider-less, veered to the right and galloped wildly past Tom, a manic look in its eyes.

The commander who had recognised the scout rode forwards towards the fallen man. When he reached the motionless body, he looked down from his saddle and turned back to look at Ardum. As he did so, Tom began to see more movement in the shadows of the forest. He squinted to try to see what it was and gasped sharply as the whole of the tree line seemed to shift. A long line of men came out of the forest and all of them were carrying longbows. Before Tom could do anything, the men brought their bows up, nocked their arrows and fired them upwards into the night sky.

"Take cover!" Tom yelled. "There are archers in the woods."

There was a faint whistling noise in the air and arrows began to rain down all around them. The commander by the fallen scout spurred his mount to try and get out of range, but he was not quick enough. As he galloped forwards, he screamed and fell face-first under his horse's hooves, his back riddled with arrows.

"Footmen! Shield wall!" shouted Ardum. "Riders fall back behind the wall!"

The riders at the head of the column wheeled their horses around and raced back towards the foot soldiers at the rear of the column. A rider near to Ardum slumped in his saddle as an arrow drove itself through his chest. Tom hung on to his horse desperately as it ran towards safety. He bounced dangerously in the saddle and was so busy trying to not fall off his mount that he barely noticed the incoming arrows until one burst into bright orange fire just as it was about to hit Lalitha. The Book was protecting her.

The foot soldiers quickly spread out into a wide line of two ranks. The front rank placed their shields against the ground and crouched behind them, while the men standing behind them raised their shields up above the men in front to form a solid wall of wood and metal. Arrows hammered down at them and embedded themselves deep into the shields in the wall.

As the retreating riders reached the shield wall, a gap opened so that the riders could withdraw behind it. Another wave of arrows rained down and many of the retreating riders were hit. Horses crashed to the ground and riders were flung from their mounts as the arrows punched through their armour. The air was filled with the screams of injured men and horses.

"Shield wall, hold firm!" Ardum shouted as he rode through the opening in the wall. The riders galloped out of range of the archers and Ardum turned to face Lalitha as the gap in the shield wall closed behind them.

"I do not know who these men are Princess Lalitha, but there are many of them and their shooting is organised. I fear that Gask has sent them here."

"What do we do?" Lalitha asked worriedly.

Ardum glanced at her, a grim expression on his face and shouted to his men. "Archers! Take your positions!"

Archers from Castle Deman formed a line behind the shield wall, each man pushing a handful of arrows into the ground in front of them. The archers readied their bows and pulled an arrow from the ground. They nocked their arrows, looked towards their targets and pulled the heavy bowstrings back until the tight sinew touched their cheeks.

"Loose!" Screamed Ardum.

With a loud whoosh a wave of arrows shot through the air and ploughed into the unprotected enemy archers. Several of them fell to the ground, but the remaining men fired another volley back at them.

"Incoming arrows!" Ardum yelled and his archers quickly took cover behind the shield wall. The enemy's arrows ripped into the shields again, but the line held, and Tom only saw one man fall as an arrow found its way between two shields and drove deep into his shoulder.

Tom estimated that the enemy archers were less than two hundred metres away. He didn't know what the range of the bows was, but he knew what the effective range of a C8 assault rifle was four-hundred metres. The archers would be sitting ducks.

"Ardum," Tom yelled. "Pull the wall back to our position here."

"But the enemy will be out of range of our arrows," Ardum argued.

"Good. Just do it and we will take over."

Ardum ordered the shield wall to come back towards them and as the soldiers walked slowly backwards with their shields still raised, Tom pulled his rifle from its leather skip and dismounted.

"Alex. Danny. Jimmy. With me!"

The team cocked the actions on their rifles as they walked towards the rear of the shield wall. The enemy's arrows were falling short of their position now and Ardum ordered the shield wall to hold where they were.

The soldiers in the wall parted and Tom led his team through the openings. They took position a few metres in front of the wall, took their Bergens off, laid down on the ground and rested their rifles on top of their packs.

"Okay. Single shots. Conserve ammo," Tom ordered.

He squinted through his scope. It was difficult to see the enemy, but the moonlight helped to make them just visible. He picked out one of the archers near the tree line and squeezed his trigger. The man fell and the archers on either side of the target looked around in confusion.

Danny fired a round at the archers and soon, all four of them were firing bullets at the enemy soldiers. The sudden noise and flash of flame from the rifles' muzzles caused the men in the shield wall standing behind Tom to flinch and move backwards, but they saw the damage that the gunfire was doing to the enemy and cheered loudly.

Very quickly, the rising number of casualties proved too much for the opposing archers and they gradually began to break ranks and run back into the forest.

"We have them," declared Ardum. He turned in his saddle and drew his sword. "Riders, prepare to charge."

"Lord Ardum, what are you doing?" Lalitha shouted.

"We must chase the retreating enemy and finish them. I cannot allow them to inflict more damage on our men."

Ardum raised his sword above his head and screamed at the top of his voice.

"Charge!"

His massive black stallion stamped its feet and neighed loudly before rushing forwards. The riders at either side of Ardum drew their weapons, charged through the gaps in the shield wall and thundered towards the tree line.

"Cease fire," Tom yelled as the horses entered their line of fire.

The four of them rose to their knees and watched as Ardum and his mounted soldiers galloped towards the forest. Tom could feel the ground vibrating with the pounding of the charging horses. As Ardum approached the trees, Tom raised his rifle and looked through his scope. He could see the riders as they stormed forwards, but... what was that? There was movement in the tall bracken in front of the trees. It was more enemy archers.

The archers stood up from where they had been hiding and quickly fired a salvo at the rapidly approaching horses. The arrows smashed into the riders and their horses, but rather than turning to retreat, Ardum and his men thundered on. The mounted charge had been hit hard by the archer's arrows, but the remaining riders raised their swords, ready to smash their way through the line of bowmen. Just as they were about to reach their targets, the surviving archers quickly sprinted back into the trees and, from out of bracken, another line of men with spears and pikes stood up, stepped forwards and set their weapons against the ground.

"Shit," Tom breathed. "It's a fucking trap."

It was too late for the charging horses to stop their forward momentum. They crashed into the wall of spiked weapons with a noise like thunder. Many of the pikemen in the charging horses' paths were crushed, but the cost to Ardum's mounted soldiers was far worse. Men and horses were impaled on the weapons of the enemy and screams filled the air. Wounded horses bucked and writhed to free themselves from the sharp weapons and their riders were thrown to the ground. The riders that survived the initial charge rained blows down on the pikemen with their swords, and fought desperately to pull their horses away to safety. Several men were dragged from their horses and Tom lost sight of them as they disappeared into a sea of pikes and swords.

The few remaining riders managed to break free of the pikemen and they galloped back towards the shield wall. As they raced back across the open ground, Tom heard a massive roar coming from the forest and all of a sudden, the tree line erupted as a hoard of armed soldiers emerged and hurtled towards them. There were hundreds of them. They screamed loudly as they brandished swords, axes and all manner of other vicious looking weapons as they ran forwards.

Tom watched Ardum lead the remnants of his mounted charge back towards the shield wall and once they had made it through the ranks of soldiers, Tom and the others opened fire again. The sheer number of soldiers charging at them was frightening. As fast as Tom and the team took their targets down, more leapt over their fallen comrades and charged on towards them.

The enemy was within fifty metres and Tom switched his C8 to auto, stood up and began firing quick bursts at the looming mob.

"Switch to auto and retreat to the shield wall," Tom yelled.

The enemy's archers were advancing behind the charging horde and Tom suddenly saw arrows hitting the ground around him. He picked up his Bergen, quickly pushed his arms through the straps and heaved it up onto his back.

"We need to get a move on, Boss!" Danny yelled as he fired another stream of bullets at the rapidly approaching soldiers.

"Okay, go!" Tom shouted.

Tom squeezed off a last burst of fire and followed the others as they ran back behind the shield wall. As soon as they were safe, the wall closed behind them and the soldiers braced themselves for the imminent attack.

Ardum's archers set up position again behind the shield wall, and began to fire at the approaching force over the top of the men in front of them. The arrows rained down on the approaching horde, but the resulting casualties did little to reduce the tidal wave of men heading towards them.

Tom pushed his way between two of the men in the shield wall and got them to open a small gap between the upper shields. He poked his C8 through the gap and opened up on the oncoming soldiers. Men fell as his bullets ripped through them, but Tom's magazine was soon empty and the attackers were almost on them. Tom pulled back to reload his weapon and the soldiers closed the gap in the wall.

As Tom slapped a new mag into the C8, the charging army hit their shield wall with the force of an express train. The crash as they smashed against the wall of wooden shields was immense. The defenders were forced slowly backwards as the enemy battered the shields with their pikes, swords and axes. Ardum's men held fast, but many were injured as the attackers thrust their swords through gaps that appeared between the shields and chopped viciously into the top of the wall with their axes.

Tom looked up and down the rear of the defensive line and saw that not only was the enemy swarming at the shield wall, but they were also trying to outflank them. The men at each end of the wall were having to desperately fight off the oncoming enemy. Tom suddenly saw that Ardum had dismounted and stood nearby. The older man had a nasty looking wound on his head and blood streaked his face. Ardum looked at Tom and shook his head gravely.

"We will not be able to hold them, Thomas McAllister. There are too many and we are too few."

"What do we do?"

"You must take Princess Lalitha and get her to safety. We will hold them for as long as we can. You need to go before they surround us and there is no escape."

Lalitha had climbed down from her horse and was standing nearby. She had heard what Ardum had said. "Lord Ardum, I will not leave you."

Ardum was about to reply but, with a mighty surge, the attackers suddenly forced their way through the wall to their right and enemy soldiers began to stream through the breach. Tom saw that Lalitha had the Book in her hands and as he watched, her eyes began to sparkle with sparks of orange fire and he could hear the whispers of the

Souls in his head. Lalitha turned towards the attackers as they hacked at the soldiers around them. She held the Book up in front of her and the Soulstone blazed with an intense light that lit up the area around her.

"Scalto!" she screamed.

Four of the enemy soldiers instantly exploded in a spray of blood and bone. The other attackers briefly hesitated, but more were surging through the breach behind them. They raised their weapons and charged towards Lalitha. Alex brought her rifle up and squeezed the trigger. Several of the attackers were thrown backwards as her bullets ripped through them.

"Scalto!" Lalitha cried again and three more attackers were instantly blown apart.

Tom shouldered his C8 and blasted at the incoming soldiers. Several of them fell, but more surged through the breach. Ardum's men tried their best to close the opening in the shield wall, but the sheer number of men pushing and hacking their way through made it impossible.

Ardum's archers abandoned their bows as the risk of hitting their own men was now too great. Instead, they drew swords and long, wicked looking knives and launched themselves into the fight. Men from both sides screamed and fell as blades cut through flesh and severed limbs.

Jimmy and Danny fired prolonged bursts of bullets at the enemy fighters as they pushed through the shield wall. They took down a dozen or more of them, but the attackers surged on like an enraged swarm of ants.

A huge figure with a two-headed axe barged his way through the dying bodies of his comrades and charged straight at Alex, his axe raised ready to cut her in two. Alex raised her rifle and pulled the trigger, but nothing happened; her mag was empty. As the giant of a man swung the axe down, she dodged sideways and the huge blade missed her by just a matter of millimetres. The attacker screamed at her, spittle spraying from his mouth. Alex ejected the empty mag and scrabbled to get a new one into the gun. The big man swung his axe back over his head and lunged at her. As he started to bring the vicious looking weapon down, Tom quickly dived past Alex, jammed his rifle into the axeman's chest and pulled the trigger. The big man's body was shredded as Tom shot through him into the rampaging soldiers behind him. Alex's eyes met Tom's and she nodded gratefully.

Another man with a short, vicious looking sword leapt over the axeman's corpse and swung his weapon at Tom's head. The strap of Tom's rifle had become snagged on the dead axeman's armour, and he couldn't lift it high enough to get a shot off.

Instinctively, Tom raised his left arm to protect his head and the sword struck him hard. Tom gasped loudly as the impact of the blow shot through his body, but it had been his left arm rather than his right. He glanced down to see a deep gouge across the surface of his arm, but as the swordsman looked on in astonishment, Tom flexed his fingers and grinned at him. At that moment, Alex slammed a new mag into her rifle, cocked the action and blasted the man in the face. His body was lifted in the air and fell back across the body of his comrade.

"Thanks, Alex," he spluttered.

"You're welcome," she replied grimly. "Good job that was your left arm. That asshole's blade would've cut clean through your other one."

"Tell me about it!" he replied.

"Frag out!" came a shout from nearby.

Danny had pulled the grenades from his pack and Tom saw him pull the pin from one and lob it over the wall into the throng of attacking soldiers. The grenade exploded with a huge boom, and chunks of both shrapnel and enemy soldiers peppered the shield wall. He did the same with another two of the frag grenades and smiled grimly as they exploded, ripping through the ranks of the enemy.

Soldiers still powered their way through the breach in the wall and two of them rushed at Danny screaming as they raised their swords. Jimmy calmly took aim and brought them down with two carefully aimed bullets.

Enemy soldiers were hacking at the men in the shield wall and the breach was beginning to widen rapidly, allowing even more of the opposing fighters to push through.

"Drive them back through the breach," screamed Tom as he fired repeatedly as more and more attackers came towards them.

The noise around them was deafening and there seemed to be men running in all directions. Ardum thrust his sword through the throat of a nearby soldier and glared at Tom as he turned to face more of the attackers battling their way through the breach.

"Why are you still here?" he shouted desperately and pointed to where Lalitha stood. "Get Lalitha to safety!"

Ardum should not have taken his eyes off the men he was battling. As he shouted to Tom, one of the soldiers in front of him swung high with his sword. Ardum raised his own blade to block the attack, but as he did so, a second attacker thrust his pike forwards. It sliced straight through Ardum's armour and on into his stomach. The soldier twisted the weapon viciously before pulling it out again. Ardum's torso erupted in a fountain of dark blood and he fell forwards into the growing pile of the dead and dying.

"No!" screamed Lalitha. She clutched the Book to her chest and Tom could feel the hairs on his arms stand up.

Danny swung round to look at her, his eyes wide.

"Boss, she's tryin' to do somethin' big. Stop her!"

It was too late. The light from the Soulstone pulsed brighter and brighter and the whispers in Tom's head turned to shrieks. Lalitha's face was a mask of absolute rage and fire blazed brightly in her eyes. She raised the Book towards the breach and roared her command.

"PYRTA!"

Instantly, a huge cascade of flame leapt from the Soulstone and blasted into the soldiers in front of her. Everything and everyone caught in the unearthly fire instantly burst into a raging pillar of flame. Burning men, both friend and foe, staggered blindly into each other as their flesh was seared and their blood boiled. The noise of their screams was terrible, but the stench of their burning flesh was worse.

"What the fuck is she doing?" Screamed Alex. "She's killing almost as many of our own men as she is theirs."

Tom looked across to shout at Lalitha, but something was wrong. As he watched her, Lalitha's eyes rolled back into her head and the light from the Soulstone went out. He looked on in horror as Lalitha collapsed slowly to the ground.

"Lalitha's down!" Tom yelled. "Come on!"

With Alex on one side of him and Jimmy on the other, Tom blasted his way towards where Lalitha had fallen. The advance of soldiers through the breach in the wall had briefly slowed because of the unbearable heat from all the burning bodies, but there were still several enemy soldiers on the wrong side of the wall who had managed to escape Lalitha's flames. One of them ran towards Lalitha, a wicked looking spiked club in his hand, and Tom only just managed to gun him down before he reached her. Alex switched her C8 back to single shot and carefully picked out her targets. Bang. Bang. Bang. Three more attackers fell and did not get up again.

As they made it to Lalitha's side, Alex quickly crouched next to her unconscious body to check that she was still breathing.

Danny and Jimmy caught up with them and fired at a group of enemy fighters who were battling their way towards them. The soldiers fell backwards in a heap as they raked them with gunfire.

"She's breathing and she's got a pulse," Alex said. "It's weak, but it's there."

"We've gotta get out of here, Boss," Jimmy yelled as he shot at more soldiers. "There's no end to these bastards."

Tom nodded. The fighting at the shield wall was still intense. The defenders were slowly being overrun by the enemy soldiers who continued to batter the wall with their weapons. The fires were temporarily plugging the breach in the wall, but that would not last much longer.

The last of Lady Castra's commanders looked at Tom from where he fought with his men to keep their section of the wall together. Their eyes met and Tom knew from the look on the man's face what was about to happen.

"Run now," the man shouted, "before it is too late. Make for the river. We will buy you what time we can."

Tom looked at the chaos and carnage around him and made his decision. He nodded at Castra's man and passed his rifle to Jimmy.

"Look after my rifle for me," he said before bending down to pick up Lalitha's unconscious body. As Tom picked her up into a fireman's lift, Danny took the Book from her hand and pushed it inside his tunic.

Jimmy and Alex shot at enemy soldiers through the breach in the wall as they tried to get past the flames and Tom had to shout to make himself heard.

"Okay. We need to run and we need to do it now. Are you all ready?"

The team all nodded and Alex quickly grabbed Tom and kissed him on the lips.

"For luck," she smiled grimly.

Tom looked back at Castra's commander and shouted over to him.

"Thank you… I'm sorry… I don't even know your name."

"My name is Treltan. Keep the princess safe. Go now!"

Tom took a deep breath and looked at the faces around him.

"RUN!" he yelled.

Alex, Jimmy and Danny sprinted south away from the battle and Tom followed as quickly as he could, shifting Lalitha's weight on his shoulder to help him keep his balance.

After running for about a hundred metres, Alex pulled up and turned to wait for Tom to catch up. Danny and Jimmy stopped with her and they all looked back towards the slaughter at the shield wall. The burning bodies illuminated the fighting around them and the noise of the battle was still loud in their ears. As they watched, there was a crash and a splintering noise and all of a sudden, the shield wall collapsed completely.

The attackers surged over the fallen defenders and the fighting became a chaotic maelstrom of men and weapons, each slashing and stabbing at the other.

The violence was horrific. Tom briefly saw a figure that he thought could be Treltan fighting with an enemy soldier before the tall man stumbled over one of his dead comrades and three soldiers with axes hacked at him as he fell to the ground. Jimmy raised his gun to try and help the few remaining defenders from Castle Deman, but all he could see through his scope was a seething mass of fighting bodies. He couldn't tell who was an enemy and who was not, so lowered his rifle and looked at Tom.

"What do we do, Boss?" he asked.

"This battle is lost," Tom answered solemnly. "We need to get to the river. If we can make it there, we might have a chance of getting away. We can't go into the forest and we won't make it all the way back to Castle Deman on foot before they catch us."

"Jesus, Boss," Danny exclaimed. "Look!"

Tom looked back towards the fighting and his stomach fell. Apart from pockets of fighting here and there, the battle seemed to be over. The army that had marched with them from Castle Deman a few short hours ago was gone. Massacred.

As he watched he saw the soldiers pause and look in their direction. One of them shouted something that Tom couldn't quite make out, but the meaning quickly became apparent as a large group of soldiers started to move in their direction. Archers formed up behind them and began to shoot arrows over the advancing men's heads.

"Shit," swore Tom. "Go right towards the river. Alex, help me with Lalitha."

Alex passed her rifle to Danny, pulled Lalitha's left arm over her shoulders and grabbed Lalitha around the waist. Tom did the same from the other side and between them, they carried her limp body as they rushed across the open ground. Behind them, Danny and Jimmy fired at the advancing men before they turned and chased after the others.

"Danny!" Tom yelled as they ran, "can the Book do anything to help us?"

"Like what, Boss? If I try to zap them all, you'll end up carryin' me too."

"Can it hide us?" Alex asked.

Danny pulled the Book from inside his tunic and held it tightly as he ran. They all heard the whispering start up again.

Tom glanced back. The chasing horde were catching them. Before long they would have to make a stand, but there were just so many of them. It would not end well!

Arrows started to fall around the team as they rushed across the open ground and Tom knew that one of them could be hit at any moment. They had to keep going as fast as they could.

An arrow streaked towards Danny's unprotected back, but instead of impaling him, it exploded in a flash of orange light. Danny grinned. The Book was protecting him. He was a Chosen!

"Danny. Come on. We're running out of time!"

Danny looked at Tom and his eyes filled with swirls of orange flame. As the whispers filled Tom's head, Danny stopped, crouched down and put his hand flat on the grass.

"Naralkos!" he said in a quiet but clear voice.

Once the word had been spoken, Danny's eyes cleared and he re-joined the others as they ran. All around them mist began to rise from the ground and after a few short seconds, the team was enveloped in a thick fog.

"Nice one Danny," Tom said quietly. "Keep heading this way. Try to stay as quiet as you can and for Christ's sake, let's not get split up."

The team rushed on through the fog. The sound of their pursuers became quieter, but Tom wasn't sure if this was an effect of the fog masking the sound, or if the soldiers had become disoriented by the sudden change in visibility.

"I've got an idea," Tom said all of sudden. "Let's use the claymores to slow these bastards down a bit. We'll have to be quick though. They're probably still right on our tail."

"I'll set them," Danny said. "It'll be safer for me to do it coz the Book is protectin' me from their arrows."

They stopped running for just long enough to allow Danny to quickly grab the claymore mines from Tom and Alex's packs. Everyone ran on through the mist while Danny stayed behind to push the first of the Claymores mounting spikes into the ground and activate the on-board infra-red tripwire. He moved forwards about twenty metres, set the next charge and quickly repeated the procedure two more times. Once all four mines were deployed in a line behind him, Danny sprinted ahead to catch up with the others. Once he reached them, they continued to move forward cautiously. They could hear voices somewhere in the fog and the team stuck close together as they moved forward as quietly as they could.

After only a few moments, the soldiers behind them got close enough to trigger the infrared tripwire on the first of the claymores and it went up with a huge boom. The explosion lit the fog up briefly and there were anguished screams as the mine's C4 core propelled seven hundred steel balls through the ranks of the oncoming enemy.

The team ran on and a minute or so later, the second mine detected movement and detonated loudly. Tom could hear the screams of injured men behind them and wondered if the rest of their pursuers would be scared off by the destruction caused by the first two claymores. His question was quickly answered as the third mine went up. No, they would not.

The devastating carnage caused by the mines bought Tom and the team some valuable time and they used it to stop briefly and catch their breath. Danny and Jimmy took over carrying Lalitha while Tom and Alex took all the rifles from them. As they set off running again, they could still hear the screaming of the mines' casualties, but they could also hear angry shouts. The crazy bastards were still coming.

They had only travelled another few metres before they heard the final claymore detonate. After the booming echo of the explosion had died away, Tom realised that he could hear something else through the fog in front of them. It was running water. The river must be close.

The voices behind them began to get closer again and as Tom looked back over his shoulder, he heard an arrow whistle past. He silently prayed that the archers were shooting blindly and couldn't somehow see them through the darkness. As he squinted into the fog, trying to locate their pursuers, Tom heard a voice not far behind him shout loudly.

"We approach the Viran. They have nowhere to run. We will catch the royal bitch and her bodyguards as they enter the water."

Tom leaned towards Alex and whispered urgently.

"We are almost at the river, but they are still behind us. Keep moving! We might have to make a stand when we get to the water."

The shout from the fog behind them had spurred them on. Tom gritted his teeth and forced his aching leg muscles to run just a bit further, but suddenly the ground disappeared from under their feet and the team found themselves careering down a steep slope covered in reeds. Danny and Jimmy dropped Lalitha as they skidded and rolled downwards in a tangle of arms and legs. Alex almost managed to keep her balance as she hurtled down after them, but her feet snagged on the reeds and she fell forwards in a heap. Tom tumbled down and came to an abrupt halt as his hip crashed into a rock at the bottom of the slope. When he looked up, he could see a wide expanse of fast-moving water stretched out into the darkness in front of them. They were at the river.

As Tom screwed up his eyes and rubbed his aching hip, he heard a voice above them and saw three figures with swords rushing down the bank towards them. He grabbed one of the C8's that he had been carrying and instinctively fired a burst of fire at the men. They all instantly pitched forwards and fell onto their faces. None of them got up again.

Tom struggled to his feet, and as he did so he felt a gust of wind on his face. He looked out over the river and could see that the fog was rapidly clearing.

A noise made Tom spin back around and he flinched involuntarily as he saw a group of archers standing at the top of the riverbank above them. Their bows were drawn and Tom swore under his breath as he looked up at them. There were over a dozen wickedly barbed arrows aimed right at them.

Tom considered trying to raise his rifle, but realised that he wouldn't stand a chance. The arrows would hit him before he could pull the trigger. Jimmy was lying face down in the dirt, Alex knelt nearby with her hands on her knees and Danny seemed busy searching the ground around him for something. There was nothing that any of them could do.

"Danny," Tom hissed. "Do something!"

"Boss, the fucking Book fell out of my tunic when I fell. I can't do anything if I'm not holding it!"

One of the men strode forwards and stared down at them.

"Wait," Tom called up to them, "you don't need to do this!"

The leader of their pursuers looked down the banking. He saw the three men that Tom had shot and he scowled angrily at Tom as he pointed down at them.

"When I give the command, kill these devils," he called to his archers.

Tom's eyes darted to Alex's face. It couldn't end like this. Not now.

Time slowed down and Tom tried to find the words to tell Alex how much he loved her, but he didn't have enough time. Before he could say anything, gunfire boomed from the darkness behind them and the men at the top of the riverbank were blown off their feet.

"Anybody need a lift?" asked a familiar voice.

CHAPTER 47

The River Viran, North-West of Derralt

As the echo of gunfire faded away, Tom spun round and a long, wide rowing boat appeared out of the darkness. Sam crouched in the bows of the boat holding his smoking C8 rifle and in the middle of the boat, Ramman shipped his oars and turned to greet them, a huge grin on his face.

"Holy shit, am I glad to see you two," Tom exclaimed. "How the hell did you get here?"

"We'll tell you later. Just get in and let's get the fuck out of here!"

"Yeah, sorry… good idea." Tom agreed. "Thanks, Sammy."

Alex and Jimmy dusted themselves down and lifted Lalitha gently into the front of the boat. Tom retrieved his rifle and passed it over to Sam.

"What's Fester doing?" Sam asked.

Danny was scrambling back up the riverbank. They saw him cock his head to one side and then after darting to the left Danny picked something up and rushed back towards them.

"Found it," Danny said as he clambered into the boat. "I dropped the bloody Book when I fell. Whatever happens, don't tell Lalitha when she wakes up."

"Fester, you are such a dickhead," Sam laughed.

"Nice to see you too mate," he chuckled.

Danny pushed the Book carefully back inside his tunic and helped Alex to climb up into the boat. She squeezed past Ramman and sat on one of the rowboat's thwarts at the rear of the boat. Tom followed suit, quickly slipping his arms from the straps of his Bergen and stowing it under the seat.

As Alex struggled out of her Bergen, she looked over to Ramman and gave him a huge smile.

"Great to see you, Ram. Thanks for getting here in the nick of time."

Ramman grinned and nodded. "I am glad to see you too Mistress Alex. I am mightily relieved that we managed to catch up with you in time."

"Me too," she winked back at him.

Danny and Jimmy pushed the boat away from the riverbank and as the current began to pull it away, they climbed in quickly and collapsed in a heap into the bottom of the boat next to Lalitha.

As Ramman unshipped his oars and started to turn the boat around so that it faced back out into the river, another group of armed figures raced down the riverbank towards them. They held vicious looking spears and they were approaching quickly.

Danny knelt up in the boat and held the Book up in front of him. His eyes instantly came alive with incandescent sparks and the voices of the souls began to whisper again. He extended his fist towards the soldiers on the bank as they drew their spears back to throw them at the boat and shouted loudly.

"Pyrta!"

The men burst into a seething mass of intense flame that set the dry reeds on the riverbank ablaze. All thoughts of throwing their spears gone, the men shrieked horribly before pitching face-first into the river. They lay unmoving in the shallow water as the heat from their burning bodies created billowing clouds of steam. The wildfire on the riverbank spread rapidly and soon a wide swathe of reeds was ablaze. Nobody else would be able to get down to the river's edge any time soon.

Sam looked open-mouthed at Danny.

"Fester," Sam gasped, "what did you just do?"

"We did it Sam," Danny grinned. "We got to Gessan and I did the Ceremony. I'm Bound! I can channel the power of the Souls."

"Holy crap!" Sam said. "Nice one, Fester!"

"I know. I'm gonna be freakin' royalty mate!"

Jimmy and Alex anxiously checked Lalitha as she lay quietly in the bottom of the boat. It was difficult to see much in the darkness, but at least they could see her breathing was regular.

"What happened back there Tom?" Alex blurted. "Lalitha went psycho and blasted as many of our own men as she did of theirs."

"She saw Ardum get killed and she lost it," replied Tom. "She lashed out so hard that the flames burned anyone in front of her. Their soldiers... our soldiers...

everybody burned. It was brutal, but to be honest it went a long way to saving us. Would we all have survived the attack from that force hidden in the forest otherwise?"

Alex shook her head. "I don't know, Tom, but what she did was insane and it cost some good men their lives. We lost whatever was left of our whole fucking army back there."

"I take it this Ardum guy was on our side then?" Sam asked. "Can I not leave you muppets alone for a few short days without everything going to rat shit?"

"It was bad, Sammy," Tom said earnestly. "Our whole plan is FUBAR!"

"Rest up for now. Let's worry about what comes next once we're clear of this place," Sam said. "I'll give you a hand, Ram. Let's get the flock outta here."

There was a second set of oars lying across the thwarts and Sam picked them up, stepped carefully over the thwarts and sat behind Ramman. He dropped the oars into the rowlocks on the boat's sides and started to row in time with Ramman's strokes.

"Come on, Ram," he said as he pulled on his oars. "Let's get over to the opposite side of the river where we'll be harder to see. Once we're close into the other bank, we'll carry on as fast as we can down river."

With both Sam and Ramman heaving on the oars, the boat cut quickly through the water and the two men guided the boat to the other side of the river. Once they were as far away from the burning river bank as they could get, they changed their course so they ran parallel with the shoreline and the river's strong current carried them quickly downstream.

With the immediate danger now behind them, the rest of the team removed their heavy packs and stowed all their gear under the thwarts. As the adrenaline left their systems and they moved further away from the battlefield behind them, they all felt overwhelmed with exhaustion. There was no sign of any of the enemy soldiers on the wooded riverbanks on their right, but nevertheless, everyone kept their rifles close and their tired eyes continually scanned the darkness for any signs of danger.

"It's good to see you, Sammy. How's the leg?" Tom asked.

"I'm good thanks, Boss. It still aches a bit, but I'm okay."

"You can't have rested very long at Ramman's farm. I thought you were going to take it easy?"

"Yeah well, something happened didn't it."

"What happened Sam?" Alex asked.

"Ram's brother, Daltran, happened."

"Did he try to do something to you?" Alex spluttered. "If he did, I hope you shot the little weasel. No offence intended, Ramman."

"There is no offense taken, Mistress Alex. Unfortunately, Master Sam did not get the chance to shoot Daltran, as much as he deserved it. My brother did not take kindly to the beating that I gave him or the threats that Master Tom made. After you left for Brentar he skulked around the farm for a while and I could sense the bitterness that ate away at him. He longed for a way to get even with me, but was too much of a coward to threaten Master Sam. The day after you left, he stole a horse and disappeared. We thought he had gone into the city to lose himself in drink and women, but he never returned."

"Initially we thought it was a good thing that Daltran had vanished," said Sam, picking up the story. "But after six days, we decided that he might be doing more than just sulking in the city. I eventually got it out of Ram's brother Tullney that Daltran had bragged that he was going to travel north to Krassak."

"To Krassak?" Tom exclaimed. "What did you do?"

"Ram here had a nasty feeling that his tosser of a brother was going to hold true to his threat to expose Lalitha, so we got the cart all harnessed up and we set off after him."

"Sam," Alex scolded, "you needed to rest. If that wound gets infected again…"

"I'm fine Moony. Honestly. Anyway, we didn't have time to piss about. We headed north and asked all the travellers that we came across on the road if they had seen Daltran and after a day or two we found a trader who recognised the description we gave him. The little bastard was heading north. He had a big head start on us so we knew that we'd never catch up with him… especially with him travelling a lot quicker than we could in the cart. I never want to travel by cart ever again by the way. I think my spine has been compressed by the rattly bloody thing."

"So…" prompted Tom.

"So… yeah… we looked at the map that Lalitha left me and we headed towards Derralt. Ram thought that if we went as fast as we could, we might make it to the city in time to meet you. We headed for the River Viran, way upstream of here and we traded the horse and cart with a fisherman for this boat. We thought we could make time up if we went as fast as we could down the river. It was a bit hairy in places and we got caught up a couple of times, but we ended up getting here safe and sound earlier tonight. Lalitha told me about her friend that lives in that big castle on the hill and we were going to go and bang on the doors once the sun started to come up. We were sitting in the boat having something to eat when we heard all hell breaking loose across the plain to the north-east. We heard gunfire and explosions of some sort and realised it had to be you guys, so we hightailed it down here in the boat. There was a bit of fog around, but we heard more gunshots and saw the muzzle flashes from your rifle on the riverbank. Luckily for you lot, we found you in the nick of time."

"Thanks, Sammy," Alex said, "I thought our number was up for a moment there."

"Ramman," asked Tom, "do you think that Daltran would have had time to make it to Krassak and tell Gask about Lalitha? How far is it from here?"

"By boat, Krassak is about six days journey. By horse it would be faster if he could negotiate his way through the forest roads."

"But Daltran wouldn't have had to make it all the way to Krassak," Alex said. "Didn't Ardum tell us that there are garrisons south of the city. If Daltran had made it to one of those, he could have alerted them and they could have sent soldiers south towards Derralt."

"Lalitha was worried that the messenger that she sent to find Ardum in Krassak might have been intercepted and told the wrong people about our plans," Tom mused. "But what if it was Daltran?"

"If Daltran was the cause of that massacre we just witnessed, he is seriously going to regret it," Danny muttered.

"Talking about our plans," Alex said, "What the hell do we do now? Lalitha's army is gone. The only soldiers she has left are sitting in this boat. How can we take on a whole army?"

Tom looked at Alex through the darkness and shrugged his shoulders.

"I don't know, Alex. I really don't know."

Everyone fell quiet as they all began to consider the implications of the night's defeat. How indeed could a group of five ex-soldiers, a carter and a young princess take on a whole army?

As everyone sat, lost in their own thoughts, Sam and Ramman continued to row downstream. They carried on deep into the night until both men looked so exhausted that Tom and Alex offered to take a stint on the oars.

"You can't row, you muppet," Sam laughed tiredly. "You'll pull your bloody arm off."

"No, I won't," Tom answered. "Lalitha fixed me."

"Fixed you? What do you mean?"

"My arm is not real flesh, but it is part of me now and I can feel things through it. I couldn't pull it off even if I wanted to."

"Really? Wow! That is fantastic, Boss."

"I know. I can't tell you how good it feels Sammy. I feel whole again."

"What did she do?"

"I don't really know. She used the Souls in that Book to attach it and make it part of me."

"How does it feel now?"

"It's like having my old arm back. I can pull, carry, fight… everything. But it's better than that. I've still got the strength of the polymer arm… and it saved my neck back there on the battlefield."

"I'm chuffed for you, Boss. I really am," Sam smiled.

"Thanks Sam, despite all the madness that is going on around us, I feel better now than I have for a long, long time. Come on, we can take over now and give you two a break."

After some early confusion and clashing of oars, Tom and Alex quickly got into their rowing rhythm and the boat was soon cutting smoothly through the water again. For the next hour, Tom and Alex recounted the events that had taken place since they had parted ways at Brentar. Danny soon fell asleep with his head resting on the side of the boat and Jimmy sat quietly next to Lalitha. He was obviously worrying about her, but until she woke up again there was nothing any of them could do.

The boat moved steadily down river and soon everyone except Tom and Alex were catnapping as best they could in the cramped conditions. A glow in the eastern sky began to herald the approach of the morning sun, and its light illuminated the landscape around them, Tom could see that the river was widening out and open water lay ahead of them. They had reached Lake Viran.

CHAPTER 48

On Lake Viran

By the time the sun had risen high above them, they had made good progress up the lake. Jimmy and Danny had taken over on the oars and Alex sat beside Lalitha, cradling the young princess's head in her lap. There were several large vessels just visible on the water in the far distance to the north and as Tom looked over the rear of the rowboat, he noticed two ships following them up the lake. He grabbed his rifle and focused his scope on the nearest of them. The vessel looked almost like a Viking longboat and Tom could see about twenty sets of oars dipping rhythmically in and out of the water. They were driving the ship on at a speed much faster than their own.

"Sam, did you see any military ships back up at Derralt?" Tom asked.

"Nothing that looked overly military," Sam shrugged.

"There were two galleys tied up at the docks near the city," Ramman said. "Elders use the galleys for transporting serfs between the great cities."

"Could they be used as troop ships?" Tom asked.

"I suppose so, Master Thomas. Why do you ask?"

"Because there are two ships coming up the lake behind us and they are catching up with us quickly."

Everyone looked over the stern of the rowboat and even with the naked eye, they could see the two ships powering their way up the lake.

"Do you think they're coming after us?" Alex asked.

"I don't know," Tom answered, "but I think it would be a fair bet."

"What do we do, Boss?" Sam asked. "We can't outrun them."

"Danny, can you do your firestarter thing again?"

"Yes, but only once or twice. If I try to channel too much power, I'll end up unconscious like Lalitha."

"Okay," Tom nodded. "If it turns out that those two boats are coming for us, then this is what we're going to do."

He filled the team in on what he had in mind and everyone nodded in agreement. Tom's plan meant letting the galleys get much closer to them on the open water, but their only other option was to land on the shore, abandon the boat and try to hide somewhere. With Lalitha still unconscious, Tom was eager to try and avoid travelling by foot again unless they really had to.

Ramman swapped places with Danny and rowed in time with Jimmy's strokes. Over the next hour, the two galleys closed the gap between them to just a few hundred metres. Tom watched anxiously as the teams of oarsmen drove their vessels closer.

The answer to whether the galleys were looking for them was soon answered. Archers could be seen readying their bows on the decks of the galleys and they soon began to fire ranging shots at the rowboat. The arrows fell far short of the team's rowboat, but as the galleys drew nearer, so did the falling arrows. Tom could hear them as they plopped into the lake's surface and disappeared.

"So, I'm thinking that they're definitely after us then," Alex commented.

"Get ready, Danny," Tom said quietly.

An arrow landed about thirty metres away from the rowboat. Tom, Alex and Sam cocked their rifles and crouched low in the boat so that they could steady their aim on the vessel's gunwale. The first of the galleys was about twenty metres closer than the other and Tom aimed carefully at the nearest ship.

An arrow whooshed through the air and splashed into the water. It was significantly closer than the last one had been. The archers were almost in range and as Tom looked through his scope, he saw that they were all now preparing to fire their weapons at the rowboat.

"You ready, Danny?"

"Yes, Boss."

"Okay... hold on... hold on... hold on... Do it!"

Danny clutched the Book to his chest, reached out with his right arm and the unearthly sparks danced in his eyes. As the whispers of the Souls grew in volume, Danny spoke the command.

"Pyrta!"

Three of the archers on the deck of the nearest galley burst into balls of intense flame. They staggered around screaming. One fell over the side of the ship and hit the water with a loud hiss but the other two fell back into the ship causing everything around them to catch fire. It only took a few seconds before the bow section of the galley was completely ablaze.

The second ship slowed down when they saw what had happened to their comrades, but it was too late for them to get away. Danny gritted his teeth and concentrated on the undamaged galley.

"Pyrta!" he shouted again.

Two of the men standing amidships on the second galley burst into bright orange flames and this ship was also soon transformed into a raging inferno as the heat of the burning bodies ignited the wooden decks around them.

"Row hard. Now," Tom ordered. Ramman and Jimmy quickly pulled hard on their oars and the boat surged forwards.

Most of the crew on the two galleys flung themselves into the cold lake water, but some of the archers continued to loose arrows at the fleeing rowboat. An arrow buried itself into one of the thwarts next to Lalitha's head with a loud thunk.

Tom, Alex and Sam opened fire. Alex hit her target and an archer fell backwards out of sight. Tom aimed carefully, but the rowboat rocked as Ramman and Jimmy rowed frantically and his shot missed. Sam waited a split second longer and his bullet found its mark. Another archer stumbled and fell.

A few foolhardy archers braved the flames to fire a last salvo of arrows at them, but their arrows fell short and plunged harmlessly into the water. Tom breathed a sigh of relief and lowered his rifle as the distance between themselves and the galleys began to open up and they moved out of range of their pursuers' arrows.

He watched as the remaining soldiers on the galleys realised that their quarry was out of reach and leapt from the burning decks into the water. They splashed loudly through the water as they swam desperately towards the shore. Alex leaned over to pull the arrow out of the wooden thwart and as she did so, Lalitha's eyes opened and she stared up at her.

"Where are we?" she demanded as she struggled to sit up. She watched Alex pluck the arrow out and throw it over the side of the boat, but then suddenly sensed something. Her head snapped round to look at Danny as his eyes cleared and he slumped forwards after the exertions of channelling the Souls.

"What are you doing, Daniel Adams?" Lalitha cried. "Give me the Book. Now!"

"Lalitha," Tom said, "Danny had to use the Book to get us away from the army that attacked us at Derralt. You were unconscious so there was no other choice."

"The Book is mine to wield, not his," Lalitha snapped.

"I am Bound too, Lalitha," Danny said, a determined look in his eye. "I have as much right to use it as you."

"The Book belongs to my family," Lalitha hissed. "You are not of the royal line. You are common-born and I do not even know why the Book chose you."

"The Book chose me for a reason. You are no better than me, Lalitha. We are the same."

"The same? You are a fool, Daniel Adams. It is my destiny to place the Book back on its altar, not yours! Once I have done that, I will use the power of the Souls to burn Gask and all his allies to dust. Everyone that opposes me will feel my wrath. Would you oppose me, Daniel Adams?"

"Of course, I won't oppose you, Lalitha, but just remember that I am Chosen too. I am not your fuckin' servant and if the Book needs me to act, then I will."

"Very well. Give me the Book then."

Danny reluctantly handed the Book to Lalitha and she hurriedly slipped it back into its leather bag and hung the bag around her neck. Her anger subsided and she sat down next to Alex. Danny seethed, but said nothing more and chose to stare out over the lake rather than add any more to the conversation.

Tom and Alex glanced at each other and Alex raised her eyebrows. The confrontation between Lalitha and Danny worried them both. The Book was a powerful weapon and the last thing they needed was for those two to be fighting over it. It was like two children squabbling over who should get to play with an armed nuclear warhead.

"What happened at Derralt, Thomas McAllister?" Lalitha asked. "I remember seeing Lord Ardum fall, but I can recall nothing after that."

"You used the Book to burn a whole load of men, but I think the effort of channelling that much energy was too much for your body to cope with and you passed out. After you fell, the enemy army pushed forwards again. There were just too many of them and they overran our defences. Your army was destroyed Lalitha. We barely managed to escape. One of Lady Deman's men, Treltan, sacrificed himself and the men he had left to buy us enough time to get away."

"The army is gone?"

"Yes. As far as we know, we are the only survivors from the battle at Derralt."

Lalitha hung her head and picked at the stitching on her bag with her fingernails.

"We travel now on Lake Viran? Do you still mean to accompany me to the capital…

even though our army is lost?"

"Yes, we are and we are going to try and get as close to Krassak as we can by water and then make our way into the tunnels under the city. If we can make it there, then you might still be able to get to the altar with the Book. It is the only option that we can think of."

Lalitha nodded her head and sat quietly as Ramman and Jimmy heaved on the oars.

"It isn't going to be easy," Alex warned. "The army we fought are bound to send riders north to warn Gask that we escaped and they will easily outpace us in this tub."

"I know," agreed Tom. "They're going to be waiting for us. I keep checking the eastern shoreline but I haven't seen any sign of soldiers yet. We're out of range of any archers on that side of the lake, but they could be still be watching our progress."

"What do you think they'll do?"

"If it were me, I would set up a perimeter around the capital and wait for us to come to them. If they also send more ships up the lake after us, they can herd us like sheep towards the forces at Krassak."

"So, what do we do?" asked Sam.

"We are too outgunned to fight them. If they do set up a cordon, we're going to have to find a way to sneak through their lines to get to the tunnels."

"Who else knows about the tunnels under the city Lalitha?" Sam asked. "Will Gask not just flood them with soldiers?"

"Only a few know of the existence of the labyrinth of tunnels that lie below the city and even fewer can navigate them," she answered. "Many of the tunnels can only be accessed if you are in possession of the Book, so Gask will not be able to block them."

"How close are the tunnels to the river?" Tom asked.

"There are a number of entrances that exist close to the river. If we can get across the lake and further downstream towards Krassak, the Book will guide us to the closest of them."

"Would we be better on foot?" Alex pondered out loud.

"We're making better time in the boat than we would if we were walking," Tom replied, "but we stand out like a sore thumb here on the lake."

Tom looked back down the lake. Beyond the two columns of black smoke that rose from the burning wreckage of the two galleys, he could not see any more ships. They were safe for the time being.

"Let's carry on in the rowboat for as long as we can," he suggested.

Everyone agreed and they all watched the two pillars of smoke as they fell further and further behind them. They rowed on northwards, swapping places regularly so that they could keep a steady pace going.

Alex settled down in the boat next to Lalitha and watched the young woman carefully.

"How are you feeling, Lalitha?"

"I am tired, Alexandra Aluko, but my strength returns slowly."

Alex burrowed in her Bergen and brought out a couple of protein bars that she had carried with her all the way from home. She ripped open the wrappers and handed one of them to Lalitha.

"Eat that. It'll help."

Lalitha bit into the bar and chewed hungrily.

"Danny is on your side, you know."

"I believe you, but this is my fight, not his. I have to take the responsibility of destroying Gask and avenging my father."

"Okay, but just remember that we are here to help you."

"Thank you. It shames me that I am weakened like this. Once I have returned the Book to the altar at Krassak, I will be strong. Stronger than you can imagine. I will have the power to obliterate Gask and anyone who stands with him. My father's Soul will witness the destruction of all those who betrayed him."

Alex took a deep breath and asked the question that she had been trying to ask Lalitha for weeks.

"What happened to you mother Lalitha? What did Gask do to her?"

Lalitha's expression hardened and Alex saw her teeth clench.

"He corrupted her."

"What does that mean?" coaxed Alex.

Lalitha hesitated, but then carried on in a quiet, determined voice.

"My mother Tella was married to my father when she was little more than a child. She stayed by his side and served him loyally for years. She bore him two children and wanted for nothing as she lived the life of a queen. However, when Gask arrived at court, he slowly wormed his way into her favour. He was always at her side, whispering to her and taking every opportunity to touch her. Everybody thought the man nothing but a fool who entertained the queen, but in the end my mother… she… she betrayed the king. She betrayed the crown. She betrayed me!"

"What happened, Lalitha?"

"That last day in Krassak, I found out that my mother was sleeping with Gask. The perfidious bastard spent months fawning over my mother and she was beguiled by the attention he gave her. He used his silver tongue to whisper his lies into her ear and they met in secret to consummate their treachery. She soiled herself by letting that animal touch her. How could she dare to betray the king in such a way?"

"Jesus," breathed Alex, "I had no idea that's what was going on, Lalitha."

"I stumbled across them that last night in the capital. I saw them in bed together. I saw what they were doing. I couldn't believe my eyes, but it was true. I ran. I hid for a time in my room, but I knew that I had to do something so I tried to find my father."

Lalitha paused for breath and Alex took her hand as a tear rolled down the young woman's face. Lalitha angrily wiped the tear away and carried on.

"I knew that I had to tell my father. He would surely have them both put to death, they had betrayed him and deserved nothing better. My mother had whored herself out to that animal and that could not be forgiven."

Alex was shocked, but knew that she had to let Lalitha continue until the whole story was out in the open.

"I tried to find my father to tell him about their betrayal, but he was nowhere to be found. I asked the royal guards that guarded his private chambers and they told me that the king had gone up into the tower with my mother. It was her who led my unsuspecting father to the altar that night. I took a dagger from my father's room and ran after them, but… but I was too late. By the time I got to the altar, my father lay dead. Gask stood gloating over his body. That is when I took the Book and ran."

"But what happened to your mother?" Alex prompted.

Lalitha looked directly into Alex's eyes and all the emotion drained from the princess's face.

"She grabbed me as I tried to escape. I couldn't even bear to look at her after everything she had done. She had conspired to murder my father. He was dead and it was her fault. She tried to talk to me but I wouldn't listen to her. I pulled away from her and I… I… I stabbed her in the chest. I plunged the dagger in my hand as deep as I could into her lying, cheating heart and I ran."

"Holy shit," Alex breathed. "Lalitha… you killed your mother?"

"Yes. My father was everything and she betrayed him. She helped Gask to murder him. She deserved what I did to her."

Alex looked up and saw that everyone in the boat was staring at them wide-eyed and open-mouthed. They had all heard.

Lalitha sat there blankly. She had stopped crying and her face now betrayed no emotion at all.

Alex made eye contact with Tom, but neither of them knew what to say. Alex put her arm round the young woman and hugged her tightly.

"You should have told me earlier sweetheart. This is too much for you to keep bottled up."

"They murdered him, Alex!" Lalitha whispered. "They murdered the king."

Alex held on to Lalitha as Ramman and Jimmy drove the boat northwards towards Krassak.

CHAPTER 49

On Lake Viran

They rowed in silence for most of the day after Lalitha had dropped her bombshell. Alex stayed with the young princess and stroked her hair until she eventually fell asleep.

The sun fell behind the trees on the western shore and the team stopped briefly to eat what rations they had left in their Bergens. The lake water was drinkable, so at least they didn't have to worry about drinking water.

Rather than pull into the shore to sleep, they decided to travel on through the night. The shores slipped by, and the rhythmic sound of the oars dipping in and out of the water in the darkness had a soporific effect on those not rowing. Lalitha hardly spoke and had retreated within herself.

As the sky began to lighten, Sam and Ramman took over on the oars, and Tom moved to the front of the bow to scour the northern horizon for movement. About three kilometres away, Tom could see a number of large ships. Around them, smaller boats could just be seen as they moved about between the ships and the shore.

"There are ships ahead of us that look like they're anchored close into the shore. Any idea what they are?"

"They are probably livestock ships," Lalitha replied. "The ships pick up pigs and some cattle from the town of Cendor on the western bank of Lake Viran and transport them to Derralt or Krassak. It is faster than herding them on land."

"Let's make for them," Tom decided. "If any ships do come up the lake after us, or if anyone is still watching us from the other side of the lake, we might be able to hide in the activity there. Worst case, we can land there and lie low somewhere in the town."

Everyone was in agreement, so they powered on towards Cendor. After about forty minutes, the ships at anchor began to loom above them and several smaller sailing vessels and rowboats passed close by.

Sam and Ramman guided their boat between the large ships and the town of Cendor could be seen on their left. A series of long, wide wooden jetties stretched out from the shore and out into the lake. Even from this distance away the noise in the town could be heard. The crying of animals, banging of shipwrights' hammers against wooden decking, men's shouts and the general hubbub of the busy port echoed out across the water. Herds of animals were loaded onto ships, and other cargo taken on trollies from the moored vessels up the jetties and into the town.

The foresail of a large ship at the end of one of the nearby jetties was being unfurled as it got ready to depart. A gust of wind blew from the shore and an unpleasant smell made Jimmy's nose wrinkle.

"What is that smell?" he complained.

"Pigs," Ramman declared. "Nothing smells quite like pigs."

Sam abruptly stopped rowing and looked at Tom.

"Boss, we're expecting to meet some sort of blockade further up this lake, aren't we?"

"Yeah, it is a distinct possibility."

"And we'll have no chance of getting through it in a rowboat like this?"

"True. If we see a blockade, we'll have to abandon the boat and try and get through the woods on foot."

"What if we hid on one of these livestock ships? We'd be a lot less obvious, wouldn't we?"

"You might be onto something there Sam. If we could hide on-board where the soldiers can't find us, we might be able to make it through any blockade that we come across. Let's head over to that ship that's getting ready to set off and see where it's going to. If it's heading for Krassak, we could see if we can hitch a ride. It's a risk, but everything is going to be risky now."

They manoeuvred the rowboat closer to the ship. As they approached the ship, the smell of pigs got worse and worse. Lalitha pulled her scarf up over her face and Alex and Jimmy followed suit. Anything to help mask the smell of the pigs.

"The smell is disgusting," Lalitha gasped. "Do you really expect me to climb on-board that ship?"

"Yes," Tom smiled. "If the stink puts you off climbing on-board, it might put any of Gask's troops off as well."

Lalitha did not look happy about the plan, but did not argue further as the rowboat pulled alongside the ship and Tom shouted and waved at the crewmen standing on deck. One of the crewmen noticed him and nudged a large man that was standing next to him with his elbow. The man turned and stared down at the rowboat.

"Where are you headed for?" called Tom.

"We set sail for Krassak," the man answered. "What business is it of yours?"

"Do you have room for seven passengers? We can pay for our passage."

"I have no cabins below decks, but if you are willing to sit up top, we could take you if you have enough silver."

"How much do you want?"

The big man scratched his head and looked down at Tom.

"Five silver each," he shouted down.

"Have we got enough left?" Tom asked Danny.

"We've got heaps left Boss, offer him a bit more and he'll bite your hand off."

"How about we pay you eight silver each. No questions asked."

"You have a deal my friend," the big man smiled. "We set sail as soon as you are aboard."

A rope ladder was thrown down to them and one by one, the team climbed up onto the deck of the ship. One of the ship's crew descended the ladder and secured a long thin rope to the rowboat before making his way back on-board. The tall man stood in front of them and eyed them curiously. He wore a heavy cotton tunic and long black boots that went up over his knees. The man was dark skinned and sported a carefully trimmed black beard.

"Welcome on-board *The Flying Boar*," the man declared. "I am the captain, Cromall. Do you have the silver?"

Tom held up a pouch of silver coins and jingled them noisily.

"We have the silver, but we'll pay you when we arrive at Krassak if that is okay with you?"

Cromall shrugged his shoulders and nodded.

"As long as you can pay, I do not mind whether you pay now or later. I have no need of silver until we reach Krassak."

The noise from below decks was ear-piercing. There was a cacophony of grunts, squeals and snorts and the smell this close to Cromall's cargo was almost overwhelming.

"What takes you to Krassak?" Cromall asked.

"We have business in the city. The nature of our business means that we need to avoid entanglements with any soldiers that we might come across," Tom answered cryptically.

"Ah, I see," grinned Cromall. "Royalists eh? Your business must be urgent indeed if you are willing to risk heading back into the city. The new regime at Krassak has been rooting out supporters of King Lestri since he died and I heard that most of those that had not yet been arrested had fled to Derralt. I do not care about such things. It makes little difference to me what you all do to each other as long as there is still demand for my pigs in the capital."

"Thank you, Captain Cromall. I appreciate your honesty."

"Ha," he laughed, "if you have silver, you are always welcome aboard *The Flying Boar*."

Tom looked down through a wooden grate near his feet and saw a multitude of pigs, all crammed together in the hold. He didn't stand over the grate for very long, as the stench that wafted up through it in waves was powerful.

"How many animals do you have onboard?" asked Tom as he moved back from the grate.

"Over four hundred fine beasts on their way to market in the capital," Cromall announced proudly. "The merchants pay me for the animals at the dockside. They are butchered close by and then the merchants take them to sell at the markets within the city walls."

Tom felt sorry for the pigs, but then who was he to judge; he had eaten enough bacon in his time.

"Where do you want us, Cromall?" Tom asked.

"If you sit out of the way up on the foredeck, you will be out of the way of my crew there and not impede the running of my ship. Also, the smell will get better up there as we set sail."

"No problem. Do you have any food that you could spare us? Our supplies have run low."

"I will see what I can do for you," Cromall said. "Now, if you would move to the foredeck, we will set sail and be on our way to Krassak."

Tom nodded and led the team forwards along the deck and then up a flight of steps to the foredeck. They dropped their Bergens onto the wooden decking and slumped down next to them.

"I think I'm gonna puke," moaned Jimmy. "This smell is bloody terrible."

"The captain assures me that it will get better once we start moving," Tom promised.

"It can't get much worse," Alex coughed. "I'm never eating pork ever again."

The sails above their heads flapped in the wind and the ropes that secured the ship to the jetty were loosened and cast off. Slowly the ship moved away from the jetty and once they were clear, the crew heaved the mainsail up and pulled the main sheets tight. As soon as the wind caught the trimmed sails, Tom felt the ship surge forward through the water. As promised, as the ship increased speed, fresh air blew over them and the stench of the pigs below decks eased a little.

Tom looked southwards over the rail as they pulled away from Cendor and saw the sails of two large vessels in the distance. If Gask had sent more ships after them from Derralt, then it was lucky that they had found passage on *The Flying Boar*. The sailing ships would soon have caught them up if they had stayed in the rowboat.

He sat down with his back against the side of the ship. Alex sat next to him and rested her head on his shoulder.

"We're getting closer to Krassak now," she said quietly, "and I've got no idea what's going to happen when we get there."

"What do you mean?" Tom asked.

"Did you not hear, Lalitha? She killed her own mother and once the Book is back on its own altar, she's going to be able to wield power like we've not seen before. Does that not worry you?"

"I hadn't really thought about it too much. I thought that she was just going to take Gask out and that would be it… job done."

"I've got a nasty feeling that it isn't going to be that simple," Alex sighed.

Tom looked at Lalitha. She was resting against the base of the foremast and Jimmy, as usual, was close by. Her face was unreadable, but she clutched her leather bag close to her stomach and met Tom's look with a steely stare.

Sam and Ramman sat down in front of Tom and broke his line of sight with Lalitha. They talked about nothing in particular for a while, but the exertions of two days and nights of rowing began to catch up with them and they all soon made themselves comfortable and fell asleep in the sunshine.

It was late afternoon when Cromall woke them all with hunks of bread and cheese and a large jug of ale.

"We can spare this food and drink for you if that is acceptable?" Cromall said.

"That's great thanks, Cromall," Tom said as he rubbed the sleep from his eyes. "How long before we get to Krassak?"

"If this westerly wind holds, our journey will be a fast one. We should arrive at

Krassak tomorrow morning."

Tom nodded his thanks and Cromall left them and headed back aft-wards. They ate about half of the food that Cromall had given them and saved what remained for later.

Alex fell back to sleep almost straight away and Tom pulled her close and mulled over the potential dangers of what lay ahead of them. The warmth and comfort of Alex's body pressed against his own made it difficult to stay focused and Tom soon found his heavy eyelids closing and he fell asleep.

When he awoke sometime later, Tom noticed that Lalitha was staring at him. He stood up slowly, being careful not to disturb Alex and made his way to where she sat. Lalitha watched him as he sat down next to her. Her expression behind the scarf wrapped around the bottom half of her face was unreadable.

"How are you doing?" he asked quietly.

"I am well, Thomas McAllister. How is your arm?"

"It is great thanks. I will always be grateful to you for what you have done for me."

"You are worth more to me as you are now, so it was in my own interest to make you whole again."

"Nevertheless, thank you," he smiled.

"I sense that you want to ask me something," Lalitha said.

Tom looked at her sheepishly and carefully considered how to ask her what he wanted to without igniting her anger again.

"What are you going to do once we get the Book to the altar?"

"I am going to burn Gask and his allies to dust."

"But what does that mean?"

"I will use the power of the Souls to destroy Gask and all those that have sided with him. The rule of law must be re-established. You have seen the lawlessness that prevails in the outlying towns and cities. Statues of the king are pulled down and stones thrown at members of the royal guard? That anarchy must be stamped out. The idiot peasants that show their disrespect to the throne must be brought back in line. My father would not stand for such subordination and neither will I when I sit upon the throne."

"I take it that you will use the army to re-establish the laws in the cities."

"Of course."

"Lalitha, just be careful how you use them to re-establish law and order. You cannot rule through force alone. I've seen it tried back home and it never works for very long. People take so much and then they always rebel. Violence begets violence."

"I appreciate your opinion, Thomas McAllister, but I know how to rule this realm.

My father taught me what needs to be done and I am more than capable of doing it."

"And what happens after you've dealt out the retribution you think everyone deserves?"

"What do you mean? Things will return to normal and we will be at peace."

"Whose normal is that? You have seen the conditions that some of your subjects live in while we've travelled across Zakastra. The serfs are not treated well and you saw yourself that some of them in Prentak were even being sold into prostitution by their Elders. Will you do something to improve what they regard as normal?"

"I agree that some of the Elders are taking advantage of their positions to abuse their serfs and those Elders will be dealt with."

"But can nothing be done to make the lives of all the serfs better?"

"Thomas McAllister, you begin to sound like the anarchists and subversives that we fight against. As I have said to you before, the serfs are fed and housed by their Elders. They need not worry about finding food or shelter; it is provided for them. Work on the land and in the cities would go undone if not for the serfs. How then would the population be fed or the cities kept clean? This way of life may be foreign to you, but this is not your world. It is mine. This way of life is normal for us."

"I realise that, but surely you can do something to make things less squalid for the serfs. You saw how they were living in Prentak."

Lalitha rolled her eyes before answering. "If it makes you happy Thomas McAllister then I promise that when I am on the throne and the country is at peace again, I will see what can be done for the living conditions of the serfs in Prentak. Does that please you?"

"Yes. Thank you," Tom nodded. He realised that this was a topic of conversation that would need to be talked about in much greater detail as soon as Lalitha became queen.

Noticing that Alex was awake again, Tom moved back to her side and sat down with a concerned look on his face.

"What's up?" Alex asked him.

"Lalitha worries me. She is so consumed with her passion for revenge that everything else seems to have gone out the window."

"She's young and she's angry. All she can think about at the moment is revenge and from what she's told us, I can't really blame her. Gask swans in, charms her mother into having an affair and the two of them plot to murder her father and steal his throne. What Lalitha did to her mother was pretty damn extreme I'll admit, but the queen sounds like a nasty piece of work. What would you do in the heat of the moment if your mother plotted to murder the father that you hero worshipped?"

"I don't know."

"Me neither. Hopefully, once she's toppled Gask, she'll get her head straight. You heard what the Book told you. We have to help her do this. If the Book trusts her to do the right thing, then so should we."

"Okay, okay," Tom sighed. "I give in. Let's just guide her where we can yeah?"

"Agreed," grinned Alex before kissing him full on the lips.

"Get a room for cryin' out loud," moaned Danny.

The Flying Boar sailed on northwards into the evening. There was no moon and the ship's surroundings were in total darkness. It began to get cold and Cromall brought blankets for them from the crew's quarters to keep them warm. There was much less noise from below decks as many of the pigs slept, and Tom soon drifted off to sleep as Alex pulled him close.

CHAPTER 50

Aboard The Flying Boar

"Tom wake up," Alex said urgently. "We've got company."

Tom blinked his eyes and rubbed his face. The sky was light, but the sun was hidden behind a band of high-altitude cloud.

"What time is it?"

"Early. There are ships ahead of us that look like they are blockading the end of the lake. We can't get to the mouth of the river without going through them."

Tom stood up and looked out over the bows of the ship. Sure enough, ahead of them at the northern end of the lake were a line of galleys. All of them were packed full of soldiers.

"Shit. This is what we were worried about," Tom exclaimed.

Cromall hurried forwards and crouched down next to Tom.

"I do not know what these soldiers' intentions are, but I cannot afford for them to find royalists on my ship. You must hide below decks and I will attempt to get us through the blockade and down the River Viran towards the capital."

"Below decks? With the pigs?" exclaimed Jimmy in horror.

"Yes. With the pigs. There is an area that is out of sight at the rear of the hold where we keep the beasts in quarantine if any become ill. You can hide in there. If you stay low, you should not be seen from the forward hatch and the pigs will not be able to nip you."

"Nip us?" Jimmy hissed.

"Pigs bite," Ramman nodded.

The team gathered their possessions and ran along the deck, staying as low as they could so as not to be seen from any of the galleys. Cromall took them to the main hatch down to the hold, swung it open and pointed down into the reeking darkness below.

"Get down the ramp into the hold and quickly make your way aft. The quarantine pen is at the rear of the hold on the left. Once you are there, lie on the floor and cover yourself with the straw bedding. If we are fortunate, you will not be seen. If you are discovered, I will claim that you are stowaways and that I know nothing about you."

"Fair enough," nodded Tom. He swallowed hard as he looked down into the jostling mass of pigs below him.

"I am not going down there," Lalitha announced. "I refuse to travel in the filth with those animals."

"If you want to get to Krassak without Gask and his army coming down on us like a ton of bricks, then you're coming down there with us. I don't like it any more than you do, but we have no choice. You heard the voices as strongly as I did. It's fuckin' real Boss!. You do want to get the Book back to its altar, don't you?"

Lalitha gave Tom a vicious look but didn't put up any more arguments.

"One of the galleys is moving towards us," one of Cromall's crewmen shouted. "They are signalling for us to drop our sails Captain."

"You need to move now," said Cromall urgently.

"Come on then," said Tom. He took a couple of deep breaths of relatively fresh air and walked quickly down the ramp into the hold.

The smell down there was appalling. Tom pushed pigs out of his way as he walked through the thick layer of foul stinking muck towards the rear of the ship. The air was rancid and Tom's eyes watered as he tried not to breathe deeply.

The others pushed their way through the squealing pigs behind him and struggled to stay on their feet as the pigs jostled against their legs. Tom reached the quarantine pen's fence and climbed over it into the straw beyond. Alex caught up with him. Her face was pale and she gagged as she climbed over the fence.

"Get down as low as you can," Tom said.

Alex looked appalled, but crouched down low behind the fence.

"Lower," Tom insisted.

"Tom, to get any lower I'll have to lie in the shit!"

"I know. Just do it."

Alex wrapped her scarf more tightly around her face and lay down in the straw. Lalitha got to the pen next, her face plainly signalling the revulsion she felt. After some arguments, she too lay in the straw. Sam and Ramman followed Lalitha leaving Danny and Jimmy to bring up the rear. Once they were all down the ramp, Cromall slammed the hatch closed and the hold became much darker.

The pigs snapped at Danny and Jimmy as they pushed past and Jimmy squealed almost as loudly as the pigs as one of them tried to bite his leg. He pushed it away from him as hard as he could and forced his way onwards through the animals. As Jimmy reached the quarantine pen, he paused briefly to throw up on the floor and then retched again violently as the nearest pig to him started to wolf down his partially digested bread and cheese.

"Boss, this is the grossest thing I have ever done in my whole life," he moaned.

Tom hauled Jimmy over the fence and pushed him down on the floor before quickly throwing the least dirty straw over the top of them all. Once he was satisfied that the team were as well hidden as they could be, Tom burrowed into the straw and lay in the muck with them. He shut his eyes and tried to block out the fact that his face was just a few centimetres above a moving layer of reeking liquid pig shit.

They felt rather than heard the galley pull alongside *The Flying Boar*. The smaller boat bumped against *The Boar's* sides and they heard boots clambering up the ladders thrown down from the ship's rail. It was difficult to hear anything above the squealing and grunting of the pigs and it was several minutes before the hatch was pulled open and light streamed down into the hold.

"This is my cargo sir," they could hear Cromall saying. "The finest pigs in the west of the realm. They will be at market tomorrow if you want to buy yourself some premium pork. Tell my friends at the market that Cromall sent you and they will give you a special price."

Tom squinted through the moving pigs from where he lay. It was hard to see what was happening, but it looked like several soldiers were walking down the ramp into the hold. They didn't get very far. The stench of the animals and the sea of muck that washed around their feet was enough to deter a more detailed search. The leader of the soldiers scanned the hold with his eyes one last time and then turned around and ordered his men back up to the deck. The loft hatch closed with a loud boom and then Tom could hear nothing more.

There was a scrabbling noise on the side of the ship and several more bumps. After another couple of minutes, the hatch opened wide enough for a man to squeeze through and then closed again. The unlucky crewman that Cromall had sent to talk to them pushed his way back to the quarantine pen and climbed over the fence.

"The soldiers have gone. We are going to pass through the blockade now. The captain says that he will let you know when it is safe to come out."

The crewman made his way back to the ramp and squeezed out through the hatch.

Tom sat up and fought down the urge to vomit. The team crouched there in the straw and muck for what seemed like forever before the hatch opened again and Cromall came down the ramp.

"The blockade is behind us," he called, "You can come out now."

The team dragged themselves back through the pigs and up the ramp to the ship's deck. *The Flying Boar* had left the lake and was moving slowly northwards down the wide River Viran. The sails had been shortened to keep the vessel's speed down now that they were off the open water and in the confines of the river. Tom looked behind them over the stern of the ship, but the river had curved away from the lake and the blockade was hidden from view.

Taking deep breaths of fresher air, the team stood and looked at each other. They were all covered in a thick layer of foul brown slime and straw clung to them. Jimmy raced to the ships rail and dry heaved over the side of the ship. Sam laughed out loud, scraped off a wad of the filth with his hand and threw it at the back of Jimmy's head. He howled with laughter as the shitball hit Jimmy with a loud splat. Jimmy turned to object, but his stomach wasn't finished and he turned back to throw up a thin trickle of bile.

Sam laughed so hard that he could hardly stay on his feet and, disgusting though it was, the others couldn't help but chuckle as they watched Sam bent double with hysterical laughter.

Cromall stood with his hands on his hips and shook his head as he watched them.

"I suggest that you all jump in the river to wash yourselves off some," Cromall suggested. "You smell as bad as the pigs."

Cromall threw a rope ladder over the port side of the ship and stood looking at them with a big smile on his face.

"We will drop the sails for a few minutes. Have yourselves a bath," he grinned. "You need it."

Cromall steered *The Boar* towards the western bank of the river and, once the sails had been furled, the crewmen at the front of the ship dropped the anchor.

"Stay on the port side of the ship when you are in the water," Cromall advised. "You do not want to be seen by any curious eyes on the Krassak side of the river."

"Port side?" asked Ramman.

"The left-hand side," Cromall explained patronisingly.

"Why not just say the left-hand side then," muttered Ramman under his breath. "What has port got to do with it?"

As soon as the ship had come to a halt, Tom and the team took their boots and belts off and clambered over the rail before dropping down into the cold, fresh water. Lalitha reluctantly placed her leather bag on the deck with the other gear before jumping down into the river after them. Everyone desperately rubbed at their hair and clothes to get as much of the foulness off themselves as they could. It was almost half an hour before they started to clamber back up the rope ladder and onto the ship.

"That is an improvement," laughed Cromall. "You still smell, but not as bad as you did."

"How long until we get to Krassak now?" asked Tom.

"We will approach Krassak before mid-day," Cromall said as he gestured to his crew to get the ship underway again.

"Let us know when we get near. We can use our rowboat to get to shore before you reach the docks."

Tom and the team hauled themselves back to the foredeck where they sat down again spreading out in the sun to dry out.

"Once we're off this ship," Alex said to Tom, "I'm never going anywhere near a pig ever again. I'm not even sure that bacon will taste the same again either. It'll just bring back the memory of lying in the hold of this ship, neck deep in pig crap."

"It'll take more than that to put me off a good bacon sarnie," Sam chuckled.

They sat and chatted in the sun as *The Flying Boar* sailed slowly down the river Viran. The river was wide and deep and the banks were lined with rocky outcrops and clumps of trees. A dusty road ran alongside the river on its eastern bank and travellers could be seen making their way in both directions. Hills rose from the floor of the wide valley and in the distance, larger mountains could be seen jutting up towards the clouds.

"Krassak lies at the edge of those mountains," Lalitha announced. "The tunnels that we seek are cut through the solid rock that forms the foundations of the capital. Some are formed by water, others by human hands and others still by more arcane forces."

"Where do we need to get off the ship?" Tom asked.

"We will need to disembark before we get to the city," Lalitha answered. "I can then lead us to an entrance to the secret tunnels to the south east of Krassak. It will not be a long walk from the banks of the river."

Tom nodded and turned to the others.

"Let's get ready to move. It won't be long before we need to make for the shore and leg it to one the entrances to the tunnels."

Everyone gathered their kit together and Sam examined all the rifles before carrying out a complete ammo check.

"How's it looking, Sam?" Tom asked.

"All the rifles are good to go and the Glocks are all fine. We've got six spare mags each for the rifles and about three each for the Glocks. We've got six claymores left altogether and three or four frags each. We only have four flash-bangs because you guys lost all yours when you got separated from your horses in the chaos on the Derralt plains. We only have the ones that were in my pack."

"Thanks, Sam. We're still looking okay for the time being then."

"Yep. The food is looking a bit dodgy though. We only have a few protein bars left."

"Well, we should be in the capital by the end of the day and who knows what happens then. At least our packs will be a bit lighter."

Sam nodded and proceeded to split the kit between the five Bergens. As he packed his own equipment, he had a sudden thought and beckoned to Ramman. As Ramman sat down next to him, Sam took his belt off and slid his holster free.

"Ram, I want you to take this," he said as he passed the holster to his friend. "We don't know what we're walking into here and I need you to be able to protect yourself."

Ramman popped the holster open and pulled the Glock out.

"Are you sure, Master Sam?"

Sam nodded and spent the next few minutes showing Ramman how to load and shoot the weapon. Once he was happy that the young man had grasped the basics, he passed him three full magazines.

"Okay, Ram, you have a full mag in the gun and another three here. That means that you have sixty-eight bullets. Just because you have lots of ammo, don't be tempted to just shoot it all off quickly bang, bang, bang. Pick your targets carefully and conserve your ammunition. It would be great if you could practice a bit to get used to the recoil, but it would attract too much attention here. You'll soon get the hang of it if you need to."

Ramman smiled broadly and threaded the holster onto his belt.

"Thank you, Master Sam."

"You're welcome. I hope you don't have to use it, but better safe than sorry."

Tom stood on the foredeck and watched as the mountains to the north grew ever closer. The team ate the last of their bread and cheese and Cromall filled up their water bottles from a large wooden barrel on the deck of the ship.

As *The Flying Boar* rounded a bend in the river, the city of Krassak came into view. The capital clung to the side of a mountain at the edge of the impressive range that stretched away into the distance to the north and east. High city walls rose up from the valley floor and fanned out around Krassak until they met the steep rocky slopes of the mountain that the city was built on. A wide road led from the huge city gates down to the multitude of buildings that stretched down to meet the river. The gatehouse itself was flanked by large stone towers and what looked like a vast portcullis hung above the entrance to the city.

Behind the walls Tom could see the tops of many towers and spires. Flags flew from many of them, their brightly coloured designs flapping gently in the wind. Impressive stone buildings rose up the mountainside in a series of wide terraces and at the top of everything stood a single enormous structure that featured battlements and towers. From the midst of this building, an immense tower soared up into the sky. The tower's peak dominated the skyline and was topped with a silver spire that glistened in the sunlight.

"Behold the great tower of Krassak," Lalitha exclaimed. "The altar that we must reach lies in the tower that you can see there at the top of the city."

"Wow," Alex breathed.

Everyone stood and stared at the awe-inspiring city that stood before them. It was so impressive that it almost didn't look real.

"Thank God we don't have to try and get through those gates," Sam said. "I wouldn't fancy our chances much."

Lalitha cocked her head as if she was listening to something and her eyes darted quickly to the riverbank to their right.

"We need to get to the shore," Lalitha said. "One of the tunnel entrances is not too far from here. It is through the trees that you can see there."

"Is it the tunnel that you used to escape the city?" Jimmy asked.

"No, but the Book knows that there is an entrance over there beyond those trees."

"Would we be better waitin' for nightfall?" Danny asked.

"It's ages yet until the sun will set," Tom reminded him. "If we get Cromall to anchor the ship here until then, we might well attract some unwanted attention. I think we're going to have to risk it and try to get through the trees without being seen. We need to get out of sight and into the tunnels as quickly as we can."

"Fair enough," Danny nodded.

The decision made, Tom went to speak to Cromall and found him at the ship's wheel.

"We'll leave you here, Cromall. Thanks for your help. We would not have got here without you."

"You are welcome," Cromall replied. "If anyone asks, you were never aboard *The Flying Boar*. I do not want to get myself a reputation for smuggling royalists on my ship."

"We won't say anything to anyone," Tom smiled as he handed over a fistful of silver coins.

Cromall grinned and tipped the coins into his belt pouch.

"Thank you. It has proven to be a very profitable day."

Cromall ordered his crewmen to slow the ship down by loosening the ropes that trimmed the main sail. As the ship gradually came to a near standstill, he pulled in the rope that was tied to their rowboat to bring the smaller vessel around from where it had been towed behind *The Boar*. A rope ladder was thrown over the starboard side of the ship this time and the team began to climb down.

"Good luck with your business in the city," Cromall said. "I hope you do not fall foul of the new regime."

"Thanks," Tom said and shook the man's hand. "Once we're back on dry land, we won't need this boat any longer. If you want to send a man with us, he can bring it back to you and you can keep it. You'll be doing us a favour. An abandoned boat this close to the city might cause us a problem."

Cromall nodded and instructed one of his men to go with them to the eastern bank. Tom heaved his Bergen up onto his back, slung his rifle over his shoulder and waited for everyone else to climb down onto the rowboat. With a last wave at Cromall, Tom lowered himself carefully down and as soon as he was safely onboard, Sam and Ramman rowed them quickly across the river.

The prow of the boat scraped up onto the pebbly bank and the team quickly climbed out onto dry land. Cromall's man set off back towards *The Boar* in the rowboat and Lalitha quickly led everyone away from the water, across the dusty road and into the trees on the other side. Thankfully, the road was clear of travellers as they hurried across it, so no-one witnessed their passing. Once the team were in the shade of the trees they crouched down and Tom turned to Lalitha.

"How far away are the tunnels?"

"They are close. We will head through this woodland and once we reach the hillside, the Book will guide me to the entrance."

"The city is quite a way from here still," Alex said. "How long will it take us to get through the tunnels, Lalitha?"

"I do not know exactly. I have never been through the tunnels this far south of the city. Some of the passages can be steep and tight and the going is not quick. I would guess that it will take us several hours to reach the tower once we are in the tunnels."

"Let's get started then," Danny said.

Lalitha had the Book gripped tightly in her hand and gestured for the others to follow her as she made her way carefully through the trees. The undergrowth was quite dense and their progress through the woods was slow. Several times one of them had to be freed from the clutches of the brambles as their long thorny shoots grabbed hold of clothes and flesh. The woods had not looked too thick from the road but it took almost an hour for them to fight their way through to the rocky hillside that lay on the other side.

As the trees began to thin out ahead of them, Lalitha sped up, eager to get to the tunnels. She burst out of the trees onto a narrow path, on the other side of which stood a wall of solid stone. Lalitha looked around to see if she could see the entrance, but there were no obvious gaps in the cliff wall.

"The entrance is here somewhere," she said as she held the Book in front of her.

The whispering voices must have told her something useful because Lalitha suddenly looked to the left and started making her way along the foot of the cliff. Everyone's focus followed Lalitha as she moved to their left and, as a consequence, nobody noticed the group of soldiers that rounded the corner to their right.

"Do not move!" the soldier at the front of the group yelled as he drew his sword.

"Shit!" exclaimed Tom as he swung round and unslung his rifle. "Danny. Jimmy. Go with Lalitha and find the entrance to the tunnels. We'll hold these guys off."

Danny and Jimmy headed off after Lalitha as she searched for the tunnel entrance and the others turned back to face the soldiers. They were advancing slowly towards them and they had all drawn their weapons. There were about twelve men in the group and they continued to move forwards. Alex and Sam moved slowly back to the edge of the trees, while Ramman pulled the Glock that Sam had given him out of its holster and held it against his side.

"What is your business here?" The soldier demanded.

"We were travelling towards the capital and were looking for somewhere to make camp for the night," Tom said as innocently as he could.

Another of the soldiers was looking suspiciously at Tom's rifle and said something quietly to his comrade. Their leader glanced at Tom's C8 and looked back into his eyes.

"Lie face down on the ground and place your hands behind your back," the soldier ordered.

Tom backed away slowly and began to raise his rifle. As he did so, one of the soldiers blew a loud blast on a horn. As the note echoed against the cliff beside them, another soldier leapt from the trees and grabbed Alex. He had a wicked looking curved blade in his hand and he held the blade to Alex's throat.

"Lie down. Now!" The officer in charge of the soldiers ordered.

Tom glanced quickly back down the cliff wall and could see no sign of Lalitha or the others. His eyes shot back to Alex as the soldier holding her tightened his grip and the knife pressed against her neck.

There was no room for manoeuvre. Tom could not risk doing anything with Alex's life hanging in the balance, so he slowly lowered his rifle and placed it on the ground in front of him before lying face-down in the dust. Sam and Ramman followed suit and the soldiers rushed forwards and took hold of them. Their hands were bound behind their backs and then they were lifted roughly to their feet.

"Where did your friends go?" the soldier demanded.

"I don't know," lied Tom. "They must have gone back into the trees."

One of their captors gathered up the weapons from the ground and the four friends were pushed into the middle of the path. The horn blast had brought more soldiers running and they were soon surrounded by over thirty armed men.

"Sorry, Tom," Alex said in a soft voice. "I didn't hear him coming."

"Be quiet!" the soldier ordered. "You will answer to Lord Gask for your crimes. Corporal, take five men and escort these prisoners back to the city as quickly as you can. I will lead the search for the others."

Tom made eye contact with Alex and shook his head slowly. This was not good.

Six of the soldiers began to push them back up the path in the opposite direction to where the entrance to the tunnel must be, whilst the remaining soldiers spread out along the foot of the cliff, looking for Lalitha.

As Tom was jostled along the path, he managed to steal one last look down the edge of the cliff. There was definitely no sign of Lalitha, Danny or Jimmy. They must have made it into the tunnels.

CHAPTER 51

On the Road to Krassak

Tom, Alex, Sam and Ramman were herded along the path as it curved away from the cliffs and looped back to the road that ran alongside the river. More men waited for them at the edge of the trees with two horse-drawn wagons and the soldiers herded them towards the nearest one. The soldiers must have been hidden in the trees as *The Flying Boar* sailed down river just a short while ago. It was a miracle that the men had not seen the team come ashore in the rowboat.

Tom, Alex and Sam were stripped of their Bergens and were pushed aggressively into the nearest of the wagons. Ramman was also manhandled roughly up into the wagon, and winced as one of the soldiers rammed the butt of his sword into his back in an attempt to speed him up. Once they were all in, two men climbed up after them and sat at the back of the wagon: their swords still drawn and their eyes watchful. The team's guns and packs were loaded into the other wagon and the soldiers quickly whipped the horses into a trot.

The wagons rumbled quickly along the track towards the city, a cloud of dust rising behind them. Tom had a brief glimmer of hope as he looked towards the river, but *The Flying Boar* had already sailed on downstream. Not that Cromall would have wanted to get involved anyway. It seemed that they had no choice other than to see how this played out, and hope that they could escape and meet up with Lalitha, Danny and Jimmy once they were inside the city.

The soldiers drove their horses hard and it was not long before they were approaching the city. People and animals filled the road to the gates, some on their way into the capital and others coming back out towards the docks that spread out along the riverbank to their left. The buildings down towards the river were mainly of wooden construction and around them were great paddocks full of livestock. Bordering the paddocks were long wooden barns and the distinct noise of animals' screams could be heard coming from them. Tom looked hurriedly away. They must be the butchery sheds that Cromall had mentioned. There lay the grisly fate that awaited *The Flying Boar's* unfortunate cargo.

Tom could see several ship's masts above the buildings where they were moored at the edge of the river and guessed that *The Flying Boar* was one of them, but there was no sign of Cromall amongst the throngs of people. Merchants could be heard haggling loudly for better prices with the ship owners, while the ship owners in turn argued the virtues of their cargoes. Around them all, longshoremen rushed backwards and forwards with trollies and carts full of produce.

The wagons turned sharply to the right, away from the bank, and the vast city gates stood before them. The scale of the fortifications was breath-taking. The gate towers loomed over them and the massive iron spikes of the portcullis hung menacingly above their heads as they passed through the stone portal.

The streets inside the city walls were flagged with large granite squares and the wagons rattled and shook as they raced along. The streets were narrow and were bordered on each side by tall grey stone buildings. Houses, taverns, grain stores, army barracks, stables and all manner of buildings flashed passed them as the wagons rushed along. Pedestrians and other travellers had to get out of the way quickly as the soldiers driving the wagons yelled and shouted at them to move.

The population here seemed much more affluent than in Prentak or Brentar. People were dressed in clothes that looked far more elegant and expensive and there were many more mounted riders here. A finely dressed couple sneered at the wagons in distain as the speeding wagons caused their horses to stamp nervously.

The buildings suddenly opened up and Tom looked on as the soldiers drove the wagons around the edge of an enormous open-air market. The marketplace was filled with the noise and bustle of people buying and selling a vast array of fruits, vegetables, breads, leather goods, clothing, ironmongery, weapons and livestock. The market must have been ten times the size of the one that they had visited in Lintar. The smell of a multitude of different foods drifted by as the wagons forced their way through the throngs of people.

The soldiers turned their horses abruptly left, away from the market and the streets began to climb more sharply. The horses panted and sweat shone on their necks as they pulled the wagons along the streets that cut across the mountainside in broad sweeping arcs. Each arc ended in a tight hairpin corner, and as the horses struggled up and around each corner to the next level, Tom realised how quickly they were climbing through the jerked levels of the city. As they rose above Krassak's lower levels, he caught occasional glimpses of the market below them and the River Viran in the distance as they rattled quickly past gaps between the buildings.

The upper terraces of the city contained more residential buildings, but these were much grander than those further down the mountain. Many of the huge houses up here boasted lush gardens that stretched out around them. This must be where the members of the royal court lived.

The wagons made another couple of tight turns and the view out over the valley suddenly became clear. Tom was lost for words as he looked down over Krassak. He could see the streets winding down below him. He could clearly see the marketplace and the streets leading down to the gate and beyond. Hundreds of people could be seen bustling through the streets. Up here they were above most of the towers and spires that rose from the buildings on the lower terraces and they had a clear view out to the west. In the distance, sunlight reflected from the river's surface and the docks heaved with activity.

Turning around, Tom looked up at the elaborately decorated building next to them. As their wagon moved pulled into the wide driveway that ran towards the front of the building, Tom realised that this must be the Royal Palace; Lalitha's home. A flight of steps led up from the driveway to a wide terrace in front of the two-story building. At the top of the steps stood a long line of massive statues, each portraying what looked like a king or queen. Banners and flags flapped along the front of the palace, and towering above it all the great tower jutted skywards, its silver spire glistening high above them.

The wagons lurched to a standstill, and Alex gave Tom a nudge as a group of ornately uniformed guards rushed down the steps towards them. The soldiers manhandled their captives down out of the wagon and the Royal Guards took hold of them and frog-marched them up the steps to the palace.

As they reached the top of the steps, they could see a wide sunken pool that stretched out across the width of the building. The pool was filled with lilies of some sort and amongst them swam brightly coloured fish. One of the guards knocked loudly on the large heavy looking double doors, and Tom heard a muffled clunk as a bolt was drawn back and the door swung open.

The guards pushed Tom and the others through the iron-bound doors and across an entrance hall. The hall had a black and white chequerboard floor, and in the middle of the room a fountain sprayed a jet of water up into the air which fell down in a cascade of water droplets into a raised circular pool. Large arched windows let the light stream in, throwing long shadows over the floor from the many statues and busts of monarchs and warriors that stood all around the room.

The guards' heels clicked loudly on the tiled floor as they guided their prisoners to the right and through another set of thick wooden doors. They entered a long, narrow banqueting hall which housed the biggest table Tom had ever seen. It would easily seat forty or fifty people. Banners fluttered from the ceiling and a gigantic fireplace stood in the middle of the left-hand wall. Tapestries depicting hunting scenes, grand looking royal feasts and battles between great armies hung from the long wall on the right and in-between them was an open space where it looked like a painting had recently hung.

Guards were dotted all around the room and they all looked at the newcomers cautiously as their captors pushed them towards the end of the table.

As Tom, Alex, Sam and Ramman stood there silently, two figures stood up from the far end of the table and walked slowly towards them. One of the figures was shrouded in a hooded cloak and the second was tall and wore black leather armour. He had shoulder length dark hair and a closely cropped black beard.

Tom had seen this man in the vision the Book had shown him. It was Findo Gask.

CHAPTER 52

The Royal Palace at Krassak

Gask walked forwards until he was standing directly in front of Tom. The two men were about the same height and Gask stared directly into Tom's eyes. Gask's eyes were a piercing blue colour; Tom did not blink and returned the stare.

"So, you are the outlanders that Lalitha has recruited to her cause," Gask exclaimed. "I do not know how you got so close to the city, but from the smell that assails my nose, I guess it had something to do with the livestock vessels that sail up Lake Viran."

Tom and the others said nothing.

There was a flurry of activity behind them, and several guards marched into the room carrying the team's packs and weapons. Everything was placed carefully on the floor and the guards backed away and stood close by, their hands resting on the hilts of their swords. Gask walked over and picked up one of the C8's. He examined it closely, turning it over and over in his hands before he put it back down and turned to face them again.

"Where is she?" he demanded.

Again, no-one said anything.

Gask gestured to his guards. One of the men drew his dagger and cut the ropes that bound the teams' arms. As they rubbed their sore wrists, the guards pushed them towards the table and forced them to sit down. Gask sat down across the table from them and placed his hands on the wooden surface. The hooded figure sat down a few chairs away from Gask and sat with his head bowed, his cloak still shadowing the features of his face. Gask glanced at the shrouded man and then turned back to face his captives.

"Was Lalitha with you? Does she still have that cursed Book?"

Tom stayed tight-lipped, but continued to stare coldly at Gask.

"Where did she find you?" Gask mused. "You do not look like barbarians, but your weapons are like nothing I have ever seen before."

"We are not from your world," Tom said in a flat, even voice. "We come from somewhere else."

"So, I have been told," Gask nodded. "I did not believe my sources when they told me this, but now that I see you, I am more inclined to believe them. How do you come to be in Zakastra?"

"We're not telling you anything Gask," Tom said determinedly. He risked a quick glance towards the rifles on the floor, but knew that they were too far away. The guards would be on him before he got halfway to their weapons.

Gask brought his fist down on the table with an echoing boom and glared at Tom.

"You do not understand the seriousness of the situation here," Gask said loudly.

"Oh, I think we do," Tom replied calmly.

Gask took a breath and forced himself to calm down.

"I am at a disadvantage," he said. "You know who I am, but I do not know your names. Who are you?"

Tom hesitated, but then decided that it made no difference if Gask knew what their names were or not.

"I am Thomas McAllister."

"My name is Alex Aluko," Alex said as Gask turned his gaze to her.

"I'm Sam Franklin," Sam announced.

"And I am Ramman, son of Sarratil."

"Very well," Gask said, "Let me try to explain our situation. I need to know where our impetuous young princess is. If she is anywhere near here, I need to know about it. What are her intentions?"

"Go screw yourself," Tom said calmly.

Gask scowled and his fists clenched tightly.

"Do you know what will happen if Lalitha brings the Book here, Thomas McAllister? Do you have any idea how many people will die?"

Tom stretched his hands out on the table in front of him and the muscles in his cheeks stood out as he clenched his jaw tightly shut.

"Does the world where you come from so easily accept mass murder?" Gask snapped.

"You are a fine one to talk about murder," Alex retorted. "You murdered the king just to steal his throne."

Gask's eyes darted to Alex.

"You know nothing about me or my intentions," Gask exclaimed. "Your beliefs are built upon the words of a spoiled child."

"A child whose father you murdered!" Alex snapped.

"I did not murder the king."

"Bullshit!" Alex yelled.

The hooded figure sitting nearby suddenly raised his hands and pulled the hood of his cloak from his face. The young man had dark hair and striking green eyes. He clasped his hands together in front of him and looked at Alex.

"Findo Gask did not kill the king."

"So, who did then?" Alex said defiantly.

"I did."

"And who the fuck are you?"

"I am Relfa, first born of King Lestri."

"What?"

"I am Lalitha's brother and I killed my father."

Alex looked at Tom and was suddenly lost for words.

"We thought that you were either dead or being held prisoner," Tom said, a confused look on his face. "Lalitha saw you in the tower covered in blood."

"That was not my blood. It was the blood of my father. Lalitha did not understand what she witnessed."

"But you were seen being led away by Gask's men."

"They were protecting me in case Lalitha came back to the city. I thought Lalitha knew that I had killed our father. She was always his favourite and she idolised him, so when she escaped with the Book, I feared for what she would do. She has a temper like my father and once roused, she is uncontrollable. She… she killed my mother in the tower. She stabbed her and left her to die."

As Relfa spoke, Gask's gaze fell to the table and Tom saw his shoulders slump. What did this all mean?

"What happened, Relfa?" Tom asked.

"My father demanded that I be Bound to the Book. I was his first-born and I was chosen by that unnatural thing when I was born. The king insisted that I go to Gessan and Bind my soul to it, but I refused. My father was furious. He planned to take me to Gessan by force and get the magi there to carry out their arcane ritual. I did not want it and I did not want the throne. Lalitha was different. She worshipped the king and everything he stood for. She coveted my father's power, but I had no interest in it."

"If Relfa had plotted against the king to steal his throne, would he not sit upon it now rather than being hidden under hoods and cloaks?" Gask said wearily.

"What happened in the tower?" Asked Alex.

"My father had heard rumours of the queen's infidelity and took her to the altar in the Tower to seek the truth from her using the Book. I followed them and watched the king as he summoned the power of the Souls. He used one of the words of summoning to command my mother to tell the truth and his suspicions were confirmed. When he realised the full extent of my mother's infidelity, he went insane with rage. He beat my mother with his fists and I thought he was going to kill her so I confronted him. I drew my dagger and stood between them both. My father looked at me and laughed in my face. He said I was weak and cowardly and that I would never have the courage to strike him. He was wrong. I stabbed him over and over again until I was covered in his blood. He tried to grab the Book from the altar to save himself, but it slipped from his grasp and fell out of his reach."

"Why did the Book not protect your father when you stabbed him?" Alex asked.

"I am chosen," Relfa grinned grimly. "The Book would never allow the power of the Soulstone to be used in a conflict between Chosen."

"By the time I arrived, the King's fate was already sealed," Gask said. "I was searching for Queen Tella and a guard that I trusted told me that she had climbed up into the tower. I feared for her safety and ran as fast as I could. By the time I got to the altar, the king lay dying, Relfa's dagger stuck deep into his chest. Relfa was crouched next to him and Tella had her arms around him. I stood over the king and watched as the life left his eyes and his Soul was sucked into the Soulstone. I don't know how long I stood there staring down at him, but the next thing I knew, Lalitha raced in and stole the Book. Then she… she…"

"She killed my mother," Relfa finished. "The kindest, most beautiful woman that ever lived and my twisted sister killed her."

Tears ran down Relfa's cheeks and splashed onto the table's wooden surface. Gask leant over and grasped the young man's shoulder. Relfa wiped his face on the sleeve of his cloak and looked at Tom defiantly.

"I regret deeply what happened to my mother, and my sister must atone for what she has done, but I do not regret killing the king. My father was a tyrant. He ruled the land and his family through fear and violence. He beat me. He beat my mother. He cared nothing about his people, all he cared about was power, influence and wealth. Anyone that said anything against him was silenced… violently. The only person who ever escaped his wrath was Lalitha… his favourite."

"He used his position as king together with the power of the Book to keep the realm in line," Gask said coldly. "Anyone that contradicted him paid a heavy price. The weak and poor were disregarded as inconsequential. To the king, they were nothing more than tools to be used to further his own ends."

"But didn't he keep the peace? He defeated the barbarians and put down a rebellion in the south," Tom said.

"A so-called rebellion led by my father," Gask nodded. "He and others like him recognised the atrocities that were heaped upon the serfs, and objected to the crippling taxes that the crown imposed on the poor. There were reports of an armed uprising in the southern cities of Lintar and Verna, but they were not true. Nestor Gaskkalt never intended to resort to violence, that was a lie that the king used to justify his use of force. Lestri took his army south to deal with what he called the 'subversives' and killed anyone that dared to stand before him. My father was hung by the neck and his corpse left on the gallows to be fed upon by the crows."

"The king did defeat the barbarians, that is true," Relfa added, "but the brutality that he used to stop their raids was inhuman. He spent several weeks aboard his royal ship and every barbarian vessel that they encountered was burned together with their crews and passengers. My father did destroy many raiding parties, but he also burned traders and their families. Men, women, children, animals… all were burned alive."

"He was a cruel and vicious man," Gask muttered bitterly. "After he executed my father, the name Gaskkalt was tainted. I had to be hidden by family friends in Lintar before the king's soldiers found me. If I had been discovered, I am sure that the king would have had me butchered too. I grew up under a different name and only adopted the name Gask when I arrived here at the capital many years later. If the king had known my real name earlier, I would have been strung up on the city walls as soon as I got here."

Tom, Sam and Alex looked at each other, their stomachs clenching tightly at what they were hearing.

"Lalitha knows that Nestor Gaskkalt was your father," Tom said.

"I trusted people here in the capital that I should not have. Lady Castra Deman was one of them. I confided in her shortly before that fateful night in the Tower. I thought that she would be a useful ally to fight against the king's tyranny, but I was wrong. She betrayed my trust and the king learned that Nestor Gaskkalt was my father. It was that knowledge that caused the king to have me followed and he then heard rumours of my relationship with the queen."

"Why did he not just have you killed as soon as he knew who your father was?" Alex asked.

"Despite my poor judgement when it came to Castra Deman, I had established several other important alliances in the leadership of the army and within the families of the royal court. Many of them agreed that changes were needed within Zakastra. I think that the king was trying to determine the best way of disposing of me without causing a political backlash. I had not confronted him or made any threats and as a consequence I believe that Lestri was biding his time before I mysteriously disappeared at the hands of Lord Ardum and his men. He did not want to upset my powerful friends and risk conflict in Krassak before he was fully prepared to move against me. To move while I had so much support would have reflected badly on him, and he would do anything to avoid the appearance of weakness. He knew that it was only a matter of time before me and my allies had enough support to challenge him, but he had the power of the Book in his hands and I think that the knowledge that he could kill us all by uttering a single word made him complacent. Of course, my fate would have been decided much earlier had he discovered my love for the queen sooner than he did. There would have been no avoiding his wrath had that happened."

"Did you plan to get close to the queen and use her against King Lestri from the start?" Tom asked.

"In the beginning, perhaps I did," Gask said sadly, "but the more time I spent with her, the more my feelings for Tella deepened. She was a beautiful and kind woman… nothing like her brute of a husband. I did not mean to fall in love with her, but it happened anyway. Lestri made her life a living hell and I take some small comfort in the knowledge that I made Tella's life more joyful towards its end."

Gask fell silent and stared into the fire as he struggled to contain his emotions.

"Relfa, did you know about Gask and your mother?" Alex asked.

"I did and I was happy for her. My father beat her regularly and treated her worse than he did his hunting dogs. She received no affection from him and was kept a prisoner in this palace. To him, she was nothing more than another one of his possessions that was brought out to impress the royal court when it suited him. When Gask appeared at court and became close to my mother, I was happy that she had someone that actually cared about her. It was a dangerous relationship, but it gave some happiness to her tortured existence."

Gask's eyes welled up at Relfa's words and he rubbed his beard distractedly.

"I loved her and she loved me," he said, his voice breaking with emotion. "Some may consider what we did as being wrong, but was it? Really? The king cared nothing for her and he made her life miserable. I could not offer her much, but what I could offer was my heart, and that gave her last few months some meaning at least."

Tom was lost for words. He looked into the faces of his friends and they too looked torn by conflicting emotions.

"Were you the hooded figure that Lalitha saw when she fell from the cliffs?" Sam asked Relfa.

"Yes. Gask needed me with him to try and reclaim the Book, but I chose to disguise myself. If Lalitha had seen me with him, she would not have reacted well."

"Why did the Book not tell Lalitha that it was you?"

"Through much reading of ancient texts, I have learned how to shield myself from the Book's gaze. I want that thing to have no sway over my life at all. I managed to conceal my identity from both Lalitha and the Book that day on the cliffs. I tried to take the Book from her so that we could bury the thing away and remove its influence over my family and the realm as a whole, but Lalitha jumped rather than give it up. The cursed thing already had her under its control. I knew my sister to be unbalanced, but I was still devastated when she fell. After… After what happened to our mother, she is the last remaining member of my family."

"Why are you both telling us all this?" Tom asked. "What do you want from us? You know that we travelled with Lalitha and that we helped her get here. Why should we believe a word that you say and why would you trust us?"

"You need to know the truth," Gask said. "Lalitha has told you how she views the events of that night in the Tower, but her opinion is driven by her unswerving loyalty to her father."

"No matter what atrocities my father carried out in the name of the throne, my sister blindly followed him and his brutal ideology," Relfa added.

"I can see that you are honourable warriors and that you believed that bringing Lalitha here to bring about her revenge on me was the right thing to do," Gask said, "But perhaps now you can see that things were not as you thought. It may be that our cause is doomed and Lalitha will use the Book to rain down fire and death upon us all. It may turn out that we have no way of stopping her. It might be that you decide to continue to support her. I know not how these matters will be resolved. All I know is that I have to do whatever I can to stop her or something terrible will happen when she lays that Book back on its altar."

"There is much of my father in Lalitha and I fear that she has a similar capacity for brutality and violence," Relfa added, "I fear that the havoc she will wreak with the Book, should we not be able to prevent it, will be catastrophic."

Gask and Relfa both fell silent and looked expectantly at the confused faces sat across the table.

"I don't know what to think," Tom stuttered. "Lalitha obviously idolised her father and all she talks about is revenge and reclaiming the throne from you. She thinks that you killed her father and she is hell-bent on avenging him."

"What do you think that she intends to do?" Gask asked. "Do we face catastrophe?"

"She is going to try to get the Book back to its altar and then use it to burn anyone who stood against the king."

"It is as we feared then," Gask exclaimed as he glanced at Relfa.

Relfa looked at Tom and breathed deeply.

"If my sister unleashes the full power of the Soulstone to kill anyone who stood against the king, then the vast majority of people in this city will burn. The only people that supported King Lestri were those that benefitted from being in his favour. Many of the wealthy families that live up here on the high terraces of the capital, the corrupt city Elders, the tax collectors and the money lenders all stood at his side. Everyone else here knew the king for what he was. Cruel and violent. They were simply all too scared to say anything against him while he was alive."

"But we've spoken to people who support him as we've travelled from the south," Tom argued. "Traders, ships' captains, ordinary people. They mostly agreed that the king brought stability."

"Stability yes," Gask agreed, "But at what price? Fear? Poverty? Death? You must have seen the serfs and those doomed to a life of squalor. What about them? What about those that are forced into servitude and worse? Stability when it is achieved at such a price is not sustainable. We have to find a better way."

"How do we know that you're telling us the truth?" Tom asked.

"You already know it," Gask said as he looked into their eyes.

Tom looked deep within himself and thought about what Gask and Relfa had told them. Knowing what he knew about Lalitha and everything that had happened to them as they had journeyed through the realm, Tom could not help but believe that what these two men had told them was true.

"Jesus Tom," Alex breathed. "Have we been fighting on the wrong side?"

"I don't know," Tom replied worriedly.

"Did my sister complete the Ceremony of Binding at Gessan?" asked Relfa.

Tom nodded. "Yes, she did."

"I knew all along that she wasn't dead," Gask muttered.

"We did not know where she vanished to when she fell from the cliffs," Relfa said, "but it was plain that she had not perished on the rocks. The Book had done something to save her."

"What happened at Derralt?" Tom asked Gask. "If you are so against violence, why attack us there?"

"You need to ask?" Gask said. "A rider came to us from the south and told a story about outlanders travelling towards the island of Gessan with a princess and a magic book. He named Lalitha and his description of her was accurate. What were we supposed to do? I do not like violence, but we had to do something to try to stop Lalitha getting the Book back to Krassak."

"Why did you not try to stop her getting to Gessan?" Sam asked.

"She would already have been to Gessan by the time the messenger arrived with news of your reappearance," Relfa replied.

"We knew that Castra Deman was plotting something and that remnants of the old royal guard were rallying to that fool Ardum's call," Gask continued. "When Castra Deman betrayed me and made her loyalty to Lestri known, we realised that Lalitha would seek to join forces with her. After that, we had little choice; we had to mobilise forces from the southern garrisons to stop Lalitha's forces before they marched north and rained destruction down on the capital. I had intended to meet with Lady Deman and discuss terms with her, but that opportunity did not present itself. I mourn the loss of life that took place on the plains at Derralt, but we had no other options. The soldiers were ordered to capture the princess alive, but evidently they did not succeed."

"Your men did not listen to your orders," Alex said accusingly. "They massacred all of Lady Deman's men and would have killed us too had we not escaped."

"I regret that this was how events unfolded," Gask said. "I wished to take Relfa and travel with the army myself, but there was not time. If we had been there, perhaps things might have been different. I fear that the men acted out of concern for their families and the people of Krassak when they decided to ignore my orders and kill everyone. However, speaking in defence of my men, if Lalitha had been allowed to march north, there is no saying how many innocent lives would have been lost. What happened outside Derralt was upsetting, but necessary."

"What was the name of the rider who brought the news of us?" Ramman asked abruptly.

Gask looked at Ramman but shook his head. "I do not know."

"I think he was called Datran," Relfa said.

"Not Datran… Daltran," Ramman muttered.

"Ramman," Tom said, turning to his friend. "We thought this might be the case, but if your brother did betray us, he might have inadvertently saved us from making a huge mistake. If he hadn't done what he had, we might not be sitting here now. Forgetting the fact that your brother is an asshole, what do you think about everything we've been told here? Does it sound true to you?"

"I do not know, Master Thomas. I know that many people in Brentar resent paying their taxes and that the serfs are not treated well, but that is the way that it has always been. There have always been stories about the king's violent nature, but who were we to question the ways of the royal house? Our farm is small and we do not get involved in politics or matters that are none of our concern."

"Just because the old ways have been adhered to for centuries, it doesn't make them right," Gask said. "The wealth and power of the rich in this realm has been built upon the suffering of the poor and weak. We have to find a different way."

Tom rubbed his eyes and rested his head in his hands.

"Boss," Sam said softly, "we need to stop Lalitha."

Tom looked at his friend. He couldn't decide what to do for the best. Lalitha had done so much to help him, but a lot of what Gask and Relfa said felt true. Could they run the risk that their own activity might bring about the catastrophic destruction that Gask and Relfa were so scared of?"

"I'm not saying we do anything bad to Lalitha," Sam continued, "but I think we need to stop her using the Book to set this city on fire."

"I agree," nodded Alex. "Let's try to get her to sit down and talk it all through before she lashes out with the Book. We need to explain that Gask didn't kill the king."

"I fear that it will take more than words to stop my sister," Relfa mused. "She has the Book and her anger knows no bounds."

"What is the deal with this Book," Alex asked abruptly. "Is it evil?"

"The Book is neither good nor evil," Relfa said. "Nobody knows the origins of the Soulstones and the Books that harnessed their power. Not even the magi on Gessan. Only the Great Book remains now and it is neither a force for ill nor good. Everything that it does is done to protect itself and make itself more powerful. That is why a Chosen can never use the Book to harm another that it has chosen. It relies on its Chosen to protect it and do its bidding in the physical world and would never risk hurting one of its own protectors. It will not intervene if two Chosen fight each other. The Book will take solace in the fact that the stronger Chosen will win any such conflict, thereby making them a better protector."

"Such power as is contained within that Book should not be wielded by human hands," Gask said. "With Relfa's help, I intended to bury the thing away in a deep dark hole. The Book is not evil, but the power that it gives its wielder over others is the ultimate corrupting force. Few can have that amount of power at their command and stay unchanged. Being able to do whatever you want with no consequences will always lead to that power being abused. This is how tyrants are created and how they cling to power. Such dictators do not survive from positions of weakness, only from positions of strength and advantage."

"Boss, come on," Sam said insistently, "We've got to do something. While we're sitting here, Lalitha is getting closer."

"What does he mean," Gask snapped worriedly. "Where is Lalitha?"

Tom swallowed and looked at Alex. She nodded.

"Lalitha is in the tunnels under the city. She intends to use them to get into the tower and use the Book to rain down her vengeance on you all."

CHAPTER 53

The Royal Palace at Krassak

After hearing that Lalitha could already be below the city, Gask jumped to his feet and raced from the room to mobilise the royal guard.

Relfa stayed seated and stared at the four seated figures in front of him.

"Why did you not tell us sooner?"

"I didn't know if I could trust you or not," Tom said.

"And now?"

"We can't run the risk of doing nothing if you are right," Alex answered. "We need to stop Lalitha."

"What do you know about the tunnels below the city, Relfa?" Tom asked.

"I know of their existence, but have never entered them," Relfa replied. "My father told me of a vast labyrinth of tunnels that run through the bedrock below Krassak. The entrances to the tunnels are hidden and even if they were known, the tunnels are difficult to navigate. It would be easy to become inescapably lost down there."

"But Lalitha has the Book to guide her," Alex said.

"That is true. That gives my sister a significant advantage. I was never allowed to remove the Book from its altar, so never dared to find any of the secret entrances and explore the tunnels."

"How long do you think it will take Lalitha to make her way through the tunnels?"

"I do not know," Relfa shrugged. "It could be any time now, or could be in a few hours' time. It depends upon how difficult her route through the labyrinth proves to be. Some of the tunnels may be harder to negotiate if she is by herself."

"She isn't by herself," Tom said. "She has two of our friends with her… and one of them was also Bound at Gessan."

"What?" exclaimed Relfa. "There is another Chosen? How is that possible?"

"The Book chose one of our friends while we were in our world. He went through the Binding Ceremony with Lalitha at Gessan."

"That is surprising indeed, but I am unsure whether what you have told me is bad news or good news," Relfa said. "If this new Chosen is less militant than Lalitha then that could work in our favour. We will need all the allies that we can muster if we are to stop her committing a serious atrocity in the city."

Gask reappeared through the doors to the hall and strode back towards them.

"After everything I have told you here today, can I trust you?" Gask asked with a serious look on his face.

Tom, Alex, Sam and Ramman all looked at each other. Sam and Ramman nodded their heads.

"Yes," Alex said.

"You can trust us to try and stop Lalitha doing anything crazy, but we've been through a lot with her and I've only just met you," Tom declared. "Trust cuts both ways. Quite how we clear up this whole mess after all the shit that has happened, I do not know, but we will do what we can to help prevent another bloodbath."

"Very well," nodded Gask. "I am mobilising the royal guard to search for Lalitha in the city. Join me. Together we will do what has to be done."

"Okay," Tom agreed. "If we find her, we might be able to talk her down."

"Follow me," Gask said as he strode from the room.

Tom and the others followed Gask out through the entrance hall and onto the terrace outside the front door. Gask stood looking over the parapet at the edge of the terrace and gazed down into the city, watching carefully as the royal guard dispersed through the streets. Below them, Tom could see groups of soldiers in their bright blue uniforms taking positions throughout the city. They had a difficult task ahead of them down there. It was going to be like trying to find a very sharp needle in a very large haystack.

"Surely, Lalitha will aim to surface near the palace, won't she?" Relfa commented.

"I agree with you, Relfa," said Gask, "but I have deployed my men through the lower levels of the city in case Lalitha emerges down there... whether by choice or necessity. If she does exit the tunnels directly into the palace, I have positioned several platoons of the royal guard throughout the hallways and the lower chambers there."

"So now we just wait here until something happens?" Tom asked.

"We wait," Gask nodded, with a troubled look on his face. He stroked his beard and glanced back over his shoulder at the palace before speaking again.

"Let us wait in the Tower. That is where Lalitha intends to go, so we should confront her there. Let her come to us."

Gask led them back into the palace and straight through the entrance hall, past the fountain and through another set of carved wooden doors at the rear of the room. They walked down a wide corridor that was lined with suits of dark metal armour, each of which held a sword up in front of them. A detachment of guards stood at the end of the corridor and Gask gestured for them to follow him.

"This way," Gask beckoned.

They made their way through a long, narrow passageway that passed through a thick stone wall and found themselves in a wide circular chamber. The chamber was illuminated by burning torches mounted on the walls by large metal brackets. Tom could see a wide stone staircase that wound its way up the circular wall until it disappeared into the ceiling above them. Similarly, another set of steps disappeared down through the floor of the chamber. Most of the guards stationed themselves around the walls whilst the remaining men climbed the steps that led up into the Tower.

"We stand above the base of the Great Tower," Gask said. "The altar lies two floors above us. The only way up there is through this chamber. Below us lie more chambers, but I have already sent guards down there to search for Lalitha and your friends."

"Okay," Tom said. "We wait here then."

"Yes," Gask nodded. "We wait here."

There were stone benches positioned around the middle of the room and a round stone plinth lay at its very centre. A large jug of water and several mugs stood on the plinth together with a large bowl of fruit.

"Help yourself to food and water if you require it," Gask said.

Realising just how thirsty they were, the team quickly drank several mugs of water before sitting down on the cold stone benches. None of them was at all hungry. The anticipation of what lay ahead of them was making everyone nervous.

The minutes ticked by slowly. There were no windows in the chamber and other than the huge stone blocks that made up the walls of the tower, there was little to look at. Tom tried to rest his eyes, but his brain wouldn't let him. Sam and Alex had taken to pacing round the chamber, their constant movement did little to calm everyone's nerves.

After what felt like well over an hour, Tom could not take it any longer.

"Could we go up and look at the altar?" Tom asked Gask.

Gask hesitated, but then nodded his head. He too was feeling on edge and needed to do something to occupy his mind. He instructed several of the soldiers with them to remain on guard here and then pointed towards the staircase. As the team made for the stairs, Gask took one of the flaming torches from its wall bracket and held it above his head as they started to climb.

"We go up," he said.

The steps were tall and climbed steeply upwards as the staircase curved around the wall. Tom's knees started to complain straight away as he made his way up through the ceiling into the next chamber. This one had a series of life-sized stone statues lined up around the edge of the curved walls. The statues were of magi, and each figure had their hands outstretched before them. In the hands of each magi was a huge candle which burned with a bright orange flame. The candles flickered gently in the draft from the stairs and the dancing light threw moving shadows across the face of each statue. The effect was unnerving as the faces seemed to move in the candlelight.

"These statues represent the magi of old that lived among us in the capital," Relfa said. "That was before the magi wars and before King Athrun exiled the magi to Gessan. These statues are centuries old."

"They give me the creeps," Alex whispered to Tom as they continued up the stairs.

The chamber above them was the altar room. In the centre of the chamber stood a tall circular altar and around it stood twelve stone pillars. The altar's surface had been carved with hundreds of symbols, none of which Tom could decipher. Each of the pillars featured similar carvings, and the top of each one had been shaped into a representation of the sun. The stones looked ancient and the room had an eerie feeling to it. Tom could almost feel the electricity in the air. He reached out to touch Alex and a bright spark leaped between them with a loud crack, making them both jump.

Around the wall, Tom could see a series of small windows. There was no glass in them, and rays of sunlight cut through the chamber hitting the stone pillars. Tom could feel a breeze on his face as air blew in through the thick walls. Another staircase wound its way up around the curved walls and into whatever chamber lay above them.

The guards that had accompanied them took positions at the edge of the room and stood at attention, their weapons clenched tightly in their hands.

Tom eyed the armed men warily and moved past them towards the altar. On its top surface he could see a representation of the Soulstone cut into it. The carving of the round stone had carved flames dancing within it and beams of light shone out towards the edge of the altar.

"This is the altar room for the Great Book," Relfa told them. "It has stood here for many centuries."

"There is no door to the altar room. Can the altar room not be locked?" Sam asked.

"There is no need," Relfa replied. "When the Book sits on the altar, only a Chosen can touch it. The Book would react badly to anyone else who ventured in here uninvited."

"Everyone in the city knows that to enter this room when the Book is in its place on the altar would be a foolhardy thing to do."

"No shit?" Breathed Sam.

Tom and Alex looked around the room. It gave them both a weird feeling thinking about all the events since that night in West London and how they had all led to them being in this altar room.

"This is where we've been trying to get to," Alex said. "Everything that we've been through was to get us here."

"All we need now is for Lalitha to arrive," Tom grimaced, "and I've got absolutely no idea how that is going to play out."

"Yeah, this might not end well," Alex grinned tightly.

"Alex, I want you to leave. I want you to get out of here until the dust settles. Things could get nasty in here."

"I know that Tom, but I have as much chance of getting through to Lalitha as you do. If anything, it should be you who leaves, not me."

"No way," Tom grinned. "I guess we'll just have to take our chances together then."

"Too right. Together we're unstoppable."

Sam and Ramman walked towards them and the four of them stood together outside the circle of stone pillars.

"I'm glad we managed to catch up with you guys," Sam said. "I don't know what's gonna happen here, but I'm glad that we're here with you at the end."

"Me too, Sam," Tom smiled. "If you hadn't found us at the river that night, we wouldn't have got here at all."

"It isn't really like we thought it was going to be is it?" Alex said. "We thought we'd be fighting our way in here and zapping the bad guy. Turns out the bad guy isn't the bad guy."

"And the good guy might be about to turn thousands of people to ash," added Sam.

"Yeah thanks for that, Slaphead," Alex quipped. "As if we weren't all thinking that already."

"I think that Mistress Lalitha will do the right thing," Ramman said quietly. "I do not believe that she is a bad person."

"You're right, Ramman," Tom agreed, "I don't think she's a bad person either, but she's a seriously angry person with a lot of power at her fingertips and that could be just as dangerous."

Alex was about to add something, but was distracted by a muffled popping noise that rose from the stairwell below them.

Alex's eyes shot to Tom and he took a sharp intake of breath.

"That was gunfire," Tom exclaimed, "they're here!"

CHAPTER 54

The Chambers Below the Great Tower

The sound of more shots echoed faintly up the stairway and Tom turned quickly to Gask.

"You need to get out of here. If Lalitha sees you, you're dead. Go up into the tower and stay up there until it's safe. Take the guards here with you; you might need them!"

Gask looked like he was about to argue, but then nodded and, with several guards at his side, made his way up the next staircase.

"We've got to stop Lalitha getting to the altar and doing something crazy," Tom told the others as he made his way down the wide stone steps.

"I will come with you," Relfa said. "It is time that my sister knew the truth."

They rushed through the chamber with the magi statues and back down to where they had entered the base of the tower.

Most of the guards that had remained in the room had disappeared and Tom realised that they must have headed down into the sub-chambers to investigate already. The four guards that remained looked nervous. They knew that something dangerous was heading their way.

Everyone stood quietly, listening carefully as Tom tried to decide which direction to head in. They did not have to wait long. From below them came the unmistakable sound of gunfire.

"They're below us. What's down there, Relfa?"

"The sub-chambers are used for storage. The rooms below us were cut from the bedrock when the tower was first constructed. I thought that there was no way in or out other than this staircase."

"Lalitha must have found a hidden entrance to the tunnel system down there,"

Sam said.

"Come on," Tom instructed them as he hurried towards the steps to the sub-chambers.

"You men stand guard here," Relfa said to the last of the guards. "Whatever happens, Princess Lalitha must not be allowed to get to the altar room. If she gets past us, do what you need to in order to prevent her getting there."

"Yes sir," the men replied obediently.

Tom quickly led Relfa and the team down the narrow staircase that led to the sub-chambers. Once they reached the bottom of the dusty stone stairs, they could see that the steps opened out into a small square room. There were no windows and the room was dark with the only light coming from a torch that burned brightly on the wall. Nearby on the floor stood a barrel and inside it was a number of unlit torches. Tom picked one of them up and held it to the burning flame. Tom's torch instantly ignited and he held it in front of him as he moved forwards.

Passages shot off in every direction from the room they were in. Tom could not see the end of each of the passageways, but noticed that they opened out into other chambers as they disappeared into the darkness.

"Grab yourselves a torch each," he said to the others. "We need to stick together down here, and be careful!"

Tom led them into the passageway in front of them. Their shadows danced around the walls and low ceiling as the group advanced with their torches. There was a noise ahead and Tom shielded his eyes as he tried to see what it was. A group of guards ran from a passage that joined from the left and then down another opening in the right-hand wall. He could hear them shout instructions to each other, but the echoing words were hard to make out.

There was a loud crack of gunfire somewhere, but it was difficult to tell where it had come from.

"Danny. Jimmy. It's us. Hold your fire," Tom called and listened as the word 'fire… fire… fire…' echoed down the passageway.

They moved forwards carefully and their passage opened out into another stone-walled room. Barrels of ale and crates filled with bottles of wine were stacked around the walls. As Tom squeezed past the crates, he could see that there were more passageways that branched out from this room.

He jumped as more shots were fired and a bright flash illuminated one of the tunnels to their right.

"Down there to the right," Alex pointed.

They rushed towards the right and turned the corner just in time to see three guards run across this passageway from the left.

"It's a frigging maze down here, Boss," Sam swore.

"Tell me about it," Tom agreed.

They moved on carefully, through another room filled with cheeses wrapped tightly in linen sacks. The smell was overpowering, but no-one paid much attention as a bright light lit yet another passageway to their left and a loud scream split the air. As Tom stood, his heart hammering, a man ran from the passageway. His body was ablaze and he did not get far before he crashed to the ground and fell silent.

Tom traded worried glances with Alex and they headed for the passageway that the man had emerged from.

"Danny. Jimmy. Lalitha. It's Tom. Hold your fire!" Tom shouted again.

Tom looked around the corner into the next passageway carefully and pulled his head back quickly as two guards ran towards him. There was a series of deafening booms from a C8 assault rifle and both the guards fell to the floor, their bodies riddled with bullets.

"Danny. Jimmy. FOR CHRIST'S SAKE STOP SHOOTING!" Tom screamed.

"Boss?" He heard a voice say.

"Danny? Cease fire!"

Tom heard voices from the passageway and risked another look. He saw Danny walking towards him, his mag-lite illuminating the floor in front of him.

"Boss. How did you get here?" Danny asked as his face came into view.

"It's a long story," Tom answered as he hugged Danny.

"I thought you'd be in a deep, dark dungeon... or worse," breathed Danny. "I'm glad to see you mate."

"Me too, Danny. Things have taken a turn though. We need to talk to Lalitha."

Jimmy and Lalitha came into view behind Danny. They were both soaking wet and dust stuck to their clothes in clumps.

"Hey, Boss. It's a relief to see you," Jimmy exclaimed. "The caves were a nightmare. We nearly got lost a couple of times, but Lalitha used the Book to show us the way. It felt like we were down there for days."

"Thomas McAllister," Lalitha said. "You escaped your captors?"

Tom looked at Lalitha's face. Her eyes were wide and he couldn't tell if she was scared or if that expression betrayed a completely different, darker emotion.

Lalitha looked past Tom and saw Relfa standing there.

"Relfa? You are alive! Did Thomas McAlister free you from your prison?"

"I was not imprisoned, sister," Relfa said. "You need to listen to me. You do not understand what is happening here. You need to stop what you are doing. It will lead to nothing but tragedy."

"What do you mean? You were not a prisoner? Where have you been?"

"I've been with Gask."

"What?" Lalitha shrieked. "He murdered our father… How can you have been in the same room as that bastard and not ripped his treacherous heart out?"

"Listen, Lalitha…"

"No," Lalitha interrupted. She was wild with anger. "He killed the king and now he and his allies will pay the price. If you are not man enough to do it, then I will."

"Sister, you have to stop. The violence must end."

"It will end… once Gask and the rest of the traitors have burned to ash."

"Lalitha," Alex said, "you need to listen to us. The situation here is not what you thought."

"Sister, there is another way," added Relfa. "You must forsake the power of the Book and we can find a peaceful way forward."

Lalitha's eyes went wide and a manic look fell across her face.

"PEACEFUL?" she shouted. "There will only be peace once I have cleansed this city of traitors. Everyone who stood against our father will burn, and when I find Gask, his fate will be far, far worse."

Lalitha reached forwards and pulled Danny's combat knife from its sheath. She looked at the blade as the light from the torches reflected from it and spoke in a soft, but menacing voice. Danny made to take it back, but the look in Lalitha's eyes stopped him.

"Gask will beg me for death before the end," Lalitha hissed, "and I will enjoy watching him suffer. He deserves it for what he did."

"Sister, Gask did not kill the king," Relfa blurted.

"What?" Lalitha exclaimed viciously. "I saw him standing over our father's body."

"You did, but Gask did not kill him."

"Then who did?" she yelled.

"I did."

Lalitha gasped and stared at her brother.

"Why?" she screamed. "He was our father! He was the king!"

"He was a tyrant!" Relfa screamed back at her. "He was twisted and corrupt and cared only about himself and his precious throne."

"NO!" Lalitha roared.

The fires lit in her eyes and Tom noticed that she clasped the Book in her left hand. The whispering started and the Soulstone burned brightly, its orange glare lighting up the passageway around them

There was a sudden noise of running feet and Tom saw torches coming along the passageway behind Jimmy. Lalitha heard the sound and turned her head to look at the guards that rushed towards them.

"Pyrta!" She muttered and the guards burst into flames as they ran.

"No!" Tom yelled, but it was too late. All he could do was look on with a sick feeling in his stomach as the guards screamed and collapsed into a blazing pyre on the floor.

Lalitha stared at her brother, the flames blazing brightly in her eyes. Relfa stepped towards her and grabbed her by the shoulders.

"I will not let you kill more innocent people in this city sister. The king had to be stopped. His addiction to that Book, and his disregard for the welfare of the people of this realm was a travesty of justice and humanity."

"You are weak and stupid, Relfa," she growled menacingly. "You have let that filthy, lying serpent Gask whisper his lies into your ears. The king was a great man. How can you side with scum like Gask over our father?"

"Because he is right! Our father had to be stopped."

"Brother, you are no better than Gask. I disown you," Lalitha spat as she shrugged her brother's hands from her shoulders. "You are a disgrace to your family and the crown."

"What about you!" Relfa screamed. "You killed our mother… The mother that bore us and loved us. The one good thing in this wretched place and you killed her!"

"SHE BETRAYED US!" Lalitha roared into Relfa's face.

"Grow up, sister!" Relfa yelled back. "Take those blinkers from your eyes and see our father for what he was. Selfish, violent and evil. He beat our mother and treated her like a dog. I don't blame her for what she did."

"Come on, try to calm down you two," Alex said soothingly as she tried to defuse the dangerous situation. "It's going to be difficult, but we can work this out."

Lalitha's anger was too far gone for Alex's words to make any difference.

"You don't place any blame on that whore for lying with our father's enemy and leading him to his death? She deserved what I did to her."

Lalitha's eyes burned more brightly than ever and the whispering increased in volume. The Soulstone burned with an angry fire that lit the passageway around them. Lalitha glanced down at the Book and then stared deep into Relfa's eyes.

"You cannot stop me fulfilling my destiny," she said grimly.

"You cannot use the Book against me," Relfa scoffed. "As much as it pains me, I am Chosen. The Book will not act against me. You have to listen to what I am telling you. If you do not, then we will have no choice my sister, we will have to stop you using force."

"Stop me using force?" She scoffed. "I may not be able to summon the power of the Souls against you, my foolish brother, but that will not save you."

Lalitha let out an animal-like growl and drove Danny's dagger deep into Relfa's ribs.

Everyone watched in shock and horror as Relfa slowly sank to the floor, blood gushing from the wound in his side. Sam crouched down to see if he could help the young man, but there was nothing that could be done to fix a savage injury like that. Relfa gagged as blood poured from his mouth and he struggled to say something, but no words came out. His eyes rolled up into his head and he sighed as his last breath left his body.

"Lalitha, what the…" Tom started to say.

"Say nothing more, Thomas McAllister, unless you wish to incur my wrath. I must get to the altar room quickly. Gask may not have struck the blow that killed my father, but I still hold him responsible. He and all the other traitors in this city must burn."

The fires in Lalitha's eyes had diminished, but she looked no less dangerous for it. Tom did not know what to do and while he hesitated, Lalitha pushed past him and set off through the passageways.

"Danny, you've got to talk her out of this," Tom gasped. "If she tries to burn everyone who stood against the king, she's going to murder half of the city and who knows what she'll do after that. King Lestri was a tyrant. Gask isn't the bad guy here and I'm scared that Lalitha is about to do something fucking terrible."

"You think she's gonna listen to me?" Danny spluttered. "Have you seen her? She's obsessed with her revenge and it's drivin' her mad. She just stabbed her own brother for fuck's sake."

"You need to stop her…"

"Boss, she doesn't trust me already. She thinks that I am tryin' to steal the fuckin' Book from her. She won't listen to anything I say."

"You need to try… and quickly. She can't use the Book against you; you're Chosen. You're the only one who can physically stop her now that Relfa is dead. In her current frame of mind, I think she'll torch the rest of us if we try to stop her. Go. Quickly!"

"Okay," Danny reluctantly nodded. "I'll stop her if I can."

Danny set off running down the passage with Tom shouting directions to him from behind. Up ahead of them, they saw a bright burst of light and the sound of loud screams echoed down towards them. Lalitha was not far ahead.

They sprinted to the stone steps at the bottom of the tower and ran up them as fast as they could. When they reached the chamber where they had waited earlier, the floor was littered with burning bodies; the Book had been used to kill the guards that Relfa had left here. Lalitha stood in the middle of the carnage and as she saw Danny, she leapt over the charred corpses and rushed up the steep steps towards the chamber of magi statues.

Danny shed his Bergen and dropped his rifle as he sped after her. The sudden reduction in weight allowed him to find an extra burst of speed and he rapidly closed the gap between them. They raced past the stone magi and on up the last set of stairs towards the altar room.

Danny was close behind Lalitha now and with a desperate lunge, managed to grasp the back of her tunic as she was almost at the top of the flight of steps. He yanked her backwards savagely and Lalitha was pulled from her feet. She fell backwards on top of him and they both tumbled back down the stone staircase. They struggled violently with each other as they landed in a heap amongst the statues of the magi. Lalitha managed to pull herself free and tried to climb to her feet, but Danny grabbed her arm and pulled her back to her knees. She grappled with him, but he was stronger than her and he managed to hold her down and get a grip on the Book.

Danny wrapped his legs around Lalitha and held on tightly as she desperately tried to break free. She paused briefly in her efforts and breathed heavily as she struggled to maintain her grip on the Book.

"Lalitha, stop this!" Tom yelled as they caught up and watched the two Chosen fight. "You need to calm down and think this all through before it goes too far."

"After everything I have done for you, Thomas McAllister, you betray me in this way," she snarled through gritted teeth. "You would stop me from punishing the traitors?"

"Lalitha," Alex pleaded, "we didn't know the full story before. Gask wasn't the only one to blame here. Relfa killed the king and you've killed him already. You can't just murder Gask and everyone that supported him now… It's inhuman. We need to talk calmly. It isn't too late. We can fix this."

"FIX THIS?" Lalitha screamed. "MY FATHER IS DEAD. HOW CAN WE FIX THAT?"

"We can work something out with Gask," Tom said. "Just don't do this… please. What you're trying to do is wrong. Your desire for revenge has twisted your mind."

"Twisted my mind? I have never thought more clearly. I will burn my enemies and sit in triumph upon the throne of Zakastra. You reveal yourself to be a traitor Thomas McAllister and you will burn with the others. All of you will. I needed you to get me here and here I am. I do not need you any longer."

Lalitha bit down on one of Danny's hands and he let go of her with a howl of pain. As Lalitha pulled away from him, Danny frantically held his grip on the Book and dragged himself to his feet. The pair fought to claw the tome from each other's hands and Lalitha kicked out at Danny's knee with her foot. The pair of them fell heavily against one of the statues and the magi figure leaned dangerously. As they struggled, the statue fell to the floor with a deafening crash, its candle extinguishing as the heavy wax cylinder rolled across the floor.

Jimmy tried to get to Lalitha to help her, but Tom and Alex held him back as the two Chosen fought for possession of the Book.

"Jimmy, what are you doing?" Alex yelled. "If you get in the middle of them, I don't know what will happen. The Book will protect its Chosen if anyone attacks them while they're holding the Book."

"He's trying to hurt Lalitha. I can't let him do that!"

"There's nothing you can do, Jimmy," Sam shouted as he joined in the effort to hold the young man back. "If you try to stop her, she'll kill you."

"No, she won't… She's my friend!"

Danny's training should have made easy work of the fight, but Lalitha kicked and scratched like a possessed banshee. They fought each other viciously, each desperate to take possession of the Book. As Lalitha pushed against him, Danny stumbled over the fallen Magi statue and she seized her opportunity. Lalitha drove her knee ferociously into Danny's groin and as he doubled up in agony, she wrenched the Book from his grasp and made for the stairs.

"You are not worthy to wield the Book, Daniel Adams," she shrieked back at him. "You prove yourself to be an enemy of the crown. When I have burned the unfaithful in this city, I will find a way to kill you too."

She turned and hurried up the stairs to the altar. Danny gritted his teeth as he set off after her, his breaths loud and laboured as he struggled up the stairs.

"She's lost her mind. You've got to stop her, Danny, or we're all dead!" Alex yelled.

Danny glanced back and then hobbled as fast as he could up the staircase. Taking advantage of the distraction, Jimmy struggled frantically and broke free. He ran towards the stairs and the others set off after him.

A flash of fire lit the walls above them and a guard crashed down the steps in a shower of sparks and flame. Danny jumped over the falling body and hurried on after Lalitha.

As Danny made it up the last of the stairs, he could see that Lalitha had made it to the altar. She slammed the Book down onto the top of the stone plinth and immediately, the symbols carved into its surface began to burn with orange fire. The whispers in everyone's head became almost overwhelming and the whole chamber vibrated. The symbols on the twelve stone pillars burst into arcane fire, the lines of the intricate carvings each blazing brightly. Lalitha's eyes were wide and the familiar sparks of light danced in them.

Danny's adrenaline spurred him on as he sprinted across the room and threw himself at her. They both crashed against the stone altar and fell, wrestling to the floor, but the sound of whispering and the light from the symbols all around them did not diminish. The Book remained in the centre of the altar, enveloped in the fire that leapt from the mystic symbols.

Jimmy rushed into the chamber, then stood helplessly as he watched the two figures fighting. The power in the room was palpable and static electricity cracked all around them. Tom, Alex, Sam and Ramman ran up the last few steps and stood behind Jimmy, transfixed by the sight in front of them.

As they grappled with each other on the dusty floor of the altar room, Lalitha clawed at Danny's eyes with her nails as he tried to grab her arms and pin them to her sides. She fought against him desperately and drove her head into his nose as hard as she could. Danny's nose blossomed into a fountain of blood and as he lay momentarily dazed, he lost his grip on her. She dragged herself to her feet and kicked at his head as she reached for the Book.

Lalitha pulled herself up on the edge of the altar and slammed her hand down on the Book. As her hand touched it, blinding bolts of energy began to shoot from the top of each of the pillars into the Book. The whispering rose to a crescendo and light burst upwards from the Soulstone. Lalitha turned to look at Tom and the team, a look of maniacal triumph on her face.

"Prepare to burn, Thomas McAllister," she roared.

Alex grabbed Tom and pulled him to her. They closed their eyes and held each other tightly as they waited for Lalitha to utter the words that would end their lives.

Two loud bangs rang in Tom's ears and he opened his eyes to see what had happened. Danny still lay on his side on the floor, but his right arm was stretched out towards Lalitha and in his hand was his Glock. Smoke drifted from the muzzle of the pistol and Tom's eyes darted back to Lalitha. She stood with a confused look on her face. Her left hand rose to her chest and blood from the two ragged holes that had appeared in the front of her leather armour began to gush through her fingers.

Lalitha stared at Danny, her features contorting with shock and then fury. She opened her mouth to scream the word of summoning that would finish them all, but Danny pulled the trigger again. Lalitha's head jerked backwards violently as the bullet blasted through her skull.

"NO!" Screamed Jimmy as he raised his rifle and charged towards where Danny lay.

"JIMMY DON'T…" Screamed Alex, but there was nothing she could do.

Jimmy pulled the trigger and fired a hail of bullets towards Danny. The bullets never reached their target, but instead vanished in bursts of orange flame before they struck Danny's body. Danny looked up at Jimmy as he rushed towards him. His eyes filled with fire and the voice of the Book boomed from his mouth.

"SCALTO!"

Instantly, Jimmy's body exploded in a grotesque shower of blood and his rifle clattered to the floor.

"NO!" Alex screamed.

Tom dropped to his knees as blood dripped from the ceiling and ran down the sides of the altar.

"DANNY…" Sam shouted furiously. "WHAT THE FUCK HAVE YOU DONE!"

The fire left Danny's eyes as he pulled himself to his feet. He looked at the blood that covered the altar and the floor around it and shook his head in shock.

"It wasn't me!" shouted Danny. "It was the Book. It wasn't me!"

"Take the Book from the altar," a voice shouted from the stairway. Gask had seen Lalitha fall and he walked slowly down the stairs towards them.

"Take the Book," he shouted loudly.

Danny staggered back to the altar, tears streaming down his face as he put his hands on the Book.

"You… killed… my friend," he gasped as he gripped the Book and struggled to lift it from the altar.

The Book's whispers rose to shrieks in their heads and Danny's face contorted in agony as he fought against it. He roared loudly and with one last effort managed to pull the Book away from the stone surface. As soon as it's leather cover was parted from the altar, the burning orange symbols faded and the bolts of energy that flowed from the pillars cut off abruptly.

Danny looked up at them, pain etched all over his tear-streaked face as he held the Book in front of him.

"I'm sorry… Jimmy… I… I'm sorry," he stammered. "I thought I wanted this… but now… I don't… I can't! The magi told me… I have to choose…"

Gask walked towards Danny, but as he did so, Danny's face changed and a single word boomed from his mouth in the voice of the Book.

"DESSAT!"

There was an ear-splitting crack of lightning and everyone was thrown to the floor. When they opened their eyes, Danny and the Book had vanished.

CHAPTER 55

The Royal Palace at Krassak

No-one found sleep easy that night. Tom and Alex lay awake in their bedroom on the first floor of the palace and in the end, they abandoned even attempting to sleep, opting instead to stand on the terrace outside their room and look down over the slumbering city.

"You can't take all this on your own shoulders, Tom," Alex said gently. "Once Lalitha got back here, there was nothing you could do to stop what happened."

"But… Jimmy… The Book killed him, Alex!"

"I know and it breaks my heart that we've lost him, but even Danny couldn't stop the Book from doing what it did. There was nothing any of us could do."

"We don't even have a body to bury… he's just… gone!"

Alex nodded and put her arms around him.

"We'll do something for him, Tom. A stone or a tree or something. We won't forget him."

Tom nodded and wiped at his already sore eyes. He breathed deeply and steadied himself on the terrace parapet.

"What happens now?" he asked.

"They're going to lie Lalitha and Relfa in state in the throne room, wherever that is," she said. "I think it's as much to show the powerful families in the city that they're dead as much as it is to show respect."

"So Gask can now take the throne if he wants it."

"Yeah, he can," she whispered.

"I keep wondering if we could have done something earlier to stop Lalitha doing what she did, you know? We spent weeks with her, Alex. I knew she wanted revenge on

Gask, but I didn't realise the extent of what she was willing to do."

"None of us did. I was as close to her as anybody else and I could see that she was hiding things, but I never thought she was capable of wanting to wipe out half a city. Was she that unhinged from the beginning?"

"I don't know. She was obsessed with revenge… we all knew that, but I think the power that she could command through the Book corrupted that desire and escalated it into something much deeper and much worse."

"I think Gask had the right idea about that Book," Alex exclaimed bitterly.

"Me too. Nobody should have the ability to wield that kind of power. It changes them."

The sky behind the palace above the mountains to the east started to lighten. Dawn was not far away now. Tom and Alex stood watching the flickering of fires and torches below them in the shadows of the city, almost not wanting this new day to start. A sharp gust of wind caused the flags behind the pair to flap noisily and they both jumped.

"When I hear a loud noise, I keep expecting Danny to reappear," said Alex as she looked back at the flag.

"Me too," agreed Tom.

"Why did he disappear Tom? He had already taken the Book from the altar. Wasn't everything okay?"

"I don't know. That same question keeps going around in my head too. I think that when the Book killed Jimmy, it showed Danny something about its nature, and that gave him the strength to fight against the will of the Book. It was as if he was fighting to control the Book rather than letting the Book control him."

"What was that about having to choose?" Alex asked.

"Don't you remember? The magi at Gessan told him that there would come a time when his commitment to the Book would be tested. I think that what happened in the Tower was the test. Gask wants to bury the Book away somewhere so that no-one can ever use it again, and that is the last thing that the Book wants. It looked as if Danny was trying to choose whether he wanted to protect the Book or side with Gask. I know the lure of wealth and power was a big deal for Danny, but I think what the Book did to Lalitha and Jimmy was enough to show him what he needed to do."

"I think you're right," Alex nodded. "I wonder if the Book sensed the conflict inside him and made the decision to do something itself? It was the Book's voice that used the summoning word that zapped them away somewhere, not Danny's. Perhaps it did that rather than run the risk that Danny would side with Gask. Where did they go though Tom? Did they go back home? Our home?"

"I really don't know."

"There is the other obvious thing as well," Alex said quietly.

"What's that?"

"Without the Book, we can't get home. We're stuck here."

Tom hugged Alex to him and rested his mouth in her hair.

"You're right," he nodded. "We can't go home."

They stood on the terrace with their arms around each other until the sun rose slowly over the mountains. Sunlight shone down through the peaks and cast long shadows through the towers and spires of the city and on towards the river.

They watched as the city slowly come to life below them, unaware of the destruction that had almost befallen it the night before. Eventually, Tom sighed and led the way back inside. They both got dressed in new clothes that Gask had arranged for them and wandered through the palace until, with the help of one of the royal guards, they found the throne room. Both were curious to see where the bodies of Lalitha and Relfa would be laid in state.

The room was only dimly lit, as the large windows that looked out over the front of the palace and down over the city faced to the west, and so wouldn't get direct sunlight until much later in the morning. Sconces in the walls still burned brightly and by their light, Tom could see the ornate wooden panelling that lined the room. Rows of chairs were laid out and in front of them was a raised dais upon which sat the throne itself. The huge ceremonial chair was made from solid silver and had been fashioned into the shape of an eagle. Vicious looking talons gripped the arms of the seat and the bird's great hooked beak stood proudly up over the back of the chair. Enormous, intricately cast wings emerged from the back of the throne and extended outwards and upwards towards the ceiling. The unfurled wings gave the impression that the chair was about to take flight at any moment. The seat of the throne was finished in a deep red velvet, and a red and silver footstool sat in front of it at the edge of the dais.

As Tom tore his eyes away from the throne, he noticed that Gask was at the front of the room giving orders to a group of guards that stood nearby. They began to move the front rows of chairs towards the side of the room, as another group of men wheeled in two large wooden platforms. Tom guessed that the platforms would be where Lalitha and Relfa would be laid once their bodies had been prepared.

There was a cough to their left and Tom turned to see Sam and Ramman sitting quietly at the side of the room as they watched the proceedings. Tom and Alex made their way over and sat down next to them.

"Couldn't sleep either, eh?" Sam said.

"Too much going around in my head to sleep," Tom nodded.

"I know how you feel, Boss," Sam agreed. "I can't get the images out of my head. Jimmy… Danny… even Lalitha!"

Alex squeezed the stocky man's shoulder and a tear ran down her cheek.

Ramman looked up at them, his eyes watery and red.

"I cannot believe that they are all gone, Master Tom," the young man said shakily before breaking down into racking sobs.

Sam turned to his friend and embraced him. Alex turned back to Tom and buried her face in his shoulder.

Gask stood watching the exchange, but left them for a few minutes before making his way towards them.

"Forgive me for intruding," he said quietly. "I am sorry for your loss. I know that you were close to your friends, but their sacrifice has saved many, many, lives."

"That might be true," said Alex as she wiped her face with the sleeves of her new tunic, "But it doesn't help yet. It will… but not yet."

"I understand," Gask nodded. "I too mourn the loss of my friend Relfa. He was the last link to the woman I loved. I feel that I have let Tella down by not protecting her son from Lalitha and the Book."

"There was nothing you could have done," Tom sighed. "If you had been with us and tried to intervene, Lalitha would have killed you too."

Gask breathed deeply and sat down next to them.

"If we had stopped Lalitha… If we could have prevented her from killing so many without her death, I do not know what I would have done. She killed the woman that I loved and I could never have forgiven her for that… yet I was not driven with the same desire for revenge that Lalitha was. My heart is filled with sorrow rather than hate."

"Mine too," Tom said sadly. "Even if Danny had managed to get the Book away from her, I don't know what we would have done. We could have imprisoned her and tried to gradually talk her around, but I have a feeling that would have driven her even further into the darkness."

"Where do you think Master Fester has gone?" Ramman asked.

"I wish I knew the answer to that question, Ram," Tom sighed. "The Book could have taken him anywhere."

"Do you think we'll see him again?" Sam asked.

"I hope so Sammy… I hope so."

Everyone sat quietly for several minutes, each of them lost in their own thoughts. One of the guards accidentally dropped a long length of polished wood and the loud bang startled them all.

"What are they doing?" Ramman asked.

"They prepare the catafalques for Lalitha and Relfa," Gask said gesturing at the two wooden platforms. "Their bodies will be laid upon them for the people to view."

"What?" Ramman asked, a confused look on his face. "Their bodies? You mean people will come here to look at their dead bodies?"

"Yes," Gask answered.

"Why would they do that?"

"Some will come to pay their respects, but most will come simply to satisfy their morbid fascination," Gask said sadly.

"That is ridiculous," Ramman said shaking his head. "City people are strange folk!"

"They are indeed my friend," Gask smiled. "But this is the way of things here. It is a macabre practice, but one that is essential if power is to be transferred smoothly."

"Why is that?" Ramman asked.

"It will prove to the powerful families in the city that King Lestri's line is ended, and that Lord Gask is free to take the throne if he can gather enough support to his side," Tom said.

"Indeed," Gask nodded. "That would be true if I did intend to take the throne, but I may have other ideas when it comes to that."

"Ideas like what?" Alex asked.

"I do not want to be 'King' as Lestri was. I wonder if a new role as Protector of the Realm would be more appropriate. I think the days of a single ruler having absolute power over the land are over. We know from bitter experience that unlimited power leads to tyranny and corruption, so I am going to propose that the country be led by a council formed from the heads of the powerful families across the realm, and representatives from the ordinary people. Decisions should be made by majority voting with the Protector having the casting vote."

"That sounds like a good idea," Tom nodded. "That is more or less how things work where we come from. Would you take the role of Protector?"

"Yes," Gask nodded, "unless another comes forward that would be better suited to the task."

"What about the Elders in the other cities?" Alex asked. "Many of them seem more than willing to abuse their powers."

"New city and town councils will be established, and the Elders who have taken advantage of their positions need to be brought to justice. The serfs must be freed. That cruel and immoral practice has to be abolished."

"Good," Alex agreed.

"It won't be easy, but I think you're doing the right thing," Tom said.

"What are your intentions now?" Gask asked.

Tom looked at Alex and Sam, and shrugged his shoulders.

"I don't know. Until Danny reappears from wherever the Book took him, assuming that he ever does, we can't get home. We're stuck here in Zakastra. We'd never envisaged anything other than Lalitha being on the throne and her sending us back home when the Book was placed back on its altar, so I'm not sure what happens next."

Gask ran his fingers through his beard as he pondered something.

"I cannot do anything to send you back to your home and I do not know if your friend Daniel Adams will ever return to Krassak. I hope that he remains alive, but I must confess that the longer the Book is kept away from the capital, the happier I will be. As it seems that you will be staying with us, would you consider joining me? I have known you all for a very short time, but it is obvious to me that you are brave and honourable warriors. You chose to stand with me to save the lives of many of my people rather than take the path of violence and destruction. I trust you and would appreciate your council as I attempt to change the ideals of our realm. There will be difficult times ahead and I believe that your knowledge and experience would be a great asset."

Tom looked into the eyes of his friends.

"What do you think?" He asked.

"As long as I'm with you, I'm happy," Alex said with a smile. "If you decide that we should stay here and help Lord Gask rebuild, then I will be at your side. The journey to get here cost us a lot. Jimmy. Danny. Even Lalitha. Perhaps if we were to help rebuild Zakastra, it would make everything we went through have some sort of purpose."

Tom nodded and squeezed Alex's hand tightly.

"Sam?" He prompted.

"I want to do what I can, Boss," he said. "I've got nobody waiting for me back home and my life there was pretty meaningless. Being here and helping you forge something better for these people seems like a cause worth backing to me. Plus, if we stay here, Danny will know where to find us if he ever comes back. What do you think Ram mate? What are you going to do? Go back to the farm?"

"No, Master Sam. My life at the farm was at an end long before I met you. I had already decided to travel the lands to find a new purpose and it seems to me that the purpose is obvious. I will stay with you and help wherever I can."

Sam clapped his friend on the shoulder. Ramman smiled back at him and nodded happily.

"What will you do, Master Tom?" Ramman asked.

Tom looked around the expectant faces of the group and felt so much pride for his team that his eyes welled up and he found it difficult to talk.

"Lord Gask," he said in-between deep breaths, "we have lost a great deal since we arrived here in Zakastra. The death of our friend Jimmy is a loss that is deeply painful for us, and Lalitha's fate was a tragedy that will haunt me for as long as I live."

Tom paused. He lifted his left arm and gazed at his hand as he stretched his fingers out and then balled them into a fist. He looked at Alex and she nodded.

"Despite what Lalitha did at the end, I still owe her a great debt. Before she died, she gave me a gift greater than any I could have ever wished for. She gave me my life back and for that I will be eternally grateful. The only way I can think of to properly repay the debt I owe is by helping you rebuild Zakastra in a better, fairer way. I just wish that we could have made Lalitha realise that there was another path to the one she chose."

Tears ran down Alex's face and she pulled him to her and kissed him tenderly on the lips. As they held each other, Sam put his arms around them to embrace them both and Ramman joined the group hug, wrapping his big arms around them all.

"I would be honoured to have you all at my side as we make this realm something to be proud of," Gask said. "Come then. There is planning to be done. We have much work ahead of us."

As Gask led the team out of the throne room, Tom took Alex's hand in his and smiled at her. The journey they had made had been fraught with danger and loss, but at the end of it all, Tom found himself feeling weirdly hopeful for the future. Jimmy's death had cut him to the core, and the regrets he had over what had happened to Lalitha were going to take some time to come to terms with, but here they were at the birth of a new nation. A better nation. He had Alex by his side and his arm was as good as new. They couldn't get home, but so what? Home was all about money and politics, technology and consumerism, waste and destruction. This place had the potential to be so much more than that.

Tom, Alex, Sam and Ramman followed Gask out of the throne room and towards their new lives in Zakastra.

It was a new dawn and Tom welcomed it with open arms.

CHAPTER 56

Epilogue

The throne room was empty. Gask and his companions had left and the catafalques were complete. The room was silent.

From out of the shadows at the back of the room, two figures slowly emerged. They both wore nondescript robes and looked around the room cautiously as they approached the catafalques. One of them ran his hand over the top of his bald head and turned to the other.

"Send word to Rellik," he whispered softly. "The time to act has come."

– The End of Volume One of the Book of Souls Saga –

ABOUT THE AUTHOR

The Fallen is the first novel in the *Book of Souls Saga* from UK-based fantasy writer Mark Ashbury.

Mark lives on the edge of the strange and mysterious Fenlands in West Norfolk with his wife Lisa, their two cats and a recently acquired robot hoover called Derek. In between coming up with ideas for the next volume of the saga, Mark works in his day job as a digital manager and spends as much time as possible outside enjoying the local wildlife from his kayak.